Finders Keepers

SANDRA KITT

sourcebooks
casablanca

Published by Sourcebooks Casablanca, an imprint of Sourcebooks
P.O. Box 4410, Naperville, Illinois 60567-4410
(630) 961-3900
sourcebooks.com

Cataloging-in-Publication Data is on file with the Library of Congress.

Printed and bound in the United States of America.
SB 10 9 8 7 6 5 4 3 2 1

"If there is a book that you want to read, but it hasn't been written yet, you must be the one to write it."
—Toni Morrison

"Color was a false distinction, love is not."
—Dorothy West, *The Wedding*

PROLOGUE

It was the evening of April 7, 1932, almost midnight. The air was still and thick and stifling hot. The black clothing that Joe Wordell wore for his covert work had been drenched in sweat and stuck to his skin with the humidity. But he pushed through, struggling to move each of the remaining heavy bags and lift them into the bed of the truck. He briefly leaned against the side of the dusty vehicle, gasping for air, to mop his face and forehead with an equally drenched hand towel, confiscated from the first-floor guest bathroom of his employer's home.

Joe looked behind him, back to the dark, locked-up house, while listening for any sound around him that might indicate anyone was aware of his presence and what he was doing. His timing was tight, and he couldn't afford to hesitate. He'd grabbed the unexpected opportunity that his boss had presented him by casually telling him that he and his family would be away for the weekend to attend a funeral in Nevada. This window of time would be all Joe had to execute his plan. It was sudden and quickly thrown together. This was it.

The big house was at least a mile from the next nearest homestead, so he pushed aside his paranoia that someone could hear the thudding of his heartbeat. Then he pushed himself straight to finish the job. Just two more of the bags to be loaded and he'd be done.

He'd get in the truck and drive home to Helen. They'd leave Central Valley at first light and the fruitless promise of a better life that he now knew was never going to happen. They could start over somewhere else—south, maybe LA—thanks to the unexpected benevolence of his employer's loose lips.

Joe climbed into the cab and carefully closed the door. He turned over the engine and let the sudden rumble of the motor be absorbed into the night. He finally let out his breath as he released the emergency brake. The truck made a starting jolt and began to roll in the reverse, out of the service entrance driveway and down the pavement. He sat for a moment longer to hear if the rattling of the truck body had drawn any attention. He turned the truck toward the path and steered in the direction of the country road. He did not turn on his headlights. He did not speed. He took advantage of the gentle incline of the path that gave the big house the impression of sitting on a low hill lined with identical stately trees. This was not the kind of house that Joe ever had any hope of living in with Helen and raising a family. But he now knew that he had been extraordinarily lucky to have been hired by Leland Sanford to be his groundkeeper, just because he'd saved the beloved family dog from drowning in a rapidly running creek on the property that ran parallel to a public back road. He hadn't been paid well at all, barely enough to rent a shack in town to live in. But there had been other benefits, and he'd been alert enough to find them. Like now.

It was only as the truck finally hit the public road that Joe sighed deeply and checked off the second hurdle of his night's work. He shifted in his seat, letting his left arm hang out the driver's window. The night air offered no relief, but Joe began to feel a rush of freedom such as he'd never known before. Certainly not since leaving home at fifteen, unsure how he would find work to support himself. Not since he met Helen and fell in love and was determined to make a living to take care of both of them, to have a real house of their own. And children. But it was not until he got wind of his boss's plans to steal a lot of money from the farm association's coffers, where he was president and treasurer, that Joe found the courage and wherewithal to take some of the money his boss was planning to take for himself. But Joe changed his mind. What the hell. He took it all.

The beauty of his plan, Joe thought with satisfaction, was that his boss would have no idea what had happened to his ill-gained riches or what had happened to his employee. Such were the sometimes benefits of being a Black man treated like he was invisible while his white boss discussed, in his presence, the intricate details of nefarious plans to steal.

Joe felt no guilt for what he'd just done. The country was a mess and it was every man for himself, especially if he was Black. He picked up a little speed in the silent dark of the night, anxious to get home. He'd told Helen not to wait up because he had no idea when he'd be returning…if at all. There was always that possibility. He made a slow turn onto the dirt road that led through the center of his neighborhood of attached wooden houses that were only thirty feet wide and identical in design. There were stray dogs roaming or sleeping on empty, narrow porches. Joe went two blocks to the very end and then turned left to approach the back of the line of houses and into a narrow alley that was only two feet wider than the truck. He stopped in front of a recessed door at the back of one of the houses, with just enough room for him to get the door open and squeeze out. The back door opened, and a slender woman gasped, "Joe," and propelled herself into his arms.

He held and squeezed Helen briefly, feeling the hard, round bump of her pregnancy pushing into him. He indicated that she was to be quiet and pushed her back toward the house. Then he made sure the bed and cab were secure, removing one small bag to carry into the house with him. It was filled with a scattering of bills in small denominations that he would use to pay their way when he and Helen left before dawn and drove south. He hadn't told her where they were going. He still had no final destination. And the less she knew the better.

Joe was confident that he'd know when they were to stop, when they'd found someplace where they would be safe and could call home.

The day Joe finished constructing the second of two secret crawl spaces disguised as utility closets, Helen went into labor. They'd only been in the house a few months, Joe working mysteriously at night and not explaining anything to his wife about why he was adding the spaces, like small, deep, but narrow closets, one at each end of the house. She only knew that they now had a house to live in. It had been trashed and abandoned by previous owners, and Joe made a convincing argument to the local municipal government for buying it on the cheap and promising to repair and fix up the eyesore. But they made it difficult. They weren't giving anything away to some stranger who'd arrived from nowhere. Why should they accommodate an itinerant Black man who'd driven into town one day claiming he was forced out of Central Valley, where he'd worked in farming, by the long never-ending droughts and ruined crops? Fine. Pay $500 and not a penny less. Joe calmly said he could do it if they gave him a month to earn the money.

The deal was set. The die was cast. He waited out the month and returned with $500, all the bills carefully soiled and abused to give the look of use and constant exchange. Joe took his receipt and immediately went to the land office to obtain an official deed of ownership. No matter what happened in the future, the house would always belong to him and Helen. And no matter what changes came about in the neighborhood, he would always have money to pay the property taxes, make improvements, live quietly, and mind his own business, trying to prevent Helen from making too many friends… and sticking to their fabricated history. Staying within the law of the city, quickly forgetting his illegal activity of the past that made this future possible.

There was a Black hospital two miles from their house, but Joe didn't want his wife to give birth there. He was afraid of having to give their names or any information to the authorities, but there was no question of Helen giving birth at home. She was in pain, screaming for help, and Joe had no idea how to help her except to get her to a doctor. Their daughter, Katherine, was born a few weeks premature. But they brought her home anyway, and Helen devoted herself for a year to doing anything and everything to help her survive. And she did. Joe and Helen doted on her.

"Isn't she beautiful, Joe?" Helen frequently cooed, as she ran the back of her fingers across the infant's soft smooth skin, the color of sweet potato custard, ready filling for a pie.

Joe stared down at his daughter, his heart catching at her beauty, her innocence. But secretly he couldn't control the sense of doom that tempered his joy in Katherine, his happiness with Helen. This was his family now. It was all he had. And then he remembered that he and Helen were rich. She didn't know that, but Joe checked often on the hidden money, allowing the piles of heavy canvas bags stuffed into two hidden spaces to calm him. Joe Wordell took good care of his family, found a railroad job that justified the money he could spend on Helen and his daughter. He grew complacent and, eventually, convinced that life was going to be very good to them. He'd already considered dozens of possibilities and convinced himself that nothing could go wrong.

Life was perfect.

CHAPTER 1

There were two men sitting on the tail of the midsized pickup truck, a third leaning against the side, when Olivia turned in the short driveway to the right of the house. A fourth man got out of the cab, slammed the door, and walked to meet her. Olivia's shoes slid on the gushy mud, a buildup from the rain the day before. It was very unusual for it to rain enough to produce dirt runoff. She stood and watched the man's approach, holding on to her open car door.

"Mario. Your call was confusing. And you sounded urgent. What's going on?"

Olivia glanced to the three other workers, all languishing in unconcern as their boss and her contractor talked.

"Sorry to bother you, Mrs. Cameron. We started inside the house this morning, in that small space next to the kitchen. We thought it was a closet or pantry. Something like that. But when we took off the molding we could see a tiny opening. Javier got close, and he said there's a space inside. Maybe a room. And there was stuff, like packages or something. We couldn't tell."

"Did you take them out? Try to figure out what it was?" She didn't bother to correct his salutation.

Olivia began carefully walking toward the house, to the wide staircase leading to the front door. She knew the steps had originally been wood, but the prior owners had replaced them with bricks and cement. She had decided that the steps should be replaced, returned to the original look, in her plans for the renovations.

"No, ma'am," Mario said with a decisive shake of his head.. "I didn't know about that space. I didn't touch anything before I called you."

Olivia reached the front door and walked in. She stopped abruptly when she realized she was about to leave a muddy trail on the wooden floorboards. Not that they were in any shape to be concerned about, but she suddenly remembered her great-aunt had lived in this house, and Olivia felt a certain respect was due. Mario rushed to a pile of flattened cardboard boxes and quickly made a path for Olivia, leading through the kitchen and out again, to a laundry room. All, including the kitchen, had been added, probably in the 1940s after the war, and maybe upgraded again later.

Olivia stopped in the hall, not immediately seeing anything that could have raised Mario's suspicions. The house was empty, with all the evidence of needing repair very visible.

"Show me," she said, turning to him. He walked around her and into the kitchen and out the opposite door.

Mario stopped, stood back, and pointed to a partial paneling in the wall that was damaged. Because of the rain the day before, Olivia could smell the damp, the rot and decay of age in the old house. Mario reached into the hole of the broken panel and pulled out the remaining wood. It crumbled into small pieces to the floor. Now she could see that the space was small but uniform. Four walls, a wooden floor where there was still water, murky and festering. Olivia briefly pinched her nose and inhaled through her mouth. She peered into the space that was filled from the two inches of water on the floor almost to the ceiling with stacked bundles; some thicker than others. The stacks were lopsided, compressed over time from the weight. She poked at one. Whatever was inside the moldy wrappings was soft. She looked at Mario. He shook his head and shrugged, just as confused as she was.

"We didn't touch anything," he repeated.

Olivia believed him. He couldn't afford to be accused of touching, moving, or taking anything that wasn't his from a job. She looked around. There were only construction equipment and supplies. Some plastic storage crates, tarps...a half-used flat of sixteen-ounce bottles of water.

"Can you set up some sort of table for me?" she asked, already thinking that she was going to be late to work.

"I have some sawhorses in the truck," Mario said. "I can put a few up with a piece of Sheetrock on top."

"That will work." Olivia nodded, giving permission, and Mario hurried off, calling out in Spanish to his men to help. Olivia returned to the hole, peering through to the stacks, looking for hints as to what they were. She braced herself, angling her torso, and reached in to try to take hold of one of the top bundles. It felt heavy, and as she tugged the long stack beneath, it rocked toward her an inch or two. Olivia let it go, stepping back, afraid that the whole would topple over.

Mario returned with one of his men, and they quickly set up the makeshift table, testing to make sure it was stable and settled flatly on the floor.

"You can put whatever you take out of that hole right here," he announced.

Olivia nodded her thanks, dusting off her hands from the debris of the bundle she'd handled. Mario looked around, found an open roll of paper towels, and handed it to her.

She murmured an absent-minded thanks, looking around again. "What were you going to do today?" she asked the contractor.

"Work in here. We were going to strip out everything, including the appliances. Remove the old cabinets. You know."

"Can you work somewhere else for a while? I want some time to check out what's in the wall. We'll just be in each other's way."

"Sure thing. I'll have the guys work outside. The rain loosened a lot of dirt on this side of the house, and now it's all mud at street level."

"That's great, thanks. I don't know how long I'll be, but I'll call if I need you."

"Okay, Mrs. Cameron."

Olivia started to speak, this time to correct Mario, but got no chance. He and the other worker were already out of the kitchen, Mario shouting orders as they stomped their way to the entrance in heavy work boots. Alone, Olivia left her purse on a counter in the soon-to-be-demolished kitchen. She pulled her cell phone from the pocket of her lightweight jacket and punched in a number.

"Hi, Lori, it's me. Something's come up at the house, and I'm going to be late… No, not my place. My great-aunt's house. The one I'm renovating. I'm okay, but I can't go into it right now. Is everything okay? Have classes started? Great. Let Mr. Booth know I called in. He can cover if anything comes up. Call me if there's anything important I should know about… Yes, I hope to get in before the kids get out… Thanks. I'll check in with you later."

Olivia put the phone away and then took off her jacket, hanging it over the handles of an equipment dolly. She glanced down at her feet. She was wearing fashionable flats…not sneakers…not exactly adequate protection on a construction site. They would have to do. Then she walked back to the torn-away paneling. Again, she reached for the top bundle, wiggling to move it and carefully lifting the pack down and out the opening in the wall. Olivia held the bundle out in front of her as it dripped water. She set it down on the makeshift worktable. She poked at it again, then felt for an opening, a way to peel away the sodden, dirty cloth.

The rough woven fabric began to shred between her fingers, falling away. She found an edge and started unwinding to a layer of what had been newspaper. It was nothing more than pulp.

She bent, looking for a language, a heading, a date. She could only tell it was in English. But what was revealed stunned Olivia. She stood staring down at distinct green-inked paper bills. Money. The first bill was $50. Olivia smoothed her hand gently on the damp bill. It did not tear; the color did not run or blur. She tried lifting the top bill, but it stuck, and she immediately stopped, afraid of doing damage. Olivia knew the money was real.

Before starting to remove each bundle from the wall, Olivia searched around and found industrial-sized garbage bags and used several to protect the surface of the Sheetrock that made up her table. Then she carried the bundles, one by one, and laid them out on the table in rows of ten. But she didn't remove the rotten fabric or make any further attempt to expose the contents. At one point, she became aware that there was a black canvas bag on the floor inside the wall, also soaked in water and somewhat hidden in the back of a shelf about level with her neck. When Olivia opened the bag, she found it half-full with loose bills in many denominations. There was probably several thousand dollars inside. After some thought, she put the bag on the counter next to her purse.

It took almost two hours for Olivia to remove the bundles and align them on the table. She only opened the last one, in exactly the same manner as the first, and found more stuck-together wet bills. The top one in this bundle was $100. She couldn't even begin to guess how much money there was altogether.

Her phone rang, and she scrambled to remove it from her jacket pocket with dirty, wet hands.

"It's Olivia… Hi, Carl… Yes, I'm fine, thanks. I just had to take care of something this morning I couldn't put off. My contractor called me as I was driving in… I had to come to the house… No, nothing…nothing…serious." Olivia hesitated, not wanting to share. "I'm still hoping to get in after… Oh, really? Okay, you're right. As long as you're on top of everything I'm going to bag it today. But I will be in tomorrow. Thanks for checking in, Carl. See you tomorrow. Bye."

Olivia sighed, placing the phone on the table. She needed to wash her hands. She needed to wipe down her phone. She needed to figure out what to do next. Olivia also felt a slight apprehension about what she'd discovered, knowing instinctively what she'd found was going to be a problem, even if she wasn't sure how. She leaned back against the wall, staring at the display on the table. There were thirteen rows of ten bundles. Not all the bundles were of even height. Then there was the bag.

She heard the thump of heavy boot steps coming from the front of the house.

"Mrs. Cameron?" Mario appeared just outside the kitchen but didn't step in.

Olivia quickly tried to position her body so that he couldn't see the table behind her with its spread of dirty packages. "Yes?"

"We're going to break for lunch. You need me for anything?"

"No, no. You can go."

"We'll come back in an hour."

Olivia smiled at him. "Take two, Mario. I know you hadn't planned on me coming in and taking over. I'm pretty sure you can get back indoors tomorrow."

"No problem," he said and left again.

Olivia went back to her thoughts. She walked slowly around the table, gnawing the inside of her mouth, her arms crossed. The water was still turned on in the kitchen, and she stood at the sink and washed her hands. She checked the wall hole again, just to be sure she'd removed everything that was hidden inside. She still couldn't get her head around finding money hidden in a house that had only been left to her by a deceased great-aunt a year earlier.

There was a clear moment when Olivia thought she could just keep the money! She owned the house. Whatever was in the house was now hers. What she'd found, so far, indicated the bills were more than fifty years old. And given their condition and the way the bundles had been wrapped, the money didn't look like it had been touched in the same amount of time. Why hide it? A fear of banks? Hiding a secret? Was the money stolen?

Drying her hands on a paper towel, Olivia again thoughtfully considered the smelly, soggy mess on the makeshift table. How would she explain to a bank if she decided to keep the money and tried to deposit it into her account? Or tried to open a new one? The possibilities began to grow in her mind…along with any number of serious potential problems.

With another sigh, she made a sudden and clear decision. Olivia picked up her cell phone, touched the icon for the camera, and methodically began to record all the bundles of money. From another angle, she photographed the entire table with all the bundles laid out. She took pictures of some of the old fabric and the blobs of pulpy newspaper. She photographed the hole in the wall as seen from the kitchen and then inside the hole, including the still-wet floor. She photographed the two bundles she'd unwrapped with the topmost bills visible and easy to identify. She shot images of the bag and the money inside.

Olivia's mind was spinning with all that had happened in just three hours. She was hungry, and she felt heated and a little sweaty from the humidity inside the house, the warm fall air, and the excitement of her find. But she knew she couldn't just leave with all the money packets on the Sheetrock table. She couldn't take the open bag with her to get lunch. She opened a bottle of very tepid water and, again, slowly circled the table, feeling that there was something she'd forgotten to do. Twice, three times around the table. She finally stopped and checked the time. Her workers would be returning from lunch in just thirty minutes.

Finally, there was really only one action she could take. Olivia reached for her phone and put in a short number. A laconic male voice muttered a scripted greeting.

"911. What's your emergency?"

"Oh...a...this isn't an emergency. I need to get in touch with the local precinct for Windsor Hills. Can you connect me?"

"No, ma'am. You have to hang up and call yourself. Here's the number..."

Olivia repeated the number silently to herself, trying not to forget as she ran off and entered the precinct number into her phone. She got another indifferent flat voice, wondering in amusement if this is how they train officers to answer the phone.

"How can I help you?"

"I have a problem. I think I'm going to need a squad car…or some of your officers…to come to my house." She gave the address.

"Is this an emergency? You have to dial…"

"No, it's *not* an emergency," she repeated patiently.

"What's the problem?"

"I'm doing some renovations on my house, and…well, this afternoon I found something buried in the house. I mean, something hidden. In the walls."

There was a moment's silence.

"Which is it, ma'am? Buried? Or hidden?"

"Hidden. Behind a panel in a wall. It's a kind of hidden space."

"And you found something in this space?"

"That's right."

Another momentary silence.

"Is it a body?"

Olivia was so shocked at the suggestion her mind went blank. Was that a joke? Was he trying to be funny? But she had to ask herself, had she checked carefully? Completely? The space was far too shallow for that. She laughed nervously. "No, of course not. It wasn't a body."

"Okay. What?"

"Money," she announced simply. "A *lot* of money."

————————

"Sorry to pass the buck along, Sloan," Lieutenant Gary Anderson said, handing a folder across his desk to the man sitting opposite him.

"No, you're not," Sloan Kendrick responded evenly, taking the folder and opening it. "One less time-consuming investigation for you and your department." He quickly leafed through each page, scanning the content, but taking a bit longer at the half dozen or so printed color images. "One more for me that will turn out to be questionable."

"Looks like an FBI case to me. You decide. There's a lot of bills in those piles you're looking at. Maybe the money was embezzled funds or a squirreled-away haul of a robbery? Bank. Business. Even the government. Procurement fraud. Money laundering..."

Sloan Kendrick closed the folder and dropped it on the edge of the desk. "What makes you think that?" He asked it not with indifference but with the knowledge that he was about to take on a case that Sloan had already guessed would be nothing but complicated trouble.

"We collected the money from a house under renovation for the current owner. Are you ready? The owner's contractors found the money hidden in a fake closet next to the kitchen."

"That's creative," Sloan said dryly. It wasn't. He'd long ago lost surprise at the number of incidents that came through his office of hidden money found in unexpected or inventive spaces.

His division at the local FBI field office was familiar with the disappearance and reappearance of large sums of money. Yet it wasn't always possible to establish that a crime had been committed or even who was to blame for the possible crime. That was the first thing to determine. It would all come down to interviewing people, checking the city records for past history of very large sums of missing money. It was now going to be his responsibility to determine the where, if, when, and who of a considerable amount of very old money, Lieutenant Anderson's report indicated, stuffed into the walls of a vacant house under renovation.

"I'll read the report. What else can you tell me?"

The officer, in his pristine short-sleeved, white shirt, with its insignia and badge signifying his rank, sat back in his spring-action chair with a shrug. "Well…the call came from a woman who said she owns the house. We haven't checked that out."

Sloan showed no emotion other than the slight raise of his brows, of doubt and amusement.

"You left that for me to do. I take it you asked the obvious question."

The lieutenant pushed forward and rested his elbows on the desk. "Sure did. Wanted to see if I could catch her off guard. She was annoyed."

Sloan nodded. "She called the police…but she was annoyed by your questions?"

"Yeah." Lieutenant Anderson considered this with a shrug. "I suspect she believed I was trying to get her to confess or give up more details about how she came to find the money."

"So I can't turn this around and hand it back to you…"

The lieutenant gave Sloan a crooked grin. "Not a chance. There's a lot of money involved, and we can't determine where it came from. And I don't have to turn it over to the cold case unit and go hunting through the missing persons backlog. Officers went to meet her, see exactly what she found. Over in Windsor Hills. Nice neighborhood. Mostly middle- and upper-middle-class Black residents. They're not a demographic for weird and violent crimes in that part of the county. The house belongs to"—he leaned forward to read the name on the police report he'd begun—"Olivia Cameron. Said she inherited the house from her late great-aunt about a year ago."

"So she doesn't live there?"

"Never has. She has her own place in Baldwin Hills."

"Another nice neighborhood," Sloan responded. "How much money are we talking about? How was it packed? Bills? Coins? Bonds?"

"All cash. I had a couple of detectives try to count the bundles. Took three days, but they stopped. There were too many bills stuck together. We didn't want to fool around with that in case some of the paper got ruined. There was no rhyme or reason to the way the money was wrapped. I mean, there were no clear ten-dollar packs or fifty-dollar packs. There was quite a haul of five-hundred-dollar bills."

"That might suggest the money was divided and portioned in a hurry with no concern for order."

"Or accountability. I see this as a take-the-money-and-run kind of thing."

"Okay. What about the woman? What have you found out?"

"You have to do your own agency thing, but so far, she seems clean. No criminal record of any kind. There's a note here about some sort of car accident about four years ago, but no citation, no fault to her. She was cooperative. I really didn't get a sense of her trying to hide anything. Actually, she seemed more concerned that she had to call out from work for the day we went out to interview her at home and take a statement. I told her we had to take the money. Olivia Cameron was more concerned when I told her the house had to be sealed until we finished our findings and had done up a report."

"Did she ask if she could keep the money?" Sloan asked.

The officer pursed his lips and shook his head. "As a matter of fact, no. I thought that would be the first thing she'd want to know. I explained the department has a protocol for trying to establish who the money belongs to and that will involve public announcements in the local press. I thought it best not to commit to any more possibilities. At least for now. Actually, it falls into your hands to decide what happens, Sloan. First *you* have to determine if some crime has been committed. And where the money came from. It's clear from the paper and the condition that the bills had been stashed in the wall for a very long time. I'm talking decades. The script style is more than fifty years old. The bill date appears to be around 1929."

"Just around the time of the Depression. I'd like to take a look at the money," Sloan said, standing and taking the folder from the desk.

"Sure," Gary Anderson said, standing and leaving the small office, Sloan Kendrick right behind him.

They silently took an elevator to a basement floor, mostly deserted of staff or activity. The lieutenant unlocked a metal door at the very end of a corridor and pressed the wall switch. The only furniture was a large table with its chairs pushed back against the room walls. Oil cloth had been spread on the surface of the table, and on top were the bundles of money, laid out in the same configuration that they were found in Olivia Cameron's house. The smell of wet, rotting cloth and damp paper wafted in the room, adding a slight damp humidity to the air.

Both men were indifferent, appearing not to have even noticed the smell. Sloan simply stood at one end of the table and silently perused the display. He finally approached and, taking a thin, metal probe from the lieutenant, inserted it along the side of one of the unwrapped bundles and carefully lifted a corner. He bent close to examine the green printed paper, studying the art and calligraphy, the wording and dates.

"We already vouchered everything, and the bundles will be transferred to the property office until the investigation is over. First we have to get all the bills dried and treated. We've already contacted a professional water mitigation service. They'll know how long that service could take."

"That's good, but my forensic guys will have to do their own procedure."

"Got it. I did have someone write down a lot of the serial numbers and signatures from the treasury department. Also photographed a few of the bills full face. They're in the folder."

"Thanks, Gary. That's enough to get me started," Sloan said as they left the room. "Do me a favor?" he asked as they rode the elevator back to the lieutenant's office. "I'd like to keep everyone, including the owner, away until I've had a chance to review your report. I'll want to see the house and the space for myself."

"Like I said, I told the owner that already, but I can't hold it indefinitely. From our standpoint, there's no reason."

"Of course. Thanks."

"Sure."

"One more thing. Call Olivia Cameron. Let her know the case is now with the FBI, but don't tell her why. Just let her know someone will be coming by to have a talk with her. I'll fill her in as needed."

"Okay."

They reached the lieutenant's office, but Sloan stood at the door, indicating that he was done and about to leave.

"Let me know when you set up that appointment," Sloan further instructed.

"You'll hear from me before the day is over."

"Thanks, Gary." Sloan started to walk away, but he slowed his steps and suddenly turned back. "What was your impression of Olivia Cameron?" he asked.

Gary Anderson seemed surprised by the question but was thoughtful as he considered his answer. "Okay, I guess. I didn't get any bad vibes. She seemed thoughtful, intelligent. Asked a lot of questions about how long the investigation was going to take. An average professional African American woman…"

Sloan stared at the lieutenant. "What does that mean? Average African American woman?"

Gary shrugged, not getting the implied judgment or characterization. "You know. Good hardworking citizen, never been in trouble. A little edgy with my officers like, not totally trusting anything they told her about what was going to happen with the money. She wasn't aggressive or anything like that. I would say Olivia Cameron is…very attractive. She has a nice voice…not sure why you're asking. Does any of that matter?"

"Just curious. Helps me get a head start on how to handle her."

CHAPTER 2

"Good morning," Olivia said as she walked past a trio of teens loitering in the hallway. "TJ, please take that pick out of your hair. If you need to comb it, go to the restroom. The bell is going to ring in"—she glanced at the hall clock—"forty-five seconds. Do you know where you're supposed to be?" She heard a chorus of falsely obedient responses behind her.

"Yes, ma'am."

At the end of the corridor, Olivia had to stop short to avoid colliding with another youngster who ran across her path, his backpack bouncing awkwardly. "Sorry!" the youngster shouted, never breaking stride as he rushed through a hall doorway and started bounding up the stairs.

The bell for first class rang just as Olivia reached the open reception area outside her office. The rumble of shouts, laughter, and conversation eventually died out as the hallways went silent and empty, and several doors slammed shut on classes about to start.

"What's up, Lori?" Olivia asked, stopping in front of her assistant's desk.

Then she became distracted by the distinct fussing and whimpering of a baby. There was another small space next to Olivia's office, an opening not far from Lori's desk. It was a converted closet, brightly painted and stocked with a haphazard assortment of baby and toddler toys, clothing, and diapers, neatly stacked on makeshift shelves or in baskets on the floor. There were also two cribs catty-corner to one another. Outside the entrance was a stroller with a baby, about six or seven months old, squirming in the curved support. Olivia had noted many times in the past several weeks that the child was growing too big for the current carriage. She made a mental note to investigate how she might help the baby's mother, one of her students, get a new one.

She bent to lift the baby into her arms, her right hand gently patting the child's back. "Where's Taryn?"

"She left Gaye here and ran off, saying she was going to be late for a test. I'm keeping an eye on the baby."

Olivia swayed gently side to side, and the child quieted. "I'll have to come up with another arrangement. It's not your responsibility to act as babysitter."

"I don't mind," Lori said under her breath as she worked at her keyboard.

"I do. The district office is not happy with me insisting that something needs to be done to help teen moms with childcare so they can stay in school."

The baby continued to whimper a little but not actually cry, and Olivia swayed side to side, carefully bouncing the little girl to soothe her. "I don't want Taryn to miss that test. She's a senior and she has to keep her schoolwork on track if she expects to graduate. What else?"

Lori responded to the light blinking indicating an incoming call on her desk phone. "Harvest Prep, please hold." She pushed a button and gave her attention back to Olivia. "A reminder that you have an appointment in about twenty minutes."

Olivia frowned, taking a chubby hand and kissing the fingers before the baby could grab her chain necklace. She continued to pace in a semicircle as Gaye now became distracted by Olivia's gold hoop earring. "Oh. Right. Someone from the local FBI field office."

Lori stared at her with a worried frown. "The FBI? What's going on?"

"I'll give you the short version later. I'm going to check with Mrs. Shih. She's complaining about Colby's brother showing up again whenever he feels like."

"Mmmm," Lori crooned with a knowing grimace. "Looking for trouble. We can't seem to keep him out of the building. He's not enrolled here. I don't know why he keeps coming around."

Olivia smiled at the cooing baby. "I suspect that Curtis is trying to turn his brother, recruit him for his crew. He's older, so I know he's probably pressuring Colby."

"You think Colby is interested? Or just afraid of his brother."

"I don't know. I'm inclined to say he's definitely intimidated," Olivia said. "Colby is not like his brother. I think that's the problem. I'll take a quick look into the classroom, see if Colby is there. Maybe I also need to speak with the district chair about locking some of the doors after school begins. Try to make it a little harder for just anyone to walk in."

"They're gonna say no," Lori responded laconically, reconnecting to the call she'd placed on hold. "They'll use the old but-what-if-there's-an-emergency excuse… Thanks for waiting. Can I help you?"

"I'll think of something," Olivia murmured, and headed for the stairwell and the walk up to the second floor, Gaye in her arms.

Mrs. Shih, the math teacher, had already begun her lessons. The eleven students in the class were opening workbooks, writing in notebooks, and otherwise paying attention. Peering through the wired glass door window, Olivia saw no sign of Curtis, the troubled high school dropout who couldn't seem to accept that his younger brother really wanted to stay in school. Olivia was relieved to see that Colby was attentively watching the equation Mrs. Shih was writing on the board.

Olivia watched for another moment and then made her way back to her office. This was one of her favorite times of the school day—early morning, just after all classes had begun. The high school students all seemed to be where they were supposed to be. Another promising start to the first month of school in the hopes that the rest of the semester would continue as smoothly. Nothing was guaranteed in the community of Harvest Prep, a kind of safe haven for students who struggled with family dysfunction compounded by the dramas and angst of just being teenagers. So far, the students at Harvest seemed earnestly committed to learning. But it was early yet, and it was never easy. Most of them had a lot of challenges to overcome.

Olivia approached Lori's desk and found the assistant watching her, giving her a nonverbal signal. Olivia missed the cue, however, instead drawn to someone standing at the corner of the corridor, his eyes trained on her. He stood staring, tall and erect, a white man who seemed inordinately alert and focused on her. Olivia met his gaze and experienced a sudden and profound physical reaction to his presence that left her momentarily dazed. It gripped her stomach, tightened her throat, and totally caught her off guard. Olivia's steps faltered.

The sensation was quickly gone but left her not only unsettled but acutely aware of the stranger waiting in front of Lori's workspace. He was dressed in dark business slacks and a white, short-sleeve shirt. He wore a tie. His presence was very official and very serious. She observed his square-jawed handsomeness, his sculptured lips, and his close-set eyes. His gaze was sharp, focused, and startling. No smile, no open greeting. His gaze was steady, and Olivia realized he was studying her with equal awareness. When she was within ten feet, Olivia stopped and faced off with him.

Their gazes met and held. It was only seconds of a silent encounter but seemed so much longer to her. Olivia became aware that she was holding on to Gaye like the baby was a tiny lifeline.

She couldn't seem to formulate a coherent thought, let alone speak.

Olivia recovered, but with a dizzying sense that her world had shifted. Her sense of certainty and even safety were no longer fixed points in her existence. She thought it was almost like what had happened several years earlier that had also rocked her life so completely, so profoundly… but this moment was without the pain and loss of that earlier time. This moment had an odd sense of predetermination. Destiny might not have been exactly what she was thinking, but it was close.

"Olivia, this is Special Agent Sloan Kendrick." Lori made the professional introduction.

Only Olivia could hear and interpret the curiosity in Lori's introduction. But she, herself, was left to deal with the intent perusal of the agent's eyes. Still. Not blinking. Holding her gaze. But it was not really the look of someone in a professional capacity who was sizing her up. She glanced away first, using Gaye's animated wiggling and busy hands as a distraction. Olivia tightened her hold on the child.

Lori was speaking. The man was speaking. Strange, guttural voice. Rough and scratchy. He acknowledged her with a brief nod of his head. Lori stood glancing from him to her, waiting for Olivia to say something.

Then the phone rang again, and Olivia exhaled. Her head cleared. She gave Agent Kendrick a calm but careful welcome.

"I'm Olivia Cameron. Sorry I kept you waiting."

The quiet and self-assured intro from Olivia Cameron immediately held his attention. It happened instantly. In just seconds, Sloan Kendrick recognized why. But he let his purpose and his long experience take over. Any other consideration didn't make any sense.

She was, in that quick instance, as totally focused on him as he was on her. Her dark gaze inquisitive, even startled. They were both engaged in intense examination, and Sloan made no attempt to end it. To acknowledge her greeting and get on with it. Like a warning of some kind, he was put on high alert with a profound physical awareness. Her mouth was full and expressive and, he was surprised, had the barest of smiles hovering at the corners. It was her smile that really grabbed his attention. It was sensual and fixed and very… warm. Sloan knew beyond a doubt that it was a natural feature and not forced or false. It very likely came with who Olivia Cameron was.

The presence of the child caught him off guard as well. Had she brought her baby to work that day?

His research to date did not indicate that Olivia Cameron had a child.

"Morning," Sloan finally responded, his voice low and textured. "Did I catch you at a bad time?"

"I was expecting you," she responded. Her arms circled around the child, holding the little girl protectively. Maternally.

He realized he was staring because her slight smile, that natural curve at the corners of her mouth seemed genuine. He didn't return

Olivia's expression, not allowing himself to be drawn in by the welcome. Still, was it possible subterfuge or coyness? Nervousness? Olivia Cameron had a compelling presence. He had to remind himself not to put his investigative process aside despite this surprising interest in her that had no place in his job right now—or anytime.

She continued studying him, smiling that little smile as she approached to stand right in front of him. He didn't move, holding his ground.

"Gun," Olivia said quietly.

He understood immediately. "Ankle."

Satisfied with his answer she turned to enter her office.

"I'm sorry I wasn't here when you arrived. I had to take care of something."

"No problem," Sloan said. She'd taken control of the situation by speaking first. It gave him time to recover, and he was aware that he needed that.

In one brief, sweeping glance, he took in the details of the small office. A desk with several messy stacks of files and papers. A mug half-filled with cold coffee. A cell phone and a box of Kleenex on a corner. A set of keys. "I can see you have your hands full. No pun intended," he said with a straight face.

She chuckled quietly but didn't take a seat at the desk. Once inside the small space, Olivia Cameron stopped and faced him. She took another silent moment as if to confirm a thought or an impression of him. Maybe something about what he'd said caught her attention, or his appearance. He wasn't used to the kind of silence that they kept falling into. Did she not remember why he had come?

"Please sit down," Olivia instructed, vaguely indicating a chair. She finally went around behind her desk, pulled open a drawer, and, bending somewhat awkwardly, began rummaging around the contents. After selecting several very small objects, she pushed the drawer shut with her knee.

Sloan watched her actions but was frankly completely baffled as to what Olivia Cameron was doing.

"It gets a bit crazy around here. It's a new school year, and it takes a while for life to settle down, especially with teens."

"Okay," Sloan responded noncommittally. She *was* nervous. Was there a reason for her to be? "Officer Anderson said first thing in the morning was probably the best time to catch you." She continued her study of him, her gaze giving her the appearance of youthful openness and curiosity. Gary Anderson was right—Olivia Cameron was attractive. "He's the officer from the LAPD who interviewed you after your discovery."

"Yes. I remember. I didn't expect it would take so long for someone to call me again."

"You mean about the money or being interviewed again?"

"Yes," Olivia responded simply.

He felt himself wanting to smile at her quickness but pursed his lips instead. "Your discovery got turned over to my agency because of the amount of money involved, why so much was hidden in an old house, and who might have put it there."

Sloan couldn't tell if Olivia was actually listening. The baby chattered away nonsensically, her contribution a comical interruption in the conversation. Sloan knew it was up to him to lay everything out. "Mrs. Cameron, I'm not going to ask the same line of questions the police used when they spoke with you. There's other information that I—"

"'Scuse me. I don't mean to interrupt," the assistant said from the office doorway. "Did you forget about your class? It's Wednesday."

Olivia started, easily adjusting the weight of the wiggling baby in her arms. "Oh. Right. Almost forgot, and I'm late."

"Why don't I…" Lori began, reaching for the child as her phone began to light up again. "Gimme a sec." She disappeared back to her desk.

Olivia was again in motion; coming around the edge of her desk, she held out her hand to him. Automatically Sloan put his hand out to take her offering. It was what Olivia had taken from her desk drawer. He briefly examined the items, three wrapped candies, and dropped them into his pocket.

"Look, maybe we should…"

Then Olivia suddenly handed off the baby girl. Sloan had no time to make an alternative decision before accepting the child.

"Wait… I don't…" he started.

Olivia was already out the office door. "I'll only be fifteen minutes," she promised over her shoulder, disappearing down a hallway.

Sloan was nonplussed, bemused, and mildly annoyed by what had happened. He'd lost control of the moment while recognizing that he never had control to begin with. He could hear the assistant in conversation on the phone…with a parent, given her placating tone and reference to a student. Sloan focused his attention back on the child in his arms, a very small human specimen with a brown face, dark button eyes, and sparse, soft black curls all over her head. The hair was parted into two small bunches of curls, each fastened just over the ears with plastic hair barrettes shaped like butterflies.

Sloan shifted her against his chest to hold her more securely, to make her more comfortable. She stopped moving, noticing him. She stared from her bright eyes as if he was a curiosity. He thought at once, she'd probably never been held by a white man before, probably had never been even close and had no reference for someone like him. She showed no fear and stared up at Sloan wide-eyed, mouth open…and drooling. The baby uttered something, pointing a tiny finger at him…and attempting to hook her finger into his mouth. He shifted again, discouraging further exploration and using the damp yellow bib tied around her neck to wipe her mouth. She laughed and bounced against his chest as if that was funny.

Sloan didn't smile back at her but examined the child in fascination. He'd never held a child this small, this…new. And he had another thought that made him equally curious.

He left the office, slipping past the assistant without her noting that he was going elsewhere in the building, the baby in his arms. He only guessed that Olivia could not have gone that far; the charter school building was not that big, only three stories high with narrow frontage. Sloan walked along the corridor on one side, peeking quickly into each room in search of Olivia. He got to the end and crossed over to the other side of the corridor to head back to the front. Two rooms along the path, he spotted Olivia. Sloan found her seated on a chair facing about twenty students who were all seated crossed-legged on the floor in front of her. They were perfectly still, silent, eyes closed. Their hands were resting on their knees, palms up. Sloan recognized, in some surprised, that Olivia was conducting a guided meditation session. Her eyes were also closed, hands on her knees like her students. Then she stopped talking and, along with the students, continued in seated silence. After another moment he returned, again unnoticed, to the school director's office deep in thought, trying to process the scene he'd witnessed, but only because the nature of the class was unexpected and seeing Olivia Cameron as the instructor raised even more questions about the kind of teacher…person and woman…she was.

The kind of class she was conducting was also an eye-opener. Meditation? For a high school class? But he knew, from personal experience, about meditation. And seeing Olivia Cameron so confidently conducting a session surprised him; she obviously had experience with the mindfulness technique as well. He wondered *how* and *why*.

Sloan's confusion over the course of events since being introduced to the charter school director was replaced with a new level of curiosity that had nothing to do with his purpose at the school but solely with Olivia. Continuing to act as reluctant babysitter, he nevertheless accepted the situation, slowly pacing around Olivia's office, holding the baby and feeling the warmth and softness of her against him. Mentally, he scrapped a lot of the questions he might have asked Olivia if he'd never had a baby thrust into his care or witnessed Olivia conducting a class meant to calm and center the kids seated in front of her.

Over the baby's head, as she waved her arms about and continued to chatter, Sloan looked around the office. A teacher's office with an odd assortment of items—clothing, books, things the students should not have brought to school—taking up space on the floor, the top of a bookcase, the windowsill. There was nothing really personal here, no photographs on Olivia's desk or pinned to the bulletin board against the wall. Her tote was next to the desk on the floor, a pair of basic black pumps discarded under the chair where he'd been told to sit. There was nothing that told Sloan anything about Olivia to fill in the kind of person she might be or her background. He was even more intrigued.

The time he spent waiting for her no longer seemed terribly important. So when Olivia calmly reentered the office, he was almost surprised to see her back so soon. She vaguely smiled what he took to be an apology for the presumption of leaving him with an infant and reached to take the child out of his arms. Sloan surprised himself, gently turning away from Olivia's outstretched hands.

"I've got her."

Olivia raised her brows and gave in, not making an issue of the situation that was already strange by anyone's imagination.

"You know, you should probably be home."

"Excuse me?" he asked, confused.

"There are a lot of kids in the building. I'm not absolutely sure how many have been vaccinated since COVID, how many have lied about being vaccinated. Have you had COVID? Are you vaccinated?"

Sloan didn't have a chance to answer as Olivia stood right in front of him. He had the distinct impression she was about to lecture him. Except there was an exclamation from the doorway as a cute and overweight young teen hurried into the office to forcefully sweep the baby out of his arms.

"Gimme my child," the young girl confronted Sloan, snatching the baby and startling her. The baby began to whine.

"Taryn, it's okay." Olivia touched the teen on her arm. "This is not an abduction. Mr. Kendrick is here to see me."

"I thought I was helping," Sloan said smoothly.

"I asked him to," Olivia added, her tone indicating it was not an issue.

Taryn glared at him suspiciously. "You can't touch my baby."

"You're right. I apologize. What's her name?"

"Gaye," Taryn muttered, trying to soothe the fussing child.

"She was no trouble. As Mrs. Cameron said, your daughter was safe with me. Cute kid."

Taryn fell silent, not having an adequate response. She glanced at Olivia.

"It was my fault, but there was no time to find you and ask your permission. I'd forgotten about the meditation class, and I asked Mr. Kendrick to step in for me to watch Gaye. Too much going on this morning. How did the test go?"

Taryn was bouncing her daughter. "Aced it," she said confidently, kissing her baby's cheek. "Thanks," she muttered reluctantly to Sloan. Then she pivoted and left the office.

Left alone together, Olivia faced him, and Sloan experienced again that moment after they'd first met that had left him a little disoriented. Almost light-headed. He blinked and took a deep breath, as if to clear his head.

"Is every day like this?" he asked.

"The start of the week is mostly okay. By Friday…"

He nodded. "TGIF sets in."

"Correct."

"Olivia?" Lori called from the outer office.

Olivia gave Sloan another apologetic glance and left her office to answer the summons. Sloan slowly trailed behind her, his mind doing switchbacks from what he'd been told, what he thought, and what a mere hour in the company of Olivia Cameron had shown about her. But all of it would have to take a back seat to a protocol he had to follow, and he couldn't cut corners.

When he reached the corridor, he found a small gathering of teens facing him, as if they'd been standing around discussing his presence. Their acute defense mechanisms had already ID'd him. Sloan quietly scanned the group and assessed that there was only mild suspicion, teen boldness, and curiosity they were going to satisfy.

"You're a cop," one of the boys, a short, chubby youngster in a too-tight school shirt, addressed Sloan. It was an accusatory statement.

"No, I'm not."

"Yeah you are. Detective, right?" another boy asked.

"No...I'm *not*," Sloan quietly repeated, his voice low and rough but not ominous.

"Tee thought you was going to cop her kid," a female student offered.

There was a tittering of knowing laughter.

"What's wrong with your voice?" a tall youngster with glasses asked.

"Nothing," Sloan said simply.

"You sound like a bad car engine," the short, pudgy kid suggested.

Sloan kept his demeanor blank, his attention on the inquisitive students. "Laryngitis."

"You hiding your gun? Where is it?"

"You don't need to know that," Olivia said, joining the hallway gathering.

She came to stand next to him, and Sloan raised his brows, knowing that Olivia was protecting him from the inquisitive students. He didn't find their posturing hostile. Just pushy and insolent. Typical teens.

"You getting arrested?" the girl asked Olivia. There was no laughter this time as they waited for a response.

Olivia glanced at him, and her calm smile of assurance told him how far he could go. "Not today."

The teens, left without a real answer, exchanged knowing smirks but also seemed to have decided that he was not a threat, or at least not the kind of white man they were used to dealing with.

"Man, we thought he's gonna perp walk you in handcuffs," chortled one of the teens, addressing Olivia. It set the others off laughing.

"All right, the halftime show is over," Olivia said, clapping her hands a few times. "Please get to your next classes."

"Is he going to work here?" someone in the group asked as they began to shuffle away.

Sloan shook his head. "I have a job."

He watched the kids split up as a bell pealed throughout the building. A few of his audience dashed through a door into a stairwell to head up to the next floor. Their interest in him had waned with their attention span.

No sooner had Sloan turned to make a comment to Olivia than he saw her attention was drawn to a lone young man, obviously not a student, who she purposefully approached. Sloan stood watching this new encounter, sensing it was different because the man clearly wasn't supposed to be there. Sloan's attention was drawn not because he thought anything would actually happen but because he was curious how Olivia Cameron was going to handle a situation Sloan perceived was not school related. He did, however, sense that there was a potential for trouble.

Sloan could not hear the actual conversation, but body language spoke volumes. The young man, maybe early twenties, was good-looking with a cocky posture that was universal, in his observations, among young men of a certain age who demonstrated more insecurity than they realized. He was dressed for the street. His clothing and demeanor spoke of someone used to being quick and clever, getting over and smooth talking his way into and out of dark circumstances. He would be the kind of person who covertly carried a weapon...a knife possibly, but certainly a gun. He had both of his hands in his pockets, making Sloan all the more suspicious, but he guessed that the young man was not likely to start anything violent with the school's director. He sensed that he had been on the premises before. Maybe multiple times and took his own trespassing for granted. Whatever his reason was for being in the school building, it was not to hurt anyone. At the moment he was drawing too much attention for that to make sense. Too easy to identify him.

Olivia calmly faced off with the unwelcome visitor, who Sloan felt was not unknown to her. As she spoke, the young man stood shifting from foot to foot and looking covertly around now and then, shrugging, shaking his head, and giving the impression that he could care less about anything Olivia had to say to him. When he did respond to her, his tone was not so much arrogant as indifferent and impatient. He was not backing down from the quiet confrontation but challenging her.

Sloan changed his position, facing directly down the corridor to where Olivia and the man squared off. He knew she probably didn't need the backup, but that was exactly what he was doing. He stared at the younger man, deliberately wanting his presence to be known. The quiet, covert glances from him let Sloan know the message was received. He slowly took one step forward and stopped, noting every-thing about the physicality of the young man.

Olivia gestured with her arm and hand. Sloan interpreted the meaning.

What are you doing here? You have to leave.

She tilted her head and leaned in a little closer to the young man. He abruptly turned away and headed to the exit. He pushed his way out with a noisy thrust against the door's horizontal release and slipped out as the door swung closed. Olivia stood for a moment star-ing at the closed door before turning to retrace her steps to him. Sloan was quick to notice that there was not even a hint of the brief but tense encounter expressed on Olivia's face. By the time she reached him, she was composed. Sloan was drawn in by her curious smile and the way the movement filled out her cheeks. Her dark eyes calmly met his gaze. But he somehow knew that Olivia was not as calm as she appeared.

"Wednesday morning at Harvest," she murmured.

"Really? If I might say so, I don't think he's your normal academic visitor." She said nothing to his comment. "I'd like to make a suggestion," Sloan began. "I don't think it's possible to have a discussion let alone an interview here. Too many interruptions and distractions. You've put out a lot of fires in the time I've been here."

"That's an interesting way of seeing things."

"Sorry. The point is, we'll have to set up another appointment. At a different venue. I'd like you to come to the local field office." She was already nodding, perhaps realizing that it was the smart thing to do. "You have a lot of responsibility here, and your students are used to getting your attention when they need it. You're used to giving it to them. That's not a criticism, by the way."

Olivia nodded again. "What do you suggest?"

"Tomorrow."

She raised her brows, surprised. "Tomorrow? So soon?"

"Soon would have been today. Any day, Monday through Friday, is going to be a problem for you. So let's just do this. Tomorrow."

Olivia sighed, averting her gaze as she obviously began thinking through all the reasons for saying no. But Sloan, reading her mind, forestalled any she might offer.

"Come during your lunch hour. That's probably the easiest time of the day for you to get away. You take a break for lunch, don't you?"

"Well…"

He casually stepped around Olivia, signaling that he was about to leave. He reached into his shirt pocket and withdrew a business card, handing it to her. "Let's make it one o'clock. Your students will be back at their first afternoon class by then. I'll make sure you can get back here before the school day ends. Will that work?"

Olivia stared down at the card, as if she needed the time to think, to take back control of their meeting, but Sloan was not about to give her the chance.

"It won't take long, Mrs. Cameron. Officer Anderson has already done much of the preliminary background check. Tomorrow you can tell me all about finding the money."

Olivia brought her gaze sharply back to him. He watched her become the person in charge again. He was, after all, on her turf. That made him want to smile, but he hid it behind the tightening of his jaw.

"I did turn the money in, you know."

"Yeah, you did," Sloan said, taking a few steps backward, away from her. "I'd still like to ask why you made that decision. See you tomorrow. One p.m., my office."

Sloan's exit was significantly quieter than that of the young man who'd left only moments before.

He wanted Olivia Cameron to remember that. Sloan felt no need to be forceful or to intimidate her. He did not want to be Olivia's enemy.

CHAPTER 3

Sloan leaned against the passenger door of his car, casually watching the thin parade of employees as they exited the security gate of the studio property. These were the worker bees of the film industry and never likely to look like they were in the business. They were functionaries, hidden deeply behind the scenes, not needing or wanting the spotlight. Unlike Krissy McKay whom, Sloan had quickly figured out, was constantly looking for an entry into a bigger, more visible position in the Hollywood universe. He let his gaze scan the small crowd and then spotted the one standout. He no longer felt any of the heightened curiosity or excitement that once accompanied meeting up with Krissy. He'd gotten pleasantly comfortable in their relationship of eighteen months. That was until Krissy, in a teary and awkward showdown, broke it off.

If Krissy had thought she could guilt him into begging her to stay or to make any definitive declaration about his feeling for her, her risky performance backfired. He was understanding and kind to her. He was unmoved and not about to change his mind. He was relieved. Sloan had been firm but not unkind from the beginning that if she was looking for more than what they had together, it wasn't going to happen. It couldn't be with him.

But he had liked Krissy a lot. Still did. She was Southern California blond, with artfully disheveled hair that she constantly had to shake or sweep out of her face. Her sunglasses were movie-star dark, as if to make anyone seeing her curious about who she might be. Did they know her? What movie had she been in recently? No and no, she'd never been in a movie. She was an assistant location scout. Not film royalty on any level but fairly indispensable.

He pushed away from the car, his hands deep in his pockets as he watched her spot him and break into a beautiful smile of perfect teeth. She was outfitted in what Sloan had come to recognize as the uniform of female film workers. Comfortable, fashionably different than anyone else but simple, tastefully revealing of an excellent body and tons of sex appeal. She also had a soft leather, oversized tote bag slung over her shoulder loaded with the accoutrements of her trade. She briefly waved, very trademark Krissy, as that was her way of greeting anyone. It was cheerful and inoffensive.

Sloan lowered his gaze to the ground, an image of Olivia Cameron forming, unbidden, in his mind from earlier that day. Mostly he was still caught by her calm, her inquisitive dark eyes…her mysterious smile that, probably totally unbeknownst to her, had a certain sensuality to it. He glanced up to see Krissy approaching, now with her arms positioned to embrace him and encouraging that they kiss. Sloan's hand automatically gripped her shoulder, shifting her ever so slightly so that his kiss ended on her lower cheek near the corner of her mouth, but not on it. If she was disappointed, it didn't really show.

"Waiting long?" she asked as he held the car door for her.

"Not at all. I left my office a little early to avoid the traffic on Santa Monica Boulevard."

"Of course. I forget that you have all the inside info on how to drive across town at the start of rush hour."

"It's called defensive driving. No inside anything." Sloan got into the driver's seat and started the car, pulling smoothly into traffic, watching it from all directions. Krissy sat at an angle so that she could watch his profile. She momentarily played with her long hair. Sloan gave no attention to her practiced gesture. He'd long ago stopped finding what she did interesting...or charming. She was very pretty, very sunny, but all of her moves had played out a while ago, over and over again. Not original and never changing.

"How was your day?" she asked conversationally.

"Fine. I had an interview this morning at a charter school." He opted not to be specific. Sloan knew that it wouldn't be interesting enough to Krissy for her to want to know more.

"Okay." She nodded. "I suppose the students were plotting to take it over and hold the principal hostage?"

"Nothing that dramatic," he responded smoothly. As far as he could tell, Olivia Cameron appeared to have a firm but empathetic control over the school and students. It didn't seem that the students had any thoughts of being subversive. What Sloan had witnessed was that the students liked and respected her.

Krissy slouched in her seat and smiled her bright smile at him.

"I'm glad we're seeing each other tonight. You know...I really miss you."

Sloan was careful and thoughtful. "I think you were very clear that you were ready to move on, Krissy. I know that you wanted something more than what we had."

She glanced out the windshield for a moment, perhaps to hide any emotions. "I always thought that maybe...you know...we would make a more permanent go of it."

"I'm sorry," Sloan said quietly. He certainly didn't want to hurt her, but honesty was all he could give her now.

"You were never in love with me, were you?" she asked easily, just curious.

Sloan slowed for a stoplight, turned to regard her. "If we go down that road, it's going to be a long, uncomfortable night. I like you very much. You're great to be with and around."

She groaned and dropped back against the head rest. "You make me sound like a rambunctious puppy. Cute but…"

Sloan remained silent.

"Well…we certainly did have a lot of fun together," Krissy sighed, suddenly resigned to not getting the response she wanted. She looked at him with a brave and fetching smile. She shrugged. "Your loss."

"It probably is," Sloan agreed graciously.

Krissy distracted herself and ended the discussion by picking up her heavy tote from the floor and digging around the contents. She pulled out a small black studio bag and held it up. "I brought you a gift. It's not every day that a former squeeze gives you a present after you've broken her heart. I know, I know." She cut him off. "You didn't break my heart. But I am disappointed."

"What's the gift?"

"Films. What else? Champagne would have been inappropriate, right? And just in case you care at all, I am seeing someone…so *there*!"

"Good. I'm happy for you. So why the invitation to get together this evening?"

"There's a film the studio is screening at UCLA." She twisted in the seat to drop the bag with DVDs on the back seat. "It's a new twist on a buddy film, and I thought you'd like it."

"What films are you giving me? Do you want them back?"

"No, they're yours. They're not recent films, but I thought you might find them different and interesting."

"Thanks. Mind if I ask about your new beau?"

She thought for a moment. "Ummmm. I think I do mind. He's not in the business. I think one of the reasons he likes me is because I don't come with free popcorn. What about you? Seeing anyone new?"

Sloan gave the impression of concentrating on the traffic and making a left-hand turn at a busy intersection, putting them closest to the campus location for the Dodd building for the screening. And then Sloan had to quickly assess not only his immediate impressions but his unexpected feelings having met Olivia Cameron.

"Not yet" was his answer.

The prospect was under consideration.

———————

Olivia accepted that she'd made it clear to a respondent on her dating app that she would agree to a public meeting with him, the first step after amusing and charming emails, to find out if he was worth more of her time or if he was interested. This was the totally harrowing part for Olivia, justifying herself. Knowing she was going to be assessed on a lot of qualities that were silent, inherent, and even genetic that she couldn't do much about. None of which said anything about the kind of person she was, the kind of woman trying to connect to a strange man.

In-N-Out Burger would not have been her first choice, but it was very public and very popular. She was coming from school but made an effort not to dress that day as if she were a teacher but a more upscale professional wearing good shoes, not sneakers. Her maybe one-time date, Wilson, was certainly presentable. Not much taller than herself but a nice-looking man. He was not so much a bit overweight as stout. A lot of muscle in his arms and thighs. His online photo did not show him with facial hair, but in person his beautiful short beard had apparently been barber treated, trimmed, shaved, and sculpted, and all Olivia could think was that Wilson was wearing some sort of black mask on the lower half of his face. There was a perfectly outlined space where his lips appeared, but the overall affect was very disconcerting. Everything so sharp and even and... theatrical. Olivia was determined not to let any of that matter. She was going to be fair. She was going to try.

"Is this place okay?" Wilson asked, looking casually around, not really affected by the presence of clusters of teens, young mothers providing a cheap dinner for their kids, or the senior singles doing the same thing.

"This is fine. I love In-N-Out burgers." Although she'd opted for just a shake while Wilson had the full deluxe meal.

"I figure, for a first introduction date, you won't fault me."

Olivia smiled. "I won't fault you."

"How long have you been on the website?" he asked, picking french fries one by one, dipping an end into a small container cup of ketchup, and stuffing it into his mouth. Repeat.

Olivia kept her gaze averted from the way he was consuming his french fries. "Maybe six months."

"Have any luck before we found each other?"

She wanted to correct him that they had not *found* found each other; they were just a choice among hundreds of others. "I'm not sure what you mean by luck. I answered several connections. They were...okay but didn't go anywhere."

"Yeah, that happens a lot." He chewed, sipped his drink, wiped his hands on a napkin. "Maybe things are about to change. You're a pretty lady, and I like that you're not scouting out all the men that have been passing by."

"If I did that, it would mean I'm not paying attention to you, right? We're here to see if there's enough of a connection to move to step two."

"Hell yeah!" he said, giving her a very suggestive grin. "I'm agreeable."

Olivia gave him a calm smile that didn't suggest much of anything. But she made an effort not to check the time…or fidget.

In all fairness, she'd hoped that this one, this app-generated date, would be better than the earlier ones. Lynn had been merciless in telling Olivia she needed to get over herself and give these guys a chance. Maybe they weren't Michael B. Jordan or Idris Elba or a really hot Lenny Kravitz, but there were lots of wonderful average guys out there who were straight, sane, and mature.

But she'd not responded to many of them on a check-out date or after two or three dinners. Olivia realized she'd not been affected by any one of them as much as she'd been by FBI Agent Sloan Kendrick. Even recalling his name, conjuring up his very masculine image was enough to send shock waves through her system. Her reactions had taken her totally by surprise…and she was still recovering.

Olivia inhaled and looked at Wilson. He seemed okay. But she couldn't get past the sharp edges of his rigidly trimmed beard, the way he stuffed french fries into his mouth. Was it really reasonable to judge anyone this way?

She watched him as he talked, but she hadn't heard a word he'd said. She blinked and tried to pay attention. It was much better when they genuinely talked about themselves. She mentioned that she was in charge of a charter school. He worked as a clerk for a county judge. He had a four-year-old son from a prior relationship. He liked working out, the Dodgers…

Olivia found there was more about her life she didn't want to share. Too soon. She was able to avoid details. Was the evening enough to warrant seeing each other again?

Wilson said he wanted to. She was willing to try. How did she feel about a casual day at Venice Beach? She wasn't interested. He suggested an upcoming concert at Disney Hall downtown. It was a group she knew. Maybe not a favorite but would do nicely for an evening together. Wilson was so charmingly pleased when she agreed that he suddenly became a tad more attractive to her. Except her perception kept sort of moving in and out. But it was done. He said he'd contact her with meet-up details. And Olivia spontaneously countered with another idea. She had a wedding to attend in a few weeks. Would he like to attend with her? Be her plus one? He thought about it for a moment and finally nodded.

"Yeah, I can do that. Big party, open bar, hopefully good food, and dancing…let's do it. I think I'm okay with not knowing anyone."

"I won't either. Except for the bride, that's it."

Olivia was relieved that a second and third date had been agreed upon. She was very sure that Wilson was not going to be a heartthrob or anything even close to it. And since she had no expectation that it could or would happen, Olivia indulged in a pure fantasy speculation about Sloan Kendrick because there was no harm in a fantasy.

He would be different. He would be an interesting date like she'd never experienced before.

———————

Olivia sat in the nearly filled parking lot in her car, with the engine still running, for a good ten minutes after she arrived at the FBI field office. She had to show ID and her name was checked on a security list before she'd been allowed to continue onto the grounds. She'd debated that morning about coming at all to meet with Sloan Kendrick. Olivia tried to talk herself into the excuse that she'd done far more than she thought necessary to cooperate with the investigation, but speculating about what would happen if she didn't keep the appointment was the first thing that had forced her hand. The LAPD or the FBI might have begun to make more of her refusal than she wanted. But the second thing that had helped her decision was that all contact with Special Agent Sloan Kendrick would be over.

The very fact that was a consideration was not lost on Olivia. And she recognized her final decision as a very bold and chancy move. But she was curious because of her initial reaction to the agent the day before. Sloan Kendrick intrigued her. She'd met many men on dating apps since her divorce. In emails and texts, many of them came across as amazing and available. The reality, however, when they met for drinks, coffee, or a simple stroll along the 3rd Street Promenade was disappointing. Wilson had been the most promising, but it was a compromise on her part not to be so picky, difficult, about his persona.

She hoped the girlfriends would be satisfied and stop complaining.

So now Olivia sat in her car and experienced a gripping apprehension that had started even on the drive over from the school. She didn't want to examine too closely what was happening. Olivia still believed her first reaction to meeting Sloan was maybe fanciful and ridiculous. There were two simple things about him that, for whatever reason, had captured her attention and produced feelings of admiration…and attraction. Instantly—the sound of his rough, ragged voice vibrating along her nerve ends and his large, strongly masculine hands and fingers firm and careful in the way he'd held Taryn's daughter.

And there was that initial gaze-meeting-gaze thing that went on between them, each waiting for the other to blink first. Olivia wondered if there was any possibility that Sloan had felt something similar. Whether he had or not, she knew that this meeting between them… just the two of them…was going to be difficult. And she didn't know what to do about it. She was impatient that she didn't know, was clueless to even understand why their introduction was affecting her so.

She took a deep breath and glanced out the window at the white stone building that housed the field office. Perhaps sixteen stories high, it was completely undistinguished. It was fortress-like, with small, tightly regimented windows, the kind that were framed for security and safety and structured not to be breached. She'd had no idea there was an FBI office in LA county, let alone where it was. Isolated. No other significant structures around it. No notable services. She was a stranger in a strange land!

Was Sloan's job that important, he so important, that he had a better facility than her students at Harvest? Shaking off her foolish insecurity, Olivia finally exited her car, walking with purpose and presence of mind to the entrance, where she again endured a security check. By the time she'd reached the eleventh floor and the elevator doors opened, she was unreasonably angry that Special Agent Sloan Kendrick was putting her through such an ordeal.

An official sitting at a desk took her name and stood up to escort her down a corridor, a left turn, and another corridor, stopping at a door that was invitingly wide open. Olivia's escort stood in the doorway blocking her view.

"You have an appointment with Olivia Cameron? She's here."

The staffer abruptly turned and walked away, leaving her unprepared.

The very first thing Olivia saw was that Sloan was wearing a sidearm holster on his right hip. It was only then that it hit her that what he did for a living was dangerous. People could be hurt or worse. He was standing behind his desk, bent over, studying a map. But the presence of his weapon fleshed Sloan Kendrick out much more than the man he'd seemed the day before.

Wide-eyed, Olivia met his gaze. And the way they studied each other was deliberate. Filled with silent meaning. For a quick instant, her gaze dropped to look at his hands, braced on the map, veins ropey and prominent on the back of each and up his forearms.

And it happened again. That instant gut-wrenching reaction.

———————

Sloan believed he'd done an excellent job of keeping his mind and curiosity focused. There were enough emails, texts, impromptu visits from coworkers, and actual phone calls to keep him legitimately busy before his scheduled meeting with Olivia Cameron. But as his morning progressed, he found himself genuinely annoyed that, since meeting her the day before, he'd been inordinately distracted by thoughts of her. He struggled to make sense of it, a brief encounter having such a monumental impact.

He failed.

When Olivia arrived, on time, and was shown to his office, Sloan knew he now had an opportunity not only to pursue her case as set up by the local police but to delve into an emotional connection he felt had been made, didn't understand, but also couldn't deny. And if he could pin it down to a specific moment he would say, at least, for the moment, that it might have happened when he stood in the corridor outside her office and Olivia appeared from a stairwell with a warm, calm smile that felt personal and with a baby in her arms.

Sloan stood at his desk, a map of the Windsor Hills area of LA, spread across his desk. He was bent over, studying the exact neighborhood of the house where the money had been found by Olivia.

Sloan glanced up, but the staffer who'd made the announcement quickly retreated. He found himself staring at Olivia. She stood, hesitant, outside his office door. But her expression was remote, maybe suspicious. He gestured her inside.

"Thanks for coming in. I know it's inconvenient."

"It is, but that's my fault. Yesterday was..."

"I agree," Sloan interjected smoothly. "Can I get you anything? Coffee? Water?"

"No thanks."

He folded the map and set it aside but did not immediately take his seat. He openly studied Olivia, trying to gauge her body language. Familiarizing himself with his own reactions to her the day before. Nothing had changed. Today she was wearing a blue denim skirt and a white knit sweater, over which was a camp shirt worn as a cardigan. Simple but professional. Everything about her spoke of careful control, a quiet presence.

"I don't suppose you had any lunch before coming in today?"

Olivia shook her head. That perpetual small smile she used hovered on her mouth. But it wasn't necessarily for him. It was just her way of responding.

"No. There wasn't enough time."

"Me either. Maybe I can make it up to you when the case is closed," he said casually, surprised at the spontaneity with which he was suggesting a nonofficial get together. Off the clock. After hours. A date. Olivia remained silent and didn't object. Sloan left it at that. The possibility was enough of a response.

"I have to explain something," Olivia suddenly began, sitting a little forward, not really relaxed in her chair.

Sloan waited, watching her.

"It's not *Mrs.* Cameron. I'm…divorced. I took back my maiden name."

"Sorry about the mistake." He felt a kind of relief at her correction. "My research stated otherwise. Married to"—he found a page printout of data—"Dr. Marcus Palfrey."

"*Was* married to. The kids at school call me missus anyway. Like a sign of respect, I guess. I don't bother correcting them anymore," she said in surrender.

"I'd rather have the truth. As long as we're making confessions, I have one." Sloan retrieved something from the desk and held out his closed hand to her. Olivia's brief gaze was questioning, but she presented an open palm and he dropped the three lozenges into the center. "I don't have a cold…or laryngitis," he added. "But thank you for the thought. And your concern."

Olivia rolled the small candies in her hand before dropping them into her open tote. "I just thought when you talk, you…"

"My voice is…hoarse." Sloan remained standing, looking for and retrieving her case file. "It changed a while ago. Long story," he murmured with a hint of irony. He gave no further explanation, making his history a nonissue under the circumstances.

"Can I ask…were you ever intubated?" Olivia asked.

Sloan's brows rose in surprise, but he managed to keep his expression otherwise blank. "When I was overseas. Bad accident."

Olivia was studying him closely. "FBI service? Or military?"

He was impressed with her interest, her questions. "Air force. I was on the receiving end of an IED under a Humvee."

"Resulting in…this?" she asked, indicating with her index finger two inches or so below her throat.

Sloan nodded, studying her thoughtfully.

"Does it hurt?"

The question was very quiet, as if she cared about his answer. Sloan shook his head. He was stunned that Olivia seemed to care. "No. Not anymore. While I was being treated and unconscious for three days, I kept pulling out the tube." He considered and then said, "I'm told my voice has…character."

Olivia stared at him, and then that curious smile of hers slowly appeared at the corner of her mouth. Sloan felt a certain gratification that he could get that response from her.

"You mean women find it sexy?" she suggested.

He certainly wasn't expecting that. It was…bold. "Not that I've been told directly. What do you think?"

She pursed her mouth and averted her gaze for a moment. And then Olivia gave him a sideways glance that hinted at coyness. He was, nevertheless, sure that was not a game Olivia Cameron played.

"No comment," she said smoothly.

Touché, Sloan thought to himself, impressed.

"I think I should remind you that this is *my* interview. You're here to answer my questions."

She nodded, seeming a little embarrassed. "Yes. I know."

Then he grew serious and pensively stared down at his desk. Then back to her. "We're going to do something a little different." He stretched his arm toward the door.

"What?" Olivia asked, standing and preceding him out the door.

"First things first, I want you to see what the FBI is really all about."

Sloan walked at a leisurely pace along a corridor, turning and changing directions now and then at will. Olivia kept pace at his side, but she was curious as she took in the wall displays, the photographs of famous people and places in high-profile crimes. There was a room they passed where the walls held hand weapons of various vintages with captions of information and details. Sloan said very little, knowing the collection spoke for itself.

Yes, the departments were rather formal but not as sterile as insurance or law offices were. He only passingly said anything about what Olivia was seeing, and she didn't ask any questions. But her interest was obvious. The last hallway was designed with the framed photos of women agents through the decades, including any number who were African American, Latin, and Asian. There had been periodic lawsuits about discrimination within the agency by agents of color, but he had never believed it was the agency itself. After all, it had hired and trained at great expense people they believed had demonstrated skills and mindset needed for the work. And Sloan had come to learn through trial and error that you can't legislate people's feelings and personal beliefs. He had learned as an adult especially that when you got talking with someone not like yourself, you found out how much alike you really were. That early awareness had been an important heads-up…and a life changer. It had helped to broaden his world view.

"Was that a tour?" Olivia asked as they made their way to a small bank of elevators.

"Maybe a little bit," Sloan said, almost smiling at her. He was not a smiler, but something about Olivia and her open curiosity pleased him. "It was a roundabout way to get to the elevators." A bell dinging announced the arrival of a car. It opened, and half a dozen men and women stepped out, all dressed in the same variation of professional dark blue or gray clothing.

Sloan boarded and faced the door. Olivia stood on the outside staring at him. He put his hand on the door sensor to prevent it from closing.

"Where are we going?" she asked, not moving.

"To get something to eat."

The door bumped and bumped, attempting to automatically close. Finally Olivia stepped in. The door closed when Sloan released it. "I thought I came for an interview."

"That's right. This is it."

He went through a security check point, the man and woman on duty nodding hello as he walked through with Olivia. Out the building and to the parking lot. There was a separate section of official agency cars, although there was nothing official looking about them. Late-model sedans without any identifying features for law enforcement. Sloan opened the door of a silver-gray vehicle and held it as Olivia slid into the passenger seat.

"I… I'm really confused," Olivia confessed, fastening her seat belt.

"Don't be, Ms. Cameron. All will be revealed." He hoped his tone indicated some humor. Yet Sloan didn't think it would suit his purpose to play too lightly with her.

They drove only a quarter of a mile to a tiny strip mall of businesses, one being a Chinese restaurant called Gourmet Garden. Once seated, Sloan handed her a laminated lunch menu.

"This is on me…and the agency," he said.

"I hope so," Olivia said tartly, scanning the options. "I would have chosen someplace with more…more ambiance," she commented officiously.

"Probably. But not as good," Sloan shot back, his voice raspy and firm.

In the silence that followed, he knew that Olivia was studying him over the top of her menu. He didn't return the scrutiny, already uncertain with how much he'd revealed. Maybe she hadn't noticed. Or it didn't matter.

They placed their order and, once again, silently confronted each other across the table. But there was a difference, and Sloan noticed immediately. The standoff of the day before, unavoidable under the circumstances, had shifted. He was glad of that. For his part Sloan had to accept that Olivia Cameron had already taken a place of significance in his consciousness. Now he only had to figure out why. He faced her squarely and got down to business.

"As I said yesterday, Officer Anderson has covered the basics of your case but I'd like to get a few more details, if you don't mind."

"I don't. I'm here." She shrugged.

"You sound annoyed."

"I think I've been very cooperative," Olivia said, a bit defensive.

"I appreciate that. You've made this process a lot easier than it might have been."

"I think you have everything from me you need," Olivia said smoothly. "To be honest, I do feel like…maybe…you think I might be hiding something."

Sloan was a little surprised by pushback from her. He had no reason to think Olivia Cameron had been treated unfairly or not shown respect. And so far, no hint that she was withholding anything.

"That's not the issue. This is a process. And I have a job to do to finish the process."

She didn't respond, and a thought came to him. Sloan leaned back against the banquet cushion, picked up the paper-sheathed chop-sticks, and slowly removed them. He thoughtfully regarded Olivia.

"Yesterday a few of the students in the hallway tagged me as a cop. I told them I wasn't, but I don't think they believed me. You know I'm not a police officer, like Anderson, but maybe you feel the same way. FBI. LAPD. What's the difference? I'm still law enforcement, right?" Her continued silence confirmed his thinking. "We both get a bad rap. Frankly, some of it well deserved."

He had her attention. Olivia blinked at him, her expression changing from skepticism to interest. Maybe even reconsideration.

"I'm surprised that you'd actually admit it," she murmured.

He carefully spread the wooden chopsticks until they snapped apart at the top into useable parts.

"If I'm not honest and real, I have no right to demand it from you. I respect how you feel, believe it or not. In my mind, yours is a really simple case. The LAPD's and FBI's interviews with you are purely formality. It has to end in a report that says Mrs...*Ms.* Cameron... has been completely cooperative. There's zero evidence of wrongdoing on her part. We can split the blankets and go our separate ways. The end."

Her eyebrows went up, and the corners of her mouth rounded her cheeks into a grin. She got the Native American reference.

"I didn't mean to accuse you, exactly—"

"Yeah you did," he interrupted bluntly. "Did I pass?"

"What do you mean?"

"Yesterday. Leaving me with baby Gaye. I'm sure that wasn't protocol. What if I'd refused, given her right back to you?"

"I would have handled it. Apologized, maybe. But yes, you passed. It was very...very..."

"In the moment."

"I…really didn't think about it when I handed Gaye to you."

"It meant, to some degree, you were willing to trust me."

"I wanted to see if I could, yes. How were you going to react. Maybe I pushed it a bit because you're…eh…*law* enforcement."

Their lunch courses were placed before them. "Mom was a different story," Sloan observed, showing knowledge and ease in the use of his chopsticks. Olivia didn't even try, reaching for her fork.

"I'm sure you know it's understandable. In general the kids are very skeptical about everything. You can't blame them. They don't hold authority in high regard. Certainly not police."

"And I passed," Sloan concluded comfortably. He didn't wait for her to answer. "I hope we've moved beyond the whole cop/law enforcement thing. The services could do a whole lot better."

"Accountability would be a nice start."

He pursed his mouth but didn't respond directly to Olivia's suggestion. She wasn't wrong…but it was complicated.

"What was the first thing you did when you found the bundles in your walls and realized they all contained stacks of money?" He glanced at her.

"Well…I roughly counted two bundles but didn't bother opening any more. I just assumed they were all the same."

Sloan let her talk as she recounted the morning of the discovery. But he was also studying Olivia, her expression and gestures. Any hesitation, anything that didn't match the story she'd told the police a week earlier when she'd call to report her find would have raised a red flag. He'd already surmised his overview was really going to be pro forma. But he was just as interested in the cadence and sound of her voice. The way she looked him right in the eyes and didn't shy away from his observation. Her eyes were very dark. He had to fit all that he was learning about her into what he'd gleaned from official records.

"What made you decide to call the police?" he asked.

Olivia gave him a look that suggested he should know the answer to that already.

"I knew right away that I had to. I didn't have any idea why money was hidden in my great-aunt's house. It was a mystery that I wasn't prepared to unravel. I did photograph the bundles…"

Sloan glanced up sharply from gripping a fried dumpling with his chopsticks. "Why?"

Olivia shrugged. "To keep a paper trail, my own record. Just in case."

Sloan arched a brow. "Were you afraid that the police would claim a different number than what you counted?"

She didn't blink. "I thought it was possible. I didn't want there to be any mistakes."

"Good idea," Sloan commented. "But how do they know you photographed everything you took out of that wall?"

"I…well…that's a good question," she said wryly.

"So you do understand why an investigation might be necessary?"

She nodded, conceding. "I do."

"It says in the first investigative report that you have a brother."

Olivia shifted in her seat, crossing her legs at the knee as she allowed herself to become more comfortable. She twirled her fork in a pile of noodles. "Jackson. He's my older brother."

"Did you tell him about the money?"

Olivia shook her head. "Actually…no, I didn't. I mean, once I knew I had to turn the money over to the police, there didn't seem to be any point. The money wasn't mine."

Sloan had to smile to himself at her tone of incredulity. Like…
seriously? No way. "You're saying you never even considered just keeping the money?"

"No."

She was indignant. But her gaze dropped briefly, not meeting his.
"And I was very surprised when Officer Anderson contacted me to
say LAPD was bringing in the FBI to continue the investigation. He
didn't say why. What, exactly, are you looking for?"

"Fair enough question," Sloan nodded. "I don't suppose Officer
Anderson gave you a full accounting of how much money came out
of that hidden cubby."

"No, he didn't."

He could see the interest in her eyes. "My field office had to take
over the count, but first we had to deal with paper that was in bad
shape. Sitting in foul water for we don't know how many years left its
mark. The estimate is just over one million." He kept his gaze trained
on her. Her expression was exactly what he knew it should be if she
were being honest. Stunned surprise. Her lips opened around a soft
ohhhh. She blinked at him.

"The bundles were different denominations but mostly in high
figures, five-hundred- and thousand-dollar bills. We checked with the
treasury department and could find no incident of a bank robbery or
corporate theft, but there's no question the money was stolen from
somewhere. Otherwise why hide it? My office is trying to go back
through the ownership records of the house, to the year the bills were
circulated, and try to match the amount to any reported incidents of
fraud, embezzlement, that sort of thing. I don't want to spend a whole
lot of time doing that to no end."

"How long do you think the money's been hidden in the house?"

"It's hard to pinpoint exactly, but at least since the early 1930s, based on the printed dates on the bills and their condition. The forensic lab captured and recorded what it could. We're still checking into records and reports."

"That's a lot of money," Olivia mused thoughtfully.

"Yes, it is," Sloan agreed. He regarded Olivia thoughtfully. "You're renovating the house. Planning on moving in when the work is done?"

"I thought about it. That was my original idea. But now…I don't know. I feel a little spooked by what I found inside. I'm not superstitious, but…I'm not so sure I want to live there. First of all, it's a huge house. I don't really need all those rooms, so much space." Olivia glanced off into the distance for a moment. "And now…I can't help thinking about the money and the previous owner and…maybe he left the house to my aunt for a reason. Like a thank-you for her care and kindness. Maybe…" She turned her gaze to him, shaking her head. "I don't know."

Sloan listened as Olivia confirmed a lot of other questions he wanted answers to but not knowing he did until she began to recite her thoughts on the inherited house.

"You could finish the renovations and sell it. Where its located, you'll do very well."

"I suppose," she said without much interest.

For whatever reason, silence fell between them, and it was inevitable that they'd simply regard each other now and again in moments of pure personal interest. Sloan made no attempt to fill the void, just letting his observations and feelings fall naturally where they may. And where they seemed to fall gave him great emotional pause. He also didn't try to make an excuse for the distance he suddenly believed was being closed between them. Olivia broke the silence, regarding him with a kind of open curiosity that he'd noticed from the start. He had the feeling that there wasn't a whole lot that she let intimidate her.

"How did you end up an FBI agent?"

He wasn't expecting that. He had to rearrange his expectations of what Olivia was thinking. "To be honest…it just happened. I'd come back from the Middle East and…"

"Middle East?"

He nodded. "Right."

Her scrutiny was focused. "Afghanistan."

It wasn't a question. Sloan nodded again. "Right."

Olivia's reaction surprised him again. She paused her eating with a fixed study of his face. Her gaze seemed to hold concern—and perhaps lots of unasked questions.

"Almost two years. I was in intelligence." And then Sloan spontaneously offered up another fact. "I met my wife after I returned stateside. We're divorced now."

She'd slowed her eating to listen to his tale. Sloan was stunned that he'd rushed in to share so much with Olivia Cameron. But there was also the feeling that he'd done so with a purpose he wasn't quite sure of yet.

"I'm sorry it didn't work out," Olivia offered quietly.

It was clear to Sloan that Olivia was caught off guard by his confession and didn't quite know what to say. Was she suddenly thinking of her own divorce? She seemed to be waiting for him to say more, but he wasn't going to. *TMI*. It was definitely time to get back to the real reason for summoning Olivia to his office.

"Question. I'm just curious. What would you do with the money if you could keep it all?"

She shrugged. "I really didn't think about it. But now that you ask…" Her brows furrowed with thought as she considered her answer. "I…I really can't think of, you know, a big-ticket item that's on my *must have* list. I can't even think of anything I need."

Sloan found her response a novelty and was secretly amused.

"Would you share some of your windfall with your brother?"

"Jackson?" she asked as if the idea was slightly ridiculous. "I don't know. He's doing well on his own, thank you. He's a doctor. Radiology." She was thinking again. "Yes, of course I'd give…*something* to him and his partner." Her gaze widened on him, as if she'd said something she hadn't meant to.

Sloan pursed his lips. "Nice gesture. But he is your brother."

Olivia took a deep breath, trying to manage the conversation, his question. "I think I'd first of all want to try to help the kids in my school. So many of them need so much."

"You can't solve all their problems, you know."

"No," she murmured. "Maybe scholarships for college or extra lessons." She suddenly chuckled. "I don't think I'll mention it yet to my girlfriends. They won't take but a fast minute to tell me what they want."

"But…what about you?"

Olivia's gaze once again went into deep space, inside to some secret wish or dream. She slowly shook her head. "If my ex and I had survived the bad time in our marriage, I would say…buy a nice home to raise a family. Travel for sure. Finish my degree…"

When she looked at him again, her gaze was still somewhat distant, as if she were actually imaging possibilities.

"Maybe I should make a list of ten things I want to do if I had a million dollars," she mused.

"Why not? I think you deserve to give it some thought. You never know. There could be lots of things you'd want for yourself."

The waiter brought the check and a small plate with three wrapped fortune cookies. Olivia reached for one, passing the plate to him. He only took the check.

"Aren't you going to open one?" Olivia asked.

Sloan shrugged. "I don't think my life lends itself to wishful thinking...or fortune cookie predictions."

"But what if something really happens just like it says?"

"Do you believe in all that?" he said, nonetheless unwrapping one of the cookies.

"I think I'm hopeful. I think I feel...*you never know*," Olivia repeated to him. "What does yours say?"

"You first," Sloan murmured, studying the slim piece of paper from his cookie.

Olivia looked at her paper again, finally reading out loud. "'A lifetime of happiness lies ahead of you.'"

"Sounds nice." Sloan nodded. "When does the lifetime begin?"

"Maybe it already has," Olivia said quietly, reading her fortune over and over. "What about you?"

"'A calm mind will help you make your next decision.'"

"Do you have a calm mind, Agent Kendrick?"

Sloan considered her question and her. "Sometimes. Why don't you take the last one?" He placed his slip of paper on the table.

They prepared to pay the bill and leave. Olivia took the third cookie and, at the last possible moment, also picked up Sloan's fortune and put everything in her tote bag.

They walked out to the car and headed back to the field office.

"I want to say something," Olivia began suddenly, to his profile. "You are the strangest FBI agent."

"You've met other FBI agents in your lifetime?" he asked, amused.

"I haven't met any before you, but…you seem…different. You surprise me."

"Thank you," Sloan said simply.

"You aren't annoyed by what I said?"

"What you just said suggests you're pleasantly surprised. Or dumbfounded that I'm weird in some way."

Astonishingly, she laughed quietly.

"No. You're definitely not weird. Just…really thoughtful."

"I take all of that as a compliment. But you can't forget I'm still doing a job."

They got back to the building, and he didn't invite Olivia to return to the office with him. There were no more questions he needed to ask, nothing else he needed to find out from her. At least as it pertained to the discovered money in her house. But…there was one thing…

"I'd like to ask you to do one more thing. Could you put off returning to the house or continuing with renovations for a while longer?"

"Why?" Olivia questioned as he walked her to her car.

"I'd like to take a look around. Just to see for myself where you found the money. See what the chances are that there are other hidden spaces in the house. I'd like to set that up quickly…maybe in the next few days. Are you okay with that?"

"If you think it's necessary."

"Good."

Sloan stood watching as Olivia got into her car, started the engine. He considered her again, knowing his gaze was more personal in the moment than he should have been. Then he turned to head back into the building.

"Wait!"

He turned back. She had the window down, leaning out to talk to him. Sloan approached and bent over to bring them closer for conversation. It was an odd moment because their faces were very close and a kind of aura between them made it feel even closer. Her eyes were deep, impenetrable pools.

"I'd like to ask you…" Olivia began.

But she seemed flustered suddenly. Was it because they were practically nose to nose through the open car window? Sloan waited her out, saying nothing.

"Would you consider letting some of my students visit on a field trip to your office? I think it might be good for them to see what you do, what the FBI is all about…and why you're not a cop."

Sloan grinned at that. "I think we can work that out. We have a Teen Academy that's just right for your kids. They're old enough to qualify. A full day of hands-on activity to see how interested some of them might be in a career here."

"That's great. Thank you so much."

"My pleasure, Ms. Cameron. Call me and we'll set up something."

He stood back up, stretching his hand in farewell, and again turned away.

"Olivia," she called after him. "You can call me Olivia."

He stopped and looked over his shoulder to find her watching him. But her expression and demeanor had already moved them out of the realm of interviewer and subject. Olivia was uncertain…but maybe hopeful?

"Sloan," he responded to her opening.

CHAPTER 4

"Hi, Taryn. Come on in."

Olivia watched as the teen entered her small office and immediately sat down in the one extra chair meant for visitors. She noticed that the young girl, usually very confident, seemed a little skittish... and unsure.

"How's Gaye?" Olivia asked to put Taryn at ease and focus her. She generally was happy to talk about her daughter.

"She's okay," Taryn mumbled, her leg bouncing quickly up and down with nervousness.

Olivia made a note. "Did you bring her in today?"

"No, ma'am. I left her with my mom. She loves taking care of Gaye, but most of the time I...you know...I want to keep her with me."

"Well, you know we're set up to babysit when needed. I just want to make sure you get to class and keep up with your work. You're a senior, so you know how important this last year is. What's up?"

Taryn finally met her gaze, straight on and with a level of anxiety Olivia had not seen since the previous year when the girl had confessed that she was pregnant. Taryn had done amazingly well during her pregnancy, attending classes until she couldn't. But then was absent for several months after Gaye was born and ignored the inquiries to her mother and from Olivia about how the school might help her return to class. Nothing had worked until, just as the previous school year was coming to a close, Taryn had returned, more mature, focused, determined…and with a new daughter. She'd worked very hard to catch up and keep up. Olivia had used all of her means and authority to make sure the young new mom got encouragement, adding her own personal resources when needed to help Taryn out. But she'd learned quickly not to probe too much into the home situation or the circumstances surrounding her pregnancy…or the identity of her baby's father.

"What can I do for you?" Olivia asked.

"I know I wasn't on the list of who was going to that academy. But I want to go. I mean…I…I really want to be there." Taryn got it out in a rush, her tone firm and assertive.

Olivia was taken aback by the demand and curious. She was well aware that none of the kids on the school list were interested in becoming police or FBI agents. But they were curious enough about getting a behind-the-scenes look at an organization that more often than not failed most of them that there was always the hope that one of them, or more, might be truly interested in what the organization might hold for them in the future.

"Why?" Olivia asked simply.

Taryn shrugged, gnawed her lip, perhaps not having thought she'd have to explain.

"I don't know anything about the FBI and what they do. But I saw this movie about an agent and she was a girl. And she had this special assignment because she was smart. Well…I can do that. I'm smart too."

"I agree, but the question is, do you really want to go into law enforcement? Are you seriously interested in, maybe, becoming a cop?"

"Why not? I work hard…"

"Yes, you do…"

"And I can learn. I can learn anything!"

"Again, I agree." Olivia nodded. She studied Taryn's posture, the intensity of her facial expressions. The leg bouncing had stopped. She braced her arms on her desk as she leaned across to address the young girl. "Okay. I'll add your name to the list. You'll have to have your mother sign a consent form…and you have to decide who will care for your daughter. You'll be at the academy the whole day. Once you start, you have to finish the course. No leaving early. No complaining…"

Taryn's expression changed instantly to relief and excitement, but she then pulled herself together to show the grown-up side she was obviously developing. "Yes, ma'am. I can do it. I can do all of that."

"Okay then. It's a go. You're in."

There was an uncharacteristic, elated, brief squeal from Taryn.

Olivia stood on the periphery of the twelve-student group selected for the special visit to the FBI field office. These were the students who'd maintained a high grade point average, had no discipline record of note, and knew how to listen. But just to keep a balance, she'd thrown in a few students who were walking the line between hopeful outcome and needing a lot more work. And there was Taryn, the only female student who'd shown genuine interest in the program.

What gratified Olivia was the seriousness with which the students participated in the daylong event. While she wasn't sure if any of the sessions changed their minds about law enforcement, they had shown interest and, so far, seemed riveted by what they were to experience. She hoped it might be life-changing for some of them in terms of a career prospect. She'd already learned through a Google search and information that Sloan had sent her that the agency covered an astonishing number of crimes that fell under federal jurisdiction, including civil rights violations. One of the sessions was meaningfully about how the FBI covered and resolved hate crimes against, specifically, people of color, women, and LGBTQ+ citizens.

Olivia watched Colby, a shy, serious kid who often needed a little push into new experiences. He had a tendency to shrink into a group, not to be noticed, and she knew it was a cultivated technique to also avoid the overpowering influence of an aggressive older brother. Here, with only his curiosity to guide him, Colby predictably asked the most probing, complex questions. And so did Taryn.

Behind her, even farther in the background, was Agent Kendrick. Sloan. Just mentally saying his name gave Olivia a start, a roiling awareness combined with a jolt of excitement. It was mysterious but thrilling. In a moment of sheer intuitiveness, she felt that they were silently flirting with one another. He glanced at her; she met the gaze and returned it. It was breathtaking, making her feel, ridiculously, like someone not much older than her students.

Sloan had met the group at security, welcomed them, but never acknowledged that he'd met a few of them during his first visit to their school. He was not exactly friendly, but he was totally accessible to their comments and questions. And he was very cool with the ribbing he got because of his scratchy voice. Had some punk judo-chopped him to the throat during a fight? Had he swallowed a pit that remained lodged in his throat?

Sloan never became overly familiar with them. He was in charge, and they were on his turf. And he was wearing his gun. Olivia wondered if that was a deliberate display of power and authority or an agency requirement. She wondered if it was loaded, even though the safety catch was on and there was a protective cover on the hand grip, making it nearly impossible for anyone but Sloan to actually gain control of the weapon.

Olivia observed him as he introduced what the day would be like, also making it clear that this was a serious, working environment and, if they couldn't obey the protocol, they would be asked to leave, a second invitation never to happen.

"Are we clear on the rules?"

"Yes" came the muted, respectful response.

Sloan walked them through some of the building, mostly those areas where they would be having lessons and demonstrations.

To the inevitable question, he added, "*No, you will not be testing firearms.*"

After that, the FBI instructor in each of the teaching areas took over and Sloan stepped out. Olivia found herself alone with him, very aware of his presence, more and more sensitive to his nearness. An interesting warmth seemed to emit from him. If she had to assign a description to it, she would say safety, protective, steady. Authoritative.

He was such a decidedly different kind of man than she'd ever met. Who was he, really? Why did he seem so very different to her as a man in nearly every respect?

They maintained small talk, but there seemed to be a kind of falseness to the levity. As if beneath the surface something else was definitely going on between them and this was not the place or the time to explore it. Bigger consideration...did she want to? Olivia was aware of a lot of covert glances. The tension between them made Olivia a little on edge. She wondered if there would come a time when she would know the reason for sure. And then what?

"Nice group," Sloan commented, his tone low and gravelly just over her right shoulder.

That sensation again.

"I wasn't expecting…what's her name? Tara?"

"Taryn. I'm really surprised she was interested. In fact, she practically begged to be added to the list."

"She's a good addition," Sloan said. "She's making the boys step up in their game."

"I'm not surprised. Taryn is one of the top students. And I was careful. I didn't want to embarrass the school and myself or make it difficult for you."

"I wasn't concerned. I trust your judgment."

"Does that mean I'm off the hook in your investigation?" she teased.

Sloan looked at her carefully, as if trying to decide how much to say. He was amused but under the circumstances kept it tamped down. "Not yet, but you're close. I have only a few more areas to flesh out, but I expect to wrap my report any day now. You worry too much."

"I have a lot of responsibility," she murmured.

"So do I. But you know, at least what you do isn't life-threatening."

She thought about that, catching a quick glimpse of Colby bent over a table with the other students, studiously examining fingerprint samples. "Sometimes," she said cryptically.

There was an hour's break for lunch, and the kids loved that they could get whatever they wanted from the agency commissary. But they sat together, already exclaiming over what the morning had been like. Olivia thought it appropriate that she sit with them, but Sloan convinced her to let them be.

"They don't need supervision for lunch," he advised. "Let them talk among themselves. I think they're more likely to share insights, ask questions. They're going to be interrogated, so to speak, in the last session. It's not helpful if any of them feel they know less than their classmates."

She looked at Sloan, this time in admiration. He really did pay attention. He did consider consequences.

Sloan found a table some distance from the students but where she could still more or less keep an eye on them. She got chicken salad on a bed of lettuce and iced tea. Sloan settled for a sandwich and coffee.

"Sorry. No fortune cookies," he said, biting into the multigrain bread.

"I wasn't going to complain," Olivia said, feeling somewhat giddy that there was just light banter between them now.

She was still at a point where she kept returning her gaze to him. Still trying to ferret out his personality and character. Still finding things about Sloan that, weirdly, made him so...appealing. But Olivia couldn't help tempering her opinion with healthy caution.

She had very good reason to be careful despite her interest.

"If I haven't already said so, I can't thank you enough for allowing the kids to attend your academy."

"You have said so a number of times. I expect I'll probably also get an official letter on school stationery thanking me and the agency. No need for your students to submit individual notes with drawings."

Olivia laughed, taken by his easy humor.

"In many ways the agency is well aware of its tenuous relationship to the communities where it has offices and personnel. This program is an outreach. It's an open-arms approach: Come and check us out. Bring the kids. Get involved. It actually works but…"

"I think I know. There's never any reporting of the good things you do, right? In New York City they've had a Police Athletic League department for more than half a century. I bet not more than ten people have even heard about the great work the officers do with kids in sports and mentoring. But it's what happens to men, women, and, increasingly, children in the streets that's the bigger news. People die, and families remember that."

He silently regarded her as she spoke, unable to stay away from the political that she was more aware of than perhaps himself. Some of her students came from situations where it was all too real. Olivia suspected his awareness was still theoretical.

He said nothing in direct response to her comment.

"I'm glad I had a chance to see you again, in a different official capacity."

The admission caught her off guard. It sounded almost personal. After a moment of thought, Olivia decided to go with her own train of thought.

"How would you feel about being a guest at our next quarterly Sports Saturday?"

"Still trying to thank me?"

She grimaced. "It's work to get the students out of the school building and doing other things, like sports. If we sponsor, somehow they think of the games as just more schoolwork. The boys all believe they'll make the NFL or ABA anyway, but right now I want them to get more physical exercise. It's distracting and healthy, parents don't worry about where they are, and they have fun. It's a three-hour event with soccer, baseball or softball, touch football. Parents and siblings come. There's a picnic."

"You're very proactive. What do you do on the weekends that's just about you?"

"You asked me that before. Embarrassing but not much, I guess. Me and my girlfriends get together for lunch or dinner. We rotate who hosts. I'd like to also be a little more creative and active. There are so many things I'd like to try that don't involve food or shopping." His cough sounded suspiciously like a chuckle, his eyes bright. "I'd like to break the cycle of predictable girly stuff."

"Let me know if I can be of any help. I think I'm pretty good at tactical diversion."

Olivia considered his boast. Was he serious? "Maybe not so much with females? Unless you have different meaning for tactical diversion than I do."

He didn't laugh, but Olivia suspected he probably wanted to.

Sloan seemed thoughtful as he finished his lunch, and raised voices from the table where the students gathered indicated they were also done, their energy level indicating they were ready for the next activity. He regarded her as they stood and gathered the debris of lunch for disposal.

"Thank you for the invite to the sports thing." He glanced at her but signaled for the students. "Can I bring someone with me?"

Olivia was surprised. He wanted to bring *someone*. "If you want to, sure." They all left the lunchroom, Sloan advising the students on the afternoon program, the final for the day. Olivia trailed behind, not eavesdropping on the conversations but aware that some of the students sidled up to Sloan for asides with him, including Taryn. As always, Sloan was attentive. She noticed that Taryn seemed to have a lot to say or ask. And he said a lot in response.

While the students were closeted away in the darkroom of a photo lab, Olivia paced the hallway outside, when Sloan suddenly appeared right next to her again.

"Your kids seem to be really enjoying the activities."

"Yes, they are," she agreed, adding a smile.

Sloan regarded her. "Feel free to contact me if you want to do this again. It's a successful program, and the agents here are really committed."

"Thank you," she murmured, pleased by his offer.

Sloan took a step back but reached to briefly squeeze her elbow. "I have to see to the rest of the afternoon. I'll be back." And he left.

She watched him retreat with a firm stride and little excess movement, very quiet. Olivia sighed when she was alone, agitated by the way she was feeling, impatient with an inability to control it. She absently rubbed where Sloan had touched her elbow, a light touch that nevertheless felt so personal. She spent the entire time alone mulling it over and finding no answer. When Sloan appeared again, he was holding a small stack of white nine-by-twelve envelopes with the FBI seal printed on the front. And he carried a plastic ziplock bag holding something she couldn't identify. He walked by her toward another room, a conference space with comfortable swivel chairs around a rectangular table.

"Come with me," he instructed her.

Olivia entered the room behind Sloan and watched as he efficiently set up the table with the envelopes and the bag that, when emptied, scattered lapel pins. In the hallway, the students' voices could be heard again. The day was coming to a close. The last class was done, and they would be leaving to board a bus that was waiting to return them to the school grounds.

The kids entered the conference room still wound up with all they'd been through, clearly not having expected so much to take place. A few mentioned firm intentions to join the FBI when they were old enough.

"You need to have at least an undergraduate degree," Sloan calmly reminded them.

"Yeah, yeah, I can do that," one student voiced with conviction.

"No, you can't," another student challenged. "You can't even pass gym."

The students erupted in laughter.

Sloan once again took charge, stating he hoped they'd found the activities worthwhile. There was a chorus of enthusiastic *yeahs*. He congratulated them on finishing the academy…and graduating. And added that they should thank Ms. Cameron for coming up with the idea to attend the academy.

Catcalls and slang props were forthcoming for Olivia, some random woo-hoos combined with wrist rotations in the air. She stood near the door merely smiling at their praise. Sloan then called out their names, one at a time, to come up and receive their certificates of graduation from the teen academy. And they were given a lapel pin, a replica of an actual FBI pin with slight modifications so that it couldn't be used unofficially for ID…or other purposes. They were not only surprised but impressed.

Olivia smiled a genuine thank-you this time for Sloan. No matter her confusion that he asked to bring someone to the Sports Saturday she'd invited him to attend. *Who?* He had been incredible the whole day, to all the students. To her.

She gathered her charges and maneuvered them toward the exit, pointing them to the waiting school bus. Olivia turned to say a final goodbye to Sloan and found him standing just out of and to the side of the main door. He gestured for her to come to him. She did.

"Did I forget something?" she inquired, frowning.

Sloan only responded with a lopsided grin. Then he boldly slipped two fingers into the V opening of her sweater. Olivia gasped and looked at his invading hand.

"What are you doing?" she managed. He didn't respond.

Instead, the tiny needle from the back closure of a pin poked through the navy-blue fabric of her top. Olivia lifted her gaze to his, but Sloan was carefully watching what he was doing and firmly attached the top face of the lapel pin to the backing.

"Now it's official," Sloan murmured.

"Official? Did…did you just pin me?" she asked, uncertain.

"Ms. Cameron…we hardly know each other." He feigned shock. It was outrageous that he could joke about it, but really, it was a clever response, and Olivia reluctantly gave him points for using humor in the moment.

"So it's official? I've successfully completed your program…like my students?"

Sloan shook his head. "Not exactly. They did all the work. Your pin is a…a congratulations, if you like."

"For what?"

"For not letting your skepticism and point of view about law enforcement, any law enforcement, deprive the kids of this opportunity. Well done."

She stared at him. "Have I been that obvious?"

"Yes," Sloan said simply. "You're tough. But you're fair. Email me the details of that sports event."

With that, he waved to her before turning to reenter the building. Olivia stood a moment longer to consider that almost nothing of the day had escaped his keen attention—or his thoughtful assessment.

What did that mean?

What did she want it to mean?

The afternoon had finalized Sloan's assessment of his opinion of Olivia Cameron. It had also solidified his interest. The one thing he was now certain of was that he wanted to continue seeing her. It felt instinctual. Until he finished and turned in his report, however, any pursuit or communication remained official. He was about to change that. His very limited contact so far was daring and risky, but he felt compelled to push the envelope to purposefully test Olivia's reaction. She was surprised with the few gestures, but she never objected or warned him off. They were small acceptances, but acceptances nonetheless.

Sloan returned to his office, closing the door and sitting at his desk to use the phone.

"Lieutenant Anderson, please, if he's available… Special Agent Kendrick… Sure." Sloan was put on hold. He sighed with relief that Anderson was around and not out on a case or at headquarters for something worse. He was impatient to move forward with his own interests. "Yeah, Gary. Hey. Sure I'm not interrupting anything? Got it. This won't take long.

"I have one more thing to take care of, but I'll be submitting my report on the Olivia Cameron case in a few days… No. As far as I can discover, there's nothing more to accomplish. That's the short version of what I'll be writing up… Your department has the final word, but I'd like to ask you to do something for me. I'd like to be officially pulled from the case. My part is done… I appreciate that… Frankly I just don't think I'm needed anymore. No need to spend the agency's or my time chasing a vague, long-ago theft. I'm convinced we'll never find the way to the start of it. I consider Ms. Cameron's money discovery pure coincidence. You know how I feel about coincidence… Thanks. One more thing. What's going to happen with the money? That's fantastic. If everything works out with the public notice, will there be a problem with me informing her?… Well, I've had the most contact with her, and I'd like to be there to see her reaction… Good enough. Let me know… That's great. I appreciate it."

Sloan sat back in his chair, feeling some relief from the conversation with Gary Anderson, as if one hurdle had been cleared. But there were more ahead of him. He checked the time. It was late in the afternoon. He hoped the rest of the day could be concluded without any outside criminal occurrences or emergencies or being put on a last-minute call sheet. He needed time to get his head around where he was moving with Olivia, where he strongly felt he wanted to go.

It occurred to Sloan in a moment of absolute truth, he'd not felt so strongly about anything since returning from Afghanistan. At that time, nothing had seemed like it would ever be certain in his life again. And so far, he'd been right. Even his brief marriage had turned out to be a casualty of that war.

Sloan, not usually given to examining aspects of his personal life, had come to the unavoidable conclusion that Olivia Cameron, for reasons still to be discovered, had very definitely become part of his personal life. He was stunned by the realization, but he was also pragmatic. She was in it.

Deal with it.

He only had to figure out how he was going to get close enough to find out more and to see if he could cultivate some interest on her part. The thing was, he knew it was there…carefully controlled and curated, maybe. Olivia was smart and fearless, in a quiet unassuming way. She wasn't afraid to speak her mind, but she wasn't combative. She wasn't hesitant about confronting him eyeball to eyeball and holding his gaze as if she was probing deep into his soul. He was sure he knew what that was all about as well. He only needed Olivia to confirm or deny the possibility of her own interest.

The other thing that Sloan had to confront was the swiftness with which his attention had been grabbed when they'd met. Their eyes meeting down the length of a school corridor and creating a fierce tension in his stomach had struck a nerve that said *you're all in from this moment.* And that subtle but lovely smile, her cheeks filling and directed at him. Her flawless brown skin. He liked the way her hair fell to her neck, smoothly framing her face. A side part swept a portion of her hair over her forehead, not quite obstructing her left eye.

She's beautiful, Sloan thought. An instant appraisal that was more true each time he saw her. Each time her magical smile was presented to him.

"Okay. We're off," he murmured to himself, standing.

He said it as if now were the start of a race or an event headed for a conclusion—or the establishing of a fact that he still had to prove.

He wandered off to thank all the agents who'd given their time and their expertise to a dozen or so charter high school kids who needed as many opportunities as they could get.

———

"For heaven's sake, Liv, it's only a date. Not even that. You just want to see if the man is worth the time and effort. Is he interesting? Presentable? You know…reasonably good-looking. Has his own teeth. Does he make you laugh?"

Olivia sighed dramatically. This was the usual drift of the conversations with Tessa. "It's too much work. I always feel like I'm keeping a score sheet while trying to have real conversation with these men. I feel like they're doing the same thing to me."

"That's the way the dating game is played this century. In a lot of ways, it's easier. Dating sites really cut to the chase and the wait time. You can meet a whole bunch of men in a short period of time. Like…in an hour, you could have a dozen responses to choose from."

"It's nerve-racking, Tessa. It's…scary."

"I get that you're scared, but you're taking it too seriously. I swear, Dr. Marcus did a real job on you after that accident. He seemed to lose his bedside manner overnight! And that excuse about his conjugal rights. Asshole! Who knew he was so shallow?"

Olivia winced at Tessa's very honest assessment of that time and her ex.

"Pretend online dating is a game. Pin the tail on the bro. Which one is the real man? Are any of them going to fit into your mythical checklist?"

"So far I'm zero for what? Ten? Fifteen?"

Tessa laughed, her head thrown back and showing excellent teeth on the desktop screen, her wine sloshing precariously in a glass. "Girl, you need to lighten up. Yeah, there are a lot of dogs out there, but there are a lot of lovely men. Gainfully employed, not living with their mothers or trying to control you. You have to be more patient and less picky."

Olivia took a delicate sip of her own wine. Tessa's comment gave her pause as she mentally sought to fit Sloan Kendrick into any of Tessa's categories. She adjusted her legs to rebalance her laptop as she and her former college roommate conducted a Zoom cocktail hour. It had become a much looked forward to weekly meetup, especially during the COVID pandemic. Even after the country began to unwisely open up too soon, there was something very cozy and safe about their wine weeklies.

Tessa had insisted it be just the two of them this evening and not the other two women in their circle, Lynn and Mallory…all together jokingly referred to as the Gang of Four.

"You know, you're right," Olivia said, pensive. "Suddenly I'm willing to consider men I would have passed over in college. I accept that we all have shortcomings. It's actually nearly impossible to find a Prince Charming or even a prince who's not a frog. And the truth is some of the men in my past have been brutal about my flaws."

"Oops. I hear the ghosts of the recent past. I know you're talking about Marcus. Only he would think your idiosyncrasies were flaws and not adorable quirks."

Olivia did not confirm. There would be no point. Her life was an open book to Tessa. They'd known each other since the first day freshman year at USC. Olivia drank more wine. "Maybe brutal was too strong a word."

"Not inappropriate. To me, Marcus was always a bit judgmental, sometimes in an unkind way. It's astonishing that he thought he would make a brilliant doctor."

"He is brilliant. Just…distant. And full of himself." Olivia felt a guilty need to clarify her opinion. "But he can be very concerned and caring."

"Mmmmm. Depending on the day of the week. Or if he could get personal PR out of a case. Okay, I get that you hate online dating, but the traditional way of meeting the opposite sex can't compete with online platforms and a catalog of eligible men. Right?"

Then how did she explain the way she'd met Sloan? Olivia considered without responding to Tessa's comments. And why was she thinking of him as eligible? Available? Desirable? How was her instant reaction to him explained away by anything else but chemistry? Or desperation.

"What *really* happened between you and Travis?" Olivia asked quietly. She knew that she was the only one Tessa would even entertain mentioning the man who had been almost *the one* to. "It had to be more than a fabulous job prospect in New York."

Tessa stared at the screen, blinking and thoughtful. She glanced off to the side and ran a hand under her thick, loose weave of curly hair. It was very becoming and looked very natural. She sighed. Drank more wine. "Didn't I tell you?"

"You weren't saying much of anything at the time of the breakup. I knew you were...devastated."

"The usual. His parents wouldn't let up. It wasn't that they didn't like me. They were really lovely to me. But they kept throwing his future in his face and the downsides of marrying someone Black. I don't give Travis credit for holding out for almost two years, telling them they had no right to dictate who he could love. He never committed to me. Maybe he never intended to, but...I know he loved me, Liv. Maybe as much as he could. Then his father brought up two magic words. Children. Inheritance. He caved. I didn't want to know which held the most clout. What was the point?"

"Did he want children?"

Tessa pursed her mouth. "I don't think it ever came up. We were busy having a great time together. Going to premieres. Traveling, partying, setting up that gorgeous place in Santa Monica. I would have loved kids with Travis. I want kids. I think. I don't know, Liv. Sometimes I'm not sure. Not a good recommendation for parenthood."

"Well, you're far more likely to meet a good man than I am. You'll date *anyone*."

Tessa's eyes widened, bringing her out of her reflection, and she roared with laughter. "*OMG*! That's true, I suppose. After all, that's how I met Travis. This cute white guy chasing after me all over Southern California was fabulous for my ego and my libido. Ummph! But…I'm not sure I'll go that route again. Every time there's a fight, you're holding your breath wondering if the Big R thing is coming up in the next sentence. It's…stressful. I won't rule it out, but I'm certainly not going out looking for that kind of relationship again."

But what if you're not looking at all? What if, out of the blue, this guy appears in your life and you're positively gobsmacked?

"So this guy that tagged you last week. Are you going to agree to meet him?"

Olivia sighed. "Maybe."

Tessa shook her head. "You are really a sad case. Coffee is not a commitment. He's not taking you home to meet his mother."

"You're not giving me any credit for seeing Wilson *twice*! That has to count for something. He's had two chances."

"And?" Tessa asked, skeptical.

With that, Olivia's insides twisted, and a vivid image of Sloan appeared in her mind's eye. Wilson wasn't Sloan. Sloan was most definitely not Wilson. She recalled how suddenly close he was to her when she'd called him back to her car to ask about a field trip for Harvest students. The way he'd stared at her, his gaze studying her features.

What did he see?

"Lynn is really good at finding guys. Some sort of extra sense. She's passed along some strong prospects to me since I broke up with Travis," Tess said with quiet admiration.

"*Please* don't say anything to Lynn about me. She's critical. She says I'm not trying hard enough. I'm not. Maybe I don't care. Maybe I'm not ready."

"Yeah, she's tough. And angry. But she's too sexual to give up. For Lynn it's all recreational sex. Healthy release. Did she ever tell you about her orgasms?"

Olivia nearly choked on a swallow of wine. "No, thank goodness. And don't you dare share!"

"I'm telling you, you wouldn't believe the things the girl has tried. You do have to be open to all possibilities, right? That's where you fall short, Livi. Don't think too much about this."

Olivia considered the remaining wine in her glass. Considered Sloan and the unexpected and bold move he'd made, slipping his warm, large, masculine fingers into her sweater opening. She'd relived the moment, the sensation, that whole night. Her stomached twisted again. She quickly drained the glass and grimaced, as if she'd just swallowed bad medicine.

Sloan was not bad medicine. He was only unexpected…and had changed the game.

"Right."

CHAPTER 5

The assistant, Lori, was on the phone when Sloan started down the long corridor. She was also multitasking, working on her desktop and, once, silently admonishing a wayward student who appeared to be loitering in the hall on his device.

Lori acknowledged his approach with a practiced, careful glance before giving her attention back to the call. As he neared the desk, Sloan heard the fretful half cry of a baby. Walking around Lori's desk, he stopped at the open doorway of the next room. He saw two cribs, two strollers, and two children. One he recognized immediately as the child he'd cuddled and held during his first visit to Harvest Prep. Gaye, he recalled. She was hugging a stuffed animal, but she was distracted by his sudden appearance. She stared up at him with great curiosity and calm. She suddenly broke into a babbling grin and pointed a finger at him. Sloan raised a brow at the baby's possible recognition of him. He stared back at the baby and, after a moment's hesitation, approached and crouched next to her stroller. He continued to study her, and when she reached out a hand to him, cooing something or other, he gently took her hand, rubbing his thumb on the soft skin, shaking it a little as a way of greeting. The other child, a younger boy, was asleep in the next crib. Then Sloan stood, heard the goodbyes from the desk, and exited the makeshift nursery to face the assistant who'd risen from her chair.

"Hi. Lori, right?"

She silently nodded, studying him.

"Sloan Kendrick. FBI. I was here—"

"Oh, right. I remember." She sat down again. "The students are still talking about that academy thing they took part in. You have a fan club going."

Sloan was surprised but remained straight-faced. "I'm flattered, but they don't get any extra points for that." He titled his head toward the nursery. He could hear Gaye babbling to herself. "Do you regularly babysit kids?"

Lori shrugged. "It's the best we can do, I'm afraid. The girls… the young parents…don't want to leave their babies at home. They still kind of see them as cute little dolls and want to carry them everywhere. But Ms. Cameron was afraid the mothers might drop out of school because of their kids and maybe never get back."

"So they bring the kids to school?"

"It's actually a growing movement. LA County is still grappling over how to establish day care in schools, how to pay for it, but they do exist. Fortunately, we only have two young children to deal with. What can I do for you, Agent?"

"I'm here to see Ms. Cameron. I thought I might catch her before school let out."

Lori shook her head, her expression suddenly puzzled. "She's not here. Haven't heard from her since just after lunch. She always calls if something came up and she's running late. Nothing all afternoon."

"I tried calling her, but it went right to voicemail. Never got a call back."

"I'm trying not to worry too much. Ms. Cameron's very responsible."

Sloan was quickly processing information from the assistant against the facts of the moment. No one knew where Olivia might be. "Maybe she's unable to call..." he murmured, instantly on the alert. "She never told you if she had an appointment of some kind?"

Lori frowned, thinking. "No. I mean, maybe I didn't pay a lot of attention once she said she'd be back in an hour."

"Sorry to be pushy, but could you possibly remember anything else she might have said? An appointment, a person, something she had to do?"

Lori frowned, shaking her head. "I think... I think she mentioned something about...the police and something they were looking for..."

"Where?" Sloan asked, his FBI persona suddenly in charge.

"Where? I'm not sure. Actually...I think Olivia mentioned her house."

"Thanks. That's very helpful," he said, smiling benignly and heading for the exit.

"School lets out in an hour. I'm betting she'll return very soon."

Sloan was already out the door.

Rush-hour traffic, in a town where rush hour was almost twenty-four hours anyway, was a real roadblock to Sloan's drive to Olivia's house. Not the one she currently lived in in Baldwin Hills but the one she'd inherited in Windsor Hills. Not that far between communities as the crow flies, but this afternoon, heading into early evening, the crow was flying all over the freeway in a stop-and-go crawl that had Sloan anxious and impatient. And his anger was also growing with what he guessed might have happened that afternoon, where Olivia had gone.

It infuriated Sloan that time was lost before he could exit the freeway and make the rest of the trip by side streets. Not as much traffic…but again, stop and go. When he drove up the hilly street of Olivia's house, he immediately saw her SUV pulled halfway into an improvised carport that was being used to store materials for use in her renovation project. But seeing Olivia's vehicle was only moderately comforting and only answered one question: *she was here.* Or might be.

Sloan could see there were two other immediate problems. The front of the house faced east, and the sun was already at the back. It was no longer bright in front. The high-powered flashlight he routinely kept in the trunk of his car might not be enough illumination if he had to search through the property. The other problems he didn't want to fully explore. Olivia was hurt. She'd had a run-in with a second party. She wasn't actually here at all, only her car. That was more than two problems, and Sloan began to imagine others. He was wearing his gun but never entertained he was going to need it.

The house was built partially on an incline, the right side, as you looked west, on the shallow downward angle. Sloan parked his car right at the top of the angle, in front of the entrance. There were no sounds. No one calling out. He got out of the car, listening closely for any movement, a voice. He started up the steps to the door. It was unlocked, and he quietly entered, stepping into the center of the foyer, a staircase to his right, looking around for a sign.

"Olivia?" Sloan called out, no chance that he wouldn't be heard in the hollowness of the empty house. There was no response.

He made the decision to move to the right, onto the floor extension that would be above a lower level. He walked through the foyer into another room. It could double as a dining area or living room or simple salon.

"Olivia?" he tried again. Then he thought he heard some muffled movement a little to his left. He made his way toward it.

———————

Olivia heard her name and thought she was dreaming.

Unbelievably, as concerned and uncomfortable as she'd become in the last several hours, she'd managed to finally fall asleep. After screaming and yelling for help, she'd given up, briefly, in tears of sheer frustration. No one was coming. No one knew where she was. When she'd fallen through the floor, there had been no time to prepare for impact. She'd landed on her left side, managing to partially brace herself with her forearm, hip, and thigh. She was sore, but nothing was broken.

In a momentary flashback, Olivia suddenly recalled her situation in another accident, not of her making, but then she'd been hurt badly. Marcus had been concerned when he was summoned to the hospital, but he had also been critical of her. Why hadn't she been more careful? Had she been speeding? Couldn't she have avoided the truck? And then he asked the doctor if she was stable or was any surgery needed. Yes. And no. He had an important meeting with his department head and had to leave her. He'd return afterward.

"I can't play savior right now. I'll be back."

A stroking of her cheek. A kiss on her forehead. And then Marcus was gone.

The truck. Her car on its side, having flipped once. The terrible pain in her back and head. The blood...

Olivia squeezed her eyes closed, took a deep breath, and coughed out dust. She looked around the cement cell of a very small room. No windows, no door, no way out. It had a musky, dank smell. It was dark. She rolled over and heaved herself into a sitting position. She didn't seem to be hurt. Olivia had reached for her cell phone in the pocket of her white slacks. Then gasped when she suddenly recalled that she'd dropped it into her purse when she began to explore the kitchen. She'd left it on a sawhorse makeshift table in the foyer.

She heard her name again, and her heart lurched. A phantom pain returned briefly in her back, her head. She gritted her teeth.

Marcus was going to be so angry.

The voice was closer. It wasn't a dream. Someone was above her. Someone was roaming the rooms, the kitchen. Their movement stopped where the pantry door had been. A duplicate to the one she'd first discovered that held piles of money. She'd found another hiding place.

It went quiet. Had she imagined someone calling?

Someone was at the pantry opening. They'd see the other panel, the hole in the floor. She saw a shadow over the hole.

"M…Marcus?"

"Olivia? It's Sloan. Where are you?"

Emotion and relief swelled in her chest. "Here! I'm down here. I'm… I fell…"

He kicked through the second door, sending some debris crashing below. A head appeared.

"Oh…Sloan," Olivia moaned.

"Watch out!" he shouted to her as he just missed making a false step that would have sent him plummeting through the floor to the space next to her.

Olivia made a small yelp as wood splitters fell around her. She crouched back against the cold, bare cement wall. Sloan squatted down over the opening. She peered up at him. Her heart was pounding in her chest. She was covered in dirt and dust from where she'd fallen. It was even in her hair.

"Are you hurt?"

She shook her head. "No. No." Her voice was hoarse. Flat. Sore. "Sloan?" She didn't plead.

"You're okay. I'll get you out."

He disappeared, and she heard rummaging, stuff being moved and shoved aside. Sloan shouted as he continued to search for anything that could be used to help her. "Is there anything down there to stand on? Bricks or wood? A crate?"

"No, nothing." He seemed to move farther away, and she couldn't hear much of anything. "Sloan?" Olivia got no answer.

"Stand back," he suddenly called down to her, standing on the edge of the opening above her, holding a ladder. He suddenly stopped, in thought.

Sloan leaned the ladder against the wall where he stood above her and detached the hard casing that housed his sidearm and snapped onto his belt. He pulled it off and set it aside and reached for the ladder again.

He knelt, lowering the ladder and awkwardly pulling it opened. It was too short. If he dropped it or let it go, it would topple over to the floor below.

"Listen to me. I'm going to brace the feet against the floor and hold the ladder in place. You have to climb up to me."

"I…don't think…I…"

"Yes, you can. Hold on and try not to move around as you climb. I'll keep the ladder steady, but you have to be quick. You're not that far below me. Olivia? Do you hear me? You're going to be okay."

Olivia stared up, seeing his eyes and a rigid determination to his countenance. He was stretched out on the floor above. She could detect Sloan's stiff, straight arm bracing the top of the ladder, forcing the legs against the cellar floor.

"Come on," he commanded. "Start carefully until you find your balance."

She squeezed between the wall and the bottom rungs of the ladder and placed her foot, taking a first step cautiously. The ladder settled but otherwise didn't move. Olivia gripped the sides and then began to climb. Only once did she feel the ladder lurch an inch or two, starting to tilt to one side. She stopped moving instantly. Sloan forced the feet of the ladder flat on the floor again.

"Keep moving," Sloan urged. "You got this."

The strain of trying not to shift her weight made her hands and arms shake. She stopped when she had only two more rungs to clear the opening, quickly glancing up and seeing Sloan's face hovering just above her. His forehead was beaded with sweat.

"I can't go any higher." The ladder swayed with her weight and indecision.

"You're almost there, Liv. *Step up*! I've got you!"

Olivia's breathing became heavy and erratic. Like she'd just finished climbing a steep hill. She made a tentative reach for one more rung.

"I'm going to let go of the ladder…my right side. When I reach down, grab my hand. Okay…*NOW*!"

They let go of their hold at the same time, but there was a fumble as Olivia flailed for his hand. They finally clasped tightly, and she made a short, startled sound. She shifted in an effort to hold on to Sloan's hand. He had a death grip on her. Her feet pushed the ladder. It began to slowly flip to one side. Sloan let his hold on the ladder go completely and swiftly reached down in the hole to circle her lower back. Olivia gasped again as she forcibly expelled air. Sloan snatched her halfway up through the hole, hauling her against his chest. She lost her breath.

He grunted as he fell backward, forcing her up in his arms. Sloan felt a sharp pain along his arm from scraping over something rough on the floor. He ignored it. He clasped both arms around Olivia and quickly twisted, landing with a heavy thud on his back with her on top. The ladder crashed to the cement floor beneath them. Olivia was clutching his shoulders, her hands shaking. He lay breathless for several seconds and then struggled to sit up while still holding her.

"Okay...okay," he muttered, his voice even more hoarse, strained, and breathless. "You're fine. It's over..."

In a burst of willpower, Sloan pushed her away so he could look into her face. Olivia's hands were cold, her skin a dull, flat color. Clammy. He forced her face up so he could look closely into her eyes. Olivia blinked, but she was dazed. He shifted her off his chest completely so he could come to his feet. One of his knees locked and unlocked as he moved, shooting pain through his leg. Sloan half lifted, half carried Olivia away from the hole, out of the tight space that was a false pantry entrance to begin with. He lowered her to the ground, kneeling over her. She was struggling for air, her chest heaving. Olivia couldn't even form words, any kind of response. He pulled her into a sitting position. Sloan's hand pressed firmly to her back, rubbing and pressing in a circular motion. Suddenly Olivia could breathe freely. She gasped, panting gulps of air.

Not letting go of her, Sloan stretched to the side, reaching for something. It was a heavy, folded tarp. Olivia listlessly watched as he folded it again and slipped it under her legs, trying to elevate them above her chest. She struggled to sit up with her legs elevated, so Sloan gently but firmly pushed her back down.

"I'm...fine...fine," Olivia kept insisting.

Sloan grabbed her wrist, putting two fingers on the pulse point and holding them there. "You're not hurt or bleeding. Your pulse is too fast."

"I...I'm trying...breathe...normal." Olivia swallowed. "I don't want to go into shock."

Sloan frowned and stared into her eyes. "You'll come out of it in a few minutes."

"I know. Water?"

"Not yet." He let go of her wrist. "Still too fast. Don't move."

"I'm cold."

"I know." He was looking around. "I don't see anything to cover you with."

Olivia pulled her face away from his exploring hand trying to force her to look at him. "Marcus...wasn't my fault...said, I'm okay."

"You will be," Sloan whispered. He stroked and tried to smooth her messy hair, her face.

His thumb pushed under her chin, and Sloan continued to study her face, looking to see if her pupils were dilated. Their gazes met... and locked. Slowly, Olivia focused. She blinked again. She let out one long exhalation in a whimper. But she felt odd and disoriented.

What Sloan did next Olivia never saw coming. It was slow motion, and she had plenty of time to move, do something. But she didn't. He shifted his sights, watching her mouth. Suddenly, Sloan pressed his mouth to hers. It was a light touch, momentarily exploring, rubbing over her lips. He withdrew barely an inch and pressed again closer, firmer. Olivia didn't feel surprised, and her lips parted, her eyes drifted shut. Sloan accepted her acquiescence, cupping her face in his hands. Olivia wrapped her hands around his wrists. If she meant to stop him, she changed her mind. She sighed, Sloan moving his mouth against hers. Or was she moving her mouth against his? Her fingers moved caressingly over the back of his large strong hands. She liked his hands.

The kiss did not deepen, but they maintained contact, and the effect was immediate and electric. Sloan didn't seem inclined to end it. He seemed comfortable where they were. Not exactly in each other's arms, her legs were still slightly elevated, but they were connected in the most fundamentally emotional way. Olivia was confused, but she liked the way she was beginning to feel kissing Sloan. She more than liked the pressure of Sloan's lips, the teasing texture of his tongue. Her erratic breathing now was not from the possibility of shock. Or if it was, she was not in any danger. Kissing Sloan was creating another kind a trauma. A different, special, never-before-felt experience.

But then, with an agonizing jolt of awareness, Olivia pulled her lips away.

"I…have to stop."

Sloan responded at once, standing to help her up. In her recovery, she'd also regained strength. She pushed at his chest. "Don't. Don't…"

"Okay. I won't touch you."

"I don't need to be rescued. You're not my savior," she said, her own voice sounding unnatural, angry, and…unreasonable.

———

Sloan was stunned. He was absolutely, suddenly chilled to the bone.

"You mean…are you accusing me of…of being…like some *white* savior?"

Olivia blinked rapidly and stared at him, her eyes blank. Her breathing was still shallow and rapid. She frowned.

"Wh…what?"

"What you wanted to say was…you don't need some white man to rescue you. I'm the only white guy here. You didn't need me to rescue you. But you definitely needed someone to help. That was me. The white guy."

Olivia didn't move, only stared at him. Was she dazed and disoriented, frightened and hypersensitive? Did she not remember what she'd just said? She looked at him, trying to focus, to see clearly. Sloan turned away from her. But he, too, appeared weary. Defeated.

"I… What do you mean?" she asked in a bewildered voice.

Due to their unplanned kiss, a show of emotion, and what could have meant more, Sloan felt a bit in shock himself.

What did she mean, savior?

"You'll be all right once you get home," Sloan said to her, calm but formal. "I'll drive you in your car. Are your keys in the ignition?"

Olivia shook her head. "No. There."

Sloan followed her pointing finger to a space somewhere over his shoulder. Her tote was on a makeshift worktable, her keys next to it. He picked up the bag and keys. He handed the bag to Olivia, not meeting her gaze. He looked around and located his gun holster, snapped it back on, and settled the firearm against his hip.

"I know you think you can walk on your own, but I'll hold your arm. Let's go." He opened the front door and waited for her to exit in front of him, firmly holding her upper arm.

He became distant, a defense against Olivia's rant. Sloan also realized that the very fact that she'd managed to affect him so quickly was also a stark indication of the depth of his desire to be someone *more* in her life. Had he really let the fast and first aura of attraction go to his head? Had he not been paying attention to Olivia's skepticism? As a Black woman, of course there were institutionalized odds stacked against her. He knew that. Had he been too cavalier in fashioning a connection between them that maybe only he could see?

Olivia had gone silent as they left the house. Sloan realized he couldn't overlook the chance that she was still on the edge of shock, that she was still very affected by what she'd gone through, alone, all afternoon. He tried to let the practical, knowledgeable, pragmatic side of him slide back into place and make sure she was okay, to take care of Olivia in a moment when she could not do so for herself.

Had he forced her to get up too soon? Could she tolerate a car ride without vomiting? He recognized he'd become distant and seemed to be getting even further away.

Sloan watched her as she walked unsteadily to her car. He opened the passenger door and held it until she got in. Olivia just sat, staring ahead. Exhausted. Sloan silently fastened her seat belt for her.

She turned her gaze to him, and Sloan realized that she was not recovered. She needed to get home. Have a shower and get some sleep.

Was he trying to rescue her?

"What...about you?" she asked.

Her voice sounded hollow. She closed her eyes. He knew Olivia was feeling slightly dizzy.

"How will you get your car?"

"Don't worry about it."

And that was the extent of conversation. Olivia was too worn-out to talk, and Sloan felt the same way. She'd nearly fallen asleep during the fifteen-minute drive to her house. He knew where she lived, how to get there, and Sloan unerringly made his way to a neat, small Los Angeles cottage. The car stopped, and as she unfurled herself from the front seat, Sloan already had the passenger door open. While she grabbed the frame to haul herself out of the car, Sloan went to unlock and open her front door. He felt a stab of pain in his left knee. The one that had locked when he'd put his strength behind hauling Olivia clear of the hole in the floor. When he turned around, Olivia had reached him at the door. She stared at him, her gaze questioning.

"Are you okay?"

His jaw was tensing, his mouth grim. "I'm okay."

Sloan ushered her through the door into her house. He took her tote from her and set it on a chair just inside the living room. He looked at her, and they stood facing one another in the late-afternoon dimness.

"I'll wait until you go shower, get into clean clothes. It's best if you don't eat anything for the rest of the night. Drink water. You're probably dehydrated. You'll be fine in the morning. I probably won't be able to talk you out of going into school, but take it easy. You've been through a lot today."

"It could have been worse, I guess. But you—"

"Don't worry about me."

She frowned, bewildered. "Sloan..."

"Go. I'll wait here until you're out of the shower."

She opened her mouth to say more but stopped. Olivia left to do as he'd ordered. She slid her hands along the wall for support as she disappeared down a short hallway.

Olivia returned twenty minutes later dressed in a kimono robe, barefoot, her hair wrapped in a terry cloth turban. He stood in the living room, his hands in his pockets with his sight trained on the entrance as she reappeared. His other observation, from his gut, was how beautiful Olivia looked. Her demeanor serene and graceful. Her brown skin glowing and clear. From where he stood, he could detect the smell of lavender.

They stood facing each other across the space of the living room. His gaze softened slightly. She looked refreshed and composed. Olivia suddenly began walking right to him, and he saw that she held a brown bottle in one hand and cotton pads in the other. She stopped in front of him.

"Let me see your arm," Olivia ordered quietly.

Sloan was confused and then felt the slight tightening of skin on the back of his arm that indicated an abrasion. He twisted his arm and glanced down, seeing the long scratch just above his elbow, but it wasn't deep enough to bleed. Olivia reached for his arm, but he pulled away.

"I'll take care of it."

"I'll do it," Olivia said, firmly taking his arm and positioning it so that she could see the wound as well.

"Should I accuse you of rescuing me?"

Sloan regretted his words and his tone as soon as he spoke. He sounded petty. And he was bewildered. Olivia didn't respond to his cold question. She opened the bottle of peroxide and applied it to several cotton pads. She took his arm, and Sloan didn't resist, watching Olivia, with her focus and sudden calm as she swabbed the scratch, the cool liquid stinging along the surface cut. She didn't look at him as she worked, concentrating on what she was doing. She didn't say anything, and he didn't either. Suddenly he was relieved that neither of them knew what to say.

Olivia completed her attention to his laceration.

"That should help. You don't want to risk an infection."

"Thanks," he murmured, his voice gruff. Olivia's actions created mixed emotions in him.

"It will heal quicker if you don't cover it up."

He silently watched as she recapped the bottle and put it aside with the used pads. Sloan reached for a glass of water on an end table. He held it out to her.

"Water. I hope it's okay I wandered into your kitchen."

She took the glass. Their fingers briefly touched. "Of course it's okay. I feel much better."

Sloan nodded. She took a few thirsty sips of water. He watched as Olivia swallowed, watched as her face settled into her usual appealing features of quiet calm. But he was still too stunned to be drawn into her charm. He could feel himself resisting being drawn in again.

Sloan abruptly turned and headed back to the door, opened it. He stepped halfway out and turned back to look at her. He had a momentary urge to ask Olivia if she wanted him to stay awhile. But he also wasn't willing to risk another accusation thrown at him.

"Get some rest. I mean it." And before she could respond, Sloan pulled the door closed behind him.

He walked to the curb in front of Olivia's house. He had a suspicion that she might be watching, peering from a hall window facing the street. Sloan didn't turn around to see. He pulled out his cell and made a quick call. It lasted less than thirty seconds. Ninety seconds later an LAPD squad car slowly drove through, stopping right in front of him, and he climbed into the back. He never glanced at the house again, to see if Olivia was watching him ride away. If he'd done so, Sloan wasn't sure how he'd feel if she wasn't there.

Sloan was fooling himself if he thought it would be simple.

In the dark of his balcony, he stared out over the railing to a view that displayed mostly the Pacific, with a diagonal strip of the free-way. The busy LA night below was quiet from where he sat stretched out in a patio chair, the cars and streetlights a tiny distraction not taking away from his deep and troubling thoughts—that his instant attraction to Olivia would now instantly go away just because a harsh possibility had suddenly reared its ugly head.

It was *not* so simple. Sloan's brows furrowed deeply over the way his gut was reacting. There was no way he had not *seen* that Olivia was African American when she turned down the school corridor toward him that first day. It was a fact that took second place to what he intuitively experienced from her smile, her eyes—*the windows to her soul*—and the way she carried herself with a presence that drew him in. It was the way she approached him totally without any suspicion or hostility. He was used to both of those. There was only one other time he could remember anything remotely similar to his response to Olivia. But he was only seven years old at the time.

The thing that Sloan had known for certain was that in the moment of their gaze meeting, somehow, he and Olivia were on the same page. That is, until the one moment in the house after he'd helped her out of a difficult situation. After he'd confirmed that she was unhurt but maybe in shock. Until what she'd said was said.

Sloan understood immediately what Olivia meant with her comment about a savior. He closed his eyes and tried to conjure up a situation in which her scenario might have happened. He couldn't. Of course, he'd never had any of the experiences that challenged her because she was Black.

Nonetheless, he knew far more than Olivia could know about the insidious assumptions and beliefs held on both sides of the aisle and had also learned how ignorant and pointless they were. He'd also learned when he was still a kid that if you just listen to someone, you were far more likely to not only learn some truths but discover surprising similarities as well. He had no idea if any of that came to mind when he'd met Olivia Cameron. But Sloan did know that once he experienced a kind of immediate recognition, there was immediate acceptance.

His intuitive and profound reaction to Olivia did not change with the confrontation after the incident at her house. His only concern was, how the hell was he supposed to deal with it now?

CHAPTER 6

Olivia's mantra today was *peace and calm.*

She'd been mentally repeating it to herself all day. Now she was sitting alone, incorporating the chant, breathing in and out through her nose, syncopated with the words. Almost a week ago, after Sloan had gotten her home, shaken and limp with exhaustion after what she'd been through at her inherited house, she'd meditated that night with *discerning*. It could have been substituted with *sympathetic* or *generous*, maybe even *forgiving*. She belatedly considered either would have been a better…fairer…attribute to Sloan. She would not have been able to sleep without the forty minutes of mindfulness she'd learned years before to incorporate into her routine. And ever since that afternoon, Olivia had lived with not thoughts of some kind of retaliation against Sloan but remorse.

She'd treated him badly.

It was mostly quiet in the corridors outside the empty and darkened gym because the students were in the last class of the day. Olivia sat on the third row of the bleachers, forward almost to the edge, with her back straight and her hands resting on her thighs. She tried very hard to remain focused on her breathing, the cornerstone of not thinking, of emptying her thoughts so that she could center. But her thoughts continually brought her back to the awful encounter and the things she'd accused Sloan of. And Olivia's stomach tightened and spasmed with her regrettable behavior.

What she wanted to do now was apologize.

To set things right.

But there was resistance. She didn't need to be forgiven. She wanted to be understood. And she wasn't sure she could have it both ways. And what was Sloan feeling, if anything? Or had he written her off as a difficult case he was well rid of?

Did it matter to him how they'd parted at their last meeting?

When her smartphone quietly chimed, as she'd set it, Olivia finished her very private meditation session. She returned to her office just as the last class of the day was ending, and the students, as was the protocol, were escorted to the exits by their homeroom teachers and dismissed. This ensured that all students had left the building and the doors could be officially locked for the day.

"You're still here?" Lori asked, surprised when she saw that Olivia was still in her office, slowly gathering her belongings to leave.

"I'm finishing up. I'll leave in a few minutes."

Lori hesitate. "Is everything okay?"

Olivia glanced at her with a quiet and vague smile. "Yes, of course. I'll see you in the morning. Bye, Lori."

Lori accepted her farewell and continued on her way.

Olivia sat staring into space. She knew she needed to call Sloan. She knew she wanted to. As much for herself as, hopefully, for him. Her angry, historic racial reference made perfect sense to her. It was inappropriate and unfair that Sloan would immediately understand that reference. Why should he be held accountable for so much institutionalized arrogance and ignorance?

But Olivia's stomach clenched even tighter as she took a deep breath, exhaled, and called him. As a precaution, she used his office number, not his personal cell. They still really didn't know one another. Their last face-to-face notwithstanding, it didn't mean she wasn't interested in some kind of outreach between them. But it had to come from her.

"Agent Kendrick. How can I help you?"

The sound of his voice, deep, scratchy, and very officious, threw her. She didn't recognize it. Olivia swallowed and pulled herself together.

"H-hi. It's Olivia."

Silence. She gripped her handset.

"Ms. Cameron. What can I do for you?"

Olivia closed her eyes briefly. This was going to be hard.

Ms. Cameron?

"Thank you for not hanging up on me."

Silence.

"There's no reason for me to do that. Did you really believe I'd do that?"

"I...wasn't sure. After what hap—"

"Is this about your case?"

Olivia frowned. He was throwing shade at her, not letting her *go there*...to what had happened. What she'd accused him of.

"Not really. But...I...I did get an official letter from a Lieutenant Gary Anderson."

"Right. He's the lead LAPD officer on the investigation."

"Oh. But I thought you were in charge?"

"Not anymore. I asked to be pulled. It was clear that FBI input was no longer needed."

"Oh," Olivia said again, suddenly experiencing not only confusion but unexpected disappointment. Had that happened before or after their ill-fated last meeting?

More silence. Sloan was not giving her anything. It had been a mistake to call…

"I know the contents of the letter by the way." Sloan broke into her thoughts. "You've been cleared. Nothing to worry about going forward."

"I was never worried," she said with a small show of confidence and resolve. Her voice was firm.

"Good."

"I think you were very decent and…and honest in how you treated me. I have no complaints."

Silence.

"I appreciate that."

Olivia took another deep breath. "I can write a letter of commendation if you like? Do agents need that kind of affirmation?" She attempted a little levity.

"No need, but thank you."

"Sloan?" Olivia couldn't help the slight plaintive question that saying his name produced. When he didn't respond, she went quickly on, getting, finally, to her point. "I didn't call about the letter. I called because—"

"No need for explanations either. I think—"

"Don't think," Olivia interrupted coolly, weary of his placating, indifferent tone. She *couldn't* have been totally mistaken in what she sensed had been their almost instant compatibility. It felt instinctive. Natural. Scary but real. "What I said… I didn't mean… It wasn't about you."

"I believe I figured that out. Still…"

"Yes, there is *still*. I was very unfair. I'm so…so sorry that I made you the target of my own insecurity. My own history. What I said was *not* about you."

Silence. And then she thought she heard a drawn-out sigh. She frowned, listening closely.

"I appreciate you telling me that," Sloan said quietly but still very formal.

Olivia waited for him to say more, any indication that he was not going to hold her unfortunate misplaced vitriol against him. Nothing.

Olivia gave up, worn-out by knowing she had to make this call to him, with no recognition that it would make a difference. Worn-out with the private admission that she wanted it to. But she was *not* going to plead or apologize again.

"I knew that I owed you that. I'm a little late…and a dollar short, but…the truth is, you did rescue me."

When the silence again stretched, Olivia was about to just hang up. And then he spoke. And there was no question that the flat, controlled cadence of his voice had suddenly mellowed.

"I'm glad I was there to help."

"One more thing," she began, her own voice softening. "It's still Olivia."

She waited a heartbeat and then ended the call.

———

Sloan stood with the two agents from his office who'd been on a local case for well over two years. The repeat robberies had now established a pattern that could be tracked. It wasn't his case or his department's, but he'd always thought it a good idea to be aware of what the field office was handling. Cooperation among the various sectors was key to solving a lot of their caseload. This particular ongoing crime, a series of local, small bank holdups, was more about a clever, persistent, and cocky thief who'd managed to continue operating despite the agents' best-known information to corner and apprehend him and his partner.

But the leader, the object of their pursuit, was the primary target. He'd broadened his target from strip mall banks to bigger branches in small towns to businesses that garnered thousands of dollars in a week. His latest feat was managing to intercept an armored car drop. This was a first and showed a distinct change in target. The suspect's new and bigger focus meant he and his partner were becoming bolder and more unpredictable. What had also been added was a level of violence—to tellers, shopkeepers, and customers—that made Sloan's office more determined to take him out of commission before his next step could end someone's life.

The signals on the police radios and car had pretty much traced the latest incident but, again, not before the two suspects had eluded capture, managing to stay two steps ahead of law enforcement. Police had actually cornered the two perps in a specific neighborhood, the abandoned getaway car hastily exchanged for another stolen vehicle. That move had apparently happened so fast that some of their gains had also been abandoned, a bag of money spilling all over the back seat and floor of the first car. They were rushed. They were getting careless.

"We have a chopper coming in. There's more data on this part of town. They're most likely trying to disappear into the community."

"Where?" Sloan simply asked over his radio. But his question was not only specific to the case and most recent holdup; it narrowed down the locale of the perpetrators to within a mile and a half of where Olivia lived. The answer came back clear and definitive. There had already been two calls to local police about strange men rushing through yards, patios, and pool decks, zigzagging between houses. At one point, the two men quickly separated, running off in different directions. Each was wearing a backpack, no doubt containing the loot from that day's heist. They'd been smart enough to keep it small, making it easier for them to move without the burden of heavy loads.

Sloan could hear the helicopter overhead targeting the neighborhood and making a low sweep with searchlights and heat sensors to pick up the perpetrators in the dark as they maneuvered their way to escape and safety. He turned away from the communications buzz and approached several officers and commanders from local jurisdictions.

"You don't need me here. I'm stepping back, but keep me informed about the pursuit. Are you guys still sure about the general direction of their movements?"

"For now," an officer responded before turning to more information coming over his radio. "They've split up, so we might have to make a decision about which one to fix on."

"Do you know if at least one of them is still heading into and around Baldwin Hills?" Sloan asked.

"So far, looks that way. One of them seems familiar with the neighborhood, so we might not get him. He'll probably know how to get outside the perimeter of the neighborhood before we can figure it out."

"Is there an officer nearby to canvass the neighborhood and warn the residents?"

"Not sure on that. I'll check."

But Sloan had already made his decision. His involvement in the official pursuit was purely self-interest at that point. Olivia lived in

Baldwin Hills. And as much as he knew the criminal pursuit was the most important focus, his concern for her was natural and unavoidable. While Sloan didn't imagine her in any imminent danger, he was concerned enough not to leave it at that but to let the LAPD officers, and agents from his field office, do their work.

Sloan sat for a moment in his car debating the wisdom of going to Olivia's to let her know what was going on, but in a way that didn't scare her. Also it was an excuse to see her again. To see if his last impression and anything about the conversation they'd had remained the same. Then he'd know for sure if he had to completely back off and move on.

He wasn't that far away, but all the way to her block, he could hear the chopper blades, allowing him to gauge how far away they were from Olivia's house. He drove slowly to the property, carefully scanning the streets and noticing which homes had outdoor entrance lights and which didn't. Olivia's was well illuminated. He parked, turned off his lights, and sat silently glancing through the windshield. There were one or two people getting home from work. Several teens on bikes or skateboards. People walking their dogs, occasionally looking up in the night sky at the helicopter hovering over their neighborhood and the obvious searchlight spreading over them. Tensing his jaw muscles, pursing his mouth, Sloan got out of the car and made his way to the front door of Olivia's house. Halfway there he became aware of voices, a conversation, coming from the side or back of the property. He changed directions and headed toward the back. A high gate was partially open, and distinct female laughter wafted out to him. It was suddenly joined by the yapping of a small dog. Sloan knocked firmly on the door and slowly began to push it open. A dog approached and sniffed at his shoes, looked up at him, and retreated back to creep beneath the safety of a chair. Silence immediately followed. The yard was illuminated with lights and candles.

Sloan was annoyed with how nervous he suddenly felt. Annoyed that there was someone who could make him feel that way. He stepped inside to find four pair of eyes watching his entrance. But he narrowed in on the pair that mattered the most.

He had not seen Olivia in well over two weeks. But they'd spoken by phone, her call to him that he'd not been expecting. Afterward, he'd had to admit to both gratitude and surprised relief that Olivia had made the first move in trying to close the distance that had been created between them. No, it had not been his fault that it had happened, but he had still been profoundly unsettled with how it had ripped up blossoming expectations.

Sloan could only take several seconds to appraise the wide-eyed incredulity in Olivia's dark eyes as she stood abruptly and stared back at him. But he also suspected that if there had been no awkward phone conversation just a few days ago, this moment would not have been possible.

Olivia came instantly to her feet, recognizing Sloan. Although he seemed to be casually dressed, it was very clear to her he was dressed for work. His gaze quickly swept across the yard before focusing on her. He didn't smile or acknowledge her in any way. Except for the personal signal that unerringly passed between them, that made Olivia's throat dry and her stomach clench tightly. She was riveted by the intensity of his gaze without being able to read anything into it.

"Hi," she said clearly, but she knew that all three of the women seated around the table prepared for a meal noticed the surprise in her voice. Was her simple *hi* too personal?

"Sorry to interrupt," Sloan said, finally moving his attention from her to the other women.

His voice and tone were authoritative and deep. He held his arms so that the presence of his gun was not obvious, although the navy-blue windbreaker with prominent yellow letters on the upper sleeves, breast, and back of the jacket definitively ID'd who he was and from where.

"I'm Agent Kendrick...with the FBI LA field office."

"FBI? Are we doing something illegal? Is Chardonnay now contraband in LA?" Lynn asked bluntly, her tone adversarial.

Olivia shot her combative friend a look, trying to tamp down Lynn's tendency toward in-your-face squaring off. Attack first, ask questions later. Olivia stepped toward Sloan and caught his gaze again.

"I'm Olivia Cameron. I live here," she interjected quickly, and could see that Sloan read her message.

He nodded. "Ms. Cameron, I don't want to scare you...or your guests, but we have a situation nearby, and there are officers moving through your neighborhood."

"Are they chasing someone?" Mallory, the comfortably chubby female of the four women, asked, peering owl-like through her glasses. She had a hand dangling to her side to allow the dog beneath her chair to be petted and lick her fingers. "Oh my God..."

Of all the girlfriends, Mallory was the one most inclined to see a worst-case scenario in any situation.

"I hear a helicopter," Tessa said without concern, briefly turning her attention toward the twilight sky to track the sounds. She raised her brows at Olivia.

"Helicopter?" Mallory asked. "That means you're looking for someone who's... Is he...dangerous?" she directed to Sloan.

"Mallory, please. Calm down," Olivia soothed.

"You're not in any danger," Sloan said, "but I wanted to make sure everyone has been alerted. As a precaution, I suggest you close and lock this gate."

"Should we move inside?" Olivia asked him. He looked at her, and she could see his jaw tense.

"I think that's best. LAPD has this. Our suspects are not looking to draw any attention, but you don't want to give them any opportunities."

"Them?" Mallory asked, alarmed.

"Two possible suspects."

"Have they done something violent? Hurt people?" Lynn questioned.

"No, ma'am. We're talking bank robbers. They haven't hurt anyone yet."

"Well, I don't want to set a precedent by being the first," Lynn declared, standing.

"Of course not. Tessa, Lynn, could you please start moving everything inside?"

The women moved to do her bidding, but she could see that Lynn was still very curious about Sloan's appearance, and she studied him with a suspicion bordering on hostility. She was naturally suspicious, and Olivia didn't want to turn the moment into dealing with her.

"I'm going to walk the agent back to the front. I'll come in through the front door. One of you let me in."

"I'll do it," Mallory volunteered, scooping up her pet and holding it to her bosom as if it might be snatched from her at any moment.

Sloan retreated through the gate, and Olivia was right behind him. She could hear one of the ladies bolting the gate shut. Sloan stopped and turned to face her in the close space of the driveway, a thick wall of shrubbery on one side. Olivia studied him, looking to see if anything had changed since they were last together. She'd not stopped reliving that afternoon with Sloan, ending in his withdrawal. Something had happened, and she knew the responsibility for the tension was on her. Having let loose the death grip she'd had for a long time on her emotions, Olivia didn't want to retreat. She wanted to see where it…and Sloan…might lead her. Seeing him now, right in front of her, made her instantly grateful that she'd taken the risk of reaching out to him first. Not so much to apologize but to thank him. That was certainly in order. She was so glad she'd put her ego and stubbornness aside to close the gap between them.

She believed, now more than ever, that there was something happening far more than casual acquaintance. Olivia had accepted that since that house incident and its emotional aftermath, everything was different. While it was confusing, it was also exciting to imagine she might be on the precipice of something new and thrilling. Might that be Sloan?

To Olivia it didn't matter that this new whatever had happened so fast.

"Sloan?"

"Yeah?" he responded after a moment's hesitation. He regarded her. In the twilight, she was losing all definition of his features, except for his eyes and his mouth.

The gravelly texture of his voice, the low, throaty growl, was now familiar and so intriguing. So innately part of him.

"Are you still very upset with me?"

He sighed deeply, briefly averted his gaze, and looked back to her. "I was not upset with you." He gestured with a hand, shifted from one foot to the other. "Maybe a little bit. I was just… I didn't know what was going on with you. When you called me, it threw me. Frankly, I wasn't thinking I'd hear from you again."

"I knew I had to call. I felt it was all on me."

"Well…I'm glad you did…Olivia."

She gave him a tentative smile and then became serious again. "You didn't have to come to warn me about what's going on tonight. Why did you?"

"To make sure you knew about our suspect. There wasn't much time to alert the community."

She slowly shook her head. "I…don't believe you. You could have sent an officer. *You* came."

There was a thick silence that seemed to cocoon them, shutting out everything around them, including the receding whirl of helicopter blades as the craft disappeared into the distance.

"Is there something…else?"

"Why would there be?" he asked, almost frowning at her.

"Because…" She took a step closer. "Because…you kissed me. That day. Suddenly. I haven't forgotten that."

He faced her, leaning slightly toward her. "You kissed me back."

Olivia felt a distinct ripple race up her spine. "I did. I'm not sorry."

There. Now it was out. An admission. Her voice was barely a whisper as she searched his expression.

"Are you sure?" Sloan asked.

"Don't you believe me?"

He shifted. Sighed. "You told me…you didn't need a savior. I understood perfectly what you were saying."

Olivia blinked, shook her head. "I think I was in shock."

"Once or twice, you kept calling me Marcus. Your ex?"

"Marcus? If he thought someone was being condescending. He was, maybe, overly sensitive to that. Black men sometimes are."

"Believe it or not, I think I get it," Sloan responded, staring at her.

Olivia frowned. "It's...complicated." Then she looked at him, this time with a small smile of regret. "I lost my pin. The one you gave me."

"Don't worry about it. I can replace it for you. If you want."

"Yes, I want."

She imagined that there was a slight shift in his demeanor, no longer stiff and formal.

"There was something else I had to tell you. After my report was done. It's one of the reasons I came looking for you at the school that day."

"What?"

"The money is yours, Liv. All of it."

Her eyes widened, and she blinked.

"*OLIVIA! Where are you?*"

Tessa shouting her name made Olivia start. "Yes! Coming!" she shouted back. She remained focused on Sloan, who was watching her reaction. "You mean...I..."

"You can call yourself a millionaire, if that means anything."

"Is it really a million dollars?"

"It is," Sloan confirmed.

His radio began to scratch with an incoming message. Olivia couldn't understand anything that was said, but Sloan answered quickly, turning down the volume button. He gave her a sideways glance, almost playful. "Your assignment, should you decide to accept, is to make a list of what you'd spend all that money on."

"Do I thank you for that too?"

"Not really. I just advised that I didn't think it was worth pursuing the origin of the money. LAPD was fine with you keeping it. Worthy recipient…"

"What makes me worthy?" she asked, curious.

"When you found the money, you immediately turned it in. You're a professional African American woman of good standing in the community…and you're ethical. Put that all together and it spells good PR for the department. But I don't think they'll advertise what happened in your situation. People will get ideas."

Olivia sighed, pursed her lips.

"Aren't you glad about the outcome?" Sloan asked.

"I don't know. I really didn't do anything to earn it."

"Then it's an even nicer surprise, right?"

"If you say so," she said, doubt making her overthink what she should feel.

"I say so," Sloan answered quietly but firmly.

His radio squawked again. He responded just as briefly as before but then continued walking to the front of the property and his parked car.

"Sloan?" He turned to her. "You called me Liv."

He searched her features, as indistinct in the twilight as were his. They only had one another's voice to go on. "Yeah…I guess I did. You remember a lot from that day."

"It was memorable," Olivia confessed quietly. And then she detected a gesture, a movement of his head. Familiar. And the way she felt Sloan now regarding her. "Didn't you want it to be?"

"I hadn't thought about it. I hadn't planned what happened. I just…wanted to kiss you. Liv? I don't know. I guess…Olivia has too many syllables."

Olivia gave him one of her signature quiet smiles. She hoped he could see it.

"I didn't think we could get past that day. What was said. What I heard…or thought I heard." His voice was a bare rough whisper, as if to make sure only she could hear.

"You want to know what I think?"

He remained still. He was leaving it up to her.

"I don't think we should overanalyze or give up." She shook her head. "I'm not a quitter. I want to know…"

"…what happens," Sloan finished.

"Or not."

It was almost dark now. There was no light along the pathway between the backyard and the front. Olivia, without thought, reached out, searching for his hand. Sloan didn't help her, remaining unresponsive and still until their fingers touched and hooked loosely together.

"Is this a mea culpa?"

She almost shyly averted her gaze, displaying a vague smile. "Let's not call it anything. Let's…"

"Maybe…wait and see?" Sloan suggested.

"I think that's a good idea. I'm glad you thought of it."

If Olivia expected him to smile or grin or have a reaction, she could see he didn't. But Sloan did briefly squeeze her fingers.

It was a small, encouraging sign.

"Are you coming to Sports Saturday?" she asked instead.

"Is that still an invitation?"

"Yes."

"I…haven't decided yet."

Maybe, she interpreted, and had to be satisfied with that.

"*Olivia?*" a peeved voice shouted from the front of the house.

"I have to go. They're going to have a lot of questions."

"What are you going to tell your girlfriends?"

"That the kind agent just wanted to make sure we were safe."

"The agent wanted to make sure *you* were safe," he corrected boldly.

"Rescuing me again?"

"I'll let you figure that out," Sloan said in a low voice. He tightly squeezed their entwined fingers, then let them drift apart. He continued walking to his car.

Sloan kept his gaze on her as he started the engine, waited a second longer as their gazes held before he slowly accelerated and drove away.

When Olivia walked back into her house, the girlfriends were standing around idly waiting for her. For a moment she wondered if any of them had eavesdropped on her tête-à-tête with Sloan outside the house.

"I'm so sorry about that. It seems the suspects the police are looking for have quite a history. They both might have gotten away tonight."

"Bullshit," Lynn said bluntly, setting an open bottle of red wine on the table. "Know what I think? Robbery suspects were not the issue. I think you've been holding out on us, Olivia. *Who the hell was that man?*"

Olivia tried not to keep glancing toward the parking lot, looking for Sloan or his car. She was never expected to attend the Saturday programs, but she always felt obligated to. The concept was hers, and so was the responsibility. If anything happened to one of the students or even staff, she would bear the consequence. It was only a three-hour event, scheduled so that everyone still had part of the day to do other things. It also gave her an excuse to put off any of the respondents to her dating website profile who wanted a coffee hookup as an introduction. Olivia suspected her finding official things to take care of was much more than finding the whole process of digital dating distasteful. She was also very afraid of not coming off as sharp, witty, attractive, desirable, sexy—had she left anything out?

Determined, yet again, not to scan the parking area, she opened the large cooler she'd packed with rations for lunch knowing that the students would never stoop to making lunch for themselves, settling, instead, on stopping at any of the convenience stores near the park for unhealthy snacks and sodas. Sandwiches were simple and easy to provide, with a side of potato salad or chips. She reached into a second tote and began to unload the napkins and disposable cutlery.

"Hi."

Olivia heard the greeting but didn't think she was being addressed. It was a child's voice.

"Hi."

She turned and found a boy holding a baseball bat in one hand and a soccer ball in the other. His handsome brown face was half-hidden under a baseball cap a little too big for his head. His teeth gleamed with braces.

"Hi." Olivia finally reacted with a questioning smile. The youngster glanced back over his shoulder, and she followed his gaze. Bringing up the rear was Sloan, a small tote over his shoulder.

She acknowledged her physical response to his sudden appearance, having given up any pretense that she felt nothing being near him. It was now routine, the sensations of attraction, feelings having locked themselves in as early as the first time they'd met and as recently as the afternoon he'd stopped by her house early one evening under the pretense of warning her about the bank robbers. Olivia was still in the what-does-this-mean stage but was now pretty sure that Sloan was definitely going to be a factor in the answer.

His stride was comfortable and leisurely, confident. He was wearing khaki slacks and a charcoal T-shirt that fit smoothly across his torso. He also wore a baseball cap, but not the dark-blue one with the yellow FBI letters on the front. And he wore impenetrable dark glasses, giving him the decidedly masculine and handsome appearance of someone with authority. Olivia briefly averted her gaze, again physically affected by his presence.

She couldn't let him see or know that.

Olivia took a deep inhale and looked up as he approached, giving him a slight smile. Neither of them spoke as Sloan stopped, standing on the other side of a picnic table from her. She knew now from experience that he kept his expression neutral. She thought that maybe he'd been trained to do that, to keep himself at a distance. Maybe it made him more effective at his job. Did he ever smile?

The little boy turned to speak to Sloan, and he gave his full attention to the youngster, nodding at his inquiry. Sloan put an arm around his shoulders, making him look again directly at her.

"This is Cooper. You said it was okay for me to bring someone so…Cooper, this is Ms. Cameron. She's in charge of the school where that all these students attend." He indicated the fifty or so students already engaged on different fields in different sports…except basketball. There was no court provided.

"Not a problem at all. Hi, Cooper. I'm glad you could come today."

"Thanks for inviting me," he said in a proper, well-mannered voice.

Olivia was charmed. She became the teacher. "You like sports? There's a lot going on and a lot to choose from."

Cooper glanced back to the many busy fields, squinting against the bright fall sun. "I like soccer. That's my favorite."

"Wonderful. You're welcome to join in. There's a coach on the field. Go over and introduce yourself."

"Okay," he said. He leaned his baseball bat against a bench and immediately turned to jog to the soccer field.

"I'll walk him over. Be right back," Sloan said, following to catch up to the boy.

Olivia watched them, observing that Cooper was energetic and chatty, saying something to the boys already in practice who beckoned for him to join. The coach blew a whistle for attention and shouted for Cooper to throw his soccer ball to him. The coach set it on the ground at his feet, and the boys went back to practice. Sloan approached the coach, and the two men shook hands and stood talking for a moment or two. Sloan stood watching the practice until Cooper settled into the warm-up routine with the older boys. Sloan then made his way back to join her.

She quickly became busy, pretending not to have witnessed the exchange, while realizing that she and Sloan were now going to be alone. She was calm and collected, or tried to be, as she organized the details for lunch, denying that her internal tension was directly related to the way he'd kissed her. That had not been far from Olivia's mind since it happened—how Sloan had kissed her and exactly how it made her feel. A little flushed. Very lightheaded, somewhat breathless. She had been the one to end the kiss abruptly, but she couldn't quite recall why.

It didn't help that Sloan apparently felt no need to break the ice between them, get that first sentence out that would have put her at ease. Olivia knew she was on the verge of accepting the hard truth. She was in trouble. Every nerve in her body, her sensibility, told her so.

It was very scary.

Olivia finally glanced at Sloan, favoring him with one of her habitual smiles. Belatedly she wished she'd thought to wear dark glasses as well. She pointed to the tote he was carrying.

"Did you bring lunch?"

Sloan pursed his lips and briefly shook his head. He set the bag down next to Cooper's baseball bat. "Never even thought of it. The bag holds his clothes and things from last night. He stayed with me. I picked him up, took him to dinner…"

"*In-N-Out Burger*?" Olivia guessed with a knowing grin.

"That's right. His mom is on a parental campaign against junk food so when he's with me I sneak it in under the radar."

Olivia's grin broadened and she laughed quietly. "I bet Cooper loves hanging out with you."

Sloan nodded. "We get along."

She began to relax a bit, thinking the brief exchange went a long way to easing any last constraints between them. Olivia was not going to bring the subject up again, but she imagined that the last incident between them still hung in the air.

"Gun," she suddenly said. A question was implied in the one bold word.

Sloan slipped his hands into the front pockets of his slacks. "Home." He braced a foot on the edge of the bench and calmly regarded her. "You're a very unusual school director," he murmured.

She heard much more in the cadence of his quiet comment. Sloan's interest and observation made her smile again.

"Harvest is a very unusual school. The students are somewhere between real potential and other people's expectations. I guess I feel the responsibility to make sure the expectations don't sabotage them. There's a lot of budding brilliance with some of them, but I know not all of Harvest's kids will reach the stars. Some of them have defeat built into family DNA. Dysfunction, emotional and mental, and troubles beyond their knowledge or control. School can't always overcome that."

"But you're still planning on building a staircase to the stars so that they all can at least try."

Olivia gave him a brief glance. "That's right. That's what all schools should be doing." With nothing else to distract her nervous hands, she stopped and sat at the end of the bench. He took her lead and sat facing her across the table.

"I'm glad you could make it today." She felt a bit shy with the confession.

"I wanted to be here," he responded, his tone serious.

She regarded him thoughtfully before visibly relaxing even more. "Okay," she sighed.

"Okay," Sloan repeated with a nod.

She took a deep breath. "Tell me about Cooper. He's such a cute youngster."

"On behalf of his parents, I thank you."

"And…how do you know Cooper? If you don't mind me asking."

"I was counting on it." Sloan slowly pushed his dark glasses above his forehead so that their gazes were unimpeded. He clasped his hands together and openly regarded her. "He's my godson."

"Oh."

Olivia saw that Sloan was waiting for her to say more or ask another question, as if he was prepared to answer them all. She knew this was the kind of moment when secrets might be revealed, a history exposed, truths would come out.

"What?" he questioned quietly, prompting her when she remained quiet.

Olivia stared into his eyes. That first moment when they'd met, it had startled her to see Sloan Kendrick had light-blue eyes, like topaz. He'd stood before her the prototypical white American male. That she'd been drawn to him seemed an affront, a betrayal. But now… Now the fact was inconsequential, irrelevant. There were other things about Sloan that took precedent…and were far more appealing.

"How did he come to be your godson?"

"I served with his father in the Middle East. I was in the intelligence unit, and Boyd was a copter pilot. He flew or escorted brass to summits, reconnaissance, or to meet with village leaders, oftentimes with me along. I worked closely with a few of the commanders, analyzing intel. Boyd and I were the only West Coast officers in the unit serving at the time.

"Friendships between the soldiers sometimes came down to where you were from. Boyd was from Oakland. Sometimes I'd do a favor for him…a bit outside the rules. He'd do the same for me, chauffeuring me by air somewhere when I wanted to get away from base and command. He was kind of exuberant and outgoing.

"People, even villagers who were naturally suspicious, grew to like him. I kept him out of a mess of trouble that might have resulted in disciplinary action. He was finally due to ship back home and be discharged…and his wife was pregnant, the result of his quick furlough stateside. He asked me to be godfather. I didn't think it would actually happen, so I said sure."

Sloan stopped, but Olivia knew by his expression and sudden

hesitation that there was more to the story. She gave no reaction, forcing him to continue.

"His copter went down just outside the northernmost region of Kabul while returning to base with three senior officers. They were all seriously injured. Boyd and one of the officers died. Not shot down by enemy fire or anything like that. Equipment failure. I guess you could call it the equivalent of *friendly fire*."

Sloan was suddenly reflective, looking down at the table, his brows furrowed. And then he went quickly on. "I was already back home myself when I got a letter from Boyd's widow, Carol. She had a boy. She wanted to honor her late husband's request that I be godfather. And that's what happened. Cooper was a year old when I first met them. Carol remarried, but Cooper and I bonded. I wanted to be true to his father's request. The family lives in Pasadena. When Cooper visits with me, and it's not that often, I pick him up at home and he stays over with me."

"I'm sorry about the loss. You obviously take the relationship and responsibility with Cooper seriously."

He shrugged. "Boyd was a great guy."

"Where are you from originally?" Olivia suddenly asked, curious.

"Oregon."

"Oregon," she whispered with genuine surprise and awe, and openly stared at him.

"It's not outer space, you know. Still on the third planet from the sun," Sloan reminded her without expression.

She smiled. "I don't think I've ever met anyone from Oregon."

"Now you have," Sloan said, starting to rise from the bench and glancing behind her. He shifted his sunglasses back over his eyes. "There's a stampede headed this way."

"I guess it's time for lunch." She searched the students until she found Cooper. He was younger and smaller than her teens, and she wanted to make sure he wasn't forgotten or left behind.

Olivia had to settle for mentally putting aside everything Sloan had shared. But his story and some history had only created more questions and heightened her curiosity about him. She stole a glance at him as he stood chatting with his very excited godson who wanted to let him know he'd scored a goal in the soccer game warm-up. Olivia grinned to herself. She would not be surprised if the older boys had somehow made it easy for him to do so.

Sloan gave Cooper his complete attention despite the chaos around them as the students staked out places at the picnic tables. There were two who had attended the academy, and they greeted Sloan as if he was now their good friend. There were no girls present, and Olivia always considered that fact her own failure, that she couldn't persuade any of the girls to at least come out for the day. As before, Sloan maintained an adult and professional distance with the students. He was not at all unfriendly, but Olivia realized that his job simply didn't allow for him to let his guard down.

But he'd certainly done so with her. It gave her a boost to recognize that. She was different to him, perhaps, and Olivia found that encouraging. She opened the cooler and stepped back as the boys, more or less, formed a line to pick a sandwich, get a paper plate, napkin, and eating utensils. They took their places at the tables to eat while the three adult coaches distributed juice or water, bags of chips.

Sloan held Cooper back until the older students had made their selections and settled down to eat and then let Cooper do the same. He was not shy about squeezing himself in with the bigger boys, who by now were treating Cooper like a favorite little brother. Olivia was glad she never had to ask them to be nice to the young boy. When the excitement had died down and the students were eating, she turned to Sloan.

At that moment, he was sitting bent over his smartphone, reading what seemed like a lengthy message. Then he stood and sauntered away from everyone as he placed a call and quietly talked. After nearly ten minutes, Sloan made his way back to the table, casually observing the talk and laughter of the teens spread out around him.

"There are more sandwiches," Olivia said, turning the cooler so Sloan could peer inside and choose something. He reached in and pulled out a small rectangular box with a colorful graphic illustration on the lid of an orange cut in half.

"What's this?" he asked, examining the box from several angles.

"Oh…that's a little potato salad and a few pieces of fried chicken…"

He released the clasp on the lid and opened the box. He glanced at her.

"We can share if you like. There's enough there."

"Great," he responded simply.

Olivia set a paper plate for each of them and served the chicken and salad between them. She gave Sloan the bulk of the salad and left the last piece of chicken in case he wanted that as well. He politely thanked her, and they once again sat opposite each other at the table to eat.

"Homemade?" he asked, biting into a crisp thigh.

"With my very own hands," she replied.

"I'm grateful for your many talents…*Ms. Cameron*."

She winced but grinned slightly, passing disposable utensils and a napkin to him. And grateful that he, at least, remembered that this was not a private picnic but an off-site school event. He remembered the protocol in addressing her. But she couldn't help also recalling the aloof and formal way he'd referred to her when she'd gotten the courage to call him, just a few days earlier, before he'd appeared at her home.

He was staring at her as he settled down to the lunch. Olivia was pleased that he seemed to be enjoying it.

"You have an extreme amount of concern for your students."

"I know. Lori tells me all the time I need to dial it back. I can't expect to teach them everything in the little amount of time I have with them at school. I'm fortunate to have some great teachers on board."

"She's right," Sloan said, a very quiet sound emitting from the back of his throat, indicating his pleasure at the food. "You like to cook?" he asked.

"I do. I find it therapeutic. I prepare more than my fair share of the lunches for my circle of girlfriends."

Sloan nodded, but he was concentrating on and clearly enjoying the chicken and salad.

Lunch was quick. Olivia reminded the kids to dispose of their trash and recyclables. They shouted thank you as they jogged back to whatever sport they were participating in. Cooper took up the rear, running after the bigger students to keep up. Olivia had to grin at his confidence. And she grinned at Sloan, at his presence, but he wasn't paying attention. Without her asking or expecting it, he had already begun to gather the remains of the lunch, sorting out leftovers from trash and anything that could be saved for another time.

He lifted the cooler and a tote. "Where's your car?"

"I'll show you," Olivia said, grabbing the last two bags and leading the way to her SUV. They loaded everything into the back.

"I'm not going to ask how you managed to bring all of this stuff by yourself."

"I managed," she boasted.

"Stubborn," Sloan added smoothly.

She was about to close the raised door when Sloan stepped in front of her and stopped her. Olivia glanced at him, curious, just as Sloan bent toward her and planted a kiss on her mouth. Before she could respond—and she wanted to—he had pulled back to gaze into her eyes.

"I know you weren't expecting that this time either," Sloan said.

"No. I—"

Then he kissed her again. This time Sloan let her catch up to him. Gave her time to respond and participate. Let her enjoy the quiet, spontaneous moment that took them both to another place. But just as smoothly as it had begun, it was over. Olivia stared at Sloan, seeing the man she'd decided to let in and show what she was made of, that she might possibly care for.

Again, he paused.

Olivia stared at him, and he at her, silently coming to some sort of mutual decision about being together in public, about no longer being strangers.

"I think it's a good idea not to rehash what happened. I don't want to stay there."

"I'm glad to hear you say so."

He nodded, with a big but quiet sigh. "So. Are we starting over?"

Olivia shook her head. "I don't think we need to go that far back, but...can we pick up where we left off?"

"I think we can make that work," he replied, his voice a rough growl.

She knew Sloan was staring at her intently through the opaque, dark glasses.

She was happy to have him spend the day with the students, who seemed to now accept Sloan without further skepticism. Without knowing or working at it, Sloan had managed a place for himself that fit. And Olivia was more than happy to have him there with *her*.

"I'd ask you out later, when this is over," Sloan began as they meandered their way back to the picnic area to wait out the rest of the afternoon. "I wanted to that afternoon the world blew up around the two of us. I thought there should be a celebration for getting the money from your house."

"That's nice of you," Olivia admitted.

"That call I took…I have something to take care of later. After I get Cooper back home." He glanced at her. "Rain check?"

"I'd like that."

"Truce?" Sloan added.

She grinned at him. "Olive branch."

For the first time since they'd met, Sloan almost smiled. Olivia took full credit.

CHAPTER 7

"This is all I could find," Mallory said.

"It's a lot," Olivia commented, accepting the manila envelope from Mallory.

They had just finished eating a boxed takeout lunch in one of the public spaces of the Powell Library at UCLA. Mallory was an associate reference librarian there. Every now and then Olivia was aware of Mallory's dog, Phoebe, her emotional support animal, swishing her tail in contentment from beneath Mallory's chair. Every now and then she also made a gentle half-hearted yelp, to which Mallory obediently responded with a pinch of food from her lunch.

Olivia opened the envelope and pulled out a sheaf of photocopied newspaper and magazine articles and other materials about an organization called The Millionaires Club. She silently browsed through the pages, occasionally stopping at a headline or photographs that caught her attention. She glanced at Mallory in admiration.

"This is great. How did you find out about the club?"

"You said you were looking for someplace that could help you set up a charity fund or some kind of platform where low-income students could apply to get money for college or professional training. Patrick Bennett used to be a pro baseball player. He stopped playing because of injuries and then became this popular national sports commentator, *and*—you're going to love this—he won the lottery a few years ago for $75,000,000," Mallory said in a some-folks-have-all-the-luck tone. "So he comes up with this idea to form a foundation that would give back to people and organizations that certainly need help a lot more than he does."

"I'm impressed," Olivia murmured, quickly scanning one article. She looked at Mallory. "Have you read all of this? Who is this with him? Jean Travis?"

Mallory became animated, pushing her glasses up her nose. "You have to read everything I gave you, okay? I think she had something to do with the founding of the club, and she now works in some unofficial capacity in the organization. She used to work in the mayor's office in New York City. *And...*she's now Mrs. Bennett!"

Olivia silently studied the image of the handsome, smiling CEO and the pretty, serene woman at his side. For a long time she examined the photo and knew she definitely wanted to know more not only about The Millionaires Club but also about this young, attractive, influential couple.

Olivia slipped the pages back into the envelope. "I owe you," she said.

"Yeah, you do, but you know I owe you more, so let's just call it square." She squinted at Olivia. "How come you can't tell me where this money came from that you're getting from the city that's going to fund your project? Do you know who those bank robbers are and you turned them in and now you're going to reap some reward?"

Olivia allowed herself a half grin, putting the envelope inside her tote bag resting on an adjacent chair. "It's not that I can't tell you. It's that I don't have enough information yet," she said in a half truth.

"You said you were getting some money because of something

that had happened in that house your aunt left you. What happened? How come you get money for it? Are you going to share?"

Olivia gave her attention to her friend. She and Mallory might never have met but for ending up in a rehab center at the same time several years earlier. That they had become friends had seemed unlikely, their lives, backgrounds, and even personalities being so different. But Olivia had also learned this to be true of her relationship with Tessa and Lynn, whom she'd met at a professional women's luncheon.

"You know Lynn didn't believe you that night," Mallory said, absently scratching under the chin of her pet who'd surface from her lair to stand on hind legs, wanting to be picked up.

Olivia watched the pet and owner interact for a moment and then frowned at Mallory, but already she was on the alert. "I don't know what you mean. What didn't Lynn believe?"

"Tessa and I felt she was overreaching, but Lynn thought there was something odd about this white guy showing up and saying he's an FBI agent. And that story about bank robbers skulking through your neighborhood didn't fly with her at all."

Olivia shifted in her chair and sighed, thinking fast. "Lynn was born suspicious. That's probably why she's such a successful attorney."

"And still single," Mallory offered dryly.

"We all are," Olivia reminded her.

"Yeah, but you hate dating."

"Not true. I hate online dating."

Mallory studied her intently. "Do you want to get married again?"

Olivia shrugged. "I haven't ruled it out, but I don't really think about that. You know, Lynn has never shown, at least to me, that she's remotely interested in getting married."

"Not married, maybe. But that doesn't mean she doesn't have a soft spot in her heart for finding someone to be in a relationship with. I think she wouldn't mind having a boo of her own."

"I don't know. She can be real hard on people...especially men."

"I think she's been badly hurt at some point. Maybe even abused." Mallory giggled. "I call Lynn a witch savant. Do *not* cross her or she will burn your ass! How did she become our friend anyway?"

Olivia sighed. "Maybe she needs us. Maybe...we need her. I sometimes think of all of us as lost-and-found souls." She stared at Mallory. "What did she have to say about Sl—that...that agent who came by?"

"She just felt it was weird, the way he suddenly showed up. She didn't believe a word of his excuse. Do you know him?" Mallory questioned.

Olivia's stomach roiled. Her mind was racing to come up with an answer that wouldn't betray her or give up secrets she wasn't ready to share. So she gave the only possible response that would shield her—and Sloan—from further scrutiny.

"No, I don't."

When Olivia and her brother, Jackson, finally left his office at ALT Imaging, she was already preparing herself for one of his haven't-heard-from-you-lately-what's-going-on conversations. It would be the start of a careful but loving interrogation of her life. She knew that. It had gotten milder over the years, as she'd grown into adulthood and he had to act less like the older brother. Even less after she'd married Marcus. As a matter of fact, she'd met Marcus through Jackson. Marcus had been something of a prodigy under Jackson in medical school before switching to a surgery specialty. Jackson once said of Marcus, "He's got great hands."

"Sorry I made you wait," Jackson said with some exasperation and weariness.

"Don't worry about it. I didn't mind people-watching outside your office. I do the same thing with students who come in and out of the school."

"Yep," Jackson agreed as they crossed the street, headed to a large commercial chain restaurant known for its all-day breakfast.

He held the door to let her precede him inside, and they were quickly seated. Jackson sighed heavily and immediately reached for his smartphone to check messages and voicemail. He didn't bother asking permission, and Olivia didn't expect it. He was a doctor at the mercy of patients and administrators and surgeons needing to schedule for his services in the radiology department.

She settled into the cushioned banquette seat and idly scanned the laminated menu. She knew what she wanted. It hadn't changed since she was eleven and Jackson had first brought her here on one of his rare visits home from the first hospital he'd worked at in Philadelphia. It had been *their* thing, their routine. And Olivia had always felt closest to her brother when he insisted on these rituals that kept them a small family unit. Their parents were now gone. Being fifteen years older, Jackson, by default, was the head of their family. She was and always would be the baby of the family. Unexpected for parents approaching middle age...as Jackson was now reaching himself.

"I just have to make one little call..."

"Whatever," she responded agreeably, beginning to relax after her own school day of teenage drama and a failed assembly program that the students didn't enjoy and were vocal about it.

Olivia sat casually examining her brother, as she knew he would do to her as soon as he finished his current call. She sighed in contentment. She loved Jackson and loved having him as a protective brother who had never failed her nor ever given bad advice. If he could be faulted with anything, it would probably be his brief, overbearing vigilance when she began to date. She could appreciate his position now. But at the time it had created stress and contention between them. Olivia was relieved that they'd outgrown what was a difficult period for both of them.

She was startled out of her reverie when Jackson put down his phone, sighed, and sat back, regarding her silently just as she'd expected.

"What's up?"

Olivia pushed the menu aside. She shrugged. "The usual. Lots of work at Harvest. A few students with discipline issues. A nonstudent who shows up repeatedly. He has a younger brother enrolled, and I'm not sure what to do about it. Not enough resources…"

"You know what I'm talking about, Liv."

"I'm fine."

He was watching her very closely, as if she were one of his patients and he was trying to ferret out what she wasn't revealing. "Mm-hmm."

"What about you? How's Brett?"

"Still in London. Teaching a course at the International School. I'm going to try to get away for a few weeks in October to visit. But he'll be back at the end of the semester in December."

"Miss him?"

Jackson gave her a wry half smile. "Of course. But it was an invitation he couldn't refuse. I guess it's no different from when I had that consultation down in Texas a few years ago. I didn't like being away, but that work looks great on my résumé. And you didn't answer my question."

They were interrupted when a waitress arrived to quickly take their order, and then they were alone.

Jackson didn't let up. He stared at her and waited. Olivia suddenly realized there was a lot to talk about with her brother and she didn't actually know where to begin. She focused on the biggest thing to happen to her that was an undeniable shocker.

"The city is giving me two million dollars I think that's their final count."

Jackson sat stone still not even blinking. Then he sat straight up and leaned on the table to regard her, eyes wide and sharp with questions.

"What did you say?"

Olivia repeated her announcement. And then she calmly and methodically detailed finding the money in their great-aunt's house, turning it into the police, followed by a brief investigation of why money was hidden in the house and what she really knew about it. From the start Olivia knew that she was severely censoring the story, completely leaving out Sloan Kendrick and his significant part in it.

She was distracted with her brother's rush of questions, forcing Olivia to focus on the discovery and how it all concluded with her being given the money she'd found.

Her pancakes, with all the trimmings, were served, along with Jackson's Belgian waffles. The entire meal was taken up with the story and details of her adventure. Of course Jackson wanted to know what she was going to do with the money. And Olivia admitted she was considering options, including establishing a fund or scholarship or grant for low-income students like the ones at Harvest who never had enough resources available to them.

"So you're not going to share with me? Your flesh-and-blood *only* sibling who's practically raised you and kept you out of trouble…"

Olivia merely grinned at his sad tale. "Oh, please. You're doing very well on your own. Mom and Daddy would be proud. And I don't need to adopt you."

"What are you going to do for yourself?"

"I'm thinking on it. The students and my girls have been ragging me about getting a real grown-up car and not that mom's SUV that I use for school. That would be fun."

"Okay. Consider it done. What else?"

"I don't know," she said, a bit impatient. "I want to do something different. I want to have fun and be daring and…and…not be afraid."

Jackson averted his gaze, thoughtfully, and slowly shook his head. "You're not afraid, Liv. You've never been afraid of anything."

"Marcus didn't think so."

"Yeah…well…I can say it now, but I came to think Marcus was a little high-handed with you."

"You never said so," Olivia said with genuine surprise. "You never even let on."

"I couldn't. You were married to the man. I couldn't criticize him to you. If you thought he was brilliant and wonderful…"

"He was brilliant."

"It's the wonderful part I had trouble with. To be honest, I always hoped you'd come to see him differently and maybe…you'd leave him."

Olivia was already shaking her head. "I loved him. I believed that all of his giving me a hard time was for my own good. That he was… you know…protective."

"His kind of protective wasn't like my kind of protective. I believe that Marcus was doing much more than being protective. He was trying to keep you in a particular place so you didn't outshine him."

"But he did love me. He could be generous and helpful."

Jackson sighed, throwing his napkin down and clasping his hands to gaze at her over the top of his knuckles. "That wasn't love. That was insecurity masked as him thinking he knew what was best for you. In hindsight, it was really about what was best for *him*."

"I never knew you felt that way."

"Didn't matter. The question is, how did you feel?"

"I wish you'd warned me," Olivia whispered, truly sorry that she'd learned too late to make changes for herself. She had wanted her marriage to work.

"I couldn't, Liv. It's not like Marcus was physically abusive. I just came to believe he wasn't good for you emotionally. But I decided to mind my own business. That was the wrong move."

Olivia was momentarily lost in reflection, mostly just remembering how it had all ended. Her in an accident, not exactly at death's door but serious enough.

"In answer to your question…" Olivia said, retreating from the topic. There was nothing more to say about Dr. Marcus Palfrey, doctor extraordinaire, overbearing husband. "I'm fine. The money I'm getting is probably the most interesting thing that's happened lately. And I'm looking into how to manage it. I'm not going to talk about it."

"Good. That's all I want to hear," Jackson said decisively, satisfied.

Olivia thought again and conjured up an image of Sloan and that sweet, unexpected kiss behind the back of her SUV. The sense of excitement she now felt around him. The phone call the next day at her office—he *knew* that neutral place would make her feel safe— when he asked if she was free yet for a celebratory dinner.

Not yet.

"There is something else," Olivia began thoughtfully. "I...think I've met someone."

Jackson's eyebrows shot up. "Really? On the internet? One of those crazy websites where the guys put up false profiles and swear it's all true?"

He was as suspicious as she was about the legitimacy of meeting someone online who wasn't weird, secretly married, or looking for a hookup and had real-world potential.

Olivia gave a small grin but shook her head, cautious again. "Actually, no."

"The old-fashioned way?"

"I'll just say unexpected."

"Well," he quietly coaxed, "where...how did you meet this person?"

Olivia stared at her brother. "At school."

Jackson's brows shot up again. "School? Well, he can't be dangerous. Weird, maybe..."

Olivia chuckled quietly.

"But not dangerous."

She considered the options. "Maybe you're half-right."

He grunted. "I'm not even going to ask which half. Go on."

"There something about him."

"You keep saying *him*."

She gnawed the inside of her lip, not because she didn't want to make a full disclosure to her brother but because even saying the name produced a subtle reaction from her. It was becoming troublesome. "His name is Sloan Kendrick. He... He works for the government."

"Hmm," Jackson murmured, nodding as if he knew exactly what that meant.

"At first I was suspicious of him. But I think I was interested right away. Totally unexpected, of course. Shocking. And…I'm pretty sure he felt the same way."

"Seriously? Suspicious of *you*?"

"No. I mean I think he was interested. *Is* interested"

"So what's the problem?"

"Maybe it isn't a problem. Maybe I'm just being too protective again. You trained me well," Olivia joked.

But Jackson wasn't smiling. He waited.

"What if I told you he was white?"

Jackson regarded her for a long silent time. Olivia guessed it was because he was trying to be…diplomatic. Maybe it was just that he was concerned about not saying too much or the wrong thing. The way he'd been with not influencing her about Marcus.

"Do you want me to meet him?"

Olivia closed her office door, checking to make sure it was properly locked before heading for the exit to the school. Lori had already left for the day, and the few after-school activities had also ended. Except for the janitor, who wasn't due in for another hour, the building was empty. Or so she thought.

There was distinct murmuring coming from the other end of the corridor. It was near an emergency exit at the back of the building. If necessary, students and staff could get out that way but couldn't come back in. Olivia heard hushed voices…and the sudden, faint babbling of a baby. She stood listening closely for a moment and then changed directions toward the sounds.

Then all was silent again, but she kept walking.

"Hello? Who's back here?" she asked with authority, letting her voice carry. In the empty hallways, she sounded very loud.

Olivia reached the end of the corridor and glanced left toward the exit. There, she found Colby and Taryn and Gaye. Olivia's reaction was one of instant suspicion. Judging from the startled expressions of the two students and their quickly averted gaze, she knew she had a right to be.

"What are you doing back here? You know you're not supposed to use this exit for anything but emergencies. Colby?" Olivia directed her firm question to the boy. She knew he was least likely to lie to her, and he wasn't very good at it. Taryn, on the other hand, was known to be practiced in the art of subterfuge.

"I was just helping Taryn." The two students exchanged careful but covert glances.

"Helping Taryn what?" Olivia asked, letting her tone come across as less accusatory. She glanced down at the baby, her features calm and her attention centered on her as she sucked on a pacifier.

"Well...I...she..." Colby mumbled.

"There was somebody I didn't want to see," Taryn interrupted. "It was...a girl in my class."

"What girl?" Olivia asked.

Taryn averted her gaze. She began to push the stroller slowly back and forth, but Gaye was not fussing or in need of comfort.

"What class?" Olivia pursued.

And then she gave up. It was very clear that the two students were hoping to get out of the building without being seen, possibly by someone they were avoiding in the front of the building. But Olivia realized that it was odd for these two students in particular to be conspiring. Colby was an introvert. Taryn was out there and fearless.

"Okay, we'll talk about this tomorrow in my office. Am I clear?"

The two students garbled an agreement.

"And if I find out either of you is routinely using this exit, things are going to get ugly very fast. Do you hear me?"

Another garbled consent. It was hard to tell if they were sincere or just placating her. But Olivia knew that there was nothing to be gained by trying to force either of them into a confession.

"All right. Go," Olivia instructed, allowing the two to hurriedly push through the exit's crash-bar doors, Taryn pushing her baby stroller out onto the street behind the school. The door slammed shut behind them, the sound echoing briefly through the corridor.

Olivia frowned at the closed door, trying to guess what the real reason might have been for two of her more promising students to be skulking around after school hours trying to avoid detection.

And she was absolutely certain it had nothing to do with any conflict between Taryn and another student.

Taryn wasn't afraid of anyone.

Olivia was very uncomfortable, already sorry she'd asked Wilson to accompany her to a wedding. She sat in his midlevel luxury car, and although the air conditioner produced a very quiet and cool environment, she was feeling mildly claustrophobic. Much worse, actually, than when she'd fallen through a floor and landed in the cement basement of the house she owned. Of course, Sloan had appeared like magic—or silent, wishful thinking—to rescue her.

Wilson had left her in his car without much explanation, the engine running, while he'd headed into a small building complex to run an errand. This was the second indication for Olivia that suggesting a day together was turning out to be a very bad idea. They were already late, and she was anxious that they might not even make the actual wedding ceremony at all. That didn't seem to factor into Wilson's plans, which, from the start, didn't seem to mesh with her own. As she fumed, annoyed by his lack of consideration, Olivia realized she should have seen the writing on the wall, so to speak. When she accompanied Wilson to the concert, it had seemed like a safe enough date. Except she didn't know anything about the group performing, found the music way too loud, and felt out of place among an audience of not only much younger attendees but also people who weren't her tribe. In other words, what had she been doing there?

And as she readied for the wedding she'd invited Wilson to, she'd been unable to come up with an excuse to disinvite him that didn't make her feel like a coward...or unkind.

Olivia was appropriately dressed for the occasion, in a simple bright-print dress and heeled sandals. Wilson had chosen to wear casual khaki slacks, an outside shirt without a tie or jacket, and what appeared to be Dockers. She'd caught her breath when he'd picked her up. Had he never been to a formal wedding before? Was he planning on going for a sail after the wedding?

As far as Olivia was concerned, Wilson had one more strike against him for the day, and she was certain he was going to get several more. She let out a sigh of relief when she finally saw him exit the building, small shopping bag in hand and sauntering toward his vehicle as if they had all the time in the world. Her body was stiff with anxiety...and growing anger.

"Got it," Wilson said, sliding into the driver's seat and putting the bag behind him on the floor.

"Are you waiting for me to ask, "Got what?""

He chuckled. "It's no big deal. I promised a designer friend I'd stop by to pick up some samples of tiles for my bathroom. Next renovation project. There's always a project when you move into a new place."

Olivia stole a covert glance at her watch. "Don't you think that could have waited until some day during the week after work? We're going to be—"

"We're not late," he cut her off, a tad impatient.

"The wedding starts in…ten minutes." Olivia tried to stay calm. She *hated* being late.

Images of an impatient Marcus were dancing in her head.

"Then we got plenty of time. Weddings never start on time anyway. I've been to enough of them to know," he chuckled, unconcerned.

"Wilson, this one is important. I'm like a special guest of the bride."

"That's great! Then she'll forgive you."

They got back on the road, heading a little north of Santa Monica. It was a pleasant but grayish day, but no chance of rain. It was, after all, Southern California. But the gray hung like a low, flat cloud over Olivia like the possibility of the day being ruined by Wilson's childish self-centeredness.

She wished she'd asked Sloan to be her plus one.

But at the time of her invitation, at the tentative start of her relationship with Sloan—whatever that was—it hadn't felt appropriate to ask him. Now, things were much better between them. Very promising. Olivia was sure that things…feelings…between them were only going to grow. Any fault now was her own insecurity, not

Sloan's intentions. Now it was all she could think of. She would have been comfortable in Sloan's company at the wedding, no matter what.

When Wilson detoured yet again, Olivia lost it. He pulled into a men's retail and shoe repair salon in a small strip mall that was also home to three Thai restaurants. Olivia's head turned sharply as she stared at his profile, in disbelief that he would dare make another personal stop. They were still ten miles from the wedding venue.

"What are you doing?" she asked, perhaps a bit sterner than was called for.

"One more stop," Wilson said without concern, putting the car in park and climbing out of the driver's seat.

"*You can't do this*! I didn't agree to accompany you on your round of Saturday chores."

"Will you relax?" he said, as if speaking to a child.

And without waiting for her response, he was headed to the shop. Olivia, her mouth open in disbelief and rage, watched Wilson enter the store and disappear. She fumed for another moment before getting out of the car and searching for her cell phone in her purse. It was a small occasion clutch, not able to hold much more than house keys, a colored lip balm, Kleenex, a card folder with her driver's license, two twenty-dollar bills, and her phone.

Olivia wandered away from Wilson's car, basically leaving it unattended as she quickly searched for her Uber icon and began trying to arrange for a car. There was no guarantee, of course, that she'd find one this far out of West Hollywood, but at the moment it was her only option. Olivia was finishing the reservation when she heard a voice behind her, annoyed and put out.

"What are you doing?"

"It's clear that you're not interested in being with me today."

"It's not like I'm going to know anybody at this wedding. You probably won't either. Besides the bride, that is. Is she a best friend or something? Old sorority sister? Colleague?"

"It doesn't matter. The bride invited me to one of the most important days of her life. If you were ever married, you'd know that."

"I was married… Now I'm not, and now I remember why!"

Olivia stared at him. "You said…your profile…"

"Yeah, yeah. Small fib, minor detail. I was married right out of college. Look, we're almost there. Get in the car. Next stop, the wedding and reception."

He turned to get back into his car, adding another package to the ones on the floor behind his seat. Olivia didn't move. Wilson climbed halfway out again, poking his head above the car hood.

"Are you coming?"

She shook her head. "No. I don't think so."

"What? You planning on walking? Hitching a ride? You're being a little ridiculous, don't you think? *What is the fucking big deal?* So we're going to be late!"

"Why don't you go on, finish your shopping or whatever it is you're doing, without me. You don't need me for company. I have someplace to be."

"You're kidding, right?"

"No, I'm not. I have no intention of getting back into your car. I don't want to ride around LA County for the next few hours, sitting in your car while you keep shopping. I'll be fine. You obviously have things to do, people to see."

Wilson stared at her for a long moment, displeasure in every feature of his face, as if he was offended. "If that's what you want. But I think you're being foolish. I can take you back home if you want."

"I don't. Bye, Wilson." She turned away, walking idly along the covered pathway in front of the row of small businesses. She heard a car door slam, the sudden change in the engine hum when he shifted into drive, and the screech of wheels as the car accelerated out of the parking lot.

Olivia was relieved that she'd never hear from Wilson again. And she made a mental note to terminate her three online dating accounts before the sun rose on another day.

CHAPTER 8

Sloan only half listened to the congratulatory toasts made by members of the bride's and groom's families, maid of honor, and best man. They were all sincere but awkward, anecdotal and personal, and too long. He would guess the bride and groom were graciously enduring this wedding ritual and, like everyone else, were ready to serve themselves from four different food stations of ethnic cuisine placed around the dining area. The ceremony had been almost an hour late getting started. Then it had been almost another hour while the wedding party and photographer roamed the property to find romantic and pretty areas to take pictures. Sloan had opted not to attend the service, sensing an intimacy about it that he knew would have made him uncomfortable. He didn't know any of the wedding party or other members well enough to invest so much emotion.

The day was getting late.

Sloan played mindlessly with the napkin ring, a white plastic rendering of the head of a bride and groom, facing each other and smiling. It didn't represent the actual couple but was meant to be a token, a souvenir for the guests, of the occasion. Sloan was also rehearsing an exit excuse that would involve an unexpected call to a new case. He didn't know either the bride or the groom but was well acquainted with the groom's father, a retired LAPD captain he'd worked with on and off for the past three years. Sloan had initially declined the invitation, recognizing that the connection was mostly professional. The resolution of the cases they'd worked together had pushed the now-retired officer into enough promotions and accolades to give him a very comfortable retirement package. Sloan had attended a post-retirement night of drinks with him and other officers and colleagues from his precinct. That was the sum total of their connection.

Sloan glanced at the couple seated at the center of the wedding party dais and saw what every guest ever attending a similar gathering saw: an attractive young man and woman in love with each other. He tried to recall if he'd felt the same when he'd gotten married. The day hadn't been this festive, dress-up affair with flowers and a tiered cake. His wedding day had been a ninety-minute ceremony followed by champagne and a finger-food gathering of near military precision. Neither his nor the bride's family had been in attendance, and the guests had all been classmates and instructors from Quantico, where they were both in training to become FBI agents.

His bride had worn a peach-colored silk sheath with not a scrap of lace or beading anywhere that stopped at the knees of her strong, shapely legs. Sloan had been in a nondescript navy-blue suit, white shirt, and pale tie. He'd never again worn the suit or tie. Sloan couldn't remember if he'd been joyous that day or not. He frowned now, twirling the napkin in the novelty napkin ring. He couldn't remember what he was feeling that day. The marriage, in any case, ended two years later. Unreconcilable differences.

Sloan made his decision. He'd congratulate the happy couple and say how sorry he was that he had to leave. He'd wish them a happy future. And say he was honored to have been included in their celebration and special day. Sloan left his table, nodding pleasantly at the other unknown guests with whom he'd had little time to chat or get to know. He walked to the main family table, and the groom's father, seeing him approach, stood up to thank him for attending. It meant so much to the whole family that someone from the agency came.

Sloan and the former officer chatted very briefly, not about the wedding. Later, in hindsight, Sloan would be grateful because of what happened next. Suddenly, there was a small but audible surprise yelp from the bride. It drew attention from several people around her at nearby tables. She jumped to her feet, her hands covering her mouth expressively, as she looked at the final arriving guest for the wedding.

"*Oh my God!* You made it!"

The pretty young bride threw her arms in the air and fluttered her hands as she bounced on her feet in joy. There were murmurs of curiosity from guests, wondering what the excitement was all about.

Everyone on the dais was now watching as a very lovely new arrival entered the festivities. Sloan turned to view the person who'd merited such a happy greeting and found himself watching the hesitant approach of Olivia Cameron. For a few seconds he openly stared, first taken by the fact that she was actually there and, second, by the stunning vision she made dressed as a guest for a wedding.

Olivia's hair was pushed back from her brown oval face, the off-center part defining the fall of her straight hair. The style was held in place by a tortoise-shell headband. Her floral dress with the boat-neck line had a stylish cut that gave a discreet hint of cleavage. No stacked stilettos, but a pair of pale-pink low-heeled dress sandals.

Olivia was smiling at the exuberant greeting as the bride left the dais to run and wrap her arms around her. By now much of the room was abuzz. But Sloan, now very alert to Olivia's gestures, mannerisms, expressions, saw something else in her posture and even the way she was breathing. He frowned as he recalled a similar reaction the day he'd found her in the basement of her house. He paid attention. As his host turned his attention to the bride's greeting of Olivia, Sloan stepped aside, looking for a place and waiting for the time to intercept her.

There was an obvious warm and affectionate history between the two women, and they were not to be rushed in their hello. The bride glanced around, finding a waiter. She said something hurriedly to a young man, who rushed away to do her bidding. Meanwhile, the bride grabbed Olivia by the hand, coaxing her to the front of the dais and facing the room and guests at large. The usher returned, giving the new bride a hand mic.

"Hi, everyone. I just had to interrupt to introduce a very dear friend of mine. Many of you will remember the accident I had a few years ago on my bicycle that resulted in a broken ankle and elbow. I was a mess! But it was my roommate in rehab who took time out from her own treatments to hold my hand when I boo-hoo'd that I'd never heal completely in time for my wedding. Olivia Cameron promised me that I would, and here I am today in heels, no limp, and ready to tear up the dance floor!

"I'm so happy to introduce you to Olivia. I owe her so much, including her friendship."

Applause broke out in the room, and the bride stood back, allowing Olivia to stand in the spotlight to accept the recognition from a room of total strangers.

Except for me, Sloan thought to himself, gratified that he could consider that.

He was not surprised by Olivia's graceful demeanor as she smiled shyly at the introduction and began to step back out of being the center of attention. And he was only mildly surprised by the revelation of another life she had. Sloan stepped out of the circle of tables so that he could better observe her. She and the bride chatted very much like girlfriends before a waiter appeared to direct her to a table for lunch. The guests had already begun eating, and the music was starting as an accompaniment and for dancing.

Olivia was seated, still settling in and acknowledging comments from the people at her table. There were several empty places, and Sloan smoothly and, for a few moments unnoticed, slipped into one right next to her. Olivia, realizing that someone else had joined the table, turned to him to say hello. Sloan was ridiculously pleased that what was Olivia's habitual smile for everyone was not the same one she gave to him from the very beginning. And with her recognition of him, *that* smile and her bright gaze rested solely on him.

"Hello," Sloan said quietly.

Her gaze widened, and her mouth opened with her own surprise. "Sloan! What…are you doing here?"

"I was going to ask you the same thing, but the bride cleared up the mystery."

He noticed immediately her blinking hesitation at his awareness and decided not to mention what the bride had revealed that resonated with him.

"I've done work with the groom's father. He invited me to his son's wedding. I almost didn't accept." He let his gaze explore her countenance, the surprise still evident in her eyes.

The small band began to play. It was danceable but still good background dining music. Sloan gave his full attention, however, to Olivia.

Her gaze quickly assessed him, what he was wearing. She smiled.

"You look like a guest at a wedding," she mused. "You look…very… handsome."

"Thanks. High praise. But if you say anything about my pink shirt—"

"Very pale pink."

"—we're done."

Olivia chuckled. She arched a brow and leaned toward him. He knew what was coming.

"Gun."

Sloan couldn't help his voice dropping an octave to disguise his pleasure at the very private repartee between them. "Ankle."

He liked very much that the two of them just silently regarded each other. He was relieved that it had taken him so long to decide whether or not to leave, prolonged by the chat he'd gotten into with the groom's father. He would have missed Olivia and the surprise of her appearance.

There was certainly now familiarity between them. But there was also a new awareness. Sloan wondered if it was because they were both still in unexplored territories of the heart. Oddly, he believed this encounter had only drawn them closer together. Had, finally, gotten them over the hump of the difficult encounter. He deliberately took it to mean there was no turning back.

Progress.

"I'm really glad to see you. Nice surprise," Sloan confessed, letting his gaze and voice convey more.

"Me, too," Olivia admitted. She placed her small clutch on the table.

Many of the younger guests had abandoned the buffet offerings in favor of dancing, including the bride with her new husband and the parents of both.

Sloan realized that a quiet tête-à-tête was not going to be possible much longer. He and Olivia were interrupted when a waiter unceremoniously informed them that they could help themselves to whichever cuisine they wanted.

"I...don't think I can eat anything," Olivia said.

Sloan studied her, suddenly noticing some tension in her. "Are you all right?"

"I... I had a difficult morning," she responded with a shrug.

"Reason why you're late?"

She moistened her lips and nodded.

He continued to study her. "Want to talk about it?"

Olivia shook her head. "I'm fine."

Sloan didn't pursue it but guessed it was not an insignificant matter. Instead, he carefully took her hand and stood up. "Come on. Let's dance."

Olivia hung back but didn't pull her hand free.

"It's kind of slow, so I won't step all over your feet," Sloan said. He gently squeezed her fingers, and finally Olivia stood and let him lead her to the dance floor.

He wisely chose not to maneuver to the center of the floor, where they would be surrounded by uninhibited, acrobatic dancers showing off their abilities and musical knowledge. Sloan had another agenda in mind. He created a space just for the two of them near the edge of the dance floor and patiently waited until the music segued into a slow number. He drew her into his arms.

Magic took hold.

––––––––––––

The minute his arm circled her waist, his large hand splayed across her back, Olivia caught her breath. A sudden and strong wave of longing swept through her. She had to briefly close her eyes to steady herself. She almost stepped on his foot. Sloan held her hand and simply swayed to the music, from side to side, letting his thighs and knees be the guiding force.

Olivia wasn't paying attention to the music, could not have identified the piece or performer if her life depended on it. She was comfortably pressed against Sloan's chest, his stomach. She allowed herself to imagine everything below his waist. Sloan used his hold around her waist to guide her into a subtle turn to his left and then to the right. They had not really moved at all, but Olivia happily let Sloan lead.

The music faded, and the band immediately went into a number that was more upbeat and required that the partners separate and move to steps that picked up the rhythm. Olivia had her gaze on Sloan's pink shirt and smiled to herself because their movements were in synch. She could not remember the last time she'd danced…with or without Marcus. She raised her eyes to Sloan's and let her smile grow. He took her hand and pulled her back to him.

They did one more dance, let go of each other, and simultaneously walked out of the reception room, out of the open french doors of the pavilion, and onto a path that meandered through the property of the event center. They didn't speak, for the time both fine with strolling. Olivia was aware that Sloan, now and then, glanced her way to make sure she was able to keep pace with him.

Ahead, on a small rise, sat a gazebo. They automatically headed for the old-fashioned octagon structure, painted white with slatted rail sides and openings above. Inside were two short benches. They each took one to sit on. The silence continued, peaceful and easy.

Olivia drifted off into a reverie, feeling no rush or need to speak.

She was feeling grateful that the day, a potential total disaster, was turning out to be such a wonderful, happy surprise. It wouldn't have been that way if Sloan had not been present. But he was, and there was no question that having him here with her made a world of difference. It was not lost on Olivia how good that felt, how much it meant that *he* made the difference.

She gave a curious, quiet look.

He noticed, gave her back the look, and waited.

"I'm surprised you don't have a plus one for the wedding and reception," she murmured.

"Why?"

"Why? I guess…I assumed there might be someone…you know…important, special in your life."

Sloan continued to study her for a moment longer before glancing away. "I waited too long to ask," he said quietly, pensive. "And you? You got here late. You were also alone."

Olivia nodded. Hesitated and then made a decision. "I wasn't supposed to be. I…did invite someone to come with me." She waited for his reaction, but Sloan gave nothing away.

He didn't ask for an explanation, but suddenly, Olivia wanted him to know that she'd felt uneasy about what had happened from the start. And at the time, there wasn't another option except to attend the wedding alone.

She and Sloan had not yet moved toward getting to know each other better. She wouldn't have asked him.

"My girlfriends have been really on my case about not being *out there*, not dating since my divorce. So…"

"You signed on for a dating website," Sloan guessed.

She shook her head. "I didn't. My friend Lynn created a profile

for me and put it on several sites. I wasn't very happy about it and…
she didn't ask. But…" Olivia shrugged.

"You wanted to see what would happen?"

"No. Actually, I didn't care. I really never expected anything to
come of posting…and I didn't much like the idea that I had to advertise myself to a bunch of men. I felt like…like I was a melon. Or…a
bottle of wine."

Sloan was totally silent, making no sound, no indication of the
humor she attempted…or anything else. She glanced at him. His
countenance was still. Thoughtful.

"Just after the thing that happened at my aunt's house, I met
someone online. We had a coffee date. But then I just… I blurted out
the invitation to come to the wedding with me. He agreed."

"So what happened before you arrived today?"

"The details aren't really important. But I began to feel taken for
granted. It was obvious to me when he picked me up that he really wasn't
interested in attending a wedding with people he didn't know. I got out
of his car, he drove away very angry with me, and I called an Uber."

"Good move. Not much fun but…you made it after all."

Just recalling the incident upset Olivia again. "I'm glad I didn't
just go home to…lick my wounds."

Sloan was shaking his head. "You didn't have any wounds, Livi.
You only wasted some time. Personally? I'm glad he turned out to be
a jerk. Maybe I should find him and thank him."

Olivia looked sharply at him. "Really? Why?"

"Now we can be each other's plus one. Okay with you?"

Olivia bestowed a smile upon Sloan that she hoped would say
exactly what she wasn't yet prepared to put into actual words. She
nodded.

It was suddenly settled that they were now at the wedding event together.

At the last minute, Sloan dropped several of the cellophane-wrapped cookies into his pocket before heading back to the table. The hall was mostly empty, as some of the guests had already left and others had wandered off to explore the spacious and beautiful grounds of the facility before they also headed out. The bride and groom had gone off with the photographer to take the last of any pictures they still wanted to capture their successful celebration.

And Sloan had finally persuaded Olivia that she had to eat something. He knew that, once revealing what had happened to her erstwhile date for the wedding, a lot of her annoyance and even relief at the way things had ultimately worked out would allow her to get into the spirit of the day. Having learned the truth of her earlier arrangement, he was also feeling rather hopeful that they were on a path in the right direction. Olivia had asked a dubious acquaintance to the wedding before she'd ever met him.

All was forgiven.

They had decided on the Asian station, among the four cuisines available for guests to choose from, and selected sushi and tonkatsu, shumai, and gyoza. And edamame. Sloan also secured two fresh glasses of champagne before the waitstaff could start to remove remaining food and beverages. The wedding cake had already been cut and served, but he and Olivia had decided to forgo the sugar and carbs in favor of final drinks.

Olivia glanced up as he reached their table, where they were the only occupants left, and he was rewarded with a smile that reached her eyes—and his heart. It was an incredible revelation, and, incredibly, Sloan felt a stab of fear run through him because of the implications of what he was suddenly feeling. And as much as Olivia's presence guaranteed his enjoyment of the day, there was a part of Sloan that was an experienced and recovered victim of past relationships still lurking within. He knew with a certainty that he had, maybe, one more chance…willingness…to risk everything for Olivia. He'd known from the start that she was the one.

It was a silent appraisal that caused a twist in the center of his chest as he looked into Olivia's soulful and warm gaze. He wasn't yet ready to say that he'd arrived, but he knew he was very close.

"This is the last one," Olivia announced, a little laugh in her voice.

Sloan handed her a glass of champagne and took his seat next to her. "You're not driving. I think you can be trusted for maybe one more—"

"No," she said decisively, taking a sip of her drink.

"I'll make sure you get home safe."

"And who's keeping an eye on your consumption?"

He cut her a skeptical glance and, as always, kept to himself his amusement and the contentment he felt being in her company. No point yet in giving everything up. Sloan was truly concerned about the consequences to himself if this all blew up. Again.

"You're not watching. You don't have a clue how many glasses I've drunk." With that, he downed a third of his current glass.

Olivia looked at him carefully. "Are you officially on duty or not?"

That caught Sloan up short, and he gazed at her with appreciation. "It's my day off. But I'll get called in if there's a need. I'm trusting the fairies will give me a break and that won't happen."

Olivia's smile broadened, transforming her features into a picture of beauty, pleasure, and cheerfulness.

Sloan casually reached into his jacket pocket and withdrew a handful of wrapped cookies. He placed all of them right next to Olivia. She looked at them blankly for a quick second and then graced him with another of her smiles.

"Fortune cookies. Are those for me?"

"I got them from the food station. I seem to remember that you not only eat the cookies, you actually read the fortunes. And you believe in them."

Olivia fingered one of the wrapped cookies, turning it over in the palm of her hand. She glanced at him. "Thank you, Sloan. It…it's really nice that you remembered."

"Did I pass?"

Her expression went blank and then she chuckled lightly. "Yeah. You pass."

There were maybe a half dozen people scattered around the room, as all the accoutrements of the reception were being cleaned up and whisked away by staff. They worked quickly and efficiently but were not inclined to rush the rest of the wedding guests away. Sloan was enjoying the light and easy conversation he was having with Olivia. No drama. No complaining. No coyness. No demands. He watched her as she revealed more about how she'd met the bride in, of all places, rehab. He hadn't forgotten the bride's explanation when Olivia arrived late, about how they knew each other.

What was Olivia doing in rehab? For what?

Sloan processed and filed away a ton of information that led to a ton of questions he wasn't going to ask her yet. But there was one thing. He was thinking over how to phrase his curiosity, how far to push the envelope and dig into her past.

Olivia judiciously divided the cookies in half. Three for her and three for him. Sloan absently watched as she pushed three in his direction.

"Those are for you," she said quietly, and stuffed her three into her inadequate clutch, snapping it shut.

Sloan stared at the cookies, hesitant. He wasn't the least superstitious. And he didn't believe in coincidence or luck…or fortune…by default. But curiosity got the better of him and he snatched up the cookies and dropped them back into his pocket.

There was a lovely dusk glow over the property. It was quiet. They looked at each other.

"Are you ready to leave?" Sloan asked solicitously. But if he took her home, that would mean the end to the day.

She was thinking. "Can we walk a little more?"

Sloan nodded and stood up. They were on the same page.

They were already out a side exit, through tall french doors, when Sloan became aware of a commotion behind them. There was the crash of a chair falling over, a female yelp of surprise and distress. A plate shattering as it hit the floor. Sloan stopped and looked over his shoulder. Suddenly, he broke into a run back into the dining hall. He had no time to say anything to Olivia as he hurried to a table to assist an elderly man who lolled back in his chair, holding his throat, trying to breathe, choking.

CHAPTER 9

Olivia heard the crashing and the noise, someone screaming, "*Help!
Please help.*"

When it all finally registered, Sloan had already reached the man
who was struggling to breathe, gasping for air. Sloan got behind the
man and hauled him to his feet. He kicked the chair aside so that
he could grip the man around his middle, clasping his hands in the
right way beneath the man's diaphragm to perform the Heimlich
maneuver. Olivia understood exactly what Sloan was doing and
stood by several people who were apparently in the company of the
sufferer.

"It's all right," Olivia soothed a distraught older and younger
woman, both in tears of helplessness. "He knows what he's doing. Go
find a manager or staff. Call 911," she instructed them as a distraction.

When she turned back to Sloan, it was to find him giving three
abrupt and forceful upward thrusts under the man's diaphragm. On
the fourth attempt, something shot out of the man's mouth, almost
three feet in front of him. Sloan immediately loosened his grip but
held on to the man while offering quiet encouragement. Sloan recovered the chair and placed it so that the man could sit down. He did,
heavily, trying to regain composure. And then, he abruptly collapsed,
falling right to the floor landing heavily on his side. Instinctively

Sloan dropped to a knee to place his hand beneath the man's head to prevent it from forcibly hitting the tile floor.

Staff appeared, one informing Sloan that 911 had been called.

Olivia suddenly moved, hurrying to Sloan's side. "Take off your jacket," she ordered. He didn't hesitate but awkwardly shrugged out of the linen sports jacket. She pulled it away. She also caught a glimpse of his gun, holstered at his ankle as he'd said, but she doubted that anyone else had noticed.

He was already checking for a pulse, breathing, other indicators. The man was sweating, his skin sallow and pasty.

The bride and groom, their parents, and the rest of the wedding party rushed in to crowd around the scene. The bride was distraught, of course, but everyone else stood as observers on the unfolding crisis.

"He's got a weak pulse," Sloan said.

"Yes, but he's sweating," Olivia observed. " I think he's having—"

"Right. A heart attack."

"Is he unconscious?" Olivia knelt opposite Sloan, the prostrate man between them. He didn't acknowledge her presence. Two managers stepped in and quickly cleared the curious onlookers out of the room, signaling to staff to close all doors She made another observation. The fallen man was beginning to turn blue. "Sloan..." Olivia murmured urgently, catching his gaze.

Sloan again went into action. He carefully rolled the man on his back and pulled open his shirt, disregarding buttons popping and flying all over. He tilted the fallen man's head back until his mouth was facing the ceiling. Sloan went to work using the interlocking fingers of his hands to pump against the man's chest, *hard*. Olivia dropped to his side, counting quietly under her breath, holding the man's wrist and checking for any pulse, now. When she got to a certain number,

Sloan switched off compressing the man's chest to breathe into his mouth, making sure the head was tilted at the right angle to force air into the lungs. They kept repeating the routine until the arrival of an EMS team, who rushed in to take over. It was less than ten minutes, but Olivia's own heartbeat, her adrenaline coursing through her body, was elevated. It felt like a much longer time. She stood up, grabbed Sloan's coat from the floor nearby, and stood back out of the way.

Standing behind the EMTs, Sloan quietly and in detail outlined everything that had happened, that he'd witnessed or taken part in, to the emergency workers. Olivia noticed that the back of his shirt and part of the front were damp with perspiration. The EMTs worked to stabilize the man, placing an oxygen mask on his face, and then quickly preparing him for transport to a hospital.

Olivia, feeling suddenly a little shaky in her knees, found a chair and sat down, composing herself. Sloan had done all the hard work, had gone swiftly into action without missing a beat. She knew what to do, but she was slower. Having to think and react she now found had taken a bit of a toll on her. But she sat and watched as Sloan, even after the very tense situation he'd found himself in, talked with calm professional knowledge to the EMS workers. He answered questions. He continued to assist where and when he saw he was needed. He once sent her a long, considering look, as if checking to make sure she was okay. To let her know he knew exactly where she was all the time. Olivia returned the scrutiny in the way she knew best. Sloan turned back to being solicitous, and she relaxed to wait for him.

Olivia suddenly remembered the day in the basement of her great-aunt's house, with Sloan arriving and finding her...and rescuing her. There was no other way to put it, and she now also remembered the accusation she'd thrown at him. But it wasn't at *him*. Olivia recognized that she'd probably suffered a flashback to the way Marcus used to treat her…like, after the accident. As if she were helpless, overly dependent, careless.

She had just demonstrated that she was none of those things. And Sloan's actions and responses had shown her even more. He was not a certified, highly praised, and admired doctor, but he was very present, very calm, and helpful in an emergency.

Sloan finally turned to her. Olivia stood as he walked toward her, with that steady and thoughtful way his gaze fastened onto her. And she could tell by the bright gleam in his crystal-blue eyes that he was also coming down from the adrenaline high of, possibly, just having saved someone's life. He stopped in front of her, reached for his jacket. Olivia held on and didn't let go. On a sigh, Sloan gave in.

A quick, silent exchanged glance and it was agreed—they were definitely ready to leave. Together they made their way to the exit. They were halfway to the parking lot when there was a shout behind them. Olivia gasped. *Not again…*

But it was just the bride, rushing after her to envelop Olivia in another affectionate embrace. And the groom's father followed behind, his hand already outstretched to Sloan.

"Can't thank you enough, Sloan. You were terrific."

"Everything okay?" Sloan inquired.

Olivia suddenly heard the controlled but clear exhaustion in his voice. It was flat and formal. He'd been through a lot as well.

"Yeah, yeah. Bert's a big eater and he doesn't know how to slow down. I think maybe he gets it now."

"Glad it worked out the way it did."

"See, I told my son—you can always be counted on. That's why I liked working with you."

Sloan was gracious but self-effacing. "Glad I could help."

"We'll stay in touch," the man said, taking his new daughter-in-law's arm to walk them back to the reception hall.

Sloan led the way to his car, a three-year-old Jeep Cherokee in cobalt blue. He held the door until she climbed into the passenger seat. Olivia sank into the thick comfort of the leather seat. Once Sloan was seated beside her, he sat staring out the window, his hands flat on his thighs. He said nothing, but Olivia became aware of a certain rise of tension in the enclosed space. She felt her heartbeat increase with a kind of anticipation. But...of what?

And then, Sloan smoothly turned to her, placing his left hand on her waist...like when they were dancing at the reception. His right arm was placed behind her shoulders, urging her toward him, and Olivia automatically let her eyes drift close, her mouth open for his lips to settle on hers. Sloan kissed her in the manner, she instantly recognized, she'd wanted him to for a while. She gave in completely to his urgency and let it awaken fully what she'd been holding back. Olivia let her hand wander up to find the hard line of his jaw, feel the movement under her exploring fingers, glide across his cheek, behind his ear, to pull him closer.

She could feel a hand gently kneading her shoulder, the other squeezing her waist as Sloan got them as close as possible in the confines of the car and awkward set of the seats. She let herself go with the force of his kiss, as he consumed her, possessed her, nevertheless with tenderness and erotic thoroughness, as if he wanted to absorb her into himself. It was heady and heated and delicious, and Olivia was suddenly no longer afraid to acknowledge that she wanted this... with Sloan.

In the car, almost in one another's arms, they had raised the arousal level to a fever pitch, and they either had to stop or do something about it.

Sloan very slowly stopped, pulling sweet little kisses from her mouth, teasing with his tongue. She could hear his breathing. Maybe he could feel hers, her breasts in her floral dress pressed against his chest. Their lips separated, and they sat staring into each other's eyes. Olivia watched as Sloan's jaw clenched and he sat trying to make a decision. She again placed her hand on his face, caressing and feeling the movement of his jaw beneath her fingers. Belatedly noticing the contrast of her skin against his.

She smiled faintly at him, her eyes bright with feeling. Sloan sighed and released her, facing forward, and abruptly turned over the engine.

"I'll take you home," he whispered, his voice low and rough with emotion.

―――――――――

Olivia got out of his car right away, not waiting for Sloan to say anything or to come around the front of the vehicle and open the passenger door. She was nervous and a little uncertain about what she was doing or what she wanted. Olivia was moving on instinct, trying not to overthink motivations—only breathlessly believing she wanted to have something different happen now with her and Sloan. Her breathing and heartbeat increased. Not with anxiety. It was all anticipation.

She was already at her door, unlocking it, pushing it in. Then Olivia turned to face Sloan, watching as he slowly followed her, stopping just a few feet away. She stayed focused on his face, his features and expression, trying to see into his habit of being unreadable. Sloan reached for his jacket again. She still held it, thrown across her arm. Again, Olivia held fast, not releasing it.

"That is my jacket," he said.

"I know," she said, glad at his detectable humor.

"It's been a long day."

"You were really…really great…what you did."

He briefly averted his gaze to the ground, put his hands into his pockets. "It's just a lot of training. I've had to use it a few times." He glanced at her. "I'm glad you were there," Sloan said.

She searched his face. "Me too."

He blinked, his blue eyes narrowed just a bit. "We…worked well together."

"I'm not certified or anything," Olivia demurred.

"But you knew what to do. You've been holding out on me, Ms. Cameron."

She gave him a slight smile and nodded. Olivia never took her gaze from him, finally seeing a change. "Are… Are you all right?"

He nodded, exhaled deeply. "I will be. I'm a little…wound up at the moment. I just need…"

She stepped back pushing her door farther in. "Come in."

Sloan appeared taken aback by her quiet command. "I…" That was as far as he got.

Olivia disappeared inside, leaving the door open. He felt foolish standing there staring at the empty doorway. He entered, closing the door behind him. Sloan was immediately thrown back to that evening he'd brought her here after what had happened in the house. He'd sent her off to shower, get into fresh clothes. He'd wandered into her kitchen to get her a glass of cold water. Now…

Olivia was waiting for him in the living room. She'd put her clutch and his jacket on the sofa. She stood looking at him, wide-eyed but oddly confident.

"Can I get anything for you?"

Sloan finally seemed to gather his senses, figured out everything. He took a few steps toward Olivia, and she held her ground, returning his scrutiny, the question in his gaze.

"That's a loaded question. Liv…listen. There is nothing I want more than to stay with you tonight."

She didn't respond, but she let the sudden gravelly texture of his voice rush over her, creating a longing that was not really a surprise.

"I think there's too much against that happening," Sloan added.

"How do you know I don't know what you want?"

"I think I have a couple of strikes against me, the two of us… getting together. I think…"

"What strikes?"

He still carefully studied her expression. "For one thing, my law enforcement background. Maybe even my military service. Do you think I'm robotic and uncaring? Are you getting me confused with the cops you see on the news?"

There was a change of emotion in her. That myth had been dispelled within the first twenty minutes of meeting Sloan.

"The other thing is me being white," he ended quietly.

"You know, you could say the same about me. There's never going to be any getting around the fact of what I am. It's not like either of us had a choice at birth. But you're wrong," Olivia whispered. "On both counts. I did test you a little bit when we first met. It was spontaneous, but I wouldn't have bothered if…if I didn't…wasn't a little bit interested. Curious."

"Right," he agreed.

"It scared me. And then it didn't," Olivia confessed. She slowly began walking toward him. She didn't have far to go. Two small steps and she stood right in front of Sloan. And she was acutely aware of his physical presence, the masculine solidity of him. "What's the worst thing that can happen if…?"

His brows furrowed. He shook his head. "I can't think of any *worst*."

"Good. Right now, I can't either. I've done enough *what if* and *suppose* and *I can't* and not giving myself enough of a chance to say *yes…why not?*"

"So you're saying…" He stopped, waiting for her to finish.

"I do like you, Sloan. Two strikes and all," Olivia said on a whisper, her voice catching on the last few words.

Olivia couldn't believe she'd gotten it out. Said. Admitted. Her heart *was* beating fast.

Could Sloan hear it?

But there was no possibility of misinterpreting her meaning. The corner of his mouth lifted, but she still didn't think it was a smile. He reached for her and Olivia walked right into his arms. Their lips met, fused, sought possession of one another. She slipped her arms beneath his and hugged his back. Sloan squeezed her to his torso, hips, his thighs. The kiss was deep and passionate, them surrendering to feelings kept under control and now set free as an honest expression of their regard. It was dizzying and exquisite.

Sloan could have lived there for a while longer but for one more consideration. He broke the kiss but let his mouth nibble its way to her ear. He pulled back, but his arms circling her kept Olivia melded to him at their hips. The position was provocative…and promising. He was already highly aroused, and the physical evidence was obvious.

He shook his head. "I can't. Don't get me wrong, Olivia, but…I had no idea we… I'm not prepared."

Olivia blinked, quickly understanding. "I'll be right back," she said, disappearing down a hallway.

Sloan used her absence to cover his face and breathe into his hands to gain control. He was beyond stunned at the turn of events. He brushed his hands back over his head, down to his neck, squeezing the nape. He was thinking what he could do to not squander this opportunity, this…gift. He was much more wound up than he'd imagined. Cortisol was having a field day in his brain. He exhaled and heard Olivia returning. She held a small box in her hand. Silently she handed it to him. Casting a curious glance at her, Sloan opened the box to find a handful of individually wrapped condoms with colored cellophane. He quickly raised his gaze to meet hers.

"They're left over from an assembly program I arranged in school a year ago. After Taryn had Gaye, I thought it was a good idea to have the talk. The kids weren't going to get it at home. I got permission from the district and had parents sign a release and made it happen."

Sloan used his finger to stir around the contents, feeling a little odd about getting the condoms from Olivia. He glanced at her again. His gaze was tired but warm with amusement. "Are these for me?"

"Us. I know what you're thinking," she said smoothly. "I just didn't think it was a good idea to leave those in my office. It's not a sacred place to the students."

"So…you've given this a lot of thought."

"Are you going to tell me you have not?"

"I have not, until right now. But I did have some pretty active daydreams," he murmured, closing the box.

She gently placed her hands flat on his chest. "I knew what you've been thinking for a while. But I knew the first move would have to be from me."

"Why?"

"Because I finally realized that you were being really careful, really…respectful. I really loved that. I'm ready to see what happens next. So. This is next."

Sloan was stunned by her awareness, her confession. He looped his arms loosely around her again, the box in one hand. He looked sternly into her eyes. "Have you felt pressure from me?"

Olivia shook her head. "You've only made me feel…like…I really want it to be you."

Sloan listened carefully, saw the bright light in her eyes…exactly as he'd seen the very first time they met, when he knew instinctively that something different and significant was happening.

"I am honored," Sloan whispered with deep and heartfelt sincerity. Wrapping his arms tighter, he leaned in to kiss her, and she was waiting.

The kiss was a slow-moving exploration, with Sloan providing erotic movements of his mouth on hers and Olivia welcoming and accommodating him. It was passionate and stimulating…but it was not escalating to a level of heat that would leave them both mindless with need. By silent mutual consent, they ended the kiss, their breathing not yet hurried but rather calm and peaceful.

And Sloan didn't want to rush. This moment was still evolving, and he wanted it to be natural. It was very much the kind of moment you have to just let happen and feel your way through. He spontaneously placed his hand along Olivia's face, letting his thumb brush the soft flawless skin of her cheek. He could feel her form a slow smile, and it was just for him.

If Sloan had any doubts before, they were now vanishing into very real possibilities.

"Come on," Olivia instructed simply, taking his hand and turning to lead the way down the hallway she had used moments earlier. They turned into a room. Her bedroom.

Sloan noticed that one wall was a sliding-glass door leading out to the backyard. But there were wall-to-wall sheer voile curtains providing a nice balance between transparency and privacy. There was a simple double bed that surprised Sloan, as he believed the world had bought into the idea of big beds. But he immediately recognized the level of intimacy possible with less room. Olivia's was painted a cream color, with the wall behind it a deep tangerine. Daring and bright and a brilliant backdrop for the several framed items on the wall. Sloan made note but knew he would want to look more carefully at the work…but another time.

Then, without anything more being said between them, he put the box of condoms on the nightstand nearest him and began to unbutton his shirt, letting his gaze meet Olivia's as he did so. For a moment she watched him before turning her back on him and reaching behind with her arms and hands, twisting in search of the zipper to her dress. It drooped from her shoulders, exposing her back down to her waist. She was not wearing a bra and held the dress to her chest as she stepped out of her shoes.

Sloan shrugged out of the pink shirt and, looking around, dropped it on top of a basket that was being used to hold magazines. He braced his feet, one against the other, to get out of his shoes, lifting one foot at a time to pull off his socks. He was watching Olivia to see how far her striptease would go, but there was a grace and elegance to the way she carefully revealed herself. She took the time to hang her dress in the closet, remove the headband that held her hair back from her face. Then Olivia turned to face him with nothing but black bikini panties on, her navel just above the edge. Her hair, let loose to fall free, almost reached her shoulders and curved gently along her face.

He stood staring, all of his impressions that Olivia was a beautiful woman in a purely unadorned way that was without pretense or play validated. He quickly removed his slacks and briefs. He made no attempt to disguise or hide his physical reactions to Olivia, and her expression, somewhat shy, seemed to indicate that she liked having this effect on him.

The last thing Sloan removed was his service weapon, strapped to his ankle. He placed his foot on the edge of the bed and unfastened the holster. Olivia reached across the bed, and Sloan gave the gun to her. She turned to the closet and placed the holstered weapon on the top shelf, stretching on tiptoe to set it back from the edge.

The entire process of disrobing was like a show-and-tell between them. *You show me yours, and I'll show you mine.* There was a bit of humor in the way they took their time peeling back protective public layers to bare themselves. Olivia pulled back the comforter, letting it fall to the floor at the foot of the bed. She slid under the top sheet and curled on her side watching and waiting for him. Sloan followed suit, and they at once pulled into each other's arms. As if there was some sort of safety there in holding on to one another.

Sloan was again surprised to discover that, for all her clear willingness to be with him in this very intimate way, Olivia was trembling.

It was not fear he got from her body signals but uncertainty. He held her, enjoyed being able to. Letting her rub against him and get used to his nakedness, his desire. She'd been married; she knew the routines. Sloan caressed a hand up and down her back, to her hip… her buttocks. Olivia flexed herself closer against him, but she was still trembling. She let him explore, but Sloan did not feel a need to make his touch sexual. To him it was enough that they were together, this close, where he felt relief and comfort and a rightness to where he was.

"It's okay," he finally voiced in a low whisper.

"I've thought so much about being with you, like this," she responded, a little anxiety mixed with bravery.

"I'm really glad to hear that, Olivia. I'm guessing it's…probably been a while." He couldn't think how to say it more gently than that.

Olivia didn't confirm or deny but sighed and relaxed into his arms. "My girlfriends keep telling me it's time…"

"*Your* time, not theirs. You have to trust when you know it's right."

"It's right."

"Now?"

"Because it's you." She quietly chuckled. "I…don't know how it happened. I didn't count on this."

"Sorry? Want to change your mind?"

"No. And, no."

Sloan breathed her name as he hugged her closer, kissing her forehead. There was no need for either to say any more. Sloan turned fully to face her. He clutched her waist and hauled her closer so that their hips were pressed together. He lifted his leg over hers, capturing Olivia. He flexed his pelvis against her. He was hard and ready but didn't want to rush. As much as it was clear he and Olivia wanted each other, he sensed she had to be eased into this physical intimacy. Every part of Sloan began to fall into a lethargic state of feeling safe and…content. Just the realization alone was enough to release weeks of concern about how he was going to deal with Olivia. He'd known he was going to be a tough sell.

The only thing left to do now was to show Olivia that her trust, her interest and desires, had not been misplaced.

Sloan slowly caressed his hand down her back to her buttock and pressed her against his pelvis. He heard the quiet intake of her breath, her stomach muscles contracting as she experienced the hard evidence of his arousal. Her fingers had begun to explore and found the smooth taut layers of flesh that were the result of healed burns. She found a few more near his shoulder and near his throat and on his side, under his arm. She gently explored them. Sloan hooked his fingers into the band of her panties, pushing them down her thighs until she could maneuver them down her legs and off. On an upward sweep, his hand trailed over her pubis area, massaging gently until he felt Olivia undulate against his fingers. He daringly probed.

"Sloan…" Olivia whispered, imploring him. She let out a small whimper.

Sloan twisted into a reclining position on his back. He reached for the night table, fumbling until he found the cellophane-wrapped condoms Olivia had given him. He quickly sheathed himself and turned back to her, capturing Olivia in his arms.

"I have to ask you something," she began, her voice muffled against his chest.

He wasn't concerned, and he was somewhat distracted by the soft, stimulating roaming of her hand and fingers.

"Why me? You don't have some weird fixation on Black women…
do you?"

He snorted, smothering the need to laugh. "I'm told I might be
weird in some ways, but that wouldn't be one of them."

She was silent.

Sloan sighed. "When I first saw you, I knew there was something special, different about you. I thought, you're really lovely. But
that wasn't what grabbed my attention. I thought… I felt you were
approachable. Your welcome came with a smile. I took it personally.
And it shone through your eyes."

"You saw all of that?" Olivia asked quietly.

"To me, none of it was hard to miss…and I wasn't even looking.
Of course it registered that you're Black. But then…I just moved
on. There were other things about you. But it was also how I was
reacting."

"Tell me," she murmured.

Sloan sighed. "No. I don't think I have to. Maybe it's not going
to make a lot of sense, but to me…I'd found you."

He was also, now, ready to move on. He was ready to show
Olivia the physical way he wanted her. But Sloan waited another few
moments for her to ask more of him. But she didn't. Instead he let
their entwined limbs dictate what happened next. And it was time.
When Olivia bent her knee, raising her leg, he took advantage of the
movement that provided space for Sloan to finally penetrate. At the
contact, Olivia held her breath, but her heart was beating fast against
his. He flexed his hip, driving closer. Olivia sighed and moaned.

He gave her what she wanted. And what they both needed.

He heard her sharp intake of breath as she wrapped her arms
around him and held on. He used his hands to guide her, to secure

their intimate connection. To help them both with a rhythmic gyration of their pelvises. Sloan went back to kissing her as she hugged him, raised her knee to force him deeper, encouraging him to love her.

They fell into a slow cadence of movement, of experiencing each other's pleasure…giving and receiving. When Olivia suddenly began to quietly pant, Sloan whispered something loving and encouraging in her ear, and she climaxed around him. The pulsing sensation sent him over the edge, and he held on to her, letting her breathing, her now-relaxing limbs guide him until the end.

They did not move for long minutes. To Sloan's way of thinking, their making love, embracing each other…this intimacy…was as open and vulnerable as it was possible to be. He and Olivia had arrived at another beginning. It was a signal from her as well that they were on the same page. Had arrived at the feelings…intentions…to keep moving forward together.

CHAPTER 10

Sloan moved when he sensed he was alone in the bed. He also could tell that it was very early morning, not even sunrise. It was quiet. He sighed deeply and let his eyes squint open. There was the promise of another Southern California perfect day showing through the sliding-glass door of Olivia's bedroom. It didn't bother him that she had obviously gotten up but that he had no recollection of it happening. Sloan's brow furrowed as he recognized that this never happened with him. In the Middle East during his service there, not knowing could be a deadly oversight. He had never been able to relax in Afghanistan. And he'd never slept well while in the country.

He quietly swung his body from the bed, sitting on the side and acclimating to the foreign space. The sliding door was slightly ajar, just wide enough for Olivia to have slipped through without making a sound. Sloan got up and padded barefoot to the door, but even before he'd reached it, he detected her sitting on a dark-blue carpet in the lotus position with her eyes closed. There was a not very deep canopy over the area where she sat, so she was protected if the weather was inclement…which it never was. She was wearing something loose and dark, her hands were cupped around each knee, and she was stone still. She'd tied a small kerchief around her head, holding back her hair in the same way as the tortoise-shell headband she'd worn to the wedding reception the day before. She looked so serene and beautiful in her meditation position. Sloan wondered how long she'd been at it.

A physical therapist had taught him meditation, under a great deal of stubborn protest, during his time in rehab after the bombing outside Kabul that kept him in a coma for four days. Sloan had learned quickly that meditation taught him how to ignore the pain of his burns, the extreme soreness in his trachea and esophagus after the intubation.

There was something sexy about seeing Olivia doing the same practice, and it was also calming. He was pretty sure they somehow had histories that warranted knowing and sharing. He yawned and turned away, not disturbing her. He wandered from the bedroom into the kitchen. He opened her refrigerator and found a container of cranberry juice. Searching for a glass, he poured it half-full and returned to the bedroom. Sloan was uncertain for a moment, not sure where to leave the restorative, but finally decided just outside the glass door, where Olivia would be sure to see it when her practice had ended and she came back inside.

He watched her for a moment longer, feeling a great deal of pleasure and affection for something they shared. And a calming awareness that what he'd suspected about Olivia from that first meeting was turning out to be true. She was a naturally calming presence.

Olivia silently repeated to herself the mantra that always ended her meditation sessions. On a sigh, she unfurled her body and gracefully stood up. She turned to the glass doors to reenter her room and immediately spotted the juice. She caught her breath knowing that only Sloan could have left it there for her. Olivia felt a catch in her throat, making it tight with emotion. She swallowed, blinking and clearing away the suggestion of tears. She hadn't heard a thing. She continued to the door and bent to retrieve the glass. One of her thoughts was that Marcus had never been this solicitous, even after her accident. She peered into the room and saw that Sloan was in bed and appeared to be asleep. Olivia was stunned by his gesture, by his awareness. And she was so glad she'd taken the chance that her first impressions of him would be borne out.

She sipped the juice as she approached the bed. He was on his back, a hand anchored behind his head, the other across his chest. She finished the juice and placed the glass on the nightstand. It was nothing but instinct that told Olivia that Sloan was watching her.

"Thank you," she whispered.

Sloan moved just a little, tilting his head toward her. Olivia peeled off the floor-length black empire-waisted dress she sometimes wore when she meditated outside. She stood naked for a moment, her infinitesimal shyness hidden under the dim interior light. She was silhouetted in front of the sliding-glass door. She reached to untie the scarf.

"Leave it," Sloan ordered quietly. He reached out his hand to her.

Following his request, Olivia dropped her arms and quickly got into bed with him. She waited until he coaxed her back into his arms. He studied her brown features in the soft morning light coming through the door. He kissed her forehead, leaned to kiss her cheek. Found her mouth and settled there on a deeply erotic and sensual kiss that drew a groan from him. He pressed deeper, undulating his body against her. There would be no stopping now.

Olivia loved when he massaged her lower back and cupped her buttocks to squeeze her to him. She loved when his tongue aggressively danced with hers and he effortlessly elicited a whimper, a moan from her. Then Sloan caught her off guard when he rolled onto his back and pulled her on top of him.

Sloan positioned her between his legs. He bent his knees to cradle her and never stopped their kissing until Olivia was starting to feel limp, hot…and ready. Sloan knew exactly what he was doing.

Her on top had its advantages. They were face-to-face. It was easy for her to bend forward to kiss him, for Sloan to run his fingers in her hair, onto her scalp, to hold her head to his kiss. It was easy for him to encourage her to find her own position of pleasure after he'd firmly thrust upward into her, gently pressing down on her buttocks to tighten the grip. To rotate her hips, or he'd rotate his until the grinding movement made her dizzy with longing. She had no idea how he was able to pace their movements, time the spiraling heat within them toward an inevitable end. But she'd already zoned out to her own needs, working against him as a delicious tightening took place in her pelvis and groin. Olivia tried to meet his thrusts. She squeezed her eyes shut, willing Sloan not to stop anything he was doing.

He was watching her, gauging the moment when he knew she was ready, her breathing labored, a joy shooting though her so strong that Olivia felt dizzy as the pulsing of her climax made her give a short cry, and Sloan pressed her down to his chest, and she could hear him. His thrusting and the strong lifting of his hips ended in his own release. She lay limp, drained, and Sloan's ride came to a climatic end, and they lay panting against each other.

His skin was damp. His mouth was damp. Sloan squeezed her

tightly as he pulled free, and still, Olivia could do no more than to lie inert on him while he cradled her.

They may have dozed then. She would never be sure. Neither of them having moved in a long while, Olivia heard his voice.

"Should I leave?"

The thought had not even entered her mind.

"Do you want to leave?" Her voice was quiet but bewildered.

"I asked first."

She tried to shake her head but realized Sloan couldn't see that. "No. Don't."

"Okay. A little longer."

They didn't fall back to sleep. And they stayed in each other's arms.

In that moment Olivia felt she wanted him to stay forever.

It was a little before nine when they woke again. Any prior awkwardness was replaced with curiosity and revelation. A lot of lazy affectionate caressing. Slow sensual kissing. Talk was informational, and they did not think beyond wanting to know more about each other. Filling in the gaps of their curiosity.

"You said you were married?" Olivia asked, curious.

"A few years. Did I mention she's also an agent? DC. She's hoping to become the first female director."

"Really?"

"The agency is not ready for that. It's still too much a conservative bastion of testosterone and inflated male egos."

"But you became one of them."

They were sitting up in bed, more or less, but still in a loose embrace. They were silently reluctant to get up and get on with the day. Olivia brushed her hand, slowly, back and forth across the flat plain of his chest. Sloan sighed, glancing away, pensive.

"That was before. I liked what they stood for. Not for what they actually are."

"Are you going to stay with it?"

She felt him shrug under her roaming hand. "I'm exploring my options."

"I think you're pretty good teacher material," she murmured.

"My mother was a teacher. In every sense of the term. I learned a lot from her, and now…" He turned his gaze at her, with warmth and tenderness. "Now I'm grateful I paid attention."

"She sounds wonderful and loving."

"She was. She died a little over two years ago of breast cancer."

Olivia snuggled closer. "You could follow in her footsteps."

"Hmmmm. I'll put it on my list."

Olivia grinned at him, at the ready way he'd accepted the idea. But she really thought so. Sloan caressed her cheek, the slumberous gaze shifting suddenly.

"I'll shower. Soon."

She giggled. "You said that a half hour ago. Whenever you want. Maybe I should make coffee?"

"Why don't we go for breakfast? Or lunch?" Sloan suggested.

"Do you really want to drive somewhere just to eat?" She was skeptical. Olivia liked exactly what they were doing together, right where they were.

"Frankly, I'd rather spend the time like this. We can talk."

"We are talking."

"Right. So how come you know about intubation? Being in shock?"

Olivia didn't pretend not to know what Sloan was talking about. And there was no point in denying it. Someone as quick and intelligent as Sloan, trained in interrogation and analysis of facts would pay attention and figure it out. What she seemed to know…and how did she know it?

"I started medical school but never finished. My… I don't think my heart was in it." Olivia shifted her body from his chest, within the circle of his arm. Her back now against him. Sloan lay still, listening. "I think I felt some pressure. My father was an internist, my mom an ICU nurse. Jackson went into radiology. So…"

"You didn't think you had a choice?"

Olivia sighed. "It's not like anyone ever suggested that I study to be a doctor. And I certainly learned a lot from my family, especially my dad. I got interested in teaching after volunteering in a teen literacy center when I was an undergraduate. But I did start medical school and learned after my second year that it wasn't a good fit. I dropped out and went on to get a master's in education. Then I met Marcus. He had finished medical school and was in his residency. He studied under Jackson for about six months. That's how we met."

She suddenly chuckled quietly at some private joke or revelation. "I didn't mind that I had stepped out of Marcus's field. He was a star, and he enjoyed that. But as I began to find my own tribe in education, he wasn't impressed with my accomplishments. Things got really…tough…when I got into a terrible car crash. Marcus seemed to lose every bit of bedside manner with me. I was badly injured but nothing life-threatening. But he behaved as if the care and time I needed were just a huge inconvenience."

Sloan sighed and shifted, and Olivia could almost sense his surprise, even dissatisfaction, with the way her husband had responded.

Olivia calmly but succinctly told Sloan about her vehicular encounter with a Mack truck in which she was the loser—a totaled car, deployed airbags, a broken arm and back…in two places.

She'd lucked out in that her broken back didn't involve her spine and she hadn't required surgery. The bad news was that the recovery was complicated and protracted. Nearly two months in rehab. Incredibly Marcus had only seen what happened to her in terms of how it affected him. Olivia decided further details were pointless and let go of Marcus's shortcomings. Like he'd waited until she was out of rehab and once again home to let her know the marriage wasn't working for him. He was busy. He'd gotten a prized assignment for his residency. He was being interviewed and profiled and asked to speak at prominent medical school programs of Black colleges and universities. Marcus hadn't denied her anything she needed toward a full recovery…except himself.

Olivia was not so much worn out after responding to Sloan's curiosity as much as saddened by having to repeat the whole episode. She would never understand how having a car accident that wasn't her fault ultimately led to her divorce. Jackson had been appropriately outraged by Marcus's handling of the situation, and his sister, but Jackson had not overly coddled her either after the accident. Olivia had to get back to work. She had to get on with her life.

"I'm sorry," Sloan said quietly.

Sloan was not going to coddle her, either. She was grateful.

His smartphone rang, and the mechanical sound seemed so out of place in the intimacy they'd created. He quickly got out of bed, walking unabashedly naked from the bedroom and returning almost immediately with his jacket. He was digging in the pocket and retrieved his phone.

"Sloan," he said simply.

Olivia was caught by how smoothly he had switched personas from lover to the man used to being in charge. He made no attempt to hide the call—personal or business—from her. He sat on the side of the bed, bending forward to rest his forearms on his thighs. Olivia threw him a curve ball because she knew he wasn't expecting her to come up on her knees, behind him, and gently plant a kiss on the back of his shoulder. But Sloan acknowledged the caress with the briefest turn of his head, even as he continued his call. He reached one hand behind him to stroke her thigh.

She went to the bathroom with the need to examine herself in the mirror. Surely there would be obvious changes. Had she gotten a bit taller, her breasts perkier with Sloan's touch? Had he left a mark of his presence that made Olivia look rejuvenated? She touched her cheeks, turned her head one way and then another. She stared straight ahead into her own eyes, dark and shining. And her smile. Sloan said she smiled all the time, a subtle show of awareness. Olivia was pleased. She had been smiling for him.

He was still on the phone when she returned to the room. Olivia went searching for her purse from the day before in search of her lip balm, her comb, and she found the fortune cookies that Sloan had given her from the reception. She'd already unwrapped one, devoured the cookie, and was reading the sliver of paper when Sloan finished his call.

"No emergency. Just updates on a few cases."

He put the phone aside and twisted his body to lie next to her, on his stomach, to see what she was doing. Olivia silently handed him the paper.

"'*Now is the time to try something new.*' Well, you've certainly done that," he said with sly inference.

"What about you?" Olivia asked.

Sloan sighed and rolled on his back, looking at the ceiling. "Olivia, I don't buy into fortune-cookie philosophy."

"You're not supposed to buy into them. You're supposed to see if any of them hold a grain of truth. You would know instinctively if there was any. Didn't you just say that mine rang true?"

"That was different. We'd just finished…" He stopped. He turned back over, taking the paper from her hand and silently reading it to himself again.

He gave it back to her and pulled himself up to sit beside her. Reluctantly Sloan reached for his jacket and pulled out the three wrapped cookies he'd kept from the day before. He ripped into the wrapping of one, broke the cookie apart, but discarded it, pulling out the fortune slip. He read it out loud, as if he was just doing so to placate her.

"'*There is a true and sincere friendship between you both.*'" He sat staring at the paper. He gave it to Olivia. "I don't think I want to bet my future on this." Still, he made short work of removing the other two fortunes from the other two cookies, reading them before turning them over to her. "What are you going to do with them?"

"Hold on to them. You never know."

"I do." He swept everything off the bed.

Sloan maneuvered to the top of the bed. He hauled Olivia up by her wrists, causing her to laugh at his He-Man action. But then he closed his arms around her and kissed her with purpose. The change in them both was instant. She enthusiastically returned the kiss, rubbing her breasts, her legs against his. Sloan controlled the kiss, his tongue playing with hers and then delving deeper and slowly to elicit the reaction he wanted. And just like that Olivia's fortune came to mind. *Try something new.*

He caressed his hand over her belly, sensing the way her skin contracted as his touch stroked over the nerves. He continued to her breast, feeling the nipple harden. Olivia sighed and rubbed herself against him.

Sloan freed his mouth and whispered into her ear. "What would you like?"

Olivia sighed again, her head falling back on his arm. She didn't answer but maneuvered onto her back. He watched her chest rise and fall. He massaged her nipples gently. And then Sloan slid his hand down Olivia's torso. She was breathing fast, and she lay languid. Helpless. He deftly, slowly, went farther to cup and explore between her legs. His fingers searching had as much of an effect on himself as on Olivia. He groaned, closing his eyes and continuing his ministrations on her body. His penis erect and ready, but he held off.

Try something new…

With that thought in mind, Sloan twisted to reach for another condom. In quick order he was done and shifted over her. Olivia drew up her knees and he settled naturally between her legs, the same as they'd done in reverse earlier that morning. This was the old-fashioned way, and he found his way into her with no coaching or assistance. She hugged him close, lifting her pelvis and falling into a rhythm that was a rocking and swaying, a pushing and withdrawal, while they kissed and made intimate little sounds that spurred them on.

Olivia, maybe inadvertently, made a move with her hips, and it pushed Sloan over the edge. He gritted his teeth, unable to hold back. He slowed his movements but kept moving with passionate purpose. He put his hand between them, and the moment he touched Olivia privately, she careened into a climax that caused her body to go limp under him as she was overcome with a euphoria that pulsed deep from within.

———————

Olivia made herself busy changing the linens on her bed, refusing Sloan's offer to help. She knew he wouldn't understand and was relieved when he went to shower, instead, in preparation for dressing and heading home.

But the ending of their little sequestered twenty-four-hour tryst was starting to have an effect…and she didn't think it was a good one. She needed the silence while Sloan showered to deal with the feeling of coming down from a high. What they had together had been extraordinary, in her experience, and Olivia was afraid of losing any of it.

They'd come together so fast, so smoothly, so physically that Olivia now felt as if they were being rent apart by their separate lives, work, and responsibilities. Were they going to be able to keep up the magic conjured out of their intimacy and their feelings for one another once they said goodbye at her door?

Was Sloan having the same worrying thoughts of *what next* that she now found herself struggling with? Being together had been a culmination of attraction, mystery, and secret desires that had bloomed beyond her expectation. It had been wonderful. It had been exactly what she'd hoped for. Sloan had not disappointed, even if she had questioned his intent up until the very moment afterward when he'd whispered, "*Are you okay?*"

She'd put the black maxi dress on again and went to her living room to wait for him. When Sloan appeared, quietly and fully dressed, they faced each other across a void that Olivia feared they'd never be able to bridge. He had not strapped on his ankle holster again and held the weapon and its holster in his hand. Sloan slowly approached her, bending to place his weapon on the coffee table. He slipped his arms around her in a light embrace.

"You look like a goddess," he murmured.

Olivia sighed, the wonder in his voice reassuring her. She smiled and looked into his light eyes. "And you look pretty in pink." His brows shot up, and she was positive he would smile. But Sloan only clenched his jaw, one of the signs she'd come to recognize as a sign of him controlling his emotions. Now Olivia knew he was pleased and amused by her comment. He tightened his arms a little, staring into her eyes.

"I'm trying to find an excuse to stay that you will agree to."

Olivia shook her head. "You can't, and I wouldn't let you. Even if I did want you to. You're busy saving humanity from itself and its worst impulses, and I'm trying to save some young lives from derailing."

Sloan nodded and kissed her forehead before stepping away. "Can't top that."

" And…maybe we both need a little time to…reflect. Get some perspective on last night. This morning."

"I don't need to. I understand exactly what happened. I wasn't disappointed, Olivia."

"Me either."

"Good." He picked up his gun and walked to the door.

Olivia didn't move, watching as Sloan was about to leave and feeling an unexpected panic and determination fighting within her. She wasn't going to succumb to her own worst fears. She wasn't going to make up a story to which she couldn't see an ending. When Sloan opened the door, he turned to her a final time to say goodbye and stopped when he must have seen the deer-in-headlights stare she couldn't stop.

He uttered something and came back to her, crushing her in his arms and whispering in her ear, "We made it this far. We're off to a great start, right?"

Sloan didn't wait for her answer, and in any case, she didn't have one, too afraid of jinxing everything. He kissed her with great feeling and depth so that she couldn't forget and she'd have this moment to replay if doubt stepped in.

"I'll call you," Sloan said simply.

And then he was gone. Olivia was unprepared for the space that he'd occupied and filled to feel so empty now that she was alone.

———————

It finally came to Sloan that Olivia's seeming reticence as he was leaving her on Sunday was not about regret that they'd found themselves past a kind of courtship phase and into the real deal of feelings and a possible budding relationship. He'd begun to wonder if she thought their intimate time together had been a one-off and that, somehow, it would change the intensity of his pursuit, that he'd quickly lost interest. Well, it had changed the intensity, but not in the way he suspected Olivia believed.

They had actually overcome curiosity and arrived at a kind of *aha* moment. At least he had. For Sloan it had solidified that his emotional instincts about Olivia had been right on target from the beginning. That sparked a possible truth that maybe he'd figured out what he was looking for. He'd left her, after a very satisfying day, feeling an unexpected hopefulness, maybe more than that—too soon?—relieved and sure of what he was looking for. It had not been easy getting here, and that had been even before he'd ever met Olivia Cameron. He had begun to wonder if his expectations were too high. Were so many women really all the same? Had they all become stuck together in a pool of monotony and little individuality? Except for Valerie, his ex. She had been consistently clear about her expectations from the moment they'd met. But now he knew he'd been looking for the wrong things in her as well. After they met Quantico, he thought he'd really lucked out in finding someone who understood service and commitment. It was a while before he realized Valerie was referring to herself—not to him…not to *them*. Someone who was confident could also translate as single-minded and determined. Someone who was fearless could also be bossy and impatient, unsympathetic.

That did sound very much like how Olivia described her ex-husband.

Sloan wondered, now, if Olivia was feeling less than he was. Should he try for a replay, getting together with her again—soon—so that the aura was not lost, or give her a little more time to see, on her own, that being together had been entirely, euphorically, real? Belatedly, he wished he'd called her after he'd gotten home. In hearing her voice, he would have known from her tone, cadence, and subtle shading how she was feeling. They could have reviewed the time together. Reminisced…been reassured.

Sloan also found himself reviewing the whole she's-Black-and-I'm-white thing, now that they'd gone all the way, to decide if that fact made any difference in where he was now. A few hours of late-night, intense rehashing of race had not been a factor in his thinking. Or his feelings.

———————

Sloan sat forward, over his keyboard, and made a Herculean effort to concentrate on the organized internal posting update on current agency cases. They were listed by date and order of urgency or prospects for violence. But there were constant interruptions from the right side of his brain as he tried to relive the experience of making love to Olivia, the sweet and moving way she'd responded to him, not holding anything back in showing how much she'd been affected by them together.

He realized she was a little hesitant but brave and everything worked. She only needed practice.

He had not been disappointed.

But what if Olivia now had second thoughts, was questioning his motives, or her own interests had been spent?

There was a quick rap on his open door.

"Hey. Did you get the news about those bank robbers who've been making merry through the county for the last two years?"

"What about them?" Sloan asked crisply, forcing his focus away from his thoughts about Olivia.

"The mother of one of them gave her son up. He did something monumentally stupid and bought an expensive car and paid cash. Mom knew he could never afford it and that he lied when he told her he'd won the money at a casino in Vegas, where he took his girlfriend for a weekend. He's never had enough money to treat his girl to anything, let alone to gamble with."

"Is he in custody?"

"Yeah, LAPD has him. They're working on getting him to flip on his partner. They don't think it'll take long."

"Don't recall how much stolen money is involved, but the department will let us know if we have to take over."

"Right. Thought you'd want to know," the colleague concluded before leaving.

The official interruption was enough to set Sloan back on track, and he had a mostly productive day...until it approached three o'clock and he knew Olivia would be finishing her school day. With no particular plan in mind, he called the school. Lori, Olivia's assistant, answered.

"Hi. It's Sloan Kendrick. Is Ms. Cameron available? I'd like to speak with her."

"Hi, Agent. She's not available at the moment. But she's around somewhere. School lets out in half an hour. She might hang around for an after-school activity. Can I have her call you?"

He was embarrassed and found it foolish that he was trying to be so proper after what had gone on between them in a less than twenty-four-hour period.

"I appreciate that. If she has the time."

"I'll give her the message."

He was only mildly disappointed that Olivia wasn't immediately available. Sloan went back to work, wishing that his day were a bit crazier so that he'd have no time to think. It was almost six and Sloan was headed to his car, having passed security out of the building, when a call came in. By then he was distracted by a number of other calls he'd been expecting as a follow-up to information on a possible abduction—the attempt had been thwarted, but the details had piled up in the course of the day.

"Sloan," he responded, unlocking his car.

"Hi. It's Olivia."

Sloan stopped, leaned back against the door. "Hey," he said, his voice a kind of surprised drawl. Despite having her on his mind much of the day, she'd managed to catch him off guard.

"Is this a bad time?"

"Perfect. I'm just leaving the agency for the day."

"Oh. Sorry I couldn't call earlier."

"It's Monday. We both have busy jobs. All is forgiven," he spontaneously tacked on and was rewarded with Olivia's quiet laughter.

"Thank you."

Sloan was listening very closely, trying to gauge any emotion from her. Any hint in her voice of how she was feeling toward him, about the day before.

"How are you doing?" he quietly questioned, his voice rough and cracked.

She signed over the line. "Well...I...I'm..." She sighed again.

"It's okay. This isn't an interrogation, Liv. It's just you and me." No response. "Want me to go first?"

"Yes."

He almost didn't hear that. "Okay." Sloan opened his car door and slid in behind the wheel. It was private there. He only wanted her to hear what he had to say. "I want you to know that the time I could be with you was... It was very special." Quiet. "The thing is, just cuddling Sunday morning was...amazing. And a first for me. It was peaceful and..." He let his voice drop, surprised by his own revelations. "It just felt so good to hold you finally."

"Do you really mean that? You're not just saying that because—"

"I'm saying that because it's the truth."

"Oh...Sloan..."

He frowned. "Were you worried?"

"I was sure you're used to something else, something more...you know...passionate and exciting and...and..."

"Olivia...it *was* passionate, and it *was* exciting. I wish I could be telling you this in person. I called because I wanted to tell you how the seventeen hours and twelve minutes we were together really rocked." He thought maybe she made a mewing sound of contentment. "I wish it had been longer."

"Maybe…next time?" she suggested.

Sloan closed his eyes and breathed with relief. "You don't have to be afraid to admit it to me. To be honest, I think I was a little afraid to call you last night. What if I'd hurt you? What if I didn't get you what you wanted or needed?" He heard a laugh from her.

"Don't you remember that movie when the heroine reminded the hero that she was responsible for her own orgasm? Without your patience and gentleness and caring, I might have failed. I didn't. We didn't."

"That's the best compliment my male ego has received in a long while."

"Liar."

He snorted.

"You know, sooner or later you're going to have to let yourself go and just laugh. You know you want to, and…"

"Olivia…we were great together. That's what I wanted to tell you. I'm glad it happened the way it did."

"Yes. I agree."

"So what are my chances of seeing you this week?"

"Hmm. Iffy. I'm on my way to meet my girlfriends for drinks. They want to weigh in on what kind of car I should buy. They don't know I've pretty much made up my mind."

"For what?"

"BMW. Jackson thought it was a good choice for me. And I have an appointment to meet with a representative of The Millionaires

Club. I think I told you I want to use some of the money to start some sort of funding."

"For your students?"

"That's right."

"Nice. So where do you and I fit in?"

"I'm pretty sure I'm free after that. Want to come for dinner?"

"You know what that will lead to, don't you?"

"Jackson says I'm sometimes slow, but I'm not dim."

"I'll have to have a talk with your brother. You're neither."

"He was teasing."

"Good. Just let me know when. And if you're up for it, I thought we could do something together this weekend."

Olivia chuckled. "I'll write that on my dance card."

When Olivia was directed to the suite booked by The Millionaires Club at The Ritz-Carlton hotel in downtown LA, she mused that it was probably the one and only time she'd ever have the opportunity to be in the rarified enclave of the very rich. It hadn't yet sunk in that she could now be considered among the very rich. The setting was très elegant, super modern, with expensive designer furnishings, but to her liking the hotel bordered on sterile. This was not her idea of comfortable.

The suite for the three-year-old foundation she was about to be introduced to was more to her liking. There was a table just inside the open doors, off of the exclusive elevator bank that served as a gateway to the suite. Olivia was greeted warmly and given a packet containing information about the monetary club, its founder and CEO Patrick Bennett, with some profiles of men and women who'd already become members. She was welcomed at the door by a woman and taken to an alcove reception area where a couple were already seated, presumably waiting for their turn to meet with a rep. Light refreshments were available, and a selection of printed testimonials from sponsors or recipients of the foundation's largesse were provided for review. Olivia, so far, was impressed.

Some of the material was familiar to her thanks to the incredible research by Mallory, but Olivia found the testimonials to be the most impressive. When it was announced that she would now be seen, she was escorted to another room of the suite, where a tall and handsome man stood to greet her. She recognized him immediately as Patrick Bennett...in the flesh. His smile was open and friendly, and when he took her hand to shake it, his was warm. Olivia couldn't help but return his smile, it was so sincere. And for a moment Patrick Bennett reminded her of Sloan.

There was absolutely no physical resemblance. Patrick Bennett had the posture and movement of a former athlete. Sloan stood erect, very military in posture, and moved silently, carefully, fully aware of his surroundings and those near him, like someone used to covert activity, possibly stalking, staying under the radar. An operative. A soldier. It was with her that he was a slightly different person. Capable of kindness, humor, even when he tried desperately to hide it. Sloan was hyper-alert and observant. But he was also incredibly tender and gentle...and loving with her. It was the most exciting discovery that Olivia had made about him.

"Mrs. Cameron. Great to meet you finally. Thanks for coming in today."

Olivia grinned at Patrick Bennett's natural exuberance. It was very attractive, and she liked him at once.

"Thanks for arranging for me to come in. And it's *Ms.* Cameron. I'm divorced."

He cringed in a sweet way. "Oops. Off with the head of the person who got that wrong on your intake form."

"Don't worry. I won't expect penitence."

He laughed outright. *This man is a winner, for sure.* Olivia considered the irony of that.

"I'm relieved. I think I'm getting better at thinking first before I speak," he said wryly.

"You're fine, Mr. Bennett. Just call me Olivia. No chance of mistake there."

The friendly chatter went on for a moment more, and Olivia knew that Patrick Bennett was appraising her every bit as much as she was him. It made everything so much easier for her that he was charming and somewhat informal. He didn't take the seat behind his desk but the empty chair in front of it, next to her.

"Tell me a little bit about yourself. How did you come into your extra cash, and what are your ideas of what you'd like to do with some of it? It's okay if you need more than twenty-five words to get all the details in."

Olivia grinned at him again and then began to answer his questions. He listened intently, nodding his head or arching a brow at salient points. He didn't interrupt her or fidget or get distracted by conversation or laughter beyond his little impromptu office. But there was one moment when a small interruption got his attention and he turned to a young woman who'd quietly approached the door.

"Give me a moment."

Patrick smiled at Olivia but stood to have a few words with the woman at the door. Just beyond her, a young boy was chatting with an adult from the organization, as he stood next to a stroller with a baby, gazing around in curiosity at all the activity.

Olivia quickly transferred her gaze to the young woman. She knew immediately that she was biracial, with a tan complexion and light brown eyes that were a little yellowish. She smiled pleasantly at Olivia, said something briefly to Patrick, who nodded and waved as the woman gathered the children and headed for the outer doors. Patrick took his seat again.

"Sorry for the interruption. That was my wife, Jean. She's taking the kids to spend the day with my sister and her family out in Irvine. You were about to say?"

"She's very pretty," Olivia commented, because that had also struck her right away. Patrick didn't respond beyond a pleased smile and nod of his head. Olivia refocused and made final comments about her intentions if she joined The Millionaires Club.

"You know from the information I submitted to your organization I run a charter school. My students are very bright and very capable but are coming from behind the eight ball and could use a few breaks to help them level the playing field. They need to understand how important education is to their future. They need to learn responsibility and focus…and hard work. They need to know it's not a cakewalk, but they're entirely up to the challenge.

"I want to set up a fund of some kind that rewards scholarships or fellowships or gives grants that could help them in the next step toward independence and accomplishments."

"Well, it sounds simple enough," Patrick said confidently. "What you want to do is pretty straightforward. To be honest, all you'd need to do is let us know how much you want to invest in your program and how many rewards you want to give each year. Your start-up money is modest, but you can do a lot with it, and it will grow as part of our overall investments. Maybe we can fashion the gifts for your funds depending on the complexity of the need. College versus a specialty training. Internships with stipend versus limited employment."

Olivia was relieved that Patrick understood so well what she wanted but was also able to break her concept down in simple language. Their meeting was over in under an hour. He personally walked her to the entrance of the suite, stood chatting with her another fifteen minutes before thanking *her* for *her* time.

"Someone will draw up a proposal and fund plans for you to review. You should have your attorney go over our submission in detail, but call us if you need help or more details. And I won't be offended if you're not interested in joining the club. It's not for everyone."

"I've already read quite a bit about your work since the founding of the club. I'm comfortable with what I've learned, but I'll take your advice about reviewing your documents."

"I'm confident enough that what you want to do fits into our mission statement to say, *Welcome aboard.*"

He waved her off in a friendly fashion, and Olivia left feeling she was close to achieving what she'd set out to do with a lot of money that wasn't even really her own.

CHAPTER 11

Sloan had parked in a municipal lot near the Mercado La Paloma and was standing near the entrance waiting for Olivia. She had not been agreeable to meeting him at first after her meeting with representatives from The Millionaires Club, but he reasoned with her that she was going to be downtown anyway. And then, after Olivia agreed to the midweek date, Sloan almost had to call to cancel himself, when a report came into the agency that looked like he'd have to respond to. He didn't though, and his rendezvous plans had been saved.

It wouldn't have been a tragedy if he and Olivia had to forego the evening together. He'd already persuaded her to meet with him for a hike over the weekend…and he had a foolproof excuse why she should stay with him for the night. The two of them had, in his mind, made significant headway in their blossoming relationship, and Sloan didn't want to lose any momentum. He'd made up his mind that Olivia was the one, and it was his responsibility to provide the emotional impetus to her to get her to think in the same way. He didn't want to lose her, and he knew that could still happen.

Sloan had also been performing a stringent self-interrogation as to why he was so sure he wanted Olivia. Maybe she believed there was too much against a *them*. He hadn't believed that from the instant he'd met her. But the pragmatist in him needed justification. Sloan didn't want to make the same mistakes he had in the past—not believing his own strong instincts or proof.

"Hi. I made it."

The calm and light announcement came from behind him, and he was immediately amused that she'd gotten the drop on him, so to speak. Olivia probably didn't have a clue that was the case. He turned to face her, and it honestly took more presence of mind than he'd ever needed before not to smile at seeing her. Sloan took a moment to appraise Olivia, noting her smile, of course, her gaze bright and open, and the way a late-afternoon breeze briefly caught her hair and blew it toward her face. She used her hand to brush the strands across her forehead and back into place.

Sloan covered his pleasure at seeing her and quickly leaned in to peck a kiss on her mouth. "Hi yourself," he said in a low growl.

"I hope I didn't keep you waiting," Olivia said. "I got a little confused about the parking lot entrance, so I think I'm around the corner or something."

"You didn't make me wait," he lied. "I'll make sure you get back to your car and headed home."

He touched her elbow to indicate she should walk with him and headed into the market. He saw that Olivia was looking around with curiosity and interest, forcing Sloan to slow his steps to keep pace with her roaming gaze.

"You've never been here before?"

She shook her head. "I avoid having to drive into downtown. Too much traffic, noise, people..." She glanced over her shoulder. "But this seems like a fun place. Bright and kind of exotic and..."

"A lot of people. It's commercial, but the food is good. We can explore the stores if you want."

Olivia grinned at him in a knowing fashion, and Sloan realized she'd picked up on when he was sincere and when he was just trying to be accommodating for her. "You don't want to spend your time shopping."

"Not really," he admitted, liking her awareness. "But I can tolerate an hour if you really want."

"I don't really want to. But I am hungry."

"Do you like Mexican? Let's go to Chichen Itza. It's actually Yucatan cuisine." He accepted her silence as assent. "It's nothing formal, but the food is great."

Olivia raised a brow at him. "Stop apologizing. I trust your decision."

Sloan couldn't think of a response. He was, by now, well aware that trust would not be a given with Olivia. The trick was just to be completely honest with her.

"You weren't kidding," Olivia observed dryly, noting that the eating arrangement at the restaurant was a casual countertop with high stools. When they were seated and exploring the menu, Sloan felt himself relaxing into the moment, into the company of Olivia. Into a sense of normalcy that was both peaceful and somewhat scary. Scary because he realized he'd begun to let his guard down around her. He'd learned to be careful around his ex-wife when he'd figured out all her motivations and decisions were about her. She always believed that she was right. He never had to worry about Krissy because he'd been clear from the start that with her it was never going to be a permanent relationship. He'd never counted on someone like Olivia or feeling the way he did now, so quickly. But he was starting to put together all the reasons why.

He ordered beer with his cochinita pibil, and Olivia ordered two tacos de pescados and sangria. Dinner was light, fun, a little messy for Olivia when the contents of her tacos squeezed out of the sides upon each bite, plopping onto her plate.

"I should have asked for a bib," Sloan teased, watching her try to gracefully manage the traditional finger food. She had a very relaxed sense of the absurd and clearly loved to laugh. He loved listening to it…and loved that about Olivia.

She confessed that the only Mexican food she'd ever eaten were empanadas, guacamole, and enchiladas.

"Hope you're not disappointed."

"No! This is all great. You have a poor opinion of me, Sloan. I love trying new things. Since my accident and…divorce, I'm determined to expand my horizon. I may have spent far too much time deferring to Marcus. He was very handsome, very smart. In the end he wasn't all *that*. I'm building my own worldview. Bring it on," she said in a challenge.

Sloan took a deep drink of his beer. "Does that new stuff include me?"

Olivia took a thoughtful sip of her sangria. She wiped her hands on her napkin but didn't look at him. Her voice dropped, however, to something a little shy but definitive. "I'd think you'd know that by now. It does."

He studied her profile until Olivia turned to gaze at him. They looked into one another's eyes, and Sloan gave her a wink. He could tell that, in her own way, Olivia blushed and gave him a look filled with warmth…and trust.

Sloan drew out their evening as long as he could. But he also wanted Olivia to get home before it got too late and driving became more horrendous than it usually was during the day on any of the LA freeways. He wanted to rush through the rest of the night because he had the weekend to look forward to.

When they finished dinner, they walked past a stand selling fresh churros, the warm, sweet smell of the deep-fried dough filling the air around them. Sloan purchased one for each of them, and Olivia bought four more, giving them to him to take home. It was the kind of simple, insignificant gesture that he was not used to and that was humbling in an odd way. Like, did he deserve this kind of sweet attention? Instead of the mostly difficult, calculated agenda of so many women he'd been drawn to in the past.

In a very spontaneous move, as they finally headed to the parking lot, Sloan asked about her meeting with the rep from The Millionaires Club. Olivia recited briefly that she was very pleased with the meeting, that she liked Patrick Bennett. He was very engaging, and she was comfortable with the discussion.

"So are you going to hand over your millions to this guy?"

Olivia laughed. "I can tell you from my research that I'm probably among the *poorer* millionaires who are members. Anyway, I will be able to set up the kind of giving I want for the students. I'll have to write up my own purpose and intentions to advertise it to schools and parents and even churches. I want the funds to go to those who really need it."

Sloan spontaneously reached out for her hand, and she curled her slender fingers around his. They continued walking for a while, and Sloan realized they weren't making much of an effort to find her SUV and get her on the road headed home. They at least had arrived at the area of the lot where she said she'd parked her car. They stopped near a lamppost and continued talking.

She became thoughtful for a moment and then looked directly at him.

"And…I've made another decision. I think it's the right one."

Sloan stood alert, waiting for Olivia's announcement. "Okay," he encouraged calmly.

"I'm going to sell the house my great-aunt left me."

"When did you decide on that? Why?"

She sighed, averted her gaze for just a moment, and then brought it back, steadily, to him.

"I think it was after you…when you had to rescue you me the day I fell through the floor into the basement."

Sloan felt his jaw clench. He knew how Olivia felt about ever needing to be rescued. Her ex had really done a head thing on her.

"Are you sure?" he asked, squeezing her hand gently.

"Yes, I'm sure. It's a beautiful house. Great structure and wonderful space, but…I won't ever feel that it's mine. Even if I put a ton of money into a renovation. I'll take care of all needed repairs, and I'll have the whole house painted. And then it goes on the market. I've already told Jackson."

"He's okay with it?"

"He doesn't really have a choice. It's my house." She grinned. "I did promise that I might gift him with some of the proceeds. He said he's so glad I'm his sister and that he didn't sell me when I was a teenager and got on his nerves."

"Yeah, me too. Otherwise, we might never have met," Sloan replied, his gaze searching her face for reaction.

She looked momentarily startled, blinked several times, and grimaced. "Oh. You're right."

Before he could add to his assessment, Olivia beat him to it.

"I wouldn't have wanted that. I…like that we met. I like…now."

"You seem surprised."

"I am. But…I'm also glad."

The full admission rocked him, sent a spiral of…of *something* shooting up his gut. He couldn't think of anything else Olivia could have said in that moment that would have made him feel more alive and hopeful. It wasn't what he intended to do, but without any thought he straightened, pulled Olivia into his arms, and held her close. She circled her arms around his waist, her hands splayed across his back, massaging him through his shirt.

Sloan kept it simple. "Ditto," he said against her temple. "I don't think you have to worry about wanting to sell the house, Olivia. You're thoughtful and careful in everything you do. At least that's what I see. Think of it this way—something great is going to come of it."

"Thank you," she said, seemingly moved by the faith he'd placed in her.

"And what are you going to do for yourself? Besides buy a new car, because that's the first thing everyone wants when they come into a lot of money."

Olivia chuckled as they pulled apart, finally stopping beside her car once Sloan had magically located her SUV in the lot.

"I want to have fun," Olivia said with feeling. "I think I'm overdue."

"Probably," he murmured, enjoying her animated features.

"I want to…to…go skydiving and learn to swim better and drive the entire length of the Pacific Coast Highway. I want to hike so I can really see the land and snorkel and learn how to make cassoulet… in France! Maybe even camping. As long as there aren't too many creepy-crawly things."

Sloan coughed, cleared his throat. She had almost succeeded in making him burst out laughing. He'd not done that in…he couldn't remember how long. But he had a feeling it might be great to let himself go.

"Make a list. If you want, we can work on it together," he said. "You should go. Traffic is not going to get any easier while we're standing here. Do you remember everything I told you to pack for the weekend?"

"Yes, sir," she responded smartly, as if she were talking to a military commander.

"I'll pick you up and—"

"I can drive to your place," Olivia said firmly.

Sloan opened and held her driver's door. "I'll pick you up. Eight. Don't oversleep."

"Grouch," she said sweetly.

Sloan's response was to gladly bend to capture her smiling mouth in a kiss he'd been putting off and waiting to do all evening. He didn't intend for it to be passionate but a strong warning of things to come. A promise. He let his mouth caress hers, inviting Olivia to part her lips so that he could engage her tongue. They briefly separated, but he kissed her quickly once more. When he drew back so that she could climb into her car, Olivia looked at him a moment longer, moistened her lips as she lightly touched his cheek. His jaw clenched against the gentle action. Olivia got into her car.

Sloan closed the door and stood back. "I'll see you Saturday morning."

She started the engine and then gave him her signature smile. "Yes," Olivia murmured, before driving away.

Sloan turned away to walk to his own car. He was feeling elated and more than a little concerned.

Slow down.

Was this all too good to be true?

"Hello?" Olivia said, absentminded, as she considered the last remaining items piled on her bed. Not all of them were going to fit into her backpack.

There was a longer-than-usual silence on the other end.

"Hello?" Olivia said again, paying attention now to the lack of response.

"I'm glad I won't have to ask for a welfare check from the local precinct," Jackson drawled.

Olivia gasped quietly, turned, and sat on the edge of her bed. "Jackson. Eh…er…Hi! Have you been trying to reach me?" she asked, knowing immediately the question was a foolish one and meant to feign ignorance and pretend guilt.

"I was waiting for you to call. As you should have last week. What's going on?"

"Jackson, I'm…so sorry," Olivia fumbled breathlessly.

"Apology accepted," he said briskly. "What's going on?" Jackson repeated.

Olivia nervously played with a small flashlight. She put it aside on the nightstand. She was not going to need a flashlight to go hiking.

"Nothing, really. I've been so busy. I—"

"Hey. It's me. Your big bro. The one you can depend on even when you don't want to. Are. You. O. Kay?"

Olivia sighed, giving in to her brother's genuine concern and annoyance. She chuckled. "Jackson, yes. I…I'm fine. And I really am sorry I missed our call last week."

"Must have been some week. Or weekend. You didn't even respond to my voicemail. Where were you?"

Olivia suddenly recalled, in vivid, minute, Technicolor detail. She was with Sloan, letting him ravish her with tender, deep soul kisses and touches, letting him guide her through the kind of physical ecstasy she hadn't known for over two years. Letting him make her feel precious…and loved.

"I was invited to a wedding…that turned into a true all-day and all-evening affair."

"Had a good time?"

Olivia grinned, although her brother couldn't see her. "I had a very good time. There…was one incident. An elderly man had a crisis. But it was handled well, and he was taken to a hospital." She saw no need to go into the exact exciting details of Sloan's part in the circumstances. Her brother didn't know Sloan. Yet. "It all sort of flowed right into Sunday, and I lost track of time. You know I'm more reliable than that."

"Well…as long as everything is fine. I do have one other question. Did this most excellent weekend happen to involve that guy you were telling me about? The one *who shall not be named*?"

Olivia chuckled silently at the Harry Potter reference.

"I…well…yes. But I didn't know that. What I mean is, I ran into him at the reception, and I didn't even know he was going to be there. We were both surprised to see each other. Really."

"Umm," Jackson murmured.

Olivia laughed. "You are so funny. Still being overprotective?"

"You're the only sister I have. I'm your only brother. Both our parents are gone. We only have each other."

"Enough. I get your point. But you do have Brett…"

"And you have…what's his name. The *only* man you've seen fit to even mention to me, who happens to be white."

There was no getting around it. And there was no point. Her brother *was* being protective.

"His name is Sloan Kendrick. I told you."

"Sloan Kendrick. If you tell me a little more about him and that there's no cause for me to worry, I promise I won't Google him."

"He's an FBI agent here in LA."

"And what had you done that caused you to have contact with an FBI agent?" Jackson asked, his voice stern.

"Remember when I told you about all that money I found in our great-aunt's house? The police turned the case over to the FBI and… and that's how Sloan and I met."

"Are you going to tell me it was something like love at first sight?"

The question was totally unexpected, and Olivia couldn't even think how to respond.

Was it?

"I'm teasing. You don't have to answer. But I do want more details eventually, Liv. You understand that, right?"

"Yes, Jackson," she answered, contrite.

"So why were you so distracted when you answered the call? Is Kendrick there with you?"

"No. But we're getting together tomorrow, and I'm still…getting ready."

Again there was a long silence from her brother before Jackson responded.

"Go finish getting ready. Don't forget to pack *everything you might need.*"

Olivia cringed. She understood. "Of course I will."

"Then have a great time."

Sloan had never been particularly fond of LA, especially after his divorce and deciding to stay with the FBI LA field office. He hadn't been sure where he wanted to live…and he wasn't sure he wanted to ultimately stay with the FBI. But there were benefits to the setting. The near-perfect Southern California weather was one of them. After more than two years of Middle East desert climate and temperatures in uniform, carrying heavy military gear, LA had been, at least, a weather bonus. And there were the many incredible parks, the mountains, the ocean.

And it was a morning like this—sunshine, no clouds, no smog or air pollution due to either traffic or burning northern fires—that made Sloan think the decision to stay had worked out. Now he had more of a reason.

He was tired of having a job that required wearing a weapon, but he had yet to identify another career, job, or position that offered as much stimulation, purpose, and structure. He was working on it.

For the time being, this morning, he felt lighthearted, a description he would have scoffed at in the past, but now something like… the future…a purpose was stirring within him. And as he was able to speed along the 405 toward the 10 to get to Olivia, he knew she was the reason. But still…

Why her?

Where had that instant thing that happened that first day come from? Why had he felt so sure then…that she was…

Why?

Sloan frowned, breathed deeply, and let out an exhausted, disquieted sigh. He was very uncomfortable feeling at odds. And he wondered how his focus on Olivia would ultimately play out. He could only say for sure that he felt so much more *himself* around her. She never seemed to ask for more than that. Not more than the real *him* that wasn't posturing because of how he'd been trained or his experiences…or what he'd lost. All of that had come together like soft clay and been molded into someone who was skeptical and alert, and who couldn't…wouldn't…smile. But Sloan was aware that Olivia was definitely making headway at breaking down his facade.

He felt…naked.

His cell began to vibrate in a pocket of his vest just as he was exiting the 10. He set the device into the hands-free stand on his console. He quickly checked the ID before answering.

"Hey, Dad."

"Hey. Bad timing?"

"I'm on my way to meet someone. I've got time for you." Sloan continued to Venice Boulevard and pulled into the parking lot of a fast-food eatery to take the call. He wanted to give his father his full attention.

"Good to hear. I won't keep you long."

"Is everything okay? You?" A sliver of guilt raced through Sloan as he asked the question, but he already knew the answer.

"Haven't heard from you in a bit. Didn't see you on the news, so I figured you're okay. Wondered if I've fallen out of favor," the elderly voice said smoothly. Not unlike his son, Sloan's father's humor was light and dry.

"I guess we haven't spoken recently. I'm sorry about that, Dad."

"Yeah, yeah, I know. Work. Busy. I'm okay. Nothing much to report."

"I get it. I don't have much of an excuse this time. I guess I've been distracted."

"As long as you're okay, Son. Have they made you director of the field office yet?"

Sloan snorted, impatient. "I'm not interested in rising through the ranks. The folks at the top are never really as…you know…"

His father laughed. "Smart?"

"I'll just say that their focus changes. It's not like they don't do the job. We keep plenty busy. But…power is an interesting aphrodisiac."

His father chuckled.

"You know what I mean."

"I interpret that to mean it can be dangerous. And political."

Sloan sighed, staring out his car window. Olivia lived just minutes from where he sat talking with his father. "Right."

There was a momentary pause. "You sure you're okay? I'm not going to nag or keep pressing like your mother used to do."

Sloan straightened, played with his steering wheel. "Okay, you win. I am a little distracted, but it's nothing bad. I'm not in trouble. Nothing like that…"

Another momentary pause.

"I've met someone," Sloan volunteered, just like a kid or teenager who knew sooner or later the truth would be wrangled out of him.

"Have you?" his father asked with just the right amount of surprise, interest, and awareness. "Serious?"

"Could be." Sloan was cryptic.

"Well, tell me about her? Or…am I keeping you from this person you're supposed to be meeting?"

"It's her. We're going hiking. Her name's Olivia." He finished on a very quiet note.

And another brief pause. "Like your mom."

"I haven't told her yet."

"Yet. So it is sort of, kind of, maybe serious. Why haven't you told her?"

Sloan silently chortled. Immediately he remembered that he'd been outwardly fighting displays of amusement at anything Olivia said to him. Part of his profile. Part of his schtick! He was pretty close to losing it.

"I don't know." Sloan gave in. "I thought it might sound calculated. Like I was using the similarity to score points." He felt a certain relief at bringing this truth out of the closet. "I want her to believe me. I want her to believe I...really care."

"Good! Good, Son. I'm happy for you. You certainly make it sound like she's special."

"There is something else... I'm actually glad you called. I wanted to ask you..."

"You know very well you don't need my permission for anything. You wanna come up, come on up. Of course you can bring your Olivia, too. I want to meet this wunderkind"—he laughed—"who's obviously got you tied up in knots."

———

When Sloan drove onto Olivia's street, he saw that her front door was ajar. As he slowed to a stop, Olivia suddenly appeared, dressed stylishly in sporting fashion. Sloan was not used to seeing her so dressed down...short of being absolutely naked, which he'd already had the pleasure of experiencing. A very quick appraisal assured him that she was dressed appropriately for the day ahead. Olivia had, once again, used a folded bandana to tie around her hairline to hold her hair back from her face, her smooth, beautiful features on full display. On top of her head was perched a pair of sunglasses. And he did notice with amusement that she was fairly color coordinated. The scarf was a print in shades of purple. Her Henley tee was pink, and the color picked up in her sturdy walking shoes. She was wearing black capri yoga pants.

And she was even wearing lip gloss in an attractive berry color on her full mouth.

"Good morning," Sloan greeted her as he got out of his car. He leaned over the hood, enjoying the pretty and cheerful vision she made in her doorway, grinning at him.

"Hi," she responded. She reached inside the door and pulled out a small knapsack, hitching it onto her shoulder before closing the door and hurrying down to his car.

Sloan went to open the trunk, and she handed him the knapsack to store. Olivia climbed into the passenger seat, buckling herself in.

Sloan got in but didn't start the engine right away. He turned on an angle to regard Olivia with pleasure. And he was also replaying the conversation he'd had with his father just moments earlier. Sloan came as close as he ever had to smiling at Olivia, an open and honest show of how he felt about her. Being with her.

"I'm not packing today. I'm off the clock, and the gun is home."

Olivia nodded. "Okay," she said simply.

" Well…you're dressed correctly. *You* pass," he teased, and was delighted that she understand the reference in her quick laugh. The same assurance she'd given him when they'd first met and again shortly after.

"I'm trusting you not to let me fall off a mountain or get mauled by anything with four legs."

"Sure you haven't forgotten anything?"

He was about to face forward, finger ready to push the start button in his car.

"Oh…" Olivia whispered.

Sloan turned to her again, slightly puzzled, and realized that Olivia was twisting toward him, lifting her head and poised to kiss him. Sloan had to quickly adjust so that he wouldn't miss her effort and the opportunity. He was in the right position when their lips pressed and meshed. But when she would have withdrawn, he placed a hand under her hair, around her nape, and held Olivia so that now he could return the gesture and kiss her again. Her kiss was light, a peck, almost playful. Sloan's was not.

He was at a point where he never lost a chance to demonstrate his feelings. It was certainly encouraging when Olivia responded so willingly with her own display of feelings.

"That wasn't what I meant," Sloan whispered close to her mouth. "But I'm glad you did."

Olivia didn't ask where they were headed, and he deliberately gave no information. Until he'd driven just a few short miles and crossed Jefferson Creek, just south of the neighborhood of West Adams. She turned sharply to frown at him.

"I live here. I mean…not that far away."

"So you know the park?" Sloan asked her.

"Not really. I've been here before, but I've never walked around much or anything."

"Do you know about the overlook?"

"I've heard of it."

"We're here," Sloan said, parking along the south side of Jefferson Boulevard, at the base of the park. A quick glance at Olivia's expression before he got out of the car showed bewilderment and maybe a little disappointment.

"You have water?"

"In my backpack." She pointed.

Sloan let her retrieve the water bottle from the trunk. "You won't need anything else."

He got his own bottle from his backpack and closed the trunk. He headed into the entrance of the park and stopped at two distinct trails that could be climbed to the summit. One was a crazy length of stone stairs that went straight to the top. Sloan pointed to the trail.

"We're going that way."

He watched as Olivia stood silently assessing the dirt trail. He couldn't see her eyes, shielded behind her dark glasses. Sloan waited but never doubted her decision. Olivia nodded and stepped next to him, inhaling.

"Okay. Let's do this." She started trekking off ahead of him.

Unseen, unaware, and with no suspicion on her part, Sloan allowed a corner of his mouth to lift slightly in satisfaction. He knew Olivia was going to be up for this challenge. He also knew she was not going to complain if she could help it. And he'd deliberately chosen a trail he believed she could manage.

It was still early morning, and the air was dry and comfortably warm. A quick glance ahead showed that they were still alone on the trail. It was a gradual incline but with zigzagging switchbacks up the hillside. It was easy to follow, with no sudden off-track paths that were man-made as other hikers may have tried to forge shortcuts. Sloan stayed just a step or two behind Olivia so that he could gauge how well she was managing the incline and natural, uneven ground. Soon Sloan pulled a little ahead of her, as he noted that Olivia had a tendency to slow down to look around, spotting foliage or a bird or whatever caught her attention. She'd stop to stare down at something on the ground or off to the side in a bush. She'd reach out to examine a branch with a cluster of beautifully formed leaves or to find an old, abandoned nest in the upper branches of a tree. Several times Olivia picked things up to inspect. Most she'd discard, but when they were important enough to her to keep, she held on to them. At one point Sloan stopped and held his palm out to her. Olivia placed a stone into the center, and Sloan dropped it into his vest pocket.

The walk was silent for long stretches, until Olivia would ask him a question about what she was seeing. This became the routine whenever the switchback suddenly opened onto another scenic angle of LA. The first they quickly came upon was a wonderful view from a steep hill south of Culver City.

"Ooooh…" she breathed, pointing to the view in front of them. "What are we looking at?"

Sloan stood next to her, the bill of his baseball cap giving shade to his eyes. He followed her finger. "That's the Los Angeles Basin. It goes from Santa Monica"—he used a slow sweep of his hand to the right—"east across to the Hollywood Hills."

"Is that downtown LA over there? All those tall buildings rising into the sky?"

"That's right," he confirmed.

"It looks so far away."

"It's not. Under ten miles from here. It's easy to forget how big and flat the county is." He glanced at her, studying her for a second. "Water," Sloan said simply, and Olivia opened her bottle without comment and drank.

Other climbers—more fit than Olivia, used to the conditions of unpaved hiking trails, or having already hiked this one at some point—eventually caught up to and passed them. Sloan kept half an eye on her, checking for exhaustion or missteps or a slowing down. Or even behaving as though she'd need his help. Although Olivia was making the trail more like a leisurely walk than a hike, he didn't care. She was interested in everything around her, didn't complain, kept moving...surprising him with her quick adaptability and curiosity. Around a corner she found another reason to stop to look and consider the view, the landscape.

Sloan realized he was enjoying their slow progress because Olivia was making it a full experience. She didn't want to miss anything, and he knew she would not only remember everything, she'd probably pepper him with a lot of questions when they were done. When they reached the top, she stood gazing out over the county spread for hundreds of miles around her, in one direction disappearing into the Santa Monica Mountains above the Pacific. To the right, the San Gabriel Mountains. Sloan could see Olivia smiling at the view.

It was spectacular on a clear day like today.

They stayed for quite a while at the top, looking out at the incredible expanse of LA seeming to go on forever, to the horizon and well beyond. Sloan occasionally pointed out something in the great distance that he knew she'd recognize. Finally, he suggested they get started back down. Quickly they reached the convergence at the top of the stone steps that would have been the straighter path to the starting place below them. He asked Olivia if she wanted to take it back to the bottom. No. She wanted to follow the dirt path again. She would see things differently from the downward approach.

"How are you doing?" Sloan asked casually when they were back at the park entrance.

She beamed at him. "That was great," she said in a slightly breathy voice.

"And you've never gone hiking before?"

Olivia shook her head. "I always wanted to. Just because I'd never done it. Marcus was never interested…and my girlfriends *really* were not interested." She studied him. "It was amazing to look over the county like we did. LA looks like it goes on forever. And to think this was right in my backyard. I could have come here anytime."

"I'm glad you didn't."

She tilted her head. "Really? Why?"

"I got to introduce you to your backyard." He turned to walk to the parked car and then stopped when she hadn't moved. "What?"

"I was thinking…I should try to plan a hiking adventure for the kids at school. Something they can do in the morning and then return to school in time for lunch."

"That'll work. Sounds like a plan. You always have them in mind, don't you?"

"I know that they've had limited exposure to a broader community, the world."

"Yeah, I suppose. They're lucky to have you."

She beamed at his compliment. It quickly faded. "Are we done? That wasn't very long, was it?"

Sloan raised a brow at her mild complaint. "One and a quarter miles. The trail is more interesting, but the stairs would have been more challenging."

She stopped. "You mean we took the easy way up?"

"More scenic, more of a hike, but…yeah."

Olivia turned around. "Well, we have to go back, do it again. We'll do the stairs this time."

"We'll do the stairs another time. I have something else in mind for now."

Olivia regarded him with her hands on her hips. "Is that a promise?"

He hid his smile, surprised that Olivia was already anticipating another time. "I swear."

"If you're lying to me, I'll never forgive you."

"I believe you. Let's go."

CHAPTER 12

Olivia leaned against a boulder that was off the path and would have made a perfect seat except it was just a little too high for her to get onto. She managed to get her small knapsack open and reached in to pull out a rectangular plastic lunch box with a wide, bright-yellow stretch band that held the lid on. She glanced at Sloan and found him doing the same thing, but what he withdrew from his waist pouch was something small enough to fit in his hand.

He turned to reach out to her with an offering. Olivia frowned at the flat, rectangular object. She took it, examining it with curiosity.

"What's this?"

"It's a protein bar," Sloan answered, opening his water bottle for a quick swallow.

As he screwed the top back on, Sloan, in turn, frowned at the plastic box she handed him. "That looks like the box from…don't tell me you brought…" He took it from her.

"No, it's not fried chicken," Olivia scoffed, setting aside the bar. "Too messy to eat. And this isn't supposed to be a picnic. Open it."

She watched Sloan carefully remove the band and lift the lid. He stared down into the contents before replacing the lid.

"Not bad. It's all healthy—grapes, cheese, and multigrain crackers. But it's not fried chicken."

Olivia gave him a wry smile, pleased with his implication. "Says the expert who goes hiking with protein bars. Disappointed with my contribution?"

"I liked your fried chicken."

Olivia turned away to look for other items in her pack. "I'll make some for you another time," she promised in a quiet murmur.

Sloan moved to find a convenient place for them to sit, using the layered rocks with their rough surfaces. The picnic tables were in a designated rest area they'd silently agreed was too crowded and noisy. They couldn't commune with nature—or each other—among the parents yelling at their kids to stop running. And she liked that they'd found a quiet little space just to themselves. They sat, shoulder to shoulder, and she liked that too.

Olivia removed the lid and balanced the box on her thighs so they could share the contents. She audibly sighed as she popped two green grapes into her mouth and smiled at Sloan, a silent signal that she was just fine. She was just…happy.

"Where are we again?"

Sloan munched a few of the crackers, a piece of cheese. Unexpectedly, he fed her a piece that Olivia accepted with a startled mew. But…she saw the corner of his mouth lift as he chewed, and her chagrin turned into a private triumph. Olivia gave no indication that she'd finally caught him off guard.

"This is called Firebreak Trail. You can see it leads right up to Griffith Observatory. We'll take a look around before we leave. If you're not too tired," he added.

"I'm not," Olivia assured him.

Still, Olivia was glad that the look around didn't take very long. It was also clear that the grounds staff were setting up for some later afternoon or evening event. They still had to get back to street level and walk a bit to the car. And then Sloan took a meandering, indirect route out of Los Feliz, past Baldwin Hills where she lived, and headed most definitely toward the ocean. Sloan had asked her to pack for the night, and Olivia had not batted an eyelash at his presumption. She was looking forward to it. She sighed, very content, as she settled into the passenger seat. In truth Olivia didn't much care where they were now headed. She didn't think the day could get much better than what they'd already done together. And she was paying attention.

When did she realize, finally accept, that being with Sloan was of major significance to her now? The level of her excitement and anticipation spoke volumes.

The snack they'd shared at the Observatory was just that, a snack. It was never meant to substitute for dinner. She really didn't feel like eating. There was something else gnawing at her insides...a very different kind of hunger. Olivia kept casting covert glances at Sloan's profile. They didn't talk very much. And she really wasn't listening, responding with murmurs and smiles. His rough, gravelly voice was... intoxicating. Seductive. It did things to her nerves, made promises. She watched his large, well-shaped hands on his steering wheel, and again her mind went into a dizzying array of fantasies.

Who knew that a few hours of hiking could produce such stimulation? Of course, she knew very well that it was all about being with Sloan. Each time they were together, there was something more compelling, more desirable about him. It came down to the way he made her feel.

Priceless.

Sloan suddenly reached for her hand, capturing it and giving her a quick glance, the sparkle of his blue eyes, the tilt of his brows, and actively clenching jaw signaling her in a way she couldn't mistake.

When they drove past the agency field office, Olivia recognized it but didn't acknowledge it to Sloan. Less than fifteen minutes later, they were pulling into a community on the edge of the Will Rogers Park but before the very expensive and exclusive real estate of Pacific Palisades. They drove up a sharp incline until Olivia could glance past Sloan and down into the crystalline shimmering of the Pacific Ocean in the late-afternoon sun. It was low on the western horizon.

Sloan pulled into an allotted parking space, turned off the engine, and turned to her. "This is where I live."

A slow grin teased at Olivia's mouth as she slowly shook her head. "Poor baby. On the outside of the gated communities looking in?"

He didn't break his habit, but there was a gleam of white teeth that was promising. "Yeah, but I do have the ocean at my doorstep… unlike some people I know who couldn't even identify a park in their own neighborhood."

She released her seat belt and climbed out of the car. "Maybe. But I have other qualities to recommend me," she said with saucy inflection in her tone.

"Affirmative," Sloan murmured dryly.

The building was small, only six stories, but designed so that all the units faced the ocean. It was stunning, and when they entered Sloan's apartment, Olivia stood for an instant, recognizing not only that she was in an unfamiliar place but it was *his* place. She knew he was watching more than her reaction; he was trying to gauge her emotions in this latest moment of discovery. After maybe a minute, Olivia headed right for the wall of the open-plan space with nothing but glass and sliding doors and another magnificent view beyond.

She stood looking out for a long time. Behind her, she heard Sloan's quiet movements. He placed something on the kitchen counter, the refrigerator opening and closing. The thud of his hiking boot landing on the tile floor. She sighed and turned around.

"I hate you," Olivia said quietly, staring at him. But she could tell from the subtle changes in his facial expression that he didn't believe it for a minute.

In fact, he slowly approached her and gathered her into his arms, letting their hips and thighs be firm points of contact. "You can come and visit anytime you want."

"That's generous of you."

"Believe me, that's not an idle invitation. And it's very rare." His voice ended on a low drawl as he kissed her cheek, ran his hand beneath her hair to angle her face, and lightly kissed her mouth.

"You don't have to justify to me," she said, running her hands up his arms and glancing into his eyes.

"That was an honest confession."

"I don't need that either."

"I know. But it's important to me that you hear it. What I want…"

He stopped and Olivia waited for Sloan to finish, but he seemed to struggle, and she knew he was monitoring his words.

"What?" she urged.

"I'll tell you later."

"Is that another promise?"

"No, Olivia. That is a truth." Sloan released her and began a conversation that was neutral and less fraught for her. "Make yourself at home. Stay awhile. The night," he said suggestively, making her chuckle.

He gave her a quick, informal walk through his apartment and put her knapsack in his bedroom. He had a queen-sized bed. There was something very reassuring to Olivia that it was neatly made. The second bedroom was an office setup with two oversized monitors and audio station, a laptop on the floor by the desk. A navy-blue windbreaker with the FBI logo on the front and back was haphazardly tossed over the back of a chair, a T-shirt hanging on a doorknob. Olivia hugged herself at the very comfortable signs of a lived-in place not in perfect orderly condition. It was a comforting sight. There were several phone lines, and although he never said so, Olivia knew they were through his office, possibly other official agencies. The answering machines on both were lit, notifications of recorded messages. There were dozens of files, binders open on the desk or the bookcase. On the wall were not posters or artwork but framed citations and awards, his Quantico degree, and a few photographs of Sloan with people she didn't recognize except—she had to lean closer to make sure she was correct—there was Sloan shaking hands with President Barack Obama.

When Sloan went into the kitchen, he announced that he'd see if there was anything decent to make a meal out of...unless she wanted to go out. Olivia didn't want to go anywhere. She took off her vest, her own hiking boots, and took up his offer to make herself at home. While he busied himself in his kitchen, she did roam but did not return to his office. In the living room she found a few haphazard stacks of DVDs. Olivia casually browsed through the casings. None of the films were new releases, and they were a broad range of genres: action adventure, drama, a few documentaries, even horror. Only one really caught her attention, and she was astonished that it would be among his collection.

The movie was *Loving*, a film about a Virginia couple whose marriage was the basis for a Supreme Court decision allowing interracial couples to legally marry. There was nothing logical about the films Sloan had, but this one was particularly puzzling. She debated just putting it back and not questioning Sloan about having it. If she began to ask questions, what was she looking for in his answer? What would any answer mean?

She wandered into the kitchen. He glanced up at her from stirring a pot of simmering water with rigatoni pasta bubbling in the slow turbulence.

"Are you okay?"

"I'm fine. I don't mind telling you I'm not feeling the least guilty that I'm not doing anything to help."

"I'm okay with that. This is not going to be beef bourguignon… or cassoulet," he said, referencing her comment from a few days ago. "Plain ol' pasta with Bolognese sauce."

Olivia raised her brows. "Yum," she moaned playfully. She pointed to an avocado in a small bowl on a counter. "How long have you had that?"

"I don't know. A few days."

She picked it up and gently squeezed. "It's almost past being ripe. What were you going to do with it?"

"Don't know that either." He casually bustled around, emptying a jar of the sauce into another pan to heat.

"I could make guacamole if you like."

He looked sharply at her. "Seriously? Is yours any good?"

Olivia had to laugh. "Or we could just slice it into the pasta. That could be interesting."

Sloan shook his head. "I vote for the guac…and I think I have chips." He reached to a pantry door, pulling it open. After a quick glance inside he reached for a bag and pulled it out, handing it to her.

"Okay. Just give me a little space to work and I'll do it. But I have a question I need to ask first."

"Yes, I have onions and…"

"No, that's not it. I hope you don't mind, but I looked through the films you have in the living room. Strange selection."

"I agree. But I didn't choose them. They were a gift. From a friend," He added after a pause, "Works at one of the studios." He concentrated on his pasta and stirring the sauce. "What do you want to know?"

"You have a copy of *Loving*. Do you know anything about the story?"

"I don't. Do you? Have you seen it?"

"I haven't seen it, but I do know the story."

"Want to watch it with me?" he asked smoothly.

Olivia considered Sloan's question, considered the seriousness… and the subject of the movie. Had he at least read the synopsis? She did want to see it with him. For his reaction. "Sure. I'd like that," she said just as smoothly. "You can come to my place and I'll make dinner."

"Or we'll make it together. Better get a fresh avocado," Sloan said with a straight face.

Olivia rolled her eyes at him. But their plans now firm, she efficiently worked around Sloan, making the guacamole and finding a shallow dish to serve it in. Sloan was plating from the stove, passing her the two prepared bowls of pasta and sauce, hastily finding place mats, utensils.

"Is beer okay?"

"Fine."

Soon they were seated at the small dining table, the sun nearly set behind the edge of Santa Monica Mountains, the orange sky melting and spreading over the ocean.

"So how was your first time hiking?"

"Well…I'm probably in terrible shape, but I did enjoy it. I liked being outside in nature. I liked feeling so free. I liked that I had to work a little bit to make it up some of the hills." She glanced at him thoughtfully. "I'm proud of myself for making it to the top."

"You done good." Sloan nodded approval. "You should know you walked about four and a half miles total."

She winced. "I guess that explains my tired legs."

"Yes." Sloan looked sharply at her. "How about your back? Any problems there?"

Olivia exaggerated a rotation of her shoulders and hips, wiggling in her chair. "Everything seems to work. I'm a little achy, but that's it."

He nodded, frowning thoughtfully. "A little achiness is to be expected. I can probably give you something to help ease that."

Olivia caught the inference at once. She glanced at him with a suspicious smile. "I bet you could."

Dinner was filled with gentle innuendos and teasing. But there was also a certain growing tension that she understood perfectly…and welcomed. Olivia felt a sudden wellspring of hope within her that her feelings were real and she needn't be afraid of them. And they were far more than just enjoying Sloan's company. He was proving to be grounded, steady, and trustworthy. Olivia was really feeling that, maybe, he would be careful with her heart. Even though the idea was scary, she was not willing to pull back. She wanted very much to know where she and Sloan were headed. Olivia knew she'd already signed up for the ride.

By the time dinner was done, the guacamole decimated— "Excellent," Sloan had murmured in surprise—dishes stacked in the washer, and the mood drifting toward serene, Olivia distinctly felt not only romantic arousal but a sense of domesticity that was comforting and welcome. Another fantasy. A playful daydream.

She was on Sloan's very spacious terrace overlooking the magic of the nighttime scene of darkened beach and ocean surf. Sloan came to stand next to her, bracing his hands on the railing. His very nearness sparked a sudden desire in Olivia that took her by surprise—not that it happened but that her desire was so strong. Palpable. His arm was lightly pressed to her shoulder, and she wondered if it was an accident. But then she placed her arm around his, her hand against his forearm. Finally, her cheek against his shoulder.

Olivia could feel Sloan turning his head, angling his face down to peer at her, but she didn't raise hers to initiate anything more. They stood silently like that for several more minutes, until a sudden cool sweep of ocean breeze took away their shared body warmth. She withdrew, retreated back to the living room. Sloan followed. He caught up to her, sliding his arms around her and drawing her back against his chest.

Olivia felt herself immediately surrendering to the embrace, the firm wall of his chest behind her. She held on to his wrists as his hands sought the bottom of her shirt and tunneled underneath. She held her breath, a sudden rush of heat and passion setting her off balance.

"Sloan..." she whispered, but was unable to utter anything more.

Her voice, her breathing, said the rest and Sloan pulled the top up and over her head, releasing her arms. Olivia's sports bra was built into the top, and now she was bare from the waist up. He slowly cupped her breasts, and she became almost light-headed with longing. Had she been waiting the entire day for this moment?

Sloan's gentle massaging, his thumbs rubbing over the nipples...

his lips nibbling kisses under her ear, drew a panting sigh from her. He turned her in to his chest and began to kiss her deeply, in earnest. The way Olivia had become used to and ached for because it was all-consuming, deep, and arousing. She circled her arms over his shoulders, her fingers caressing his neck.

She was abruptly let go and was slightly dazed watching as he removed his top in one swift move and got out of his cargo shorts, and briefs in another movement. Sloan didn't give her a chance to finish undressing but squatted to pull down her capri yoga pants and panties, and she stepped out of them. He stood and took her hand, leading her to his bedroom. Sloan didn't bother with pulling back the comforter but helped her onto the bed and crawled partially on top of her and began to kiss her again, rubbing and twisting his mouth over hers, invading to dance with her tongue, drawing a reaction that left them both mindless.

Of course he remembered one final preparation step, removing the sealed protection from his nightstand. She felt shameless, wanting Sloan to hurry, wanting him to envelop her. He did not maneuver her onto her back but kept them on their sides, facing each other. He positioned himself between her legs, like the very first time they made love, with her upper thigh over his and leaving Olivia vulnerable and open when he thrust forward, inside. She held her breath at the first slow, deep strokes. They found a rhythm, Sloan's hands splayed open across her back and pressing her close so that she could feel not only his control but his innate knowledge of what felt good for her.

And they kissed, a heady, druglike melding that rocked them from top to bottom. Olivia knew it wasn't going to last. They were both too needy, too hot after the day of exercise and sunshine, too filled with abject lust and prolonged waiting to draw it out. Maybe next time.

Sloan brought his hand down to stroke her thigh, to inch over to where they connected, and the touch was enough to make her come. Olivia buried her face in his neck, panting and holding on until the heightened euphoria slowed into warm satisfaction. She felt the pulsing of Sloan, deep within, and tried to squeeze her legs tighter around him to facilitate his climax. He moaned, long and deep. He grunted, his breathing hot against throat, her chest. She could feel his heartbeat. His breath became slow and even.

They didn't move. They didn't speak. Olivia would never know if either of them tried. She sighed deeply, infused with happiness and well-being. Lying entwined, they fell asleep.

Sloan came awake smoothly, carefully. Another part of his training that brought him instantly alert to where he was. His eyes opened to note that it was still night. He glanced at the digital clock and read it was just after two a.m. Good enough. The timing was right. But he exhaled, suddenly very reluctant to awaken Olivia. His mental scan outlined exactly where she was. Now on his back, one of his arms held her secure to his side. Her cheek was resting on his chest, her open hand flat and sandwiched in between. One of her slender legs pressed against his.

Sloan wanted to forget what his plan had been for the middle of the night that meant getting up. He was suddenly so much at peace with right where they were. In each other's arms. He glided his hand over Olivia's lower back and up again to her shoulders. She sighed and undulated her hips and pelvis infinitesimally. He debated with himself but finally lost out to the fact he knew Olivia would not want to miss the scheduled event best experienced in the next hour or so.

He stroked her shoulder, gently massaged her nape. "Olivia," Sloan whispered in his rough voice. "Wake up." She moved but only to get closer to him. Sloan rubbed his chin in her hair, shook her shoulder. "Sweetheart...wake up."

She moved, at first very slowly but then struggled up. Sloan swung his legs to the floor and stood. He left the room and quickly returned, holding a garment in his hand.

"Sloan? What's going on? What's wrong?"

He held it out to her. It was his FBI jacket. "Nothing's wrong. Put this on. I want to show you something."

Olivia silently obeyed, but she was dazed. "Is it work? Do you have to go?"

"No, nothing like that. Come with me."

He was naked but taking her hand, leading Olivia through the darkened apartment to the terrace. Sloan slid the door open and stepped out, carefully guiding her behind him. His eyes adjusted to the black night, and he knew hers would too.

"Wha...what are we doing? It's cold." Olivia's voice sounded shocked.

"I want you to look up. Look up. Keep looking."

Sloan left her, returning to the bedroom to pull the comforter from his bed. He swung it over his shoulder, like a great cape, encasing himself. He hurried back to the terrace, where Olivia was hugging herself against the chilled night air. His windbreaker provided cover but not any warmth. It stopped above her knees, the sleeves longer than her arms. Sloan stood behind her and wrapped Olivia tightly within the comforter, hugging her against his body.

"Aagghh!" she uttered in relief, grabbing what she could of the comforter to tighten it even more around their bodies. "What are we doing out here?"

"I thought you'd want to see shooting stars. Look in the sky, over there." Sloan quickly indicated with a briefly exposed hand.

Olivia stayed still, trying to focus her gaze. They stood huddled together, silently for perhaps a minute, when...

"There!" Sloan said.

She moved her head about. "I... I don't see..."

"There's another," Sloan said, pointing again.

"I can't... I... Oh, Sloan! There it is! I see it!"

Sloan tightened his arms. She bounced excitedly once, on the balls of her feet. Before he knew it, he let out a quick, low chuckle near her ear. In another moment, Olivia rested her head back, and he heard her long exhalation.

"Sloan," Olivia sighed.

He wasn't sure if she was responding to the quick lines of light that streaked across the sky before burning out and disappearing or to the uninhibited sound of pleasure that escaped from him. Sloan waited for her to acknowledge that moment, but instead she kept exclaiming over the abundant light display.

"It's the Orionids," he offered. "A meteor shower."

"Yes, yes! How could I forget it was happening? I tried to arrange something so the students could view it. But the district office wouldn't approve my plans. Transportation was an issue. I think Colby, maybe you remember him from your academy class, he said he would ask his mother if she'd take him and some of the other students. I don't know if she was able to."

"That's too bad."

"They get excited about new experiences, what they've never done before or even knew about."

"You mean like you?"

Olivia nodded. "Mmmm. Today was the best day."

"You mean yesterday," he mused. "I'm glad," he said simply.

Sloan enjoyed the display for another ten minutes before deciding that they should get back inside. They weren't exactly dressed for stargazing. He hustled them back to the bed, crawling under all the bed linens and spooning, hugging and rubbing each other until the chill left their bodies.

"You didn't mind, did you? Taking me hiking yesterday?"

Sloan thought about that. In some ways he was sure he'd gotten far more out of the day with her.

"You forget I suggested it. Don't worry about me. I got what I want."

"Did you? Tell me?"

Sloan hedged, the true answer silent in his head.

I wanted you with me.

"Sharing the sun and the stars with you."

Olivia didn't respond. But then… "My hero," she crooned in a high-pitched, comic heroine voice of adoration.

Sloan struggled. And then he lost it. He burst out in a ragged bark of laughter. Once, twice.

Olivia giggled. "Gotcha," she murmured, triumphant.

Sloan nuzzled her neck and shoulder, squeezed her against him. "You sure do."

CHAPTER 13

Olivia paid attention to her driving but was conscious of Sloan, in the passenger seat of her brand-new car, distracted with inspecting all the dashboard features and capabilities. She was particularly pleased that he trusted her driving skills enough that there was no hint of him being a backseat driver.

He'd gotten off work early after attending a case briefing at LAPD headquarters with officers and commanders. Just a review of standing problems with a potential of sudden violence. The cooperating agencies were generally successful in nipping in the bud anything explosive, but sometimes they misjudged.

"Have you tried out the stations and settings? What's this?" Sloan asked. He didn't wait for an answer but began pushing the console button. There were music, talk, commercials, Spanish, and, finally, an officious voice reciting traffic details. "That's not a station. Or—"

"One of the salesmen set me up with a traffic report channel. It's twenty-four seven, so I can access local information anytime I'm in the car if I need to."

Sloan continued to play with the tuner and check out other stations. "Very cool," he murmured. Having explored all the internal toys of the BMW, he gave her steady scrutiny and then a quick nod. "You done good."

She chuckled. "Thank you for not adding 'for a girl.'" Sloan snorted, his version of a chuckle. "I was going to ask you to come with me when I went car shopping. I thought maybe you could stay a little in the background so the sales team would know I had knowledgeable backup. Because you're a guy, they'd respect you."

He shook his head. "You didn't need me for that. I bet you did a lot of research, did a test drive. I would have come if you'd really needed a guy. Nice to know I might be good for something."

She laughed.

They'd driven to Santa Monica Pier and opted to stroll the boardwalk holding hands, talking, and exchanging personal insights. Sloan was enjoying an extraordinary period of routine nine-to-five days without any critical need for his attention on anything. Olivia mused that it had been glorious to have him to herself, as they naturally learned more about each other and their backgrounds. Getting closer…more intimate. And she was so far along in her comfort zone with him that she trusted the regard she got from Sloan was real.

Olivia was now totally invested in their growing relationship. She had to trust that Sloan felt the same way. Any revelations to the contrary at this point would be devastating for her. It had already been such a leap of faith for Olivia that she trusted her feelings for Sloan. There'd been no one after her divorce until she and Sloan had met in what she called a fateful afternoon. It was scary that she had nothing to judge the relationship with now but her heart.

The plan was that they would finally watch the DVD Sloan had been given of *Loving*. They were looking forward to the movie, but Olivia knew enough about the actual family it was based on and their circumstances to be interested but nervous about Sloan's reaction to the film about an interracial couple who changed American history.

He'd driven from work to get her for their afternoon adventure and drive in her new car. Olivia parked on the street in front of her house, having left her driveway open for Sloan to leave his car. They later reversed the situation so that it would be easier for Sloan when it was time for him to leave. There'd been no decision about when that might be.

They'd already had one night, the weekend before, thwarted when Cooper, Sloan's godson, called to ask if Sloan would take him to fly a kite he'd gotten from a grandparent. Olivia and Sloan had planned to return to the Overlook at the Baldwin Hills Park to do the trail again, this time taking the torturous and challenging stone step path.

Plans had changed with the call from Cooper.

"Mom said she's sorry if she messed up your plans for today. She had to get her hair done."

"Seriously?" Sloan asked, after agreeing to accommodate his godson's mother.

"Really," Olivia responded, hearing the reason after Sloan's call with Cooper. "It's a big deal, especially if she and his stepdad are going to an important or formal event."

"My stepdad got a po…por…promotion, I think."

"Does this mean you're sleeping over?"

"Yeah. Mom said it's okay if you bring me home in the morning."

Olivia had given a sidelong glance at Sloan's profile as they headed to an area with space for testing out the flying capabilities of Cooper's kite. If Sloan was disappointed, he was a very good sport about it. Olivia smiled to herself at his calm and easy acceptance of time they'd lost to spend alone.

But the kite flying turned out to be great fun, with Cooper offering to show Olivia how it was done. Sloan stood observing the two of them trying to figure out how to catch the wind that sent the paper-and-wood kite swishing back and forth across the sky but also falling to the ground when the wind suddenly died.

They'd taken Cooper to In-N-Out for a child-friendly dinner, and then Sloan had taken her back home. He'd only stepped into Olivia's house long enough for a kiss that was deep and filled with longing that wouldn't be satisfied that night.

"You know, I had fun," she teased, smiling into his face.

Sloan grimaced, releasing her. "I'm glad one of us did. And Cooper."

"And you. Don't try to hide it, Sloan. You know you adore your godson."

Olivia and Sloan had eaten fast food on the Pier and neither wanted anything else to eat, but she still made a large bowl of the obligatory popcorn and grabbed bottles of beer. They started the film, turned out the living room lights. Sloan propped his legs on the end of the coffee table, but Olivia sat next to him with her bent legs drawn up to her thighs. The opening line to the film grabbed both their attentions. Provocative and telling. And they watched, riveted by the developing story.

Within twenty minutes, Sloan had changed positions. He sat up, feet back on the floor, leaning forward with his forearms braced on his thighs. There was no chatter or commentary between them. What happened on the flat screen completely drew them in. At one point during a poignant conversation between the couple, Sloan reached to place his hand on Olivia's thigh, slowly stroking up and down for several seconds. She completely understood the gesture, the need. It was empathy and understanding for the difficult and legally challenging lives the couple had been forced into.

In the last few minutes of the film, Sloan finally sat back heavily against the sofa cushions, as if drained by the story. When Olivia clicked the remote to stop the movie and turn off the TV, she silently regarded Sloan, who seemed quiet and introspective about what they'd watched.

She reached for his hand, threading their fingers. "What do you think?"

Sloan sighed. "I'm glad they won in the end, but…what they went through was so… It was incredible. Unbelievable." He turned to regard her, squeezing her hand. "I don't have to ask you what you think."

"I think the film was deeply moving and true to the couple's story."

He grew thoughtful. "I think my favorite line in the movie was when the husband said to the civil rights attorneys, '*Tell the judge I love my wife.*' He was very clear about that."

"Of course he was," Olivia affirmed. "And he was willing to fight for his love. It's beautiful."

"Yes," Sloan said very quietly, his answer a single-word drawl.

They put away the uneaten popcorn, finished the beers, and turned to face one another. Time seemed to stop, and Olivia felt like they were transfixed. It was a new moment, and they had moved away from what they were, what the relationship had been, just a few hours earlier. They studied each other with a kind of new awareness and desire…and maybe even truth. Olivia moved and Sloan moved, and they came, spontaneously, into an embrace that was so…so *loving* and a safe harbor. She thought maybe they couldn't say in words what they were ultimately feeling. Maybe the timing was unexpected, but the experience of someone else's story resonated with them. Certainly for Sloan. What they couldn't say in that moment, they demonstrated.

They held each other with tenderness and a reverence that made Olivia say to herself, *This is it.*

They ended up in her bedroom, disrobing while exchanging increasingly more passionate kisses and touch. They prepared for the ultimate moment of surrender, tumbled onto the coverlet, and spent quite a bit of time on foreplay. This didn't demand rushing or intense satisfaction. This was about discovery and exposing themselves to the next level of need and giving. They created heat and urgency, Olivia letting herself surrender to his mastery over her body and senses. She sometimes held her breath, forgetting to breath, when he touched her in places that made her heart race.

Olivia pushed herself as close as she could get, letting Sloan envelop her in the safety and strength of his arms. She felt protected. And desired. And loved. Sloan took a long, lazy time exploring her intimately, his fingers soothing over tender tissue and secret wet places, kissing her all the while. Olivia touched Sloan in the same way, shyly at first and then boldly when he responded with pleasure.

Olivia awoke in the middle of the night. Sloan was on his back, an arm thrown over his head, the other looped loosely around her. She lay with her head on his shoulder, an arm laid across Sloan's stomach. She could feel the steady rise and fall of his chest with his breathing. In that moment, she was overwhelmed with one extremely clear realization, as she lay against Sloan. Olivia closed her eyes tightly, as if to fortify herself.

"I love you," she whispered, almost inaudible, to herself. Her voice trembled.

Sloan suddenly inhaled and exhaled deeply. His arm around her moved for a moment and then stopped. He slept.

Olivia was relieved that she'd actually acknowledged her feelings.

And she was equally frightened that now *it was out.* Her truth. But she'd cheated because she hadn't actually said so to Sloan. It was as if she was conducting a test. Could she say those three words? The time was right to admit to it, at least to herself. She'd tell Sloan. Soon.

And then she, too, slept.

———————

Sloan finished buttoning his shirt, stuffing the tail into the top of his slacks and fastening the zipper tab. His mind was still grappling over a thought he'd awakened with. That Olivia had said something to him in the middle of the night. Only Sloan didn't actually know what he'd heard or if he'd heard anything. Was it a fragment of a dream? Was it merely suggested because of the movie he and Olivia had seen together? Or was it a thought that he'd created for himself, wanting to hear from Olivia what she felt for him? Maybe wishful thinking because it's what he felt for her?

Sloan wandered into the living room and spotted her packed tote bag on the floor near the front door. She suddenly wandered from the kitchen, in bare feet, holding a mug and a tumbler. She approached as he slipped on his shoes and reached for his gun belt, on a high shelf of her bookcase.

"Your choice," she offered, holding out the mug and glass.

Sloan looked into the mug. "Coffee. And that?"

"Orange juice. I didn't squeeze it with my own hands, but it does have pulp."

Sloan lifted a corner of his mouth and accepted the coffee. "Thanks. I could use the caffeine."

"I have to hurry. Homeroom is at eight thirty. What about you?"

"I have time to stop home."

Sloan suddenly realized that there was a real sense of domesticity in the way the morning was going. But instead of doing all the morning details alone and silently, he was here with Olivia in her place. It felt a little odd. He was used to being alone, except when he very briefly chose otherwise. But now Sloan felt a warm level of comfort with Olivia that was normalizing him. When he awoke, it had been because she was gently stroking his chest and stomach. When he had abruptly opened his eyes, not yet accustomed to a woman on the other side of the bed, he was met with a ready kiss from Olivia. It was so unexpected, and so loving, that he felt disoriented. He wasn't used to a gesture where someone was thinking solely about him.

"Okay." Olivia came to stand in front of him as he finished adjusting his gun belt.

"Okay?" he asked, enjoying the way she looked at him.

She shrugged. "Did I thank you for such a wonderful, wonderful time?"

"You don't have to thank me." Sloan placed an arm around her, looking into her gaze. "Is there something else you wanted to tell me?" The question a quiet probe.

Olivia drew her bottom lip in, focused her gaze on him, and shook her head. She seemed a little ambivalent. "Not yet."

He let it go at that.

Sloan had to go soon. It had just never seemed this hard before. There were last-minute hugs and caresses, making the parting endurable.

Olivia stood at her door watching Sloan as he got into his car. He started the engine and then leaned out the window.

"I heard a rumor that you're going to make your world-famous chicken and have me over for dinner. True?"

She laughed with a rueful shake of her head. "So the rumor goes."

"Is that a confirmation?"

"How about the end of the week?"

"I'm yours. I'll be here."

Sloan pulled out of the driveway and waved to her out his windshield as he reversed and drove away.

Olivia watched him disappear down the street, feeling as if she could explode with happiness.

———————

"Look at you!" Olivia exclaimed when Taryn rolled down the corridor, pushing a new and larger stroller. Her daughter, Gaye, was fast asleep in the comfortable, roomier seat. Taryn stopped as Olivia bent to peer at the baby, but she also examined the carrier.

"You have new wheels. Very nice. And very expensive," Olivia said smoothly.

She noted that the stroller was a top-of-the-line model that went for hundreds of dollars retail. And she knew it would be very inappropriate to question how the girl could possibly have afforded the stroller. Maybe it was a gift from her mother.

"Thank you," Taryn said flatly. She offered no explanation. And she seemed a little nervous.

"Has she started to walk yet?"

"She pulls herself up. As long as she has something to hold on to, she gets around the living room pretty good. Anything she sees on a chair or a table that's in her way, she throws on the floor."

"Then it won't be long before she's into everything."

"I know," the girl mumbled. "That's what my mama said." Taryn adjusted the blanket covering the baby. "You have new wheels too."

Olivia smiled. "You mean my new car. Yes. It was a treat to myself."

"You must be rich," Taryn observed, a little in awe. "My mama wants a new car, but she can't afford it."

"Well," Olivia said, a little uneasy. "Maybe one day soon she will."

"You should drive some of us around in it. I don't think I ever was in a brand-new car."

"You think it will be a treat?" Olivia asked, surprised.

"Yes, ma'am," Taryn affirmed. "We don't get to do stuff like that at all. I know it sounds stupid."

"No, it doesn't, Taryn. It's a simple enough wish. Nothing wrong with that. Are you leaving Gaye in the center?"

"Just for the first class. Mrs. Monroe don't mind if I have her in the English class. When she's awake, she makes all kinds of funny sounds, and it cracks up the class. Mrs. Monroe even gave us an assignment to write about it: What does my baby sound like when she makes all that noise?"

Olivia smiled. "That's very clever. I hope the class didn't mind."

"Nah. Everybody thought it was funny. Some of the stuff that was written was funny."

"Good. Well, roll her into the room. She has it all to herself this morning. And you better hurry up or you'll be late for your first class."

As she turned back to her office, Olivia heard her cell phone vibrating on her desk, and she hurried to pick it up.

"Ms. Cameron."

"Hello, Ms. Cameron."

"Hey, Lynn."

"What are you doing this evening?"

"This evening…I have plans for this evening. Why?"

"I wanted to stop by and drop something off to you. It won't take long. Just a quick minute. I have plans myself, so I wasn't planning to stay."

"It's a good thing," Olivia said dryly. "This is not an evening for surprises, and I—"

"Oh, don't worry, this will literally take, like, five minutes."

"What is it?"

"It's a surprise. One that I think will please you. That's all I'll say because I do want it to be a surprise."

Olivia frowned and chuckled quietly. "To be honest, Lynn, I don't like the sound of this. You know you and I don't always agree on things."

"I promise you, you'll like this. I'm not saying another word, and you can't make me. See you later." With that, she laughed and hung up.

Olivia held the device, considering Lynn's airy excitement. Almost immediately the phone buzzed again.

"Hello?"

"Ms. Cameron." It was Sloan.

"Mr. Kendrick." She smiled at his introduction.

"Checking in. How are you?"

"Friday morning. TGIF. The students get really antsy because they know it's the weekend. But I have a lot of official things to clear from my desk."

"Are we still on?"

"Yes. Unless you've made other plans."

Sloan grunted from his chest. "I'm looking forward to your chicken."

Olivia sighed, but there was a huge smile on her lips. "You do know you're being ridiculous. It's chicken, Sloan, not filet mignon. And there is this stereotype about chicken and Black people."

"Don't know that one. Don't care."

"Well, all right then. Get your taste buds ready."

"I'm on it. Bye."

———————

All while she was making final preparations—finding a bottle of wine, some beer in her pantry—she smiled with expectations that made her feel lighthearted. It was happening more and more when getting together with Sloan. It was not as if he'd never been to her house before or they'd never eaten a meal together, but to Olivia, this was starting to feel like a habit was being formed. More than that was an expectation in everything that she and Sloan did. Not all of their time was spent between the sheets, treating and teaching one another to a bevy of new sensations and ways of intimacy. Olivia was happy with all of it, Sloan helping her to levels of sensuality she'd never experienced before, knowing that Sloan wanted her. But there was no definitive and detailed idea of what that could mean for a future. Once past her initial doubts and wishful thinking, Sloan had fulfilled even the simplest of her desires—to be treated with kindness, handled with care.

They never talked in advance about what would happen after dinner, how the evening might end. That was always the biggest surprise of an evening, and in truth, Olivia looked forward to it. While she might expect that Sloan would ask to stay, she did like that he didn't take it for granted. Sometimes he didn't, and sometimes she had to say no. She wanted more, but experience in a failed marriage had taught Olivia to keep one foot in reality…and firmly on the ground.

It was a nice evening, and she slid the glass doors leading to her small, enclosed yard a little open. She'd placed hurricane lamps outside along the length of half the glass and lit them for a calming and serene setting. Maybe she and Sloan would sit out there before dinner or after. With a final glance around the dining and living room, Olivia changed into a denim skirt and a boxy, pale-yellow knit top with dolman sleeves. Dangling earrings so she didn't look so totally like a teacher. She'd combed her hair so that it swept just below her hairline, across her forehead, to fall along a cheek to her chin. She was just slipping her feet into a pair of ballet flats when she heard the ringing of her doorbell, followed by loud knocking. It seemed so urgent that she hurried through the house to answer, wondering why Sloan was so loud.

"Coming," Olivia called as she reached the door and quickly opened it.

She'd forgotten Lynn's warning from earlier in the day and was genuinely caught off guard as she faced her girlfriend...and someone else standing just behind her, peering at her in curiosity. A Black man of average height waiting politely in Lynn's shadow. Olivia gave him a blank stare. He nodded but said nothing.

Olivia didn't have a chance to recover as Lynn entered, heading right for the living room, the man close behind her. He made eye contact with Olivia, and they both managed a polite murmured hello. He recovered first.

"Looks like we took you by surprise. I thought Lynn told you we were stopping by..."

"I certainly did," Lynn said. She quickly absolved herself of any culpability for the awkwardness between Olivia and the stranger.

"Yes, she did call, but said *she* would be stopping by. I told her I had plans. Lynn was only going to stay for a *hot minute*," Olivia emphasized, cutting Lynn a speaking glance. She turned back to the man, and an awareness grabbed her that made her throat go dry.

Lynn wouldn't… She *couldn't* be trying to…

The man, good-looking, with a trim beard and mustache, was well dressed in business casual. Olivia was struck not only by his demeanor but by a sense of self-confidence that said *nothing surprised him that he couldn't handle.* He was quickly sizing up the scenario, and she knew he was drawing the correct conclusion: Olivia was furious. The man seemed a little embarrassed. Olivia quickly recovered and took command of herself and the situation.

"I'm not sure this was such a great idea," the man offered, trying to get Lynn's attention.

"All I was trying to do was cut to the chase and make sure you two met. Olivia, Jonathan and I met at a social event last month for the legal profession. He's running for judge in the—"

"That's not important, Lynn." He took a step forward, past Lynn, and faced Olivia. "I'm Jonathan Daniels. And I'm sorry you weren't told—"

"She said she had a surprise for me," Olivia said calmly, fighting her fury at Lynn. She didn't want to take it out on the man who appeared also not to have been informed about Lynn's cockamamie idea to spring an unsuspecting guest on her—as in a potential suitor. So unlike her but…very much what she was capable of. A very tough and effective attorney but a bull in a china shop. Her methods worked better in court…not so much with friends.

Olivia found it within her to smile pleasantly at Jonathan. "I had no idea you were the surprise."

"Me either," he said graciously, studying her for a moment. "Under normal circumstances, we might have met without all the drama and…you know…let things happen as they may. For now I think I should leave. Maybe this will come together another time, but this was not a particularly good idea." He turned to Lynn. "I forgive you," he said with surprising humor. "We'll talk soon."

"You both are being far too serious about this. It's an introduction, for heaven's sake, not a march to the altar. I see possibilities."

"I knew the plan was for me to meet you," Jonathan said forthrightly, speaking directly to Olivia. "I just thought you'd be in on the plan."

"I wasn't," Olivia stated. "As a matter of fact, I can save us all any more embarrassment and…and just say…I'm seeing someone." Her gaze went from Lynn, who was so stunned her mouth dropped open, to Jonathan, whose expression showed regret.

"That doesn't mean you can't possibly see anyone else in life, Olivia. Am I right, Jonathan?"

"Not in this case. You're not paying enough attention, and Olivia is saying she's not interested," he observed.

Olivia nodded but remained silent. Jonathan shrugged. He reached a hand toward her. Olivia glanced at the offered hand before reluctantly taking it and giving him an apologetic smile. It wasn't his fault that Lynn thought it clever to make a game of meeting her, and it wasn't her fault that she didn't care. Maybe three or four months earlier, but not now.

"I'm glad I got to meet you. As the saying goes, 'a day late and a dollar short.'" Jonathan headed for the door. "I'll wait in the car," he said to Lynn and left.

Olivia only half noted that he didn't close the door completely, leaving it slightly ajar, maybe expecting Lynn to quickly follow.

Olivia was more focused on Lynn, looking to see if she was the least embarrassed by the unfortunate and unnecessary scene she'd caused. No, she wasn't. And that was also very Lynn.

"What in the world were you thinking?"

Lynn shrugged, unrepentant. "Trying to be a good friend. I felt if I pushed you a little, you'd realize you are ready to get back in the game. And I thought the minute I met Jonathan that he had real possibilities. I thought it was worth a shot."

"Maybe. But not by your rules. You're not my mother, my marriage counselor, or my personal matchmaker."

Lynn looked affronted. "I'm a friend who's been very concerned about you. I thought you were still moping after Marcus."

"I wasn't."

"Honestly, girl, he isn't worth it. He looked good on paper, but there were definitely character flaws."

"I know that now." Olivia nodded. "I'm not losing sleep over him."

"Was that just a ploy you gave to Jonathan? That you're seeing someone? Who? Why haven't you said anything?"

Olivia took a deep breath. "Yes, it's true. And I haven't said anything, especially to you, because I didn't want to be questioned to death."

"Well, who is it?" Lynn asked, impatient.

Olivia hesitated. "You've seen him. One night in the yard..."

Lynn's mouth dropped open again. "Oh my God! You're not talking about that...that...*white* man who said he was an FBI agent. You can't be serious."

"He *is* an FBI agent. And I am serious."

"I don't believe it! Have you lost your mind?"

"Lynn, I don't want to discuss my love life with you anymore.

You're really making too big a deal out of this. And I don't question you about the men, or lack of, in your life."

Lynn narrowed her gaze. "Don't you worry about my love life. At least I—"

"Exactly. So don't you worry about mine. You have to leave. He should be here soon for dinner. And...I don't want you here. I don't trust you not to make a scene."

Lynn seemed nonplussed. Olivia didn't want to be unkind to a friend who, in many other ways, had been helpful and empathetic when they'd first met at a women's seminar. It had been put together by Lynn and her law office to help women who found themselves facing divorce. Lynn confessed that she had already faced that decision and had learned a lot about how women, in particular, needed to be informed and armed to protect themselves.

"I don't appreciate what you did tonight, but I do appreciate that you were concerned about me. Thank you for that. But you have to go."

Olivia could see that, while Lynn was prone to argue to win her point, her imperial attitude was deflating, and she was about to surrender.

And then the door behind Lynn slowly pushed open, and Sloan stood in the doorway.

CHAPTER 14

Sloan had no idea what to expect when he entered. But the unknown man getting into a car in front of Olivia's house, the partially opened door, and the tense conversation and raised voices from within between Olivia and another woman lent him license to take a professional stance and not a personal one, to make sure Olivia was all right. Sloan hoped this was not a come-to-the-rescue moment, which would not play well with her.

Conversation immediately ended when he pushed open the door and stepped into the entrance. He made eye contact with Olivia first but was aware that there was another woman in the room. Olivia's expression and body language spoke volumes. There had been arguing between the two women. The other woman acknowledged him with her cold awareness on his gun, belted on his right hip. He always removed it once inside with Olivia, but there'd been no time for that. Now he took an observe-and-wait attitude, following Olivia's lead and cues. The situation, as he read it, didn't call for anything else.

Sloan could tell Olivia was glad, but cautious, to see him. It was clear that what he'd walked into was uneasy.

"Hey," he said smoothly, holding Olivia's gaze, but she transferred hers back to the other woman, who addressed her, no-holds-barred.

"Really? A white man?"

"Are you bothered by that?" Sloan responded at once. Better wisdom wouldn't allow him to remain quiet. He felt Olivia's gaze turn sharply to his, but she said nothing.

"Personally? Yes. But I can see it's not my call."

"Thank you," Olivia said in a tight, strained voice.

"I was suspicious the first time I saw him," Lynn said tartly. "I was just leaving," she announced. "In any case, I'm too late." She turned and gave him a slow once-over.

"Have we met before? Sorry, but I don't remember that," he said.

"I'm Lynn, one of Olivia's good friends."

"Okay. One of Olivia's good friends," Sloan recited. He didn't mean it to be humorous, but he also didn't want to escalate the already uncertain scene. He looked at Olivia. "Bad timing? Want me to leave?"

She hesitated for a bare second and slowly walked to stand in front of him. He could feel the heat of her agitation. He caught a whiff of lavender, Olivia's soap of choice. Sloan resisted touching her but was encouraged when Olivia slipped her hand into his. And he knew that Lynn was fully aware of the move.

"I told Lynn I had company coming. We were just finishing our conversation."

"Well, no, not really. We were just getting started. And it was important."

"Lynn, I think you've said it all. The rest can…"

Sloan gently squeezed Olivia's hand and then released it. He addressed Lynn. "If you'll excuse us for a moment." He didn't wait for her answer but gently maneuvered Olivia into her living room. A very brief glance showed Sloan that everything was set up for the dinner they were to have together—that he'd been looking forward to.

He stopped near the glass doors to the yard and positioned himself so that he blocked Lynn's ability to eavesdrop…or read lips.

"I'll make her leave. I'll—"

"Don't," he insisted, his voice very low and rough and very firm. "Did she know I was coming tonight?"

Olivia shook her head. "No. I just said I had *someone* coming. I wasn't keeping you hidden or anything like that, but it wasn't any of her business. Lynn doesn't know everything about me, even when she thinks she does or should. And I want—"

"Listen to me. If I stay right now, it's not going to be a good thing. I realize that she's screwing up our evening, but I don't think it's a good idea for me to get on her bad side. I think I'm already there anyway. I'll leave."

"Sloan." Olivia strongly objected, her teeth clenched.

"If I stay, your friend is going to try and start something with me. I might forget myself and just square off with her. But she's your friend. I don't want it to get ugly."

"You're more important," Olivia said, her voice a quiet plea.

He blinked at her, his gaze warm for a moment before he got control. "I'm glad to hear that. And that's all I need to know."

"*Excuse me*! I'm not invisible, you know," Lynn declared, annoyed.

"I'm leaving," Sloan announced calmly. "You and Olivia need to finish your talk. I'll only be a distraction. And I might say something… inappropriate."

Lynn looked vindicated—and victorious.

"A man came out just as I arrived. Is he waiting for you? He got into a car parked out front."

Lynn sighed, briefly rolling her eyes. "I'll speak to him. He'll wait." She looked sharply at Sloan, as if she wanted to say something just to him. Lynn glanced at his gun again and back to him, suspicious and hostile. He stared her down, waiting. She abruptly pulled the door open and stepped out. There was mumbled conversation, but Olivia and Sloan couldn't really hear what was said. Suddenly, Lynn was back but only stood on the entrance.

"Jonathan and I have to go. He's probably annoyed with me too. Why not? Everyone else is. You call me," Lynn ordered.

"You don't have to worry about me," Olivia said firmly.

"Call me," Lynn repeated, just as stern. Then she left.

Sloan stood with Olivia, holding her hand, trying to see into her face, to read her expression. He could tell she was still angry. A car door slammed outside. The engine started, and the car pulled sharply away. He turned to face her.

"Look at me."

She raised her face. He stared into her eyes.

"What's going on?"

Olivia swallowed, blinked a few times, and only then did the tension seem to seep from her.

Sloan led her to the sofa. "Sit down."

He waited her out. Olivia finally recovered her equilibrium and was now just bemused. She looked at him, and Sloan saw something soft and very thoughtful in the way she studied him. A very subtle smile began to play around her mouth.

"Lynn arrived with a new boyfriend for me."

The announcement caught him off guard. "What?"

"She, more than my other friends, thinks it's time to get back out there and meet eligible men."

"*Black* men," Sloan added, just to make sure he understood clearly.

"That's right. I never added any qualifiers."

"That's good."

Olivia stopped him from speaking, rushing on before he could betray himself, his feelings. "Just so you understand, Lynn was my attorney during my divorce. She was tough and brutal with my ex, not giving him an inch. She made sure I got what I deserved, and I think Lynn was fair. We became friends, and she's been like a guardian angel."

"With fangs and claws," Sloan added caustically.

Olivia nodded. "Yes, over-the-top. I think it's because she's represented too many women who didn't do as well as I did. I also had Jackson adding support. My brother introduced me and Marcus, so he felt somewhat responsible when the marriage went south. I told him that was stupid and I don't blame him at all."

"I'll give him points for wanting to take the bullet for you. Sorry for the analogy."

She shook her head, dismissing his comment. "I'm grateful Lynn's my friend. She's been good to me, but I want her to stop thinking of me as someone who needs watching out for, who needs to be fixed. I told her I'm seeing someone. I didn't tell her it was you."

"Now she knows," he murmured.

"I don't want anybody else."

Sloan noted that Olivia's voice dropped and she was barely audible. But he heard every word.

She now looked right into his eyes so there'd be no misunderstanding. Sloan needed that. His jaw tightened as he was overcome with a complex sweep of emotions. Not the least of which was relief. And profound gratitude. For those few moments he was speechless, unprepared for his own reactions to what Olivia was confessing.

"We found each other…all by ourselves."

With that, Sloan pulled her into a half embrace, bending to first kiss her with a quick burst of emotion and then to just hold her. "Liv," he murmured fervently.

"You got here just in time for me to tell you…not Lynn or anyone else…that I love you."

"Liv…" Sloan said again, foolishly, unable to find his words. He stood, pulling her into his arms. He cupped her face, looking into her eyes, his thumbs lightly caressing her cheeks. The movement encouraged one of Olivia's smiles.

But she studied him with some doubt clouding her gaze. "Maybe I overshot my intentions. Sloan, I was only talking about…well… how I…"

He kissed her lightly, gently. Then again. It stopped the flow of her excuses, since he didn't see that any were needed. The kiss was a prelude to Sloan settling his mouth over hers with a certain reverence, capturing her lips in a deep kiss that claimed her as his own. That was all he wanted Olivia to know. They wrapped their arms around one another, and it was silently settled that they'd finally arrived at where they both belonged.

It had not taken that long after all.

———————

Dinner was forgotten.

The chicken never got fried, and the potatoes sat in lightly salted water waiting to be boiled. Sloan had brought a ripe avocado that made Olivia laugh. It did not become guacamole. All was containered and refrigerated for another night, to be determined.

They did not follow their inclinations into the bedroom to make love. That was also postponed for the time being. The thing they most wanted to do was talk. Olivia hadn't realized, when the evening began, that Lynn's impromptu and unasked-for visit had inadvertently signaled to her and Sloan that it was the perfect time to reveal their feelings for each other. Lynn had forced them to stop beating around the bush. But she and Sloan were ready. Right?

Olivia couldn't talk at all for a long time. Sloan was focused on kissing her with such deep need that she wasn't about to stop him. If he was put off by her sudden confession, it wasn't being conveyed through his actions or the sweet things he growled against her lips. Her habit of clasping onto his wrists when he held her a certain way Sloan seemed to understand was her way of not letting him go. It was possessive, and it was tender.

When her emotional eye-opener had fully sunk in, Sloan became thoughtful, as if considering how he wanted to respond. He suddenly stood up, taking her hand and heading for the enclosed yard. They stepped out into the still night, and he settled them on the love seat rocker that bordered a hand-laid stone path curving around the outer periphery of the space. Sloan sat with an arm stretched out along the back. He encouraged Olivia to hug close to his side, seated on an angle with one leg pulled up beneath her.

She was content to wait, realizing that Sloan was somehow processing the evening in a much different way than she had. She was angry enough with Lynn's presumptions to have had it out with her, maybe even risking the end of a friendship. But Sloan's appearance had put an immediate stop to things escalating. Instead, Olivia knew she'd perhaps forced her relationship with Sloan into the realm of open-air discovery that couldn't be taken back. She wasn't sure what to expect next, but she was no longer nervous.

She had spoken nothing but her truth.

Suddenly, from the very quiet of the night and her yard…

"That first time, when I saw you in the hallway of your school…I knew."

Sloan spoke with a kind of finality and reverence that suggested he hadn't expected what was going to happen that day. Olivia closed her eyes, remembering as well. And that memory caused a sudden wash of emotion to flow through her, very like what she'd felt when she first saw Sloan—the odd sensation of awareness that gripped her insides. Magical and very scary.

"From that very moment, I was all in." He silently shook his head. "I didn't understand what had happened. I thought…this is crazy. I didn't even know who you were or anything about you."

His voice was a barrel-hollow rumble from his chest, filled with wonder and awe. "It was the damnedest thing," Sloan revealed in a deep, heavy murmur. He briefly brushed his chin against her forehead. "But for sure…it's you. From the beginning. And I found you right there in the hallway."

The caress made Olivia sigh. It was such a relief to know what he'd gone through mirrored her own bewildering and electric reaction. She splayed her hand across his chest. She could feel his inhalations and exhalations. She didn't say a word. Sloan seemed to know now exactly what he wanted to say.

"Everything that's happened since then only confirmed everything I felt, that I thought, that day." He snorted. "Was it love at first sight? I don't know what that's supposed to feel like. I had no clue. But everything from that day changed for me because of you.

"I felt…hope. I felt peace. When I'm with you, I feel safe. Does that make any sense at all? Do you know that you smile all the time?

Or maybe I only think you do. But I always think you're smiling just for me. Did you know that?"

Olivia sighed. She was pretty sure she did *not* go around smiling all the time. She did know that she had a tendency to smile at Sloan. Like she wanted to give that to him. It was all she had to give at the start.

"You once asked, '*Why me?*' I've been thinking a lot about that. I bet you know what the answer is."

Olivia nodded against his chest. "Now I do: Why not?"

"Right. You're not going to understand this yet, but you're one of the bravest women I've ever met. And that's including my ex who I always thought was strong and tough. A take-no-prisoners type. But you're stronger, Olivia, because you're still…soft. And loving. That's what I want. That's what you give me. Like…I'm worth being with. I could be a…a…keeper."

She laughed. "You could be my…boo."

He grunted. "I'm afraid to ask."

"It…it's a girlfriend term for the man in her life."

He was quiet for a moment. "Oh. Black."

"Don't like it?"

"I'm thinking about it." He stroked her hair, brushed a thumb across her cheek. "Does it make me special?"

"To me. Extra special. But you really don't need a tagline, you know. I think you and I have got this figured out." Her voice was a quiet, contented whisper.

"This is what I've been looking for," Sloan said earnestly. "None of it came to me as a color, Liv. What I see in you is character. Heart. Honesty. Maybe I didn't realize that until we met. I'm in love with you."

Olivia stroked his cheek, felt the muscle in his jaw clench against her fingertips.

"I beat you," she teased on a whisper. "I knew in about three seconds. After that, everything else was denial. I was afraid of what was happening to me. Too sudden. So sure. But it… it felt like love."

Sloan sighed. "Yeah. That's what I'm talking about."

She felt something vibrating somewhere in their clothing. It was Sloan's smartphone, and he released her to pull it free. Olivia moved again, a little light-headed and dazed. In love.

Sloan responded, his voice suddenly full in-charge-and-no-nonsense mode. He stood and paced in a small area while he took the call. Olivia watched him, a little dreamy-eyed at his ability to be so loving one minute and then quickly switching to all business. She stood and was about to step back into the house when Sloan called out to her. She turned to him as he reached her side and placed his hands on her waist. Olivia held on to his forearms as he studied her.

"I suppose you have to go?"

"Not until the morning, okay? I might be pulled into a local case. It might become federal as it develops. Maybe not."

"It's Saturday," Olivia reminded him quietly.

"I know. Won't matter, Olivia. I'm twenty-four seven. Look, we've been lucky ever since we met. No work interruptions that interfered with us getting to know each other." He pulled her against him. "Thanks for that. For dealing with the program. I really needed to know."

"This is…I mean…*we're* really happening?" Olivia couldn't help asking.

"Did you mean it when you said you loved me?" Sloan asked. His voice was deep, searching, quiet with emotion.

"Every word."

He nodded, sighed. "I've been waiting a long time for you. So…
yeah. We're on."

––––––––––––

Sloan's attention was split between waiting patiently as his hand was
methodically cleaned, swabbed, disinfected, and wrapped with gauze
to cover and protect the gash on the back. Then it was wrapped again
with an Ace bandage. There was some dried blood on his forearm, a
few smears on his khaki slacks and the left side of his shirt. It wasn't
serious.

His gaze was focused on a dazed and weeping woman seated in
the back of a squad car being questioned by two detectives. They
were preparing to transport her downtown for an official interview
and statement. There were about a dozen officers taking notes and
checking out the house where an attack on the woman had taken
place. A hulking man with bowed head, his hands handcuffed behind
him, was being held by two officers leading him to another waiting
car. He was under arrest. When the woman caught a glimpse of the
man, she cowered, withdrawing farther into the protective interior
of the squad car.

The last part of Sloan's awareness had to do with seeing Olivia
later…and it was already late. He was prepared to continue his oversight role in the drama that had played out earlier that day. A tip
from a friend of the female victim had suspected a distraught and
angry boyfriend was plotting revenge and violence to his ex-girlfriend,
who'd ended the relationship weeks before.

There was something about her *no*, she didn't want to see him
anymore that he, apparently, didn't understand and would not accept.

Sloan and another agent from the field office had only served as adjunct to the LAPD, who had done an excellent job, but the unexpected had, nonetheless, happened. The ex-girlfriend had been taken hostage after the police had arrived hoping to ward off exactly what had happened. After several hours, an attempt by the desperate boyfriend to escape had created a rush by officers to take him down before gunfire came into play and anyone could be hurt. But Sloan and a police officer were hurt, fortunately only requiring on-site attention and care. He wasn't going to make a thing out of being hurt. He knew about hurt, and the cut on his hand didn't qualify. It was moments like this that he had a rapid flashback to a much more deadly encounter in Afghanistan that could have cost him his life. Then his injuries had been serious and painful.

Sloan glanced at his bandaged hand as the EMS worker said he was okay to leave, with brief instructions on care of his injury. He nodded…and was now trying to decide if he should beg off going to Olivia's. He didn't want to have to explain to her what had happened, either in the confrontation or to his hand. But he couldn't deny that the pull was definitely toward going back to Baldwin Hills to her. He would not have had a problem months ago opting for a time-out, informing the lady of the moment that he couldn't see her. That's not how he wanted to treat Olivia.

Until her, Sloan would not have believed that love could make a difference.

He had reports to write up and file, a follow-up medical visit to check out his hand and report on that. Conferring with LAPD command since his department had been called in on their case. That could take days. He didn't want to wait that long. Sloan called her as the squad cars, emergency vehicles and equipment, and the SWAT team dispersed and cleared the area. Only the forensics department photographer remained to finish up his work.

He sat half in and out of his driver's seat, his door open as he called Olivia.

"Hello?"

Sloan sighed. She sounded so reassuringly normal, quietly curious. "Hey. Sorry to be calling so late."

"It's not late. How did... I guess you had a case after all."

"No. Still LAPD, but it turned out I needed to be at the scene."

"Okay."

Sloan waited out the second or two of silence.

"I wanted to check in with you. I..."

"I was holding dinner for you if you like. It's everything we didn't have last night. I know it's been a long day, and you probably want to go home."

"Since you're asking, I have no intentions of passing up a home-cooked meal. Want me to bring anything?"

"Just you."

Sloan's chortle of contentment was lost in his throat, and he knew that she would not have detected it.

"On my way," he said, ending the call.

Sloan was standing at the glass doors to Olivia's yard, staring out into the neat, small space, with its border of perennials near the fence line and her pillow and shawl for periodic meditation neatly stacked just outside the door to the left. He'd found Olivia in a silent sit several times and quietly made himself scarce until she was finished. He had his own practice but had become notoriously lazy about it. Sloan took that to mean he didn't need it as much anymore and he'd learned how to use his breathing to ground himself when needed.

He felt her hand carefully laid against his back to announce her presence. They'd finished dinner, talking around what had happened in his day with distracting conversation about her school and one student who'd placed in the state science fair.

Sloan gazed silently at her. "Want to sit outside for a while?"

Olivia nodded and slid the glass door open so they could step out. The night was totally silent in the residential community. An occasional bark of a dog being walked. A plane or helicopter overhead in the sky. They sat together on the top step that led down into the yard proper. Olivia slipped her arm around his, and Sloan squeezed it against his side.

"Are we going hiking again? Up that staircase at the Overlook?"

"You still want to do that?"

"I don't want one hike to be all of what I do. I really enjoyed it. I want to get better, do more."

"Fine. Maybe before Thanksgiving. You can work up an appetite. I suppose you have plans for Thanksgiving," he murmured.

She sighed, shrugged. "I don't know. Jackson hasn't said anything. Last year he and his partner, Brett, went to Brett's family in New York. I made plans with Mallory, one of my girlfriends. She has a difficult family thing going on and doesn't spend a lot of time with them if she can help it. It was nice." She tilted her head to look at him. "What about you?"

"I'll go to my dad's. He's in San Luis Obispo."

"Really?"

"He moved there after my mom passed away. I was still in country when that happened, so... He got a job offer at the university's math and science department." Sloan suddenly became quiet, glancing at Olivia again thoughtfully. "And now he has a girlfriend. Nancy. A divorcee who owns a café. She used to be a librarian."

Olivia met his gaze, frowned at the way he hesitated. "Okay," she said, encouraging him to continue.

"I…eh…I never told you that my mom was a teacher. And…her name was Olivia."

Olivia's brows rose in surprise, and a ghost of her smile appeared. She remained silent.

Sloan changed his position, staring out into the shadowed yard but taking her hand. "I don't believe in coincidence or chance but… after I met you and…"

Olivia chuckled, rubbing her chin against his arm. "Got spooked? No pun intended."

Sloan frowned. "Frankly, it's a lousy pun."

"I'm glad to hear you say so. I guess I understand that you couldn't believe the similarities. But there is something kind of…sweet and maybe magical about it, don't you think?"

"Like maybe my mom was watching out for me? I don't know…I don't believe in…"

"You don't have to, you know. That fact that it even crossed your mind, that you're still wondering about it…maybe you, *we*, should just be believers. Sometimes it's as simple as that."

"You're probably right."

Olivia squeezed the hand holding hers. "Can I see?"

"What? My hand? There's nothing to see." Sloan pulled it loose, releasing hers. "It's just a scratch, like I said."

She turned a little to the side and regarded him calmly. "It's not just a scratch. It's probably a laceration. This is not a Band-Aid. The injury is wrapped in sterile gauze to protect against infection. You should have had stitches. Did the medic apply an antiseptic cream? Something? Did they give you a tetanus shot?"

Reluctantly, Sloan nodded.

"And don't tell me you feel nothing."

"It's…sore," he admitted.

"Okay, I'll accept that. You should take a—"

"I already have. Tylenol. One and done."

"I don't want you to argue with me if I want to check it in the morning, clean and rewrap your hand."

"Liv, I don't want you to be my doctor."

Olivia took his hand back. "I'm not the least interested in being your doctor…or nurse. I can't help knowing what I know. The way I see it, Sloan, I'm committed to you in a way I haven't known in some time, maybe ever. That means I am concerned about what happens to you. I want to care about you. That's part of what love means. That's what I believe. Let me."

Sloan gave in. He put his arm around Olivia to pull her closer to his side, to kiss her cheek. "I'm not going to fight with you about it. The love part is…really nice," he said in a low voice.

"Good," she said decisively. "Do you want a lollipop?" Olivia added in a quiet, maternal tone.

Sloan held out for as long as he could and then burst into a barking laugh. He caught himself but gave Olivia a broad, surprised grin, his love for her shimmering in his clear eyes. "If it's okay with you, there's something else I'd like instead."

She returned his grin, mirroring his expression of love. "Me too. I'll let my brother know I have plans for Thanksgiving."

Sloan studied her features, an interesting curve to his lips that suggested a smile. "Do you ever think about returning to medicine?"

"No, I don't. You know, medicine is in my DNA. But I really love teaching."

"Maybe you still have some of it in your bones." Sloan looked at his bandaged hand, turning it over, slowly flexing the palm.

They returned to the house, closing and locking the sliding doors, drawing the curtains. Turning off all but the yard security light.

And finally retiring for the night, when they curled into each other's embrace.

And nature took over.

"So what is going on with you and Lynn? I called her to see if she wanted me to pick her up and bring her tonight. She was very... very..." Tessa tried to articulate about Lynn.

Mallory humphed. "Righteous. We all know Lynn can be that way. The woman is brilliant, and I don't ever want to get on her hissy side. It spills over, especially if it's about a man."

"What man is she mad at now? Was she dating someone I didn't hear about?" Tessa asked.

Olivia was silent, trying to decide how she was going to respond to the questions and her girlfriends' curiosity about their other friend. Everyone agreed that Lynn was, in many ways, a valued fourth in their group. But there was no denying Lynn's toughness and take-no-prisoners attitude on many issues, while insightful and helpful when needed, left room for her to believe she was always right. And pissing folks off.

Olivia was a few steps ahead of Tessa and Mallory as they shuffled out of the movie theater with a few hundred other moviegoers. They had no idea what had happened between her and Lynn. And apparently, Lynn hadn't said anything to Tessa and Mallory.

"I think Lynn's radio silence has to do with me. We had a falling out over someone I met…know…someone I'm interested in."

Tessa and Mallory exchanged covert glances. "The FBI guy," they murmured simultaneously.

Olivia wasn't sure there was no judgment in their observation.

"His name is—"

"Sloan," Mallory said with satisfaction. "He introduced himself that night at your house. I thought that was classy. And I liked his name."

"Mmmmm. Yeah. He was kind of…*hot*," Tessa mused.

"Maybe it was his scratchy voice…and the gun," Mallory conjectured. Tessa chuckled.

Olivia calmly humored their teasing. It was complimentary, actually. And mostly true.

"So how did Lynn get herself mixed up in your affair? It is an affair, right?" Tessa asked.

Olivia gave the two women a decidedly suggestive grin, arching a brow. "I think it's much more than that," she responded. Straightforward. True.

"Ohh. A secret. I want to know what Lynn did that caused you two to go into separate corners of the ring," Mallory said.

She was casting a sideways glance at her, and Olivia knew both Mallory and Tessa were expecting all the details…sordid and otherwise.

As they meandered through the mall parking lot, with the repetitive sound of slamming of car doors and engines turning on, Olivia gave her friends the short version of the night Lynn showed up, unasked and unexpected, trying to hook her up with, admittedly, a very attractive Black man with whom it was impossible to even think of developing an interest. Olivia knew that she and Sloan had not yet declared themselves to one another, but it was that crazy encounter with Lynn that had solidified what they felt for one another, admitting to being in love.

Tessa and Mallory were riveted by her tale, adding murmurs, gasps, grunts of affront for what Lynn had presumed in the most annoying and thoughtless way.

"Girrrrl…maybe we need to cut her loose. How could she?" Mallory said.

"We all know Lynn's hot buttons. *We*, maybe, need to use them more often. Push back and don't let her get away with being…"

"A bossy bitch," Mallory snorted in glee. "Love her to death, but…"

"Before we kick her to the curb, and I'm not saying I even want to do that, I, at least, need to draw the line in the sand and tell Lynn she has to stop being angry on my behalf. First of all, she was totally wrong. Second, I don't need a bodyguard. Third, she needs to put her own house in order."

"Amen," Mallory muttered.

"And I'm prepared to tell her that. I can take care of my own business. But that's coming from me. I think each of us has to decide how valuable, or not, Lynn's friendship is."

Tessa sighed. "Yeah, you're right. But…I have to know. Forget Lynn for now." They were stopped by Tessa's car, and she held her keys in her hand and gave Olivia a probing, pensive gaze. "Are you serious about this guy?"

Olivia considered all that she might say, how she would explain not only her feelings but how she'd arrived at them. She also knew that her girlfriends were certainly going to question the speed at which the connection had happened. But it all came down to the moment she and Sloan crossed paths and their eyes met and she smiled at him. So her answer was simple.

"Yes."

They said their good nights and separated, each to her own car, exit from the mall parking lot, and heading home. Olivia's drive was distracted as she considered the excitement and passion she knew being with Sloan. Along with the bliss was an undeniable concern that she had fallen too hard, too fast. What if it wasn't real and couldn't last?

Olivia believed that Sloan gave off all the signals of sincerity, and he was very loving and attentive. She'd also believed that Marcus was *it* in every way as a partner, a husband. Until he wasn't. In the end, he had been reckless with her heart. It had hurt, badly. Shaken her confidence in herself as a wife, a woman. In an instant, Olivia felt a wave of hot doubt wash over her, making her mouth dry. She swallowed.

Her cell, placed in the dashboard cradle, vibrated. It was Sloan.

"Hi," Olivia said. She sounded a little breathless. Her heart pumped past the momentary fear she'd manufactured in her head.

"How was the movie?"

"It was fun. A rom-com. You know."

"Actually I don't. Was it as good as the movie we watched together?"

Olivia slowly smiled because Sloan actually remembered. It was very reassuring. "Different kind of movie, so, no. Tonight was just a girls' night out."

"You're fortunate to have such good friends," Sloan murmured.

"I am. I'm on my way home now."

"Are you using your traffic alert system?"

"To be honest, I mostly forget to turn it on."

"You have to get better about that. There's an accident on 10, and there're only three lanes open out of six. It's a mess for miles. Get off, if you can, and take the surface roads."

"I'm coming up on an exit now. I'll get off."

"Good."

"Did you call just to warn me? That was very thoughtful of you."

"It wasn't the only reason."

She waited, and when he spoke again, Sloan's voice had changed. Lower, quiet, craggy.

"I wanted to say I love you."

It was a whisper. Olivia swallowed again. The relief and gladness that came over her was palpable. Sloan's admission could not have come at a more important time.

" Oooh…Sloan. I feel the same," she responded with equal fervor.

Olivia didn't underestimate the enormous safety net that Sloan's words provided her. But she was taken by surprise, and bewildered, by what awaited her the next morning that had nothing to do with love but the vagaries of life.

Her car was gone.

CHAPTER 15

The next morning, Olivia was so stunned by the unexpected empty space where her car was normally parked that she stared at the vacant spot wondering if it was a trick.

She stepped onto the front pathway, glancing up and down the street, and it slowly dawned on her that her almost-brand-new BMW was, indeed, gone.

"No," Olivia moaned to herself as the sudden twisting of her stomach muscles signaled awareness of something gone wrong. She walked to the end of the driveway, looking both ways up and down the street again, hoping for a reasonable and obvious explanation. But the reality still came down to the fact that her car was gone. Not missing, but taken.

"No," she uttered again, this time with disbelief...and annoyance.

For several seconds, Olivia's mind went through a short list of what she should do. It was very telling that the first thing was to call Sloan. But she didn't. Turning and retreating quickly into the house, Olivia dropped her purse, tote, and other necessary objects for the day on her sofa and dug out her cell phone, her hands trembling slightly.

She called the police.

Olivia was sure that the answering desk officer was the exact same one who took her call months ago when she found money in the house she was going to renovate. He was just as blank and bored, while she was indignant and firm in her aggrieved announcement that her car had been taken, right from her driveway! There was an unnecessary silence.

"Was anything of significance left in the vehicle?"

"Well…what do you mean, significant?"

"A kid. A pet."

"*No*! No…"

"Okay, hold on…"

He cut her off before Olivia could launch into another argument of urgency. The officer she was transferred to interrupted her repeatedly with a litany of scripted questions while typing in her answers in a computer form. No offer to send an officer to investigate, no suggestion that she come into the local precinct to file a report. No show of sympathy or encouragement that the police would get right on looking for her vehicle. Quickly Olivia figured out that in the great scheme of things, her missing car was not on the priority list of we'll-get-right-on-it.

When she got off the call, Olivia felt exhausted from the twenty minutes of dealing with a personal issue that no one else, even law enforcement, cared about. Then she realized she was going to be late for the first period at Harvest Prep. She called Lori.

"Hi. I'm coming in, but I'm going to be late for first period."

"Are you okay? I tried to give the Wednesday morning meditation class, but the kids didn't take me seriously. The little boogers laughed when I couldn't get down on the floor."

Olivia smiled to herself. "Don't worry about it. As long as you kept them distracted until the next class. I…eh…something happened this morning and I had to take care of it."

"Are you okay?" Lori asked again, now with real concern.

"Yeah, yeah…well…actually, my car was stolen and…"

"Oh *no*."

"And…and… It'll be okay. So don't—"

"I'm so sorry. What are you going to do?"

Olivia sighed, very annoyed that she felt on the far edge of tears. It was anger and frustration and helplessness.

"I already called the police. They were not empathetic to the fact that my new car had been stolen. But the officer did tell me that I could request something called BMW Assist that will track the car."

Lori humphed. "Do you have any idea how many and how often cars, especially new ones, get taken in LA? No, the cops probably didn't care. But at least your car can be tracked. I hope that works."

"Yeah, but I need a car now." Olivia said somewhat frantically. "I'm going to call my insurance company. There's probably a rental benefit on my policy, but I don't know how long it will last."

"Right. And if you don't get your car back, you're probably talking replacement."

Olivia sighed again. She fingered her hair, gnawed her lip, anxiety beginning to grip her. "You're right. Anyway, not your problem. Just wanted to report in."

"You have a lot to deal with. I wouldn't worry about coming in today. Everything's cool. The usual manageable high school drama. Nothing I can't handle."

"What do you mean?"

"Well, I caught Colby's brother, Curtis, hanging around as the students were arriving this morning. He wasn't trying to get into to the school or anything. More like he was waiting for something. Or someone."

"I wouldn't worry about him, then. As long as he stays out of the building. I'd better go. I have some calls to make, and I have to see about a loaner car."

"Don't worry about here. I've got it covered."

"You're the best. Thanks, Lori."

Olivia hung up but was momentarily disoriented as she tried to plan her next move. She called Jackson, but it was just to inform him of what had happened. She didn't need more sympathy or suggestions of what to do. But he did offer both. Jackson also said he thought it was time to get rid of the things they'd stored in the garage after their mother had died. Olivia had returned to live with her mother after her divorce. It had never been her plan to stay in the house in Baldwin Hills where she'd spent her adolescence.

The insurance company was the easiest to deal with, and she supplied all the information they asked for, and they informed Olivia that she did have rental privileges on her policy. All she had to do was submit a police report as soon as possible. She arranged for a Lyft to the police station and couldn't believe that obtaining the report was a rigamarole taking almost two hours. It was early afternoon when Olivia was finally handed the report. She asked the officer when she should expect word on her missing car. The officer didn't even bother to hide his amusement. He shrugged, turned back to his computer.

"Maybe in a few days, if you're lucky. Maybe never."

Olivia sat in a waiting area of the station house, feeling dispirited. She was alone and finally tried to settle down. She closed her eyes. She focused on not blaming herself for everything that had gone wrong. Marcus certainly would have.

Olivia considered how much more needed to be done to get through the day and prepare for the next. Feeling in control again, she finally called Sloan.

"Agent Kendrick."

He sounded so official. "You know who this is," Olivia said quietly.

His voice retained his irregular ragged texture, but now very alert. Attuned to the emotions emanating from her.

"Liv? What's up? Everything okay?"

Olivia felt some relief just hearing his voice, his concern. "For the most part. I…I was leaving for school this morning…"

"And?"

"And…when I left the house I saw…I *didn't* see my…my car was gone. Missing. I don't know…stolen."

It was odd to hear the way Sloan, so effortlessly, was able to maintain the authoritative tone of his voice. In command. But it was definitely underscored with compassion and warmth. Immediately he began asking quick, concise questions. Details about the car, specs and VIN number. Had she left any valuables in the car? Olivia was being interrogated about her loss, something even the LAPD officers never bothered to conduct. Sloan's attention countered the sterile, stark indifference she'd received since calling the police early that morning.

"Look…I don't have authority to search for your car, Olivia. I can't do much of anything, actually. But I do have good relationships at LAPD, and I think I can call in a favor and get some follow-up or a BOLO."

"What's a BOLO?"

"It stands for '*be on the lookout*.' You don't really know when or how the car went missing. There's nothing to go on. So I have to be honest and warn you that…this might not have a good outcome." His voice lowered. "You might not get the car back. Or if it's found it might be…chopped."

"I understand." Olivia sighed deeply. Sloan was silent while she considered the possibilities. "Well, I can't worry about *what-if*! I have to get a usable car right now. I have to get to work. I have to be able to have a daily life. I have to have a car. LA is a total car culture."

"That's right."

"My insurance company will pay for a rental for a week or two. But…I have to start thinking about getting a replacement."

"I'm sorry, Olivia."

That heartfelt comment from Sloan made her feel cared for. "I appreciate that, Sloan. I shouldn't have called, feeling sorry for myself," Olivia said with a short laugh. "Bad form."

"Want me to come over? Or I can pick you up from wherever you'll be later, take you to dinner."

"You don't have to do that. I'm a big girl. I can take a hit and stay standing."

She heard Sloan's peculiar habit of stifling his laugh…but she'd already caught him out, so it was a pointless effort. She wanted to hear him laugh. She wanted to be responsible for that.

"The least I can do is say something that might help you feel better about today."

"I'll take whatever you got," she murmured in amusement.

"I love you," Sloan said softly.

———

She didn't change her mind about having him come over, but Sloan knew that was Olivia's way of exerting a little bit of independence. Not expecting him to make things better. He had to accept that Olivia hadn't yet come to the fact that he would willingly do a lot of things just for her.

It was a new awareness, for sure, for him. His ex-wife never really needed him. She was more than capable of taking care of herself, but it did include sometimes taking care of him. In fact, he also realized that in her own way, Olivia might be among the very few rare relationships in which it was sometimes about him. Her caring was subtle, natural, intuitive, and that made it all the more special to Sloan because it was so like her. The *her* he'd come to know. Declaring his love to Olivia was not spontaneous but an accumulation of time spent with her, her calm and charming sense of humor, her generous ability to consider other people and their feelings. His feelings.

So he was on his way to her in Baldwin Hills, ignoring her brave decision to tough out a very bad day by herself. It was precisely that brave front that made the decision for Sloan that he was going to be with her anyway. To support and comfort her. To love her.

But a brief surge of doubt pumped through his heart as he wondered if Olivia would be annoyed or pleased at this gesture. He rolled up in front of her house, and the absence of a car in front was a solid confirmation of her missing brand-new car.

Sloan shut off the engine and reached for the plastic bag on the passenger seat. Quietly closing and locking the car, he headed to the front door and rang the doorbell, hearing the soft chime on the inside.

In less than a minute, the door opened cautiously, and Sloan saw Olivia's pretty face, her eyes wide with curiosity. And widen even more when she recognized him. And brighten as a smile transformed her features.

"Sloan!"

Sloan's smile was not as obvious, very small and not full-blown, but it was only for her anyway. He knew Olivia would read the feelings behind it honestly. He lifted the plastic bag for her to see.

"I come bearing gifts," he said.

Her smile grew bigger, her face showing surprise and pleasure.

"Oh...*Sloan*." It was a small mew. She stepped back and opened the door wide so he could enter.

Olivia closed the door and came to stand in front of him, staring as if he were some magical apparition. Sloan stood, watching her every move, the look on her face and in her eyes. The reception was more than he'd hoped for. Olivia continued to gaze at him as if he was the greatest thing since chocolate milk. He held the desire to chuckle at the image in check.

"I didn't know, of course, what your plans were for dinner, since you turned me down on the phone. But number one, you have to eat. Number two, I knew you weren't going to feel like cooking for yourself, and one is the loneliest number. And number three...I didn't think you should be alone. I brought you dinner. And me."

Olivia drew in a little gasp and released it in a small laugh, her eyes bright as she took in the reality of him right there in front of her. She didn't say anything, but it wasn't hard to read her next move. Sloan quickly put the bag on the floor and opened his arms as she walked right into them, hugging him with her cheek against his chest. He couldn't have scripted a better hello, a warmer reaction or tender greeting. He held her close, taking in Olivia's reception as just what he had hoped from her. A little TLC never hurts.

"Are you angry that I went against your wish to be alone?"

"No! Oh, no. I'm so happy that you ignored me. Seeing you is the best moment in the whole day."

"Well, it wouldn't have taken much to give you that."

"But you're the one who made it happen," Olivia murmured.

She finally pulled back to gaze at him. "Thank you. Until this moment I didn't realize that the last thing I needed, wanted, was to be alone."

"You and I both understand it's just a car, Liv. But it was *your* car you picked out for yourself and paid for. The loss is not catastrophic, but having it taken is still significant."

"I thought I was overreacting," she admitted.

He snorted. "A man would have gone into a rage, killer instincts surfacing in a burning heartbeat."

"Too extreme." She smiled at him.

Sloan guessed what she was going to say next, and they spoke simultaneously. "*It's just a car.*"

When Olivia tilted her face upward, he met her halfway with a quick and gentle kiss.

"Thank you. What did you bring?"

"Chinese."

"Wonderful."

Sloan took up the bag and followed her into the kitchen. Olivia suggested eating in the backyard, and Sloan went to find the collapsible table to open and set up two chairs. Olivia had emptied the bag of half a dozen containers, warm, aromatic flavors wafting into the air. When she reached a small white food container that was very light, she turned to him.

"What's this?"

Even as she was about to open the square box, Sloan deftly lifted it out of her hand and set it out of reach. "That's for later. I did forget to get something to drink."

"I have wine. I could make a pot of tea…"

"Wine is fine."

Within fifteen minutes of his arrival, Sloan and Olivia were seated in the early evening in her yard, enjoying a casual and easy dinner. She'd lit three large hurricane candles along the top steps outside the living room glass doors and dimmed the lights mounted on corners of the house. Beyond asking about getting a temporary car, they didn't talk about Olivia's stolen car. Sloan was sure that was what happened; it was stolen. Olivia had persuaded the car rental agency to send someone to pick her up from the house the next morning and take her to get her rental. Sloan was silently amused that she'd accomplished that. Acting as chauffeur for customers is not on rental agreements, but he was not surprised that Olivia had managed it with a little bit of charm and, probably, an eloquent argument.

Sloan was enjoying being with her, bottom line. It was easy and undemanding. No upheavals or controversy. No complaining or bad temper. Nothing special about the evening—take-out dinner and small talk at a kind of picnic setup in Olivia's backyard. For him, it was terrific just because it was *all of the above.*

"What's in the box?" Olivia asked. They'd finished eating and were just lingering at the table over wine as night filled the sky above.

Sloan quickly returned to the kitchen to retrieve the package. In the yard again, he silently handed it to her.

Because he'd offered no introduction, explanation, or hints, Olivia cast a silent stare at him, accepting the box and opening it. Then she broke into a grin.

"Fortune cookies."

"Of course."

"How did I get started collecting them?"

"You really don't remember?"

She was already ripping cellophane from a cookie, but she looked at him steadily. Sloan could see that, of course, she remembered.

"You took me to lunch when I came to your office. It was the day after we met." She passed the broken cookie pieces to Sloan to eat as she read the thin, white paper insert. She glanced at him briefly again and quoted the paper out loud. "'*You display the wonderful traits of charm and courtesy.*'"

Sloan met Olivia's gaze and held it for a long moment. "That's a good one. And it's true."

"I think it holds true for you too," she said.

Olivia appeared to read, and reread, the paper several times in silence. Sloan didn't miss her covertly putting the slip of paper into the pocket of her denim skirt. She stood and began to clear the table, gather the garbage, close containers with any leftovers. They efficiently worked together to put everything away. The dinner, the evening, was essentially over. But there was this sense of not knowing how it would actually end.

They returned to the living room, but Sloan didn't sit on a chair or the sofa to settle in for after-dinner conversation. While Olivia finished whatever remained of cleanup in the kitchen, Sloan nervously paced a small area in the living room. He still held his wineglass and he stared into it, frowning at what remained. Olivia returned quietly, and they faced each other. He couldn't read her expression, and he was lost for a moment about what to do next.

Sloan quickly downed the rest of his wine, rolling the bowl of the glass between his palms. "Well…I enjoyed dinner. I know it wasn't much…"

"It was perfect," Olivia commented, watching him. She approached and carefully took the empty glass from him.

"I'll get going. I just wanted to try and…"

"I thought you'd stay awhile longer."

"You must be wiped out after all that's—"

"Until the morning?"

Sloan watched her, glad that Olivia had made the offer herself, clarifying their mutual desire. He didn't want to be pushy. And he was ever careful not to give the impression that he was, again, rescuing her. He didn't want to stoke her insecurities.

He took several steps toward Olivia and stood studying her. "You want me to?"

She didn't avert her gaze. She nodded. "Can you?"

"Absolutely," Sloan said so definitively that she broke into a grin. He didn't wait for another word or a signal but gathered Olivia into his embrace and kissed her with all the desire and intent that had been building within him all evening. But he was slow, taking his time to grow their desire and need, using his lips to control and massage hers until Olivia went limp against him.

Of course he wanted her. That was the simple truth of it.

Olivia hugged him back, clung to him, raising her arms to circle his neck. She let her small, slender fingers burrow into his hair. Her touch was light and caressing. Sloan captured her mouth, rubbing over her lips and invading the opening to find her tongue and to delve deeper… slowly feeling a rising passion take them to the next level. But they both seemed riveted to that one spot in the living room, in each other's arms, content for the moment to hold on to each other, letting their beating hearts, their deep hushed breathing, satisfy them. But their mutual need wanted more, and their bodies, pressed tightly together, indicated as much. Sloan was in full arousal. He slid his hand to Olivia's lower back and pulled her in closer so that she could not mistake the change in him.

They swayed, and Sloan broke the kiss. He looked into her eyes, slumberous with longing. Her lips moist and parted. Sloan kissed her deeply again and then turned Olivia in the direction of her bedroom.

Olivia broke from him to adjust the window blinds, to draw the curtains. He'd left his weapon in his office. He took off his shirt, his shoes. Then Sloan stopped disrobing to come up behind her, sliding his arms around her waist. She immediately relaxed into his arms, her back against his chest. His mounting urgency caused her to undulate into him as he pressed his hips forward to meet her. He groaned softly into her ear. She reached a hand up and behind her to stroke his cheek.

Sloan held her like that, in control, with something else in mind. His left hand deftly unzipped the top closing of her skirt. The right hand slipped beneath her white boatneck T. He bent to nuzzle beneath her ear, along her jaw and her neck. He left a trail of sensual kisses while deftly unfastening her bra. The slight weight of a breast was cupped by his hand, and his fingers massaged the rounded soft flesh.

Olivia softly moaned his name. She arched her back, forcing her breast into his palm.

He gave her what she wanted.

Olivia twisted in his arms. She broke the contact and faced him, letting him once again consume her with his ardent kisses. Sloan maneuvered her to the edge of the bed, lowering her to sit. Olivia leaned back to brace herself with her elbows. She lifted her hips so that Sloan could pull away the skirt, her panties. Balancing on a knee pressed on the bed right next to her, Sloan relieved her of the T-shirt and bra in one motion.

He stared down at her slender brown body, at her chest heaving with anticipation and need. With her eyes closed and lips parted, Olivia lay waiting for him. Sloan wanted to be careful with her, to treat her with thoughtful reverence and show his love. He removed the rest of his clothing and the cellophane packet from his trouser pocket. In just a few seconds, he was bending over Olivia, smoothly shifting her body to the center of the bed, and positioning himself to lie on top of her. He lowered his weight and gently pinned her beneath him. Sloan went back to kissing her, as she hugged him, raised her knees, encouraging him.

Sloan thrust into her in one smooth stroke. He came onto his forearms so that he could look into her face, see the emotional changes as they made love to each other. His kisses were slow and erotic.

Only when she quietly panted through her climax and ended on a deep sigh did Sloan let himself go. Olivia stroked his back, smoothed his hair, and cupped his face. Sloan opened his eyes to find her staring into his with drowsy peace and warmth. He sighed and closed his eyes again, giving himself up to the ride until the end. Sloan let himself lie still and heavy, relaxed on her body. They had not lasted very long, the tension of the day and its unexpected events having resulted in a quick quenching of their needs. And when they'd given themselves ample time to recover, to cuddle with roving, caressing hands, they began to make love again. They took their sweet time over every nuance and movement because they had all the time in the world.

CHAPTER 16

Sloan left his colleagues at the elevator as they all dispersed in different directions to their offices. He entered his and did two things. One was a habit of checking his computer for any emails, notices, or directives from his director or FBI headquarters in DC. And the second was a curious and odd newly acquired action: randomly rotating a weirdly shaped rock on his desk, next to the computer. It was the rock Olivia had picked up and he had dropped into his vest pocket the first time he'd taken her hiking. For several weeks Sloan had forgotten its presence and, in truth, when he'd finally discovered it, his inclination had been to toss it back to nature. But he hadn't.

He reasoned that Olivia must have had a reason to collect and keep this particular rock, and he felt he couldn't let it go. Even though she'd not mentioned her find since that hike. When Sloan first absently began to turn it over, flip it around, put it on various angles, the rock never seemed to be much more than a stone with a kind of triangular shape from any angle. It was the afternoon of her car having been stolen that, as he sat debating surprising Olivia with a visit and take away dinner, that his absently studying his lodestone that it appeared, very obviously now, to have the appearance of a heart. That's when Sloan realized that no matter which side the rock rested on, it was still heart shaped.

He was not about to start dealing in premonitions but realized that Olivia had probably noticed this startling feature right away and had saved the stone. For him. Sloan experienced that it was a gift, maybe of profound meaning, but at the very least that Olivia had been thinking of him, with love, almost from the beginning.

Now, when he entered his office, Sloan's first move was to change the position of the rock to see what side presented itself and what he could see on its face. He'd never spoken to Olivia about his discovery, or the unexpected feeling of magic it gave him, that made her even more special, important to him. Sloan reflected for a long moment, doing a mental inventory of women in his life in the recent past. One inexplicable marriage, too many short-term affairs...or one-night stands. A comfortable relationship for easy dates with little effort, emotional or otherwise. And, finally, Olivia.

Sloan had reached a point where he was beginning to push the boundaries of the relationship with Olivia. What might be next? Where were they headed? He might think there was a slam-dunk ending, but he was pretty sure Olivia would hesitate. He had no doubts that she loved him. Heaven knew it was mutual. But she had a history Sloan knew made her cautious and self-protective. He had to respect that. But he also wanted to overcome that. But how?

Sloan sat forward, checked the time. School had ended an hour ago. He called her.

"Hello?"

"You sound breathless. What's going on?" He was always comforted by the sound of her voice. Pure and straightforward. Never a pretense or even caution.

"I...just bought...another car."

"Really? I didn't know you'd made the decision."

"I was driving myself crazy thinking about it. And my insurance company informed me what they'd give me. I had to get one, you know, but…"

"Scared?"

"Do I sound silly?"

"You sound like someone who's recently had a bad experience and is gun-shy. Could it happen again that it gets stolen? Should I have bought a used car? A bicycle?"

She laughed. "You're funny."

"I don't believe you're afraid of much, Olivia, but you're still getting over a bad experience. It's left a bad taste. Stop beating yourself up. The theft of the first car wasn't your fault."

"I haven't heard anything from the police."

Sloan sighed quietly, giving himself time to come up with a reason that wouldn't seem hopeless. "Remember that hundreds of cars get stolen every day."

"Mine is not that special."

"Yours is not that special," he repeated, confirming her realization.

"It probably won't be found in one piece."

"It probably won't be found in one piece. I don't mean to be cavalier."

"You're being honest."

"So what did you get?"

Another BMW. Sloan listened to Olivia briefly describe the experience, but he could tell she'd kept overzealous salespeople in check, threatened to take her business elsewhere if they dared try to oversell her…and she got what she wanted.

"Want to take me for a spin tonight?"

"Sorry. Jackson asked first. I'm picking him up from the hospital. It's Tuesday…"

Sloan grinned to himself. "You're taking him for tacos."

"He's taking *me* for tacos."

"Have you told your brother about me?"

"Of course. Almost as soon as we met. Because…I thought…"

"I know. Me, too. Did he give you any advice…or threaten my life?"

She chuckled. "I gave Jackson no reason to think he'd have to resort to violence on my behalf. He's working on not being over protective. He told me to have fun. And be careful."

"I like him already," Sloan murmured.

"You'll meet him. Soon."

"I'll let you go. Congrats on the new wheels."

"Thanks. Are we still on for Sunday?"

"If you're up for it."

"You did promise."

"Then we're on. Speak with you soon."

Olivia was taking slow, deep breaths, trying not to pant. That's what Sloan had taught her. Find a rhythm, match it to your footsteps. Count slowly in increments of ten. Start over. And he'd said, if you have to stop a moment to rest, do it.

Olivia stopped and took the advice. She used the moment to look behind her, at how far she'd climbed. By her count she'd managed about seventy-five of the irregular stone steps. That left just over a hundred more to go. Some were not a step at all but sometimes required a ninety-degree leg lift to push herself up. Sloan had also instructed her to take a few sips of water every ten minutes. As her breathing got back to normal, Olivia glanced upward. She couldn't see the top of the steps where they ultimately ended at the overlook, and she certainly couldn't see Sloan. And she still had a very long way to go. She took a deep breath and started again toward the top.

When they'd reached the park, she'd asked if he could start up without her. She wanted to make the climb alone and meet him at the top. Sloan had not liked the idea at all, and they'd had a lengthy and slightly heated discussion about the wisdom of someone with little experience in climbing hikes doing the killer stairs on her own. She'd insisted. Sloan had finally given in, although it was clear he wasn't happy about leaving her. Olivia had bribed him.

"If you let me go up by myself, I will do whatever you want for the rest of the day. It's not about not wanting you to be with me. It's about me proving to myself I can do this on my own."

"Okay. Okay…" Sloan very reluctantly gave in. "You have your phone? I expect you to *use it* if you can't make it, all right? If you need me."

Olivia had been so buoyed, so thrilled by his demand. But she had no intentions of doing as he'd asked. She'd waved him off as he started the climb.

"See you at the top…"

She kept her attention on the steps, careful not to trip as she particularly monitored the ones that were higher than average. She paid no attention to the folks moving faster, some with the aid of walking sticks, or young teens and kids who didn't know the meaning of the word "exhausted." She ignored the markers that would have kept her informed of how much progress she was making on the climb up. And Olivia ignored the trickle of sweat that rolled down her spine and down her chest, between her breasts, from her exertion. She hadn't counted on that discomfort. She kept going. And she lost track of time.

Sloan paced, maintaining a calm concern each time he approached the top landing of the stairs and gazed down into the crowd of climbers. He was looking for his navy-blue baseball cap he'd given Olivia to wear with the FBI letters large and yellow above the bill. No one would take it as authentic, but it would certainly stand out. He'd taken the bright-orange scarf she'd started with, wound around her hair like a headband, and tied it around his neck. He told her she could focus on looking for it, and him, as she neared the top. Sloan hoped that Olivia had remembered to be sparing and careful with her water consumption.

By normal considerations the climb could take forty-five minutes. He had managed in thirty, but his incentive was different. It was not to be the first or to win. It was to make sure he was in place when Olivia got to the overlook.

As he paced, Sloan eventually became aware of the level of his worry. He'd never gone through the emotions he was experiencing just then. He'd never worried over anyone this way, certainly not for climbing a hard but doable hill. But then again, there had never been anyone like Olivia in his life before. And it was scary to know, so fully, that she was his equal in all the ways he wanted it to matter. Sloan was a little beside himself to think of anything happening to her.

He loved her that much. He didn't want to lose her.

And it was only a hike up 282 stone steps.

Sloan spotted the large yellow letters first. Olivia was walking on the extreme right side of the ascending stairs. If she happened to glance up, he would wave his arm as her target. She didn't look up. But she was moving steadily, if slowly, and was within about a hundred feet of her destination. Sloan took a deep breath and slowly released it, relieved. He stood with his hands braced on his hips, gaze riveted to her progress. And only when she was within about a dozen steps from the top did she look up. She found him immediately...and smiled.

The last thing Olivia would want just then was to be fussed over. The last thing Sloan wanted to do was fuss over her. She'd made her point and he was going to respect that. Olivia reached the top step, stood for a few seconds to get her balance, steady her legs, then she walked right over to him. She looked up at him...triumphant.

Sloan didn't touch her but couldn't prevent a crooked grin from shaping his lips. He silently *humph*ed in his chest and shook his head in amusement.

"Champion of the world," he uttered.

She raised her hands straight up, overhead à la Rocky. He grinned.

Sloan had reached security and was about to swipe through the exit turnstile at the field office when a guard got his attention.

"Agent Kendrick? Before you leave, several teens arrived about a half hour ago looking for you. They didn't have an appointment, but I tried to put a call into your office...let you know they were down here."

Sloan listened but hadn't a clue why teenagers had come specifically looking for him.

"Any names?" he asked the guard.

"No, sir. But they said you knew them."

Sloan frowned. Nothing came to mind. "Okay. Where are they now?"

"Right outside," the guard said, pointing out the door and signaling to the left.

"Have them come in, let me have a look, see if I recognize anyone."

Sloan stood back from the security desk, to the side of the X-ray scanner. He would be able to see the teens right away, before they saw him, giving him a moment to assess them. In just a minute, the guard returned with four teens trailing behind him. He let them walk ahead through the revolving door, pointing to where they should wait.

As soon as the kids came into view, Sloan knew exactly who they were. Black teens from Olivia's charter school. He knew two of their names, from the Teen Academy they'd attended at the field office shortly after the school year had begun—the tall, skinny teen with glasses, that was Colby. And the only girl in the group was Taryn. The young mother of baby Gaye. And baby Gaye was also in attendance, carried in Taryn's arms, peering around at all the bigger people around her. Sloan stepped forward. Colby saw him first. He waved shyly.

"Hey, Agent Kendrick. Remember us?"

"Sure. Colby. Taryn. And…"

The other two students identified themselves. Sloan remembered them as well from the class but had not recalled their names.

"What's up? You wanted to see me?"

They looked uncertain. Uncomfortable. One of the two Sloan was not as familiar with was eyeing his sidearm, a gaze of fascination and unease having him shift from one foot to the next. Sloan knew them to be bright and alert kids, and realized that the official setting where they stood, without benefit of a teacher as chaperone, had intimidated the four of them into nervous silence. Sloan looked to Taryn. He remembered thinking of her as fearless.

"Taryn?" he opened.

"We need to talk to you about something important." She glanced in the direction of the security guard who was openly listening to the conversation. "In private," she said bluntly.

Sloan nodded. "Okay." He spoke to the guard. "Let them pass

through the scan. When they're cleared, I'll take them into the main floor reception center."

Then Sloan did something totally unexpected. He reached out and lifted Taryn's daughter into his arms. The child did not act surprised, confused, or frightened. She stared for a moment into Sloan's face and then broke into a babbling sound of joy.

He held Gaye intuitively, exactly as he had that first meeting when she was thrust into his care by Olivia.

While the teens were being processed, Sloan took a visitor's pass for each of them from a rack next to the guard's desk to be worn around their neck as they were cleared by the guard. He then silently led them to a large, glassed-in room down a corridor from the entrance. There was no one inside, and Sloan held the door as the kids entered and took seats around a rectangular table. He stood by the door, once again studying the four. He came to the head of the table to give each a long hard look, to see what they revealed, if anything. He remained standing.

"Are you in some kind of trouble?" Sloan asked bluntly.

"No," they all answered over one another.

"Not really," Colby clarified. "I mean, not us. I don't think."

As he tried to listen carefully, Sloan was also trying to manage Gaye's baby movements. She wasn't fussing so much as still trying to communicate without the skills or language yet to do so.

"I'll take her," Taryn said, reaching to take the baby back.

"I got her," Sloan said smoothly. He glanced around the group. "One of you can explain. I'll listen and ask questions, okay?"

"Yes, sir" was their respectful answer.

Sloan waited for one of them to take the lead.

"Does this visit have to do with school? Something going on

there?" Sloan began, trying to cut to the chase and find a way into the reason for their visit.

Olivia came instantly to mind.

The students exchanged looks but averted their gaze from meeting his.

"No," one of the boys muttered.

"Kind of," Colby responded, looking thoughtful…and scared.

"It's about Ms. Cameron," Taryn finally clarified.

Sloan's jaw tightened. But he didn't otherwise move or show expression.

"Is Ms. Cameron okay?"

"Yeah. Sure," the fourth boy affirmed.

Sloan remembered he was the one with a little bit of a comic streak.

"Okay. Then…what?"

They exchanged furtive glances again. Suddenly Taryn glared at the three boys and sucked her teeth, a show of impatience. "Come on! Just say it!" she exclaimed.

Colby blinked behind his glasses, pushed them back up his nose with a finger. "We know what happened to Ms. Cameron's car. Not the new one. The first new one," he said to clarify.

Sloan stared at Colby. Then his gaze swept over the other three, looking for confirmation. They were looking at him for reaction. "I take it none of you has spoken with Ms. Cameron about what you know."

They mutely shook their heads. "We wanted to. We like Ms. Cameron. But if we did that, then…it will cause a lot of trouble," one of the teens said.

Sloan sighed. They were protecting someone. "It's already caused a lot of trouble. How do you think Ms. Cameron feels, having her car stolen?"

"We know, but...if we tell her what we know, then someone might go to jail. Maybe sent away to prison," Taryn reasoned.

"That's possible," Sloan agreed, thinking. "But maybe not. Depends on the circumstances of the theft. What happened to the car? Is there any chance of getting it back? Was Ms. Cameron targeted for a reason? Who knew where she lived in the first place to take the car from her home driveway? Understand what I'm saying?"

They nodded, all looking ambivalent at all the possibilities. Sloan knew he was onto something and the details were probably not all that complicated. He slowly walked to the other side of the table and sat down across from the kids. He settled Gaye on his lap, and she comfortably lay against him. He spotted a large Sharpie on the table. Making sure the cap was on tightly, Sloan was about to give it to Gaye to play with, keep her distracted, but Taryn quickly reached into a compartment of her knapsack and pulled out a small stuffed animal in the shape of an elephant. She silently held it out to her daughter. Gaye grabbed the toy, examined it for a moment, and promptly shook and waved it about.

Sloan looked at each of them, getting another impression and making a decision. He leaned a little forward.

"Who wants to tell me exactly what happened? What you know and *how* you know it." He looked from one to the other and, finally, back to Taryn, the unofficial group leader. He waited.

She sighed, squinting at him. "We'll tell you everything. That's why we came. We need you to help us. But you have to make a promise."

Sloan raised his brows, pursed his mouth. "Depends on the promise."

"You can't tell Ms. Cameron what we tell you. We know you can figure out what to do. We don't want anyone to go to jail. But what happened with Ms. Cameron…well…it's not fair. She's real nice. She's a great teacher."

"And she taught us how to meditate," the chubby teen said, somewhat in awe and knowing that was a special skill.

"First of all, Ms. Cameron was very upset when her car was taken, not knowing how or why. Of course her insurance will cover most of the cost of replacing it, but that's not the point. I think you all know that."

"Yeah, we know," was the group response.

"Question. What made you decide to come to me, to trust me with what you know? Why not confess everything to Ms. Cameron?"

Again, the silent exchange of glances.

"We know you like her," Colby said confidently. "And we didn't want to get in trouble either, so…we figure, you're not a cop. You said so. We weren't afraid that you'd arrest one of us or the person who stole the car. But maybe you could, you know, help Ms. Cameron."

"That's right," said Taryn. "And maybe there's a way of helping the person who did this and they won't have to get in trouble either."

Her simple logic made her excited, as if she'd figured out how to make it a win-win situation. She seemed *very* set on the culprit not being put behind bars. That, in particular, caught Sloan's attention.

Sloan sat back more comfortably, Gaye resting against him. It was not as bad as he'd imagined, but bad enough. "Let's go back to the beginning, to when it all happened. Obviously one or all of you, A, know the person responsible and, B, don't particularly want anything to happen to that person. You'll have to explain to me why that matters so much. I want you to tell me everything that you know. *Everything*. Then I'll see what I can do. Are we clear?"

"Yes, sir" was the contrite and relieved answer.

"Colby." The teen started when his name was called. "Why don't we start with you? What do you know?"

Colby slid down in his chair, his spine curved, his skinny legs splayed open from the knees. One knee began to bounce under the edge of the table.

Sloan didn't have to say any more as Colby began to unravel the story that involved, more than any of them, his brother, Curtis. Yes, it was known that Curtis made it a habit of sometimes getting into the school when he wasn't allowed on the premises, but it was not to steal anything. It was to try to see Taryn. And his daughter.

Sloan, again, was very careful not to let any expression show. He remained still and curious as the details unfolded.

Taryn didn't want anyone to know that the father of her baby was also the brother of one of her best friends in school. That the father was a dropout and petty thief. She didn't go into details about how she hooked up with Curtis or why; now she wanted to help him. Sloan reasoned that now was not the time, but eventually, all would be revealed. Colby swore that no one knew who Gaye's father was, but Sloan wasn't sure of that. Kids, teens, were not known for being discreet or capable of keeping important secrets. Sooner or later, it all came out.

"All right." Sloan nodded at the revelation. "I take it the order to stay away from the school had no effect on him."

"Yeah," Taryn said, exasperated. "I kept telling him don't come to the school. I didn't want anyone in school to know *all* my business. But he kept showing up anyway."

"Why couldn't he come to your house to see you?" Sloan asked.

Taryn looked down. "I didn't want my mom to know about me

and Curtis…and that he's Gaye's father. She thinks he's a loser and has no future."

Colby, uncharacteristic of him, chortled. "My brother thinks he's smarter than anybody. You can't tell him anything."

"But he does help out with Gaye. I can't let my mom know, but…"

"I think you're underestimating your mom. I bet she wouldn't want anything to happen to the father of her grandchild."

"Yeah, he's real good about buying diapers and things. He got her three stuffed animals," one of the other two teens offered.

As if that gave Curtis extra points.

"And he did buy a bigger stroller…" Colby trailed off.

"You don't know how or where he got the money," Sloan asked.

"No," Colby muttered with a shake of his head.

Sloan nodded. "Okay, so Curtis is at the center of this whole thing, right?"

No one responded.

"Let's get to the car. How did that come about?"

Sloan had known from the beginning that the theft of Olivia's car was simple and straightforward—knowledge met with opportunity, and the time to pull it off. The full details of Curtis's plan were to steal the car and sell it to a middleman who would dispose of it. Colby didn't know where or how. His brother's plan was to give some of the money to Taryn. And spend the rest on himself.

And it was at that point that Taryn realized she couldn't remain silent. Colby had put everything together and suspected his own brother of the theft. But…what to do about it?

It was nice that Curtis was trying to help out financially with his daughter, but Taryn didn't want him to steal in order to do that. She and Colby didn't want Ms. Cameron to be the person he stole from. Was there a way for Curtis to confess to what he did…but not have to go to jail?

Sloan wasn't sure that was possible. But he very much liked that these four students, maybe among Olivia's best and brightest, were plotting how to make it all come out right and help Ms. Cameron. He listened for almost an hour as the kids traded ideas about how to fix things. He was impressed that they were using critical thinking, and their affection for Olivia, to save the day.

"What do you want from me? How do you think I can help you?"

The students sat quietly, thinking, trying to reason a solution.

"Maybe you can bring Curtis to the police and make him tell everything."

"I can't make him do anything. And I can't just drag him to the police. On what grounds? What you've told me isn't enough. It's hearsay, not proof. But let's say he's arrested and arraigned, a case presented to the DA's office…"

"That's complicated," Colby murmured, shaking his head.

"And you don't want Oli—Ms. Cameron to know any of this? She'll have to, you know. Once the facts come out about her car."

"Yeah. I guess," Taryn said, her brows furrowed as she tried to sort out what could be done. She looked at Sloan. "Maybe you could talk to her?"

"About what exactly?"

Colby shrugged. "Don't know. But we do know you'll figure out something. You'll help make it right."

CHAPTER 17

Sloan was pretty sure that anything he said to Olivia about her car was going to affect her. As much as he hoped for a smooth explanation, he sensed that was not going to happen. In truth there were a lot of aspects of his talk with her students that she probably wasn't going to like. He didn't either, but he knew he was caught, firmly, between a rock and a hard place.

Sloan found himself taking several days to figure out an approach with her. She was going to ask a lot of questions. She was going to want to know *who* had taken her car and what had happened to it. She was going to ask how he knew so much about it. And therein lay the problem. He couldn't tell her.

Perhaps he'd be able to count on Olivia's empathetic nature making her happy to know at least part of the truth and not insist on names or too many details. But he was also left with the need to actually deal with the person responsible for the theft. Sloan didn't believe the culprit should get off scot-free. But to what degree should the perp be punished?

It wasn't his call.

He was *not* a cop.

Sloan made the decision that the conversation had to happen before Thanksgiving. That was less than two weeks away. He was already concerned that it could carry over and ruin his holiday plans with Olivia. But mostly, he admitted to being concerned about Olivia's reaction. His plans were further complicated by Olivia having informed him that she'd forgotten she was to help serve Thanksgiving dinner at a shelter near Inglewood, south of Baldwin Hills. The event was sponsored by a local church, and this was the second year she'd volunteered. The excitement of having Thanksgiving with Sloan and the knowledge that she'd also be meeting his father had briefly wiped the shelter commitment out of her mind, she noted to him. But Olivia was going to keep her promise…and she would do the three-plus-hour drive to San Luis Obispo by herself from LA on Thanksgiving, after her commitment.

Ten days before the holiday, Sloan talked Olivia into a movie night. They'd done it once more since the screening of *Loving* and found out how much they enjoyed watching together and then talking about the movie afterward. This time he didn't much care what they saw. He was already preoccupied with the discussion he needed to have with her.

When Sloan reached Olivia's, dinner was simple and easily prepared and, finally, with Olivia's fried chicken she'd been promising. As they toasted with a glass of wine, Sloan had given her a small envelope with her name beautifully scripted on the outside. It felt a little lumpy.

"What is it?"

"It's sealed, so obviously it's supposed to be a surprise. You can open it after Thanksgiving dinner."

She arched a brow at him, fingering the envelope and pretending she was about to tear off an end. Sloan watched her pointedly without saying a word, as if daring her to cheat. Finally, Olivia removed the envelope to a shelf on the bookcase in the living room…next to his holster and gun.

She sipped her wine thoughtfully. "This sounds too mysterious. Why give it to me now?"

"I want you to anticipate what it could be. Something to look forward to."

"You mean you want to torture me," she said airily.

"I don't. But I think you'll be pleased and surprised."

She studied him closely for a moment, nodding. "I can wait."

"I promise, you'll like it."

When they were almost done eating, Sloan considered Olivia for a moment before pushing away his plate.

"I…eh…I've been wanting to ask you something. About the theft of your car."

She was caught off guard. Olivia regarded him with curiosity. "My car? Why?"

"Have you ever wondered what might have happened? Who could have taken it right from outside your home?"

"Of course I have. But when the police showed no interest in trying to track it down, it seemed pointless to speculate on all the possibilities."

"But you did have some ideas, right?"

Olivia was drawn into his questioning. She shook her head. "I stopped thinking about it. I stopped wondering. It… It was frustrating."

"Well…I gave it some thought."

"Why?"

He shrugged. "It's what I do. Maybe on a bigger, federal level, but I still like to figure out how a crime happens. For instance, I've always felt that somehow your car theft was…personal. The more I thought about it, the less the theft seemed random. The car went missing from the front of your house. Perhaps by someone who came to know a lot about you. Where you live. The fact that it was a brand-new car."

She frowned. "I don't... What are you suggesting?"

"That you might actually be able to figure this out. What if it turned out to be someone who is known to you? Maybe someone who works around the school, knew your habits. A klepto former teacher who didn't like you..."

She burst out laughing. "I mean, I doubt that I'm beloved by every staff member, but I hardly think someone I worked with would go that far. Too much to lose if caught."

"Okay. A student? Past...or present? Friend or relative of?"

Olivia suddenly became uncomfortable, shifting in her chair. Frowned and shook her head. "No. No, I don't believe that. I can't think that... You're just guessing."

"I could be. But what if I'm onto something? What if I'm right?"

She stared at him, and Sloan could see the conversation was becoming worrisome for Olivia. He knew then that she had thought about what happened. Why hadn't she been willing to explore all possibilities as a way to eliminate them? Yes, she would have liked to have her car back, but why wouldn't Olivia want to find the thief and see them held accountable?

"It doesn't matter anymore, does it?" Olivia said flatly.

"Only you can answer that. What would you do if you knew who it was?"

Olivia blinked at him, studying him closely.

Sloan knew he completely had her attention.

"Why...why are you bothering with this, Sloan? What are you thinking?"

"I'm…curious. You must be too." He held her gaze and leaned toward her, across the dining table. "Do you have any ideas?"

Olivia blinked at him again, her eyes wide and her gaze suddenly suspicious. "You know something, don't you? Who have you been talking to? How? Why would you even suggest that a student could be involved?"

"I never said that. But it's a thought. I believe you might suspect that as well."

She gasped, staring at him. Abruptly Olivia stood and began to clear the table. "No. None of my students would ever…"

"I only suggested it could be a student who is involved. Not that they actually were."

"Semantics!" she said, almost angry. She stopped stacking dishes to stare at him. "Who have you been talking to?"

Sloan couldn't lie, so he said nothing, staring down at the table. It had not been a mistake to get into it with Olivia. But her reactions only confirmed what the students had told him. That information and her response now suggested she had unraveled more than she was willing to admit. Why not say something? Why not pursue it to get to the bottom of her car being stolen?

Of course she'd question why he would even raise the issue of the car when she'd already received the insurance payment and had replaced the stolen vehicle. Sloan now knew the *who* and the *how*. But it wasn't an easy thing to put all the details out there and do something about it. It wasn't up to him. It had to be Olivia's move. Would she?

He sighed. "Someone reached out to me. They're concerned about what could happen if the whole truth came out."

"*Who?*" she questioned sharply. Agitated.

Sloan slowly stood to face her. He knew in that instant that if he continued to push Olivia, things would get…bad. He could sense that happening already. And they, he and Olivia, maybe stood to lose everything.

"I can't say," he responded flatly. "But however it all happened, I don't think you should be in the middle. And I certainly don't think you should forget about it. I'm hoping that you can find a way through this so that no one gets hurt. Including you. Right now, if you think about it, a lot of people will pay the consequences…in one way or another."

"You're doing it again, aren't you?"

His jaw tightened. His gaze narrowed. Sloan knew exactly what Olivia was referring to. He'd hoped that they wouldn't go down that path again.

"No. I'm not. But that's exactly why I can't and I won't tell you what I know, Liv. This is…hard for me. But you've set the boundaries for how you want to be treated. I'm not going to risk crossing the line in the sand that you've drawn.

"Listen to what I'm trying to say. I think you understand exactly. I won't beat around the bush about one thing. I know you're very close to the students at Harvest. You care about them deeply. But you can't always save them, Olivia."

He stopped, seeing clearly that her posture was now mutinous. For a moment Sloan thought to stop talking and switch tactics, just sweeping her into an embrace and holding on and gently saying, "It's going to be okay." Instead, he stood still fighting his urge, believing that Olivia would reject it.

"Olivia…they're not your kids. A little tough love might be a better response right now. Instead of…of getting angry with me. Remember, I'm not involved."

"Are you trying to protect someone?"

"Just you."

He came around the edge of the table to stand next to her. She glared, but he returned her hard gaze, seeing not just her anger but defensiveness.

He was pushing too hard, but there was no turning back. Sloan suddenly didn't doubt that Olivia understood *exactly* what he was suggesting to her.

"I'm not accusing you of anything. I already know you wouldn't forgive me if I tried to…to…"

"Act like the white man in charge," Olivia said bluntly.

Sloan blanched. *Okay. Here we go.* "I hope that's not what you believe."

She shook her head, staring at him as if trying to read him, get inside his head…or his heart. "I'm not sure I like what I'm hearing."

He sighed, struggling to stay balanced and to the point. But Sloan knew he was already in trouble. He couldn't keep to the point without implicating himself in the worst way. A way that could destroy everything.

"Let's not go there, okay?" he asked quietly. "Frankly, I'm…not comfortable with what you're suggesting either."

"Who have you been talking to?" Olivia questioned bluntly.

"I can't tell you. Right now I am asking that you trust me. You once said that you did."

"Now you want me to just believe you on your say-so?"

"That is exactly what I'm asking." Sloan stared long and hard into her eyes, willing Olivia not to reject him. *Them.* He slowly moved away. "I think I'd better go. I don't want to risk…"

"Risk what?" she asked, her tone quiet and curious.

"Everything," Sloan said just as quietly. "I have very selfish reasons for getting involved at all. I believe you have your student's welfare in your heart. I have yours in mine," he said clearly.

Olivia didn't move, didn't face him or look at him.

"You're interfering in what I do as an educator, what I think is right for my students."

"Maybe I am. You haven't asked for my help…and I'm not offering now. You've got this. Your confusion about what to do can be overcome. And right now I'm not sure you'd accept anything from me. I'll have to deal with that."

"Why can't you just tell me?"

"I promised, Olivia. I was hoping you'd understand. I had a feeling you weren't going to be happy with what I had to say to you. But I promised. I will keep my word. I'm trying my best to stay on the outside. I don't want to get too much in the middle. But I don't deserve to be blamed for what you're afraid to do."

"I'm not afraid. I'm not!"

Sloan walked close to Olivia. He could see, feel, the stiff way she held herself just then. Controlled. Annoyed. What would happen if he tried to touch her? Tried to pull her into an embrace so that his love could radiate between them? And she would know that was the only thing that mattered between them.

"Liv…okay, I get that you're angry with me right now." He gently cupped her elbow. She didn't pull away, but she didn't soften toward him. He released her. "This is not that complicated, and you know what you have to do. Think carefully about what that will be…what it could mean. Especially for you and me."

Olivia still said nothing, even when he turned and walked away. The fact that she silently let him caused Sloan's gut to tighten, twist in momentary anxiety. He needed to leave. Sloan went into the living room to retrieve his service weapon. He noticed the envelope he'd given her on the bookshelf. He suddenly hoped Olivia wasn't going to discard what he'd given her, but he decided not to draw her attention to it again. He turned around and found her standing in the kitchen entrance, her arms wrapped around her waist, her eyes wide as saucers, dark and troubled.

"I want to say one more thing. You told me recently, when you checked out the wound on my hand, that taking care of me, worrying about me, was all part of loving me. Your concerns were part of the whole package of how you felt. Well, that works both ways; wanting to protect you, even rescuing you if I see the need, is what I do to love you." Sloan averted his gaze, inhaled deeply as he pursed his lips. He faintly shook his head and then looked at Olivia. "I'm not going to call you. I've said all I intend to, except…the bottom line is…I just want to be the man you love. And I want you to love me just as I am."

Sloan headed to the door of her house, opened it. In the terrible silence that followed him Sloan couldn't help wondering if this was going to be the last time he saw her or that they would ever speak. Could it, unbelievably, happen in a heartbeat, that their relationship would end on a principle and pride?

Sloan said nothing more to her. He quickly left without a chance to hold Olivia. Or to kiss her with reassurance and hope…and love. Without Olivia having assured him that she felt the same way.

CHAPTER 18

The level of Olivia's anxiety had maxed out.

She'd gone from an abundance of confidence that she knew what she was doing and Sloan had overstepped his influence to shrinking into insecurity that he had understood far better than she both the simplicity and complexity of the theft of her car and how it tied into students at Harvest.

Olivia had spent a weekend feeling self-righteous in her decision not to stir the pot of controversy over an unfortunate incident that would eventually fade away as a bad dream. That was until she, once again, connected the dots and realized that it was never going to go away because the fallout was already happening. Olivia wanted to call Sloan and let him know he won. But her stomach knotted with the certainty that he would say to her, not boastful or noble, that no one wins. It made sense that one or more of the students had spoken to him. They had won. Olivia finally realized she was the one who had to get on board because only she had the power to make everything right.

And he didn't call her, which she'd fully expected him to do. He was very good at setting things right, even when he wasn't the one at fault. That was also part of his training. Resolution. Not assigning blame. But Olivia was also grateful that his abilities were not only

Sloan's strength but inherently a huge part of who he was as a person, a man.

Had she thrown Sloan over, lost him, in a quest for her own respect?

Why should that be his responsibility when not even her ex-husband had given it worth?

She was miserable and scared when the silence stretched out for days. It was only marginally easier when, unable to stand the gulf between them, Olivia got confirmation from Sloan's office that he had been called to headquarters in DC for an important update on changes in his field office. Business first. He wasn't deliberately ignoring her. Maybe.

But she had work to do first. And it was probably the only way to begin to mend a rift that she'd created. Again.

Olivia dove right into it, questioning the first person she'd ever believed knew something about her stolen car. Colby's show of sympathy the day after the theft had seemed precipitous and detailed. He seemed to know details he shouldn't have. But Olivia didn't believe for a minute that he had anything active to do with the theft. Almost a week after her talk with Sloan, Olivia asked Colby if she could see him after school let out. She met him at the schoolyard door through which the students exited the building at the end of the day. Olivia could tell immediately that Colby was cautious and nervous. She wasted no time in getting to the point.

"Colby, I need to speak with you about my stolen car."

He blinked rapidly adjusting his glasses. His gaze dropped to the ground. His shoulders rounded as he stuffed his hands into the pockets of his school hoodie. He said nothing, but he was fidgety.

"I've been thinking. When you said how sorry you were that my car was stolen from where I live. How did you know it was taken from my driveway? How did you know where I live?"

When Colby showed all the signs of going into a panic attack, Olivia began to talk to him in a soothing voice. She assured him he wasn't in trouble and nothing was going to happen to him. But... how did he know?

It took all of a minute for Colby to cave, his voice quavering, tears of embarrassment and fear rolling down his cheeks, his nose starting to run. Olivia guided him past Lori's desk and into her office, closing the door so passing students, his friends, wouldn't notice. The sensitive, shy teen gave in to the truth, confirming one of the theories she had formed from the beginning. Colby's brother, Curtis, had pressured him for information about her. That had been just a few days after she'd first driven her car to school. His plan was to break into her house to steal any valuables...to punish Olivia for always giving him a hard time, treating him badly. When he cased the property and saw the bright new car in the driveway, Curtis switched plans and aimed to take the car instead. In the middle of the night. Easy. No witnesses. No damage. No fingerprints.

"When did you realize that your brother had taken the car?" Olivia asked.

"A few days later. He told me. My brother had already had a fence for the car. He said he was getting a lot of money for it. He told me to keep quiet about what happened. He told me not to even tell Taryn."

And that had been the second revelation that Olivia added to her arsenal of information and proof. She listened, soothed the distraught boy, and, yes, promised that she wasn't mad at him.

Olivia didn't know if she was relieved to have her initial question answered so quickly or saddened. Because Olivia knew there was more. She next asked Taryn to meet with her for a few minutes. The time and place were the same, although Taryn had not brought her daughter to school that day.

Olivia could tell that the girl was suspicious, giving monosyllabic responses and not volunteering anything. Taryn was smart, and she didn't want to trick the girl into saying something where she might compromise herself. Olivia began by not asking Taryn leading questions but by openly speaking on what she already knew.

"I think you know why I want to speak with you, Taryn."

Taryn sat with tightly closed mouth, staring into space and stubbornly refusing to meet her gaze.

"But let me start by telling you what I know to be true. Curtis stole my car and has sold it."

Taryn began to blink. Closed her eyes and gnawed on her bottom lip.

"Colby told me how it happened. But he didn't tell me how you're involved. I have my suspicions, but I'd rather you be honest with me. I don't believe for a minute you had anything to do with what Curtis did. Are you involved in some way?"

"*No*! I didn't do nothing. I didn't even know Curtis was going to take your car."

"I believe you," Olivia said at once, relieved when Taryn, quick to defend herself, inadvertently gave up the true culprit. Curtis. "I've told Colby I will not tell on him. But I can't promise what might happen if I go to the police. I think it's only fair that I tell you, I will have to report what happened."

"You don't! You don't have to say anything. You…you got another car. He won't do anything else. Curtis, I mean. He won't."

"Why are you so concerned about Curtis or what might happen to him?"

Taryn's expression changed, collapsed. She shook her head help-lessly. Ambivalence and confusion seemed to paralyze her. Olivia, sympathetic from the beginning, now tried to find a way to soothe the teen, let her know she was going to be okay.

"Taryn, listen to me. Listen." Taryn quieted, struggling not to cry, but her lips trembled. "I think…" Olivia began quietly and slowly, "that Curtis is Gaye's father." Taryn began quietly crying. "You've been trying to protect yourself, maybe ashamed to admit it. Now you're protecting him. He gives you money for your daughter. He's trying to take responsibility. You know he's not going about it the right way. He could get caught. He could go to jail. Then what? What can he do for you or his child if he has a record?"

Olivia wisely let Taryn cry for several minutes, passing her the box of Kleenex that always sat on her desk for emotional meetings such as this.

"I want you to know I'm *very* impressed that a group of you went to Agent Kendrick at the FBI office trying to get help, not wanting anyone to go to jail…or get hurt. That was very smart… and very brave. And you need to know that Slo…Agent Kendrick did not betray your confidence. He didn't reveal anything you shared with him. He merely said it was up to me to help you guys out of a terrible and difficult situation. He trusted me to figure out what had happened and how so many of you were connected.

"Slo…Agent Kendrick kept his promise to you. That's what I'm going to do."

Olivia could see that Taryn responded as if an enormous weight was lifted from her shoulders, of guilt and shame for, inadvertently, having taken part in the cover-up of what had happened. And now that she had definitive answers to some of her own questions, she knew exactly what had to be done, what she needed to do, to set things right. Most especially for her students who demonstrated a degree of honor that they should be proud of.

———————

Olivia was much later arriving in San Luis Obispo than she'd hoped. It was a pleasant drive but long and meandering with holiday traffic… and her worry about seeing Sloan again. Until the recent revelations about her stolen car and his trying to steer her in the direction of a resolution, a week was the longest they'd gone without being in touch since they'd first met. Now, the silence made Olivia insecure, made her wonder if her stubborn effort to shut Sloan down about the car theft had, somehow, created an irrevocable rift between them. The very idea that it might have caused damage to the relationship had given Olivia several very restless nights. Was Sloan deliberately not attempting to reach her, or was the DC trip complicated and time-consuming, leaving him no time for personal agendas of any kind? Olivia chose to believe the latter.

Any other possibility was…torturous.

She began to calm down as she finally turned onto the residential street, looking for the house number. The anxiety ratcheted up again when she turned into a lovely tree-lined approach to a two-story country-style home. The closer Olivia got to her final destination, the more the knot in her stomach tightened.

What if Sloan was angry with her? What if he had stopped expecting her to join him for the holiday? What if…

Olivia was in agony. And she loved him. What if it was all over… and he wasn't even here? What if…

There was a car in the driveway, but it wasn't Sloan's car. The garage door was up but no other vehicle in the two-car space. She rolled slowly to a stop in front of the house rather than pull behind the car or into the garage. She didn't know how long she'd be staying. She sat staring at the door. Did no one hear the car drive up? Was anyone home? No longer expecting her? There'd been no way for her to confirm. She'd sent a text to Sloan but got no answer. But...here she was.

Olivia took a deep breath, feeling her heart fluttering around in her chest. She got out of the car...as the inside screen and front door of the house were opened. She jumped at the sound, turning to face whomever was standing in the opening as she lifted the lid of her trunk. She peered around the edge of the raised top. It wasn't Sloan.

"Hey there" came a cheerful greeting from the man smiling at her. He started down the front steps to greet her, wearing an apron. Olivia's mouth went dry. She knew this was Sloan's father, and she was completely on her own to introduce herself. He had a full head of wavy, white hair. And very bright blue eyes...like Sloan's. She couldn't account for the smile, since her experience with the son was that Sloan never smiled and grinned very sparingly. Olivia counted herself fortunate that she'd come to see either at all. But the few times he'd laughed had been memorable.

Olivia gave a hesitant smile in return with a small wave of her hand. "Hello. I...I hope you're expecting me. I'm a stranger in a strange land."

The man laughed heartily. It was then that Olivia saw the obvious resemblance between father and son. It was reassuring. He was only a few inches shorter than Sloan, but of sturdy build and very handsome. Olivia secretly smiled to herself.

This is how Sloan will age, she considered.

"No stranger. We knew you were coming. Sloan's been like a nervous cat, stalking in front of the windows and doors. But he's not here."

Olivia stood straight, staring at the announcement in disappointment. "Oh…"

"Not to worry. He had to make a run for me in town. He'll be back soon, but he's not going to be happy he wasn't here when you arrived. I'm Matt, Sloan's dad."

He held out a large, masculine hand. Just like Sloan's. Olivia grabbed it and found the hold firm but easy.

"Hi, Mr. Kendrick—"

"Matt."

"Olivia."

"Yes, yes. I know who you are. Glad you could make it for Thanksgiving. You're our guest of honor."

"Oh, no!" Olivia murmured in surprise and consternation. "You don't even know me."

"Well, that's going to change, you can count on it. Now, what can I help you with?"

Matt was just removing her weekend suitcase out of the trunk and Olivia was balancing a large pie carrier with one hand and grabbing a canvas tote with the other when they both turned at the sound of a car turning into the driveway, continuing into the garage.

Olivia didn't hear another word that Matt spoke, her gaze riveted to the driver's door of the Outback. The passenger door opened as well, and a woman exited. She was petite and not fully visible to Olivia from where she stood. But she couldn't hear or understand anything the woman was saying either. Olivia's attention was solely on Sloan as he climbed out of the car and stood. He faced her, and she tried to read his expression. He slammed the car door and began a slow, even stride toward her, and it was as if she and Sloan only had eyes for one another. Everything else was background noise.

Her heart began to beat like crazy. She couldn't move.

The petite woman, closer to Matt's age than to her or Sloan's, deftly took the pie carrier from Olivia.

"Hi, I'm Nancy."

"Hi...Olivia."

Nancy smiled at her. "I'll take that. Does it need to be refrigerated?"

But she didn't wait for a response. Nancy headed for the house with the authority of someone used to coming and going. She paused long enough for Matt to kiss her cheek. He took Olivia's canvas tote and, chatting cheerfully, followed Nancy up the steps and through the front door. But Matt stopped to speak over his shoulder to his son.

"Sloan, grab Olivia's suitcase, will you? You know where to put it." The front door closed silently.

Olivia couldn't move her gaze from Sloan and his own expression. His gaze gave no clue to what he was thinking or feeling. *So like him*, she thought, agitated.

He seemed to be taking forever to reach her. Olivia had no idea what to expect. And then he spoke.

"Ms. Cameron," he uttered in greeting.

The tension twisted in her stomach. Was he teasing? Was the formality serious and real?

"Sloan..." was as much as she got to say, but Olivia was oddly relieved by the familiar rough texture of his voice. "I'm a little..."

He reached beyond her and bent to lift her suitcase. But he didn't touch her.

"I—" Olivia tried again.

"Let's get inside," Sloan interrupted bluntly, walking away with her suitcase in hand.

Olivia retrieved her purse from the passenger seat of her car. She hurried to catch up with Sloan, who was holding the door for her. The minute she was inside, he headed for the carpeted staircase to the right. She followed, aware of the light conversation coming from the kitchen, through the dining room to the left. Olivia was awed by the beautiful and seasonal table setting for Thanksgiving that she took a hasty moment to admire.

She hesitated on the stairs. "I should offer to help with…" she began, but Sloan had already reached the second-floor landing and could be heard walking down a hallway. She followed, hurrying to catch up again.

The corridor was empty, but there was a door open, and bright Thanksgiving sunshine spread from the room out into the hall. When Sloan quietly appeared again half his face was shaded, and the sunlight reflecting on the other half made his blue eyes eerily light and translucent. He stood watching her until Olivia walked toward him, his gaze beckoning her. He walked inside and waited for her. The large room confined them, closely together. She immediately felt a rush of emotion engulf her. She was here. With Sloan, finally. Would everything they had been to each other a week ago still exist? This was a defining moment for Olivia, when she realized that her weekend with Sloan, his father, his father's girlfriend, a Thanksgiving roasting turkey whose warmth and aroma wafted through the charming house were going to set the tone for far more, maybe even the future. She was nervous but hopeful.

"This is our room," he said in a low growl. "Okay?"

Our room.

"Yes. I like it. It's...very cozy." She turned her gaze back to him, back to his intense questioning stare. "I thought...hoped...you'd call," Olivia said quietly.

Sloan sighed. "I felt it best that I not do that. You were angry with me again. To be honest, I wasn't happy about that."

She shook her head. "I wasn't, really. Jackson said I was unfair to you. Difficult. I didn't want that."

He raised his brows. "You told your brother about what happened?"

"My brother has never held back from telling me the truth, being honest. Blunt, if it was called for."

"What else did he say?"

"That I was scared. That I was letting Marcus get into my head again."

"Yeah. We have to do something about that."

She shook her head again. "No. *I* have to do something about that. When I thought I'd pushed you away forever, that scared me, too."

"Not forever. But I needed some space."

She nodded. "I understand. But...it still scared me," Olivia voiced with quiet meaning.

Sloan shortened the distance between them, a small step. "I wasn't sure you'd come," he murmured, sounding a little surprised.

Olivia responded wearily. "I wasn't sure you still wanted me to."

"The way I feel about you hasn't changed," he added.

"Me either." She sounded breathless.

"That's good. I'm glad to hear—"

"I do love you, Sloan. So much—"

His arms stretched out toward her, and Olivia walked right into them. Sloan's mouth descended on hers in a powerful, all-consuming kiss, and he crushed her against his chest. Olivia reveled in the way he seemed to wrap himself around her, absorbing her in the strength and warmth of his arms. His lips were mobile, caressing over hers, his tongue exploring with erotic tenderness. She was so happy to be back here. Olivia let his kiss absorb her urge to cry, turning their emotional reunion into a bond of vindication and a wellspring of relief.

There were distant voices from the floor below, some laughter. They were being summoned to dinner. Sloan groaned. Any doubts that Olivia brought with her during the long drive from LA vanished in the reality of the moment and their embrace. Their passionate greeting answered all questions about absence making the heart grow fonder.

Absolutely.

––––––––––––

"What did you say to your dad?" Olivia whispered, anxious. She and Sloan stood on the porch outside the front door, watching and waving as Matt and Nancy drove away back to her house for the night.

"Just that you and I have a lot to talk about this evening and were going to be lousy company, and we had all day tomorrow, over turkey and cranberry sauce leftovers, to get better acquainted. I said I had other plans for us…and then I think my dad laughed and said he understood."

"Well, I don't. It was rude of you to kick the man out of his own house."

"Liv, he got it. Trust me. Dinner was really fantastic. But I just want us to be alone."

"I feel awful, Sloan. You make it sound like we're two hot and bothered teens who can barely keep our hands off each other."

They made sure all the extra food had been refrigerated and went back upstairs to their room, with what remained of the wine and two glasses. Being together was more companionable than lustful, and they finished the wine over quiet, loving conversation as they eventually undressed for bed. Sloan set the stage by setting up his smartphone on a small bed stand speaker, the sound just a very low wave of music in the background. He found a large votive candle on the dresser and lit it. Olivia remembered the envelope he'd given her the last time they'd shared dinner at her house, with the instruction to save it until after Thanksgiving. She was now very glad that she'd brought it along, still sealed. She silently held it up to him as if to say *should we open it now?*

Sloan's silent response was to climb into bed with her. He stared at the envelope and nodded. "Sure. Open it."

Eagerly, Olivia ripped off a short end and shook the contents into her hand. Little slips of white paper fell into her lap, along with something else; small, solid, and hard. Sloan silently observed what she was doing, leaving her to discover what he'd given her and what it all meant.

Olivia picked up the small object first, turning it over to examine. She made a quiet sound of pleasure and gave Sloan a smile.

"It's an FBI pin. Is this a replacement for the one I lost in my great-aunt's house?"

"You seemed really disappointed not to have it, so…it's not an official pin, of course. There are rules about how they are given out."

"This is very real to me because you gave it to me. Anyway, I know it's not real. That's not the point. *You* are." Olivia smiled at him. Sloan rewarded her with a quick kiss.

She gathered up the slips of paper…all inserts from about a dozen fortune cookies.

"I thought you didn't believe in these?"

"I'm reconsidering them. The thing is, every time I read one of these now, I think of you. And...I started thinking that a lot of those sayings remind me of you. Us. Maybe there is some truth in what they say."

"Thank you," she whispered, as Sloan took her gifts and put them on the nightstand.

Then he planted a wet kiss somewhere in the vicinity of her lips, settling down and pulling her into his arms. "No more talking. We've got the whole weekend to finish making up for lost time. I have other plans for the next ten or twelve hours."

Olivia curled against him but sighed. "Your father is going to have a terrible opinion of me," she murmured.

"He won't. He did ask if you are that one in a million. I said, not only that but that you're a keeper. Do you know what that means?"

Olivia smoothed her hand across his stomach, back across his chest, over the uneven damaged skin from the explosion he'd survived. "Yes. I know what that means." She was silent for a moment. "Isn't this room on the other side of the house from your dad's?"

"Yeah, it is."

"Then...he and Nancy didn't have to leave. Nancy must think I'm—"

"Relax. No one thinks anything...except that I love you. And if they had any doubts, I think it was cleared up the minute you got here."

"Okay," she said, quietly contrite. And then, "Sloan?"

"Mmmmm?"

"I'm glad we're alone. I'm glad I came."

"Amen."

"I thought…"

"Shh. I did a piss-poor job of trying to explain about the car and the theft and who did it."

She sighed, snuggling against him. "You didn't. I just became stubborn and unwilling to listen. I'm relieved you forgive me."

"I understood the dynamics, Liv. I tried not to take your annoyance personally but…it did get to me."

"Because…you love me?" she asked quietly.

"Exactly," Sloan said, just as quietly.

"While honoring your commitment to keep the secret of a few scared teens. I had a talk with Colby and Taryn and…"

"Great, great. You know, I want to hear how it all worked out. But I really don't care right now. Tell me in the morning."

"But let me just say…"

Sloan rolled almost on top of her. He stopped her attempts at explaining by capturing her mouth, delving into the warm cavern to twist and turn with her tongue, to slowly stroke until a certain mindless stupor settled in, sending waves of anticipation to her sensitive nipples, her groin, where Sloan languidly stroked eliciting short sighs.

"I always knew that you'd figure out what to do…"

"I contacted…Detective…An…Ander…son at… He's going… going…oooooh…"

"What?" he asked, his voice slurred with longing, seductive and eager.

His caressing hands, roaming fingers stripped all resistance from her, leaving Olivia open and pliant in surrender. She heaved her hips against his as Sloan settled between her legs.

"Yes…it can wait," Olivia managed. "We have…time."

Keep reading for an exciting excerpt from
Sandra Kitt's *The Time of Your Life*
Available now!

CHAPTER 1

When Eden Marsh came through the heavy main doors of the Guild Society, just a few blocks from the Department of Labor in Washington, DC, she was greeted by a hollow silence and a reminder of why she was there. A solemn acknowledgment of the recent passing of a man who'd had a profound effect on nearly everyone who'd known him, including her. She advanced to the center of the large lobby, with its Italianate marble floor, feeling herself beginning to give way to the emotional significance of the day. Eden took a breath to clear her head, determined that her personal sense of loss would not take away from the purpose of the day. To celebrate Everett Nichols.

Alone in the austere hallway, she felt drawn into the grand first floor salon, off to the right, by evidence that the room had been set up for some sort of event. Eden frowned as she glanced into the room. The dark and formal setting had been laid out with all the trappings for a reception. Or a meeting, or some sort of celebration. A table at the end of the room displayed a variety of glasses for an open bar. Two tables on the longer sides of the room were set up for buffet service, awaiting the delivery of food. It was everything she'd ordered for Everett's affair. But this was not the room she'd booked.

It was a distinctly masculine room, meant to be used by society members, once solely men, to welcome guests, business associates, family visiting for a few hours for an event, or just a place for members to gather to reflect on their good fortune, having achieved Masters of the Universe status.

Everett would hate it, Eden thought.

"Hello, are you Eden Marsh?"

Eden turned to the voice and the short, slender man approaching her. "Yes. Mr. Madison?" She shook his hand.

"Nice to put a pretty face to the voice on the phone," Mr. Madison said in an effort to be friendly. "As you can see"—he waved into the salon—"everything is ready. I'll have the catering staff bring in the refreshments shortly."

"But not here," Eden said clearly.

Surprised, the manager frowned. "Excuse me?"

"This is not the room I was originally shown. This is not the room I wanted. I chose the renovated reading room on the second floor. The room that the club commissioned Mr. Nichols to redesign and renovate several years ago."

The manager's expression turned to one of guilt, but he quickly recovered. "I'm so sorry. But that room is being used for another function. I believe our *director's* secretary," he said with emphasis, "asked to use it for her daughter's bridal shower. In any case the grand salon is our most popular rental space. It's so historic."

Eden shook her head, her gaze expressing a sort of "gee, that's too bad" gesture, as she opened her satchel and pulled out folded papers. "I'm sure it is, but it's not what I agreed to. I have a signed contract, Mr. Madison. It clearly says that the reading room will be set up for a memorial service lasting two hours for seventy-five guests." Eden held out the document to the flustered Mr. Madison. "Would you like to see it again?"

"No, I remember the contract, but…"

"Good. You just need to transfer the refreshment setup to the second floor. That shouldn't take too long." Eden looked at her watch. "The guests will be arriving in under an hour." She smiled sweetly at the manager to soften the blow of her digging in her heels. "I'm sure you can explain to the bridal shower party about *my* agreement. They can use the salon. It's big and cozy…and historic. Thank you for doing this," Eden said with self-deprecating politeness, not allowing the club manager to attempt more excuses.

"Of course," Mr. Madison conceded, giving in to the utter charm with which Eden made her case. He turned away to do her bidding.

Eden was alone again, with the silence of the building and the odd stillness that hung in the air. She immediately forgot Mr. Madison, confident that he wouldn't dare ignore the signed contract…and risk the consequences.

She continued to the wide staircase and climbed to the second level. The landing opened right in front of a bright room with high ceilings, its late-twentieth-century furnishings more in line with the earlier styles of the salon. No chrome and glass here. But it was modern and comfortable, one wall entirely devoted to an enormous built-in filled with monographs, atlases, and attractively bound series and sets. It wasn't a library, but definitely a reading space for club members that was bright, relaxed, and uncluttered.

Everett didn't like clutter, either. *Keep it simple* had always been one of his mottos.

Eden sighed and blinked, focusing. Here, there were three round tables set up for a luncheon. The tablecloths were pink, and there was a large, ornate bouquet in the center of each table. This layout was what the club manager had expected to function for the bridal shower.

Eden heard sounds beyond a partition at the end of the room, and two young men in black slacks and pristine white shirts, waitstaff, appeared with a rolling service cart.

"We're here to move the flowers downstairs. We'll be back for the tables in a sec," one of the men said.

"Thank you. I know this is last minute, but could you hurry? My guests will be arriving soon."

She watched as the two men quickly loaded the cart with whatever would fit and headed back to the discreetly placed service elevator. Eden returned her attention to the room, quickly assessing if there was a need to rearrange furniture. She was relieved that there wasn't. Maybe just repositioning some of the chairs into small clusters and placing the small side tables conveniently for glasses and plates. She began to do some of the moving on her own.

The manager reappeared and rushed to assist Eden when he found her attempting to shift a club chair so it faced the center of the room.

"Ms. Marsh, please. You don't have to do that. My team will take care of everything."

"I don't mind," she responded agreeably. "I can move a chair."

"Yes, yes," the manager said with a nervous chuckle. "I can see you're very capable, but I don't want to add a line item on the contract that includes coverage for injuries."

She stepped back and turned to look around again. Satisfied that it was all coming together, Eden headed for the staircase.

"Ah…is there something else?"

"I just want to check how things are going in the kitchen. I don't want my food platters to end up as hors d'oeuvres at the shower."

"But…"

Eden was already halfway down the stairs, carefully maneuvering in her two-inch pumps. She did a light and graceful jog down the hallway, past the entrance, in the direction of the catering department. She could hear the activity and the shouts and orders among the staff as they hurried to accommodate two events scheduled at the same time. She caught a glimpse of the folded tables for the buffet, a short stack of tablecloths, a box with other wares and supplies, and an easel, all stuffed into the little elevator. The two men Eden had already seen working on the second floor managed to squeeze in, the doors closed, and the elevator ascended.

She looked around and spotted several platters of food. "I'll take this up," she announced. And without waiting for a response, she lifted one of the plastic-wrapped trays and headed back to the staircase. Eden heard the main entrance door open behind her as she walked past. A cool wave of late-winter air wafted over her, but she didn't look to see who'd come in.

She checked her watch and frowned. Thirty minutes and counting before guests arrived. Eden started up the stairs. She hesitated, deciding against holding the banister. But trying to hold the tray with one hand was *not* a good idea. Instead, Eden balanced the tray in both hands, off to one side. She started up again, looking down to watch the placement of her feet on the steps.

Beck Dennison pulled open the entrance door of the Guild Society and entered the lobby. He momentarily stopped in his tracks as a young woman hurriedly marched by with a large, cumbersome tray in her hands. She was focused on the obviously unwieldy tray and didn't notice his presence at the door. He, on the other hand, was caught

by her erect bearing and her slender figure confidently rushing to a
destination. The lush dark curls of her natural hairdo, mostly at the
top and back of her head, bounced gently with each step. He quickly
noticed she was tastefully attired in slim black slacks, and a short
bolero-length jacket in black-and-white tweed with a stand-up collar.
It was sophisticated but simple attire, still feminine but unlike what
many of the females in DC would choose to wear. Her silver hoop
earrings reflected the hall lighting as she walked. Beck came out of his
focused appreciation of the attractive, stylish picture she presented
when he realized she was actually going to attempt to walk up a flight
of stairs in heels, carrying a tray of food.

He rushed forward, taking the stairs two at a time until he reached
her, almost halfway up. So as not to startle her, he reached out, placing
his hand beneath the tray at the center. His left hand hovered at her
back, but not touching her, in case she lost her balance.

"Let me take that," he said with quiet authority. He lifted the tray
away from her.

Surprised by the sudden action, Eden glanced over her shoulder
at him. She blinked, gave him a slight smile, and turned to continue
up the steps.

Beck heard her murmur, "Thank you." He followed her. When
they both reached the landing, she went striding off into the bright
room straight ahead, where several men were busy covering buffet
tables, setting up for an open bar, and strategically placing small stacks
of cocktails napkins on several tables. He maneuvered off his cross-
body mailbag and left it on the floor against the baseboard near the
entrance. Beck could see that this was a setup for an event and walked
the tray over to one of the catering staff, a young Black woman with
an attractively arranged pile up of long dreadlocks.

"I've got it. We'll take care of the rest," she said, taking the tray.

"Thanks." Beck nodded, looking around for the young woman he'd helped. She was busy giving directions to other staff in a quiet but commanding voice and willingly lending a hand where needed. He went over to introduce himself. She turned and saw him but gave him no chance to speak.

"Oh, good," she said, signaling him over. "I need your help. Could you please shift this love seat forward and on a slight angle? I think that will make the space cozier."

"Yes, ma'am," Beck responded agreeably and went to do her bidding. He hid his amusement and fleeting annoyance that she was, unknowingly, abusing his services. She was clearly an employee of the catering company hired to provide for the occasion, in charge of making things happen. He positioned himself behind the sofa and began to push it. Beck glanced at her again, not yet willing to admit he admired her presence. She wasn't aloof and bullying, and her directives were more…thoughtful. Things were to be done *her* way, the right way. And thank you very much. He allowed himself a slight grin. It was hard to say no to someone so charming *and* pretty.

Beck followed her movements as she, in turn, watched what the staff was doing in the placement of the trays. One side of the room was finger food items. The opposite-side table was laid out with desserts.

She turned, giving her attention to the approach of a short middle-aged man in a business suit, speaking and gesturing in disapproval.

"Ms. Marsh, I have to insist…"

"I know, Mr. Madison. But we're almost finished, and your staff has been amazing. I'll make sure they're compensated."

Mr. Madison fell silent as she again adroitly avoided a face-off.

Beck finished repositioning the love seat while eavesdropping on the exchange. He had to grin. The woman probably didn't work directly for the club, but she was certainly in charge at the moment.

He reached into his pocket and withdrew a business card from his wallet. He approached her, ready to introduce himself. But the young woman's attention was again caught by something near the refreshment table. She walked away before he could speak, not realizing that he was behind her.

Beck waited patiently. She bent to pick up a folded easel from the floor, opened it, and placed it in a prominent spot facing toward the open room. When she bent again to lift a large, flat rectangular item wrapped in brown paper, he stepped forward.

"I've got it." He passed his business card to her as he took the flat package out of her hands. She barely glanced at the card before slipping it into the pocket of her jacket. She stood watching as he removed the brown paper. The board underneath was a mounted black-and-white photograph of a seventy-something white male. His image took up nearly all of the frame of reference. In the background was an out-of-focus crowded bookshelf with models and oversize catalogs and manuals, evidence of a workplace setting. The man was leaning back in his chair, his brawny arms up with his hands locked behind his shaved head. His open-necked shirt had the sleeves haphazardly pulled up. He was staring right into the camera, and he wasn't smiling.

Beck stared, caught off guard by the suddenness of seeing the larger-than-life face of Everett Nichols, whose memorial he'd been invited to attend. Beck was also caught off guard by the sadness that coursed quickly through him. For a moment he was transfixed, a rush of memories flashing in his head. So was the young woman next to him. Beck reached in front of her and placed the dramatic photo on the display easel. It was eye-catching and very revealing, but only to those who'd known Everett Nichols well. Beck suspected the number was relatively small. He heard a small, almost inaudible sound from the woman. He turned his head to look at her.

She was standing with her arms wrapped across her waist, hugging herself. Beck was trying to figure out what it meant, that she now seemed so self-protective. What was she feeling? And why? If this was a simple work engagement, where did her personal reaction come from? Abruptly, she turned and walked away. Beck watched her go, having no idea what to make of her reaction to the portrait of Everett Nichols.

What's up with that? he wondered.

ACKNOWLEDGMENTS

Finders Keepers is the third book of the Millionaires Club trilogy, a multiyear project with many moving parts! First and foremost, I want to thank my agent, Lisa Erbach Vance, for her professional support throughout the process of creating and writing these three novels. I also want to add a sincere and heartfelt thank you to Lisa for her support as I worked my way through a plethora of challenging issues.

I also want to acknowledge Special Agent Raymond B. Hall from the Office of Public Affairs of the FBI in Washington, DC. Agent Hall was patient, making himself available to answer my endless list of questions. His input gave the FBI agent in my story a voice of authenticity.

I'm grateful for my introduction to the late FBI agent Bruce Yarborough who, in a chatty and informative conversation many years ago, gave me the idea that a special agent would be a great character for a future book. That book is now *Finders Keepers*.

Finally, a huge shout-out to the Sourcebooks promotion team with Alyssa Garcia and Pamela Jaffee who kept me company while I autographed 1,000 copies of my book for a special book event!

ABOUT THE AUTHOR

Prior to breaking into the mainstream, Sandra Kitt was considered the foremost African American writer of romance fiction and was the first Black writer to ever publish with Harlequin. Sandra is the recipient of a Lifetime Achievement Award in Contemporary Fiction from *Romantic Times*. Romance Writers of America presented Sandra with its 2002 Service Award and the New York chapter of the Romance Writers of America with a Lifetime Achievement Award. In 2010, Sandra received the Zora Neale Hurston Literary Award.

A native of New York City, Sandra holds a bachelor's degree and a master's degree in fine arts from the City University of New York and has studied and lived in Mexico. A one-time graphic designer and printmaker, her work appears in corporate collections including the Museum of African American Art in Los Angeles. Sandra is a former managing director and information specialist in astronomy and astrophysics at the American Museum of Natural History in New York and illustrated two books for the late science writer Isaac Asimov. In 1996, Sandra wrote the last show script for the Hayden Planetarium, narrated by Walter Cronkite. A frequent guest speaker, Sandra has lectured at NYU, Penn State, Sarah Lawrence, and Columbia University, and was an adjunct in publishing and fiction writing.

Sandra Kitt's first mainstream novel, *The Color of Love*, was released in 1995 to critical acclaim from *Library Journal*, *USA Today*, and *The Black Scholar* and was optioned by HBO and Lifetime from a script by Sandra. The anthology *Girlfriends* was nominated for the NAACP Image Award for Fiction in 1999. *Significant Others* and *Between Friends* appeared on the bestseller list in *Essence* magazine, and Amazon has named *Significant Others* among the top twenty-five romances of the twentieth century.

Website: sandrakitt.com
Facebook: SandraKittAuthor
Instagram: @SandraKittAuthor